---------- ★ ----------

As he approached his car, he saw it. Eleven empty beer bottles set up like a frame for ten-pin bowling. The extra bottle was placed in front of the bottle at the triangle's apex, which pointed toward the car's windshield wipers. A twelfth bottle lay on its side, pinned beneath one of the wipers. Deliberate. A mute message.

He returned to his kitchen, dug around in the closet and located a pair of rubber washing-up gloves and a large paper sack. Back outside, he pulled on the gloves and put the bottles inside the bag. Perhaps Jamie could work on them off duty, he thought, then folded the top of the sack closed. He stood there for several seconds, staring at his car, aware of the weight of the bottles. Again he asked himself the unanswerable question: what was going on and who was doing this?

The gravel area where the car was parked held no hints. No footprints, no cast-off shirt button, no blood splatter. Still, the detective in him was too strong to ignore, and he carefully stepped away from his car and walked around it in a wide circle. Nothing.

He set the bag on the car's passenger seat, intending to drop it by Jamie's house later in the day, then got into his car and drove to Noah's Ark. The bottles haunted him all the way to Chesterfield. Was he the trapped, fallen beer bottle?

---------- ----------

SIREN SONG

JO A. HIESTAND

W🌐RLDWIDE.

TORONTO • NEW YORK • LONDON
AMSTERDAM • PARIS • SYDNEY • HAMBURG
STOCKHOLM • ATHENS • TOKYO • MILAN
MADRID • WARSAW • BUDAPEST • AUCKLAND

For David—There are not enough superlatives in the English
language with which to laud you. I can never thank you enough
for your untiring help in setting up McLaren and the core of
this story. Or for your repeat reading while the postmistress got
acquainted with the nick. *Diolch!*

Recycling programs
for this product may
not exist in your area.

SIREN SONG

A Worldwide Mystery/July 2012

First published by L & L Dreamspell

ISBN-13: 978-0-373-26809-2

Copyright © 2010 by Jo A. Hiestand

Printed in U.S.A.

Acknowledgments

Sincere thanks to my friend Paul Hornung,
St. Louis–area police detective, who rewrote fight scenes and
gave me good and bad news about the manuscript.
A handshake also to Detective-Sergeant Robert Church
and Detective-Superintendent
David Doxey (ret.), Derbyshire Constabulary, for answering
questions while preparing to attend the Cheltenham jumps.
Heartfelt thanks are also due to Richard Brook, for his
suggestion about the classic car, and to Dr. Ruth Anker
for the medical information.

Despite David's tutelage, I have made one mistake:
giving McLaren access to the case reports in the police
station. This was a misunderstanding on my part;
I apologize for the error.

My deep gratitude goes to all my friends and readers of my
Taylor & Graham mystery series for giving me the support
and confidence to continue writing. I hope the McLaren series
retains your readership and that you'll love him as much
as I do. Thank you for five wonderful years so far!

Jo Hiestand

St. Louis, March 2010

Characters

Michael McLaren: former police detective, Staffordshire Constabulary
Jamie Kydd: friend and constable, Derbyshire Constabulary
Dena Ellison: McLaren's former girlfriend
Gwen Hulme: McLaren's sister

Marta Hughes: murder victim
Alan Hughes: Marta's husband
Chad Hughes: Marta and Alan's teenage son
Neal Clark: Marta's brother-in-law

Verity Dwyer: coworker with Marta at Noah's Ark animal shelter
Emlyn Gregg: shelter's resident veterinarian
Derek Fraser: boss and owner of Noah's Ark

Karin Pedersen: hiker
Linnet Isherwood: Marta's friend
Sean FitzSimmons: Linnet's friend
Tom Millington: Alan Hughes's neighbor
Rick Millington: Tom's teenage son
Danny Mercer: Rick's friend

Lloyd Farmer: police sergeant, Derbyshire Constabulary– retired
Ian Shard: police constable, Derbyshire Constabulary
Charlie Harvester: former colleague of McLaren's in the Staffordshire Constabulary
Tyrone Wade Antony: convicted burglar

ONE

"I'D LIKE YOU to solve a murder."

Of course, her statement had the desired effect. She had obviously rehearsed what to say during the drive to see him. Yet now, watching the amazement in his face, she didn't smile. The subject was too serious.

McLaren straightened up from the pile of rocks, cocked his right eyebrow, and eyed the woman with the accumulated years' experience of a police detective sizing up a reliable witness. She was tall, with hair the color of new corn silk, and she seemed oblivious to the dampness encircling the hem of her long skirt. She had waded through a pasture of dew-drenched grass and carefully picked her way between the small mounds of sheep dung and clumps of thistle to reach him. Now, near the top of the hill, the wind whipped a stray strand of her long hair, and for a moment McLaren thought how it mimicked a stalk of greater tussock sedge that danced under the light, breezy buffeting.

He slowly wrapped his fingers around the stone he held, torn between getting back to work and satisfying his curiosity. His cop's inquisitiveness won. He said rather reluctantly, "Whose murder?"

"Marta Hughes."

"Who's Marta Hughes—personally, professionally, and otherwise, Miss…?"

"Oh, sorry." She extended her hand and spoke in a remarkably steady voice for having legged it up this steep hill. "Bad habit of mine. I get tunnel vision at times." She paused, as though debating how to proceed now that she had opened the subject. "I'm Linnet Isherwood. Marta's a friend of mine. She's married. Sorry. *Was* married." She flushed slightly and McLaren thought fleetingly how attractive the pink of her cheeks accented her green eyes. Linnet glanced at the stonewall he was repairing before adding, "They've a son. She worked at an animal shelter. Everyone said it was the perfect—"

McLaren held up his hand. "Is that where she was found, at work?"

Linnet shook her head. "No. She'd gone missing several days before the police found her body outside Elton. She—" She pulled in the corners of her mouth, as though what she was about to say was distasteful. "She'd been dumped alongside the road. Like a sack of rubbish."

Watching Linnet fumble for a facial tissue in her skirt pocket, he said, "What's the matter with the police?"

Linnet blotted her eyes, then stared at him, the tissue crushed in her fingers. "Pardon?"

"The police. The coppers, the PCs, the local constabulary. The bill. They investigated the case, I assume."

"Well, yes."

"So?" He said it with a hint of sarcasm, as though his suggestion was laughable, or he already knew the outcome of similar investigations. But something more laced his simple question: an underlying tone of fatigue. With the police, with people, with his life. He exhaled heavily, slowly, waiting for her answer, his arms crossed on his chest, and wondered how she had found him. Not "why," particularly. His home village was rife with the knowledge of his previous career. And the circumstances that had led to his return there.

So he waited, eyeing the woman, and was forming the response he'd give her when she said, "They never found out who killed her."

The information had no more effect on him than a fly settling on a stonewall. He sighed, unfolded his arms, and said as though he'd recited it a thousand times, "I'm sorry, Miss Isherwood. I'm not in the job anymore. Plus, I'm too damned hot." An understatement, he thought, as he tried to swallow; it was the hottest June he could remember. He wiped the sweat from his forehead. "Talk to a solicitor." He turned from her and picked up his work gloves, silently dismissing her.

"But the killer's got away with murder!"

"Tell me about it. We live in a world of injustice." The words were muffled as he bent over the rock pile.

"The person they suspected at first now has a blot on her name that will probably stay with her the rest of her life."

"Relative of yours, I take it."

"No. Not at all."

"Friend, then."

"No. A coworker of Marta's, actually. I don't really know her."

"So why—"

"Because she's innocent. Because," she added when the words had not moved him, "I heard that you fought against injustice."

TWO

"ABHORRED IT, ACTUALLY," she said as McLaren slowly turned to face her. She eyed him, suddenly aware of his great height and muscular shoulders. From moving rocks about, she thought, her gaze shifting to the stonewall. He tilted his head slightly, waiting for her to continue, and a shaft of sunlight fell across his face. His skin had tanned to the golden hue of a fox or newly born fawn, accenting the brightness of his hazel eyes. Holding his gaze, she added, "Abhorred it as only personal experience could produce."

His face went deathly white, as though he'd received a fatal medical diagnosis. He opened his mouth to reply, but Linnet rushed on, having gained the advantage and his attention. "Which is why I took the trouble to find you. I thought if you heard about Verity's situation, you'd want to take on the case." She paused, waiting for his repeated refusal to help her. Her words had hit his inner being; she had no doubt of that. The look in his eye—was it pain or a challenge?—underscored her statement. But if she had gone too far, had revealed more about his character than he was willing to acknowledge, she had just killed any chance at getting him to help. She dabbed her eyes again with the tissue. Speaking of Marta these days drew forth her tears as easily as turning a tap brought on water. If there were a possibility that McLaren would tackle the old case… She added unnecessarily, "The case has gone cold."

McLaren snorted again. "They sometimes do. It's usual for a case to go cold, Miss Isherwood, if the police either can't identify the victim or are unable to find out where the victim or a suspect went. If there's no trail to follow, no locality or time in which to place the suspect, the case grows cold, as you said. They come to a stonewall." He stopped abruptly, aware of the simile, feeling momentarily uncomfortable at having spoken harshly.

Linnet thrust her chin out, looking resolute and hurt simultaneously. "Sorry. I didn't mean to insult your intelligence. Perhaps I'm intruding on your time after all."

She started to turn when McLaren said, "Verity…who?"

She smiled tentatively and grasped the sides of her skirt. Pulling it up so that her calves were exposed to his sight and to the air, she shook the garment slightly so the damp hem would catch the breeze and dry more quickly. McLaren's gaze never left her face. She waved the skirt a few more times before releasing it, then replied, "Verity Dwyer. Marta's coworker at the shelter. They're friends besides being coworkers. Verity gave Marta the money for her casino outing—stole it from the shelter, actually." Linnet's face flushed with embarrassment at the situation. "It was terrible. The police thought it motive for Marta's death, you see, since Marta didn't live to replace the money from the cash till. And when the money from Marta's casino win wasn't found…well, that's when Verity was suspected. She lives in Youlgreave, but—"

"When was this?"

The question caught her off guard. She grasped the ring strung on a silver chain around her neck, her fingers sliding over the polished metal as though she was saying the rosary. Or feeling it as worry beads. Her eyelashes caught the sunlight as she blinked, and she asked what he meant.

"I mean when did it all happen? When was the murder, when was the body found, how was the body found, by whom? You mentioned she was found near Elton…" His voice had turned from the earlier hint of sarcasm to take on a hard edge. As hard as the stones of his wall. As unyielding in its quest for facts.

And interested. Despite having left the job a year ago, he was still intrigued with a good story, still a cop at heart. He crossed his arms on his chest again, as though mutely challenging her to persuade him, and said, "Let's have the story first. You want to sit down?" He grabbed the bucket that had held his jacket, trowel, string, chisel, and work gloves, and turned it upside down. "Or if you'd rather sit in my car…" His voice trailed off as he glanced downhill at his car, mentally seeing its interior. It was presentable, the rear hatchback section holding a few of his stonewall tools, the passenger seat free of work clothes or CDs or his guitar.

"This is fine," she said, perhaps more emphatically or quickly than she had meant.

His right eyebrow shot up again.

Wanting to smooth any choppy waters, she added, "I'm all right standing. Actually, I love the outdoors. I sit inside too much. I'm a secretary. I work in Chesterfield." She smiled hoping he wouldn't think her reluctance to sit closely confined with him in his car had prompted her decision to remain where they were.

McLaren nodded, his eyes still on his Peugeot 207 as he asked again for the facts of the case. He concentrated on Linnet's face as she began, on her emerald-green eyes that seemed bottomless and filled with pain.

"Last June, Marta and I had a girls' night out. Oh, nothing wild," she added as McLaren frowned. "Just a few hours away from the dullness of our lives."

"Away from the husband and kids," McLaren supplied. "You mentioned earlier that she was married and had a son. You?" He eyed her, trying to put her into a convenient slot. Her left ring finger was bare, but that didn't put her into the

Unmarried category. He'd known many women who wore no wedding rings.

"A boyfriend. Sean FitzSimmons. He's a writer."

"He's okay with your girls'-night-out thing?"

"Of course. I'm not chained to him."

"Marta isn't to her husband either, I assume. Her child is also old enough that she can escape the confines of home, leaving the dad to babysit."

"Yes. Chad—her son—is seventeen."

"Right. So you and Marta spent a few carefree hours doing…what?"

Linnet took a breath, as though steeling herself for a long recital or a tale told one too many times. "We went to a casino. We don't make a habit of playing—"

"Which one?"

"What? Oh."

McLaren nodded at the name of the Nottingham room. "When was this?"

"Last year. Eleventh of June. We'd been playing the slot machines for an hour or so. Won enough to make a small profit, but really no great luck. Nothing like we hoped. So we both switched to roulette. We'd been playing for twenty minutes or so when Marta screams. I had just ordered a drink, so my back had been turned from her. I hadn't seen what had happened. I thought maybe some berk had grabbed her handbag or spilled his drink down her back. But when I saw her standing up and yelling and waving her fists, I knew she was excited. I still remember the croupier pushing the stacks of chips toward her. I thought the table would tip over." She paused, as though reliving the scene. "I'd never seen so much money. It was like a miniature skyline of skyscrapers, or the Pennine mountain chain. The croupier kept corralling the stacks of chips and scooting them toward her. People were clapping and slapping her on the back. A man in a dark suit near the entrance to the room glanced in our direction at first—I thought he was going to come over and say we'd done something wrong—but he stayed at his post. I helped Marta gather up the chips and we left the table."

"How much did she get? Do you know?"

"Of course! We took it into the Ladies' and counted it. Then took it to the cashier to cash it in. I'll never forget the sum—it was huge. Two hundred fifty-three thousand, five hundred pounds. A *fortune*. We counted the chips over and over, making sure it was right before we cashed it in. Then, when we traded it in for the notes, we took it back to the Ladies' and recounted it. We'd counted it at the window, of course, but we counted it again in private. I— Neither of us had seen so much money at once. It was like a fairy tale."

Or a folk song, McLaren thought, the song "The Female Highwayman" running through his mind. "So, was Marta killed outside the casino, then? Someone noticed her big win and killed her?" He eyed Linnet, wondering how she had escaped injury if this were true.

"No. Not at all. We weren't so elated by the win that we forgot to be vigilant. I know that's a common happening, some bloke following the winner and then robbing her. So we looked around us as we went into the Ladies' and the cashier's window and again as we left the casino. No one was overtly following us. I would stake my life on that."

McLaren didn't comment on the inappropriateness of the phrase. Or that Marta had been the one to forfeit her life. He said, "So you made it outside without being mugged. What happened after that? How and when was Marta killed?" He had not been taking notes—he had nothing to use for that— but he was taking it all in with a cop's mind for facts. He would remember everything.

"I don't know."

"What?"

"I mean, I know how she was killed but not when. The pathologist gave all that at the inquest. She was shot. In—" Again she paused, not wanting to relive the nightmare of Marta's death, as though merely recounting the events would thrust her into the middle of the players. "She was shot in the head. Nearly point-blank range, if that means anything to you. I suppose it does," she added, watching McLaren's reaction.

"Where on the head? Back, front, left side…"

Linnet screwed up her face and mumbled, "Back."

"What about the ballistic findings? Caliber."

"Oh. A thirty-eight."

"Was it traced to a specific revolver or pistol? Did the police seize all thirty-eight-caliber weapons around Elton and other relevant areas, and test fire them?" God, what a job of work that would have been, he thought, envisioning the house-to-house requests, the confiscating and testing of weapons, the cartridge cases compared via ballistics…

She shook her head, glancing at her feet. "I don't know."

The answer surprised him. "Why not? You were at the inquest, weren't you?"

"Yes."

"So why—"

"I stepped out of the room around that time." She looked at him, hoping he would not be angry, hoping he would not think her the stereotype of a dumb, frivolous blonde. "I felt ill, like I was going to faint. All that talk about Marta's body and the bullet wound…" Her eyes silently asked him for understanding. "I heard something later that the bullet could not be tested, but I don't know why."

"Was she in her car, either when her body was found or when she was shot?"

"The police didn't think so. They found her car at her house, in Chesterfield, and—"

"At her *house!* How'd it get there if her body was discovered outside Elton?"

"No one really knows, but the police surmise that either she drove home and met someone, got in that person's car where she was killed…" She paused, again reliving the testimony of the inquest, recalling the stuffy oak-paneled room, the warmth of too many people, the rumors and speculation and whispered fanciful accusations, the tiresome drone of legal and medical jargon. Linnet swallowed, then added, "Or they drove to Elton, to the place where her body was found, and they got out and she was killed there."

"What's the significance of Elton?"

"Pardon?"

"Did Marta have a friend there? A family member? There's some reason why she went or was taken to Elton."

Linnet shrugged, her eyes downcast. "I'm sorry. I don't know of anyone."

"So she ends up in Elton and her car is at her home in Chesterfield. Her car was examined thoroughly, I assume. What was the result?"

"There was no blood in the car, nor any hair or fingerprints that weren't hers, her husband's or her son's."

"Which eliminates her being shot in her car, then. Evidently her casino money wasn't in the car, either." He sighed as Linnet shook her head. "In her purse—was that with her body?"

"Yes. It held the usual things: latchkey, car key, wallet, lipstick—"

"But not the two hundred and fifty-three thousand, five hundred pounds."

"Nor did the police find it near her body. It disappeared."

McLaren refrained from saying, "How surprising," and asked, "So what about Marta's body? Any defense wounds? Bruising on her hands or forearms, skin under her fingernails…" Probably not, he mutely answered himself. Shot in the back of the head signified she never saw it coming, never had a chance to fight for her life.

"No."

"And she was found…"

"Ten days later. Twenty-first of June. Near Elton, as I said. She had been dumped along the B5057. Just off the road, actually, which was why no one found her body immediately."

"It's a rather uninhabited place."

"A lot of ramblers like the spot," she said, her voice tightening.

"I just meant it'd take a while to find her, or anyone, in that area. A lot of moorland to contend with."

"Yes."

"So the police had no idea where to search originally for her the night of your big adventure, I assume. Elton's a bit of a distance from the casino in Nottingham." In Derbyshire, he would have added if the region's geography weren't so obvious. Nottingham was in Nottinghamshire, the county east of Derbyshire. Another police force, another mode of life.

As though privy to McLaren's thoughts, Linnet said, "I know it's odd, being so far from where we were that night. Even from our homes."

"And yours is…where?"

"We both live in Chesterfield."

McLaren did a quick mental calculation. Nottingham was perhaps twenty or thirty miles from Chesterfield, nearly on the Derbyshire-Nottinghamshire border. And about the same distance from Elton, which put the village on the western side of this triangle. "Why go to Elton to dispose of a body?"

"I don't know," Linnet said. "No one does. The police didn't catch the killer."

"Or they're not closing in fast enough, at any rate," McLaren clarified. "Who found her?"

"Some rambler. I can't recall his name."

"Someone above suspicion, evidently."

Linnet reddened but ignored the remark otherwise. "Neither Marta nor I know anyone who lives in Elton. She has a brother-in-law who lives in Matlock, but no one in that part of Derbyshire. I can't understand it."

"When did you two separate? You didn't drive down to Nottingham together?"

"I know it sounds odd, Mr. McLaren, but we were coming from different directions that evening. It was a Friday, which is Marta's half-day at the shelter. She gets off at noon. And since it was her half-day, she drove to Matlock to visit with her brother-in-law there and have lunch. We had arranged to meet at the casino at six o'clock, at the blackjack tables. I get off work at five every day, so I easily got there on time. Marta was a few minutes late. We played a few hands, as I said, then had dinner and decided to try the slot machines and the roulette table."

"Then you both drove home in your cars. Did you follow her?"

"What…like making certain she wasn't followed?"

"Not necessarily, though that would have been a laudable precaution. I just want to know if you drove home together, or when you separated. Helps me make sense of when her car appeared at her house."

"She *had* to have driven home. Otherwise the police—"

"Would've found a third party's DNA in the car."

Linnet bit the end of her fingernail, trying to recall the night. The sound of sheep bleating carried downwind, reminding McLaren of the unfinished stonewall that stretched over the hill. But he made no move to resume his work. Several minutes later, she said slowly, "I *think* we split up on the other side of Ripley."

"Ripley!" Clearly, McLaren hadn't expected the parting

to be so near to Nottingham. Ripley lay approximately equidistance between the casino and Matlock, farther northwest.

"I believe so. We'd driven up the A610 and then I turned north onto the A38, heading for home. I've tried to recall exactly when we split up. The trouble is, one set of headlights in a rear-view mirror looks remarkably like another."

"You weren't following her, then."

"No. I had started out that way, riding shotgun, as you said." She allowed herself a slight smile, as though envisioning an old American Western film, then said, "But we'd changed places quite soon after leaving Nottingham. A lorry was ahead of us and we both passed. Marta pulled back in line, behind a second lorry and probably assumed I would, too. I couldn't see the sense of that, so I passed the second one, thinking she'd follow me and get ahead of me again. The road was quite busy—well, being late Friday night, it would be. I waited for some time, oh, probably several minutes, before I saw a car pass the lorry and fall in behind me. I assumed it was Marta since the car stuck quite close behind me."

"You don't know for certain if it was she or not."

"No. But the car stayed with me all the way to Ripley, as I said. Right on my tail."

"And outside Ripley you turned right onto the A38, heading for Chesterfield."

"Yes. I don't know when I realized that the car following me hadn't turned."

"You didn't turn into a lay-by and ring her up on her mobile? Weren't you concerned with her driving home alone with that amount of money?"

"She'd told me before we left the casino that she was thinking about going back to her brother-in-law's. So when the car behind me disappeared, I figured she decided to do that and had continued on toward Matlock. I really didn't think much about it until much later that night when her husband rang me up to say Marta wasn't home and she wasn't at her brother-in-law's."

A lamb called to its mother somewhere higher up the hill before McLaren said, "Matlock isn't really that far from Elton, where her body was discovered. Certainly, it's not next door and there are closer places, but it's not ridiculously far away like Manchester, for instance."

"No, I suppose not." The words came slowly as Linnet pictured the distance between the two places.

"But Elton could be significant."

"Because it's out of the way, you mean?"

"That may be part of the reason it was chosen, yes."

"But not the main reason." She studied his face, trying to understand what he was reasoning. "Why? What do you think?"

"Elton is close to Matlock."

"You can't think her brother-in-law—"

"I don't think anything one way or the other right now, Miss Isherwood. Except that this friendly coworker of Marta's, this Verity Dwyer, lives in Youlgreave. And Youlgreave is about three miles from Elton. As I said, suggest anything to you?"

THREE

THEY ENDED THE TALK unsatisfactorily—Linnet walking back down the hill disappointed and angry, and McLaren having heard enough to convince him the woman was on a fool's errand. If the Derbyshire Constabulary had not been able to find a murderer by now, who was he to open up a can of worms one year later with his amateurish effort?

But the case nagged him, whispered to him the rest of the afternoon as he worked on another section of the wall, murmured questions as he sat at his kitchen table over tea, rumbled over the dialogue of the television program he was trying to watch. Finally giving it up, he switched off the telly, grabbed a beer from the refrigerator, and sat at the dining room table, a map of Derbyshire, a pen, and a sheet of paper in front of him.

Ten days Marta's body laid in the heather and grass alongside the road. Ten days for the insects and animals to work on her. He'd seen enough corpses to know what time, exposure, and carrion produced. Sometimes you ended up with a body barely recognizable. Sometimes it was recognizable enough to be unbearably heartbreaking. In the warm summer months, when a body goes off much more quickly, that ignoble end comes faster. He shook his head at the shameful end of life, wondered briefly how her husband and son had handled it, then forced himself to think as a detective once more.

How long he had worked, he didn't know. Time ceased to flow as he jotted down questions and bits of information from the case. He stared at the map, trying to make sense of the site where Marta Hughes' body had been found. Other than Elton being a fairly isolated village, did it offer another significant reason?

Linnet had said that the casino money had not been found on Marta's person, giving weight to the police theory of a robbery gone wrong. If no one from the casino had trailed her, how did Verity Dwyer know about the casino win? Was that mentioned at the inquest? Had Marta rung up Verity on her way home to tell her the good news? Was their friendship that close that Marta would do that?

Without mobile-phone records, McLaren had no answer to his first question. And without knowing Marta or Verity, he couldn't answer the second. Her car had been parked at her house, locked, her car key in her bag. The car sustained no damage, so Marta had not been forced off the road. It appeared as if she'd merely left it in the driveway, about to walk into her house at any minute. No one heard her scream or fight off an abductor; nothing like broken twigs on bushes or shoe scuffs on pavement marked a kidnapping. Didn't this point to an arranged meeting and continuance of the evening's fun? With someone other than Linnet…if Linnet told him the truth about that.

The more he thought of the case as Linnet recounted it to him, the more he knew he had no resources to help with the investigation. Assuming he would even dream of taking it on. And he was no longer a cop. Wasn't even a private detective. He was a laborer, now. A builder and repairer of dry stonewalls. Even if he wanted to help, he was hesitant to do so. Even if his professional police life had been in Staffordshire and the Marta Hughes case was here in Derbyshire, news traveled. Traveled about cases and coppers who had been disciplined or who had mucked up. Traveled with the excited whispers of back-stairs gossip. Especially in police departments. Was there a cop in England who hadn't heard

of him, hadn't heard what had happened to force him from
the constabulary? He took a long drink of beer, trying to push
the horror from his mind, trying to ignore the words that
still echoed in his head. But the map danced before his eyes,
the face—imagined though it was—shimmered beneath his
handwriting on the page. If Verity Dwyer hadn't killed Marta
but she was wrongly suspected of it, lost her job and friends
due to it, and living with that residue, as Linnet had said…

The glass slammed down onto the beer mat as the familiar
feeling of rage washed over him. Injustice. As Linnet pointed
out in the first minute of their meeting. She had known how
it would affect him. She had learned, somehow, of his past.
The word rattled in his brain, taunted him, dared him to up-
hold his values.

He got up, shoved his chair into the table, and got out his
guitar. A large Martin Dreadnought model that laid a rich,
full foundation for his voice and the voices of the members
of his folk singing group. He launched into "Travel the Country Round," not bothering to tune the instrument, not thinking of the song's lyrics. The third verse and chorus slid by
before the significance hit him. He'd sung about squander-
ing money. Was his subconscious whispering to him about
Verity Dwyer? Cursing his song choice, he began the introduction to "Cold Haily Rainy Night," a favorite of his and
one of his group's most requested songs. But the words died
on his lips before he had finished the second verse. Music
could not penetrate his black mood, as it usually did, lifting
his spirits. Perhaps Marta and Verity preyed too heavily on
his mind. And heart.

He put the guitar back in its case and got another beer from
the fridge. There was more than one way to quell the madden-
ing rush of words that persisted in his mind even through his
singing. He wandered into the back room, plopped down onto
the sofa, propped his feet on the coffee table, and downed

half of the bottle before he saw the framed citation on the wall. He stared at it, not reading the words he had memorized years ago, yet knowing what it said.

Chief Constable's Commendation. Detective Sergeant Michael Ross McLaren. You are commended for the professionalism, commitment, and determination you showed whilst carrying out your role of Family Liaison Officer during the investigation into the death of Hadley Davis. The sympathy and consideration you showed to the family undoubtedly helped them cope with not only the death of Hadley, but also with the distresses of the police investigations. Your effort helped to secure the successful conviction of Larry Tomkins at Nottingham Crown Court on 3 December 2004.

Here he was, a year after Marta Hughes died, refusing sympathy and consideration to another murder victim's friend. Was the Chief Constable's commendation merely words? Had his role then been a sham? Was it a sham now? Had he abandoned every principle he had ever believed in merely because he had suffered an injustice?

He woke the next morning, questions still echoing in his head. The night on the sofa had been comfortable enough, he supposed, for he didn't remember falling asleep. Frowning, he turned off the table lamp and glanced at the far wall. The commendation still glared at him from behind its glass cover; the photos of familiar faces smiled at him from their wooden frames. One in particular seemed to silently chide him. Dena Ellison, his former fiancée. She constantly commended him for his sense of right and integrity. Had he changed so much in the year since he had left her?

Wanting to block the memories, his eyes shifted to a photo of himself and another cop, his mate through police training. They'd had the good fortune to be appointed by the same constabulary after leaving university and worked together for ten years. He'd lost track of the man when they eventually drifted to different departments. Now McLaren started at his one-time friend before looking at his younger self. They were incredibly happy back then, ignorant of what could happen to a career, unaware of backstabbing and lies. McLaren's hazel eyes seemed alive with hope for the future, his smile bright and unforced. Sun lit his blond hair, giving him a healthy glow that hinted at a long, robust life. He snorted, averting his eyes from the photo. What the hell was he doing—playing at fortunetelling?

He grabbed the bottle sitting on the coffee table and downed the remaining beer in one long gulp. It was flat and tasteless. Seeing Dena's photo smiling at him from over the top of the bottle, he put the bottle back on the table. Nothing marred its smooth surface but the brown glass bottle and the television remote. In fact, nothing much occupied the room—or his house. Like the kitchen, the rooms were sparse in furniture and personal items. He had disposed of a quantity of things when his life turned upside down last June, ridding himself of painful memories by boxing up or throwing out his epaulette number pins, tie tacks, and other uniform items. Shoved numerous boxes of framed commendations and photos into the attic, not wanting to see his nemesis' grinning face, consigned police manuals and notebooks and police themed knick-knacks to the dust of garage shelving. But it hadn't cleansed him as much as he thought it would; he still carried their memories and that June day in his mind and soul. So why were these few photos and this particular commendation still on the wall to taunt him? Sure, he had seen them during his year of emotional exile. He couldn't have boxed them up and relegated them to a dusty corner if he had wanted to do. Something had stopped him.

Dena's mocking gaze pulled his eyes back to her but he quickly glanced at the adjoining wall, feeling strangely uncomfortable. Several nails protruded from the apple-green-painted surface, mute reminders of the sequestered photos and certificates that had decorated the space. Why haven't I removed those nails? Because I'm lazy? Because I never saw them? Because I haven't had a chance to hang the new family photos? He shook his head, opening up to the truth that he had barricaded from his mind and heart. The admission hit him as hard as a stone. Because deep down in my soul I still love the job; I want to be part of it. The reason, once acknowledged, left him shaky yet feeling empty, as though his heart or brain was missing. He leaned forward but stopped as he reached for the bottle. What would his life be like now if it hadn't been shot to hell last June? What would this room be like now—full of Dena's laughter and scent and the myriad things that made a house feminine, lived-in, and loved?

The doorbell's sharp ring burrowed into his thoughts. He glanced at the clock. Just on to half past five. Hell of an early hour to be calling. Exhaling loudly, he struggled up from the sofa, pushing his fist into the scatter pillow for leverage. The bell rang again, longer, seemingly incessant, as if the caller were eager to be let in. Or it was an emergency. Shouting that he was coming, McLaren stumbled into the front room, grabbing chair backs or edges of bookcases as he walked. He misjudged the corner of the display cabinet and slammed his thigh into the edge. Grimacing and grabbing his leg, he hobbled to the door and yanked it open. "Yes?"

No one was there.

McLaren limped outside. The sun was peaking over the eastern horizon, tinting the gray pre-dawn landscape with splashes of rose-hued light. Ashen shadows still claimed the western sides of the trees and shorter vegetation, wallowing nearly black in the thickets of roses and in the deeper wood.

But the air at his front door was releasing the darkness and McLaren could just make out images, rather like the slow evaporation of fog along a seacoast. He ignored the dew-laden grass that shed its moisture on his shoes and stepped onto the patch of lawn. The willow near the far side of the house waved its leafy boughs, startling him with the impression someone stood there. But the breeze parted the dense, hanging branches to reveal nothing unusual at its base. Neither did the ancestral oak harbor anyone. Nor the clump of daylilies outside his bedroom window. The birdbath, too, stood alone, offering no sanctuary but for the birds frequenting it for water. He peered at the hedgerow lining his side of the road, but could discern no one crouching there. Besides, a person would have to be daft to hide in those brambles. Dafter yet to ring his bell at this hour. And why? He stood on his front step, taking one last glance around the area. No, no one was in the garden, drive or road. No vehicle other than his own was in sight. Muttering, he marched inside and slammed the door.

An emphatic pounding on the kitchen door halted his return to the back room. He yelled again that he was coming before giving his thigh a quick massage. When he opened the door, no one was there. He cursed the impatient visitor in a rush of anger as he dashed down the steps.

Again, only the gray light greeted him, the half-hinted shapes of trees, rock wall, and bushes. Nothing moved to suggest human flight.

This time McLaren walked around the house, calling to the visitor. He tripped over a tree root, unseen in the hazy light, and fell heavily, knocking the breath from his lungs. He lay there, cursing in pain, getting his wind back, then rolled onto his side and eased up from the damp earth. A check of the front and back gardens, his car, and the blind side of the stonewall revealed nothing. Anger and frustration prodded him into the road, and he walked several hundred yards in both directions before admitting defeat. Minutes later he reentered the kitchen without having heard from or seen anyone.

He paused at the electric kettle, thinking he would have a cup of tea. But the effort seemed too great at the moment, so he returned to the back room. A minute later he was oblivious to the dull aches in his thigh and chest; he fell asleep.

He woke in what seemed like no time, but the clock indicated he'd been napping for nearly a half hour. Groaning, he grabbed the empty beer bottle and slowly stood up. The room was cold and dim in the early-morning light, reminiscent of the aftermath of a party. He stretched, feeling in his back and neck the effects of his rock lifting and night on the sofa, the aftermath of excessive drinking and his fall, and the lack of sleep pounding in his head. Stumbling over to the window, he angled his head from side to side. His neck vertebrae popped, relieving some of the stiffness. He shoved the curtains open and daylight flooded the room, making him squint and lower his head. Without looking up, he left the room.

He rinsed out the bottle at the kitchen sink, put it in the glass recycling bin by the back door, then wandered into his bedroom. The bed was unmade from the previous night's sleep, the way it usually was except for the weekly change of bed linen. He hadn't come to make up the bed, though. He went to the linen bin inside the closet, pulled out the shirt he'd worn yesterday, and grabbed the scrap of paper from the front pocket. Unfolding it, he returned to the kitchen. He paused in the doorway and stared undecidedly at the phone. It was one way to dam the whispers in his head. But was it the best way? He glanced at the beer bottle lying in the nearly full recycling bin, the sunlight glancing off its shiny surface. There were other ways to drown the voices, to bring peace. But the paper in his hand seemed to exert a stronger pull. Maybe it was his cop's curiosity. Maybe he didn't want to drink himself into oblivion in order to forget. After all, that was a dangerous path on which to embark. So he filled the electric kettle with water, flipped on the switch, put a tea bag into a ceramic mug, and dialed Linnet's phone number.

He had nearly talked himself into hanging up when she answered the phone. He could have hung up or apologized that he had a wrong number, but something within him made him answer her expectant "Hello?" He poured the boiling water into his mug and said, "Good morning, Miss Isherwood. Michael McLaren. I've thought it over and I'll investigate the murder case."

FOUR

In the few seconds before she answered the phone, he looked around his kitchen, perhaps truly seeing it for the first time. Though why, he could not later remember. An ordinary room, perhaps smaller than most, comprised of white appliances standing stark against royal-blue walls. Police-lantern blue, his mates in the job joked on seeing it when they had descended on him for poker or to watch the game on the telly. Nothing adorned the walls except a battery-operated clock. Navy-blue-and-white cotton curtains bracketed the windows; the electric kettle and a toaster were the only smaller appliances he owned. Essentials for his life in an equally elementally furnished room. Now, as he listened to the phone ring, he gazed at the walls. He had vowed to repaint them last autumn, needing to cover up the reminder of his days with the police.

Yet, he was about to plunge into detective work again, he told himself as he listened to Linnet's excitement. Was he kidding himself that he could investigate a case alone? What would happen when the Derbyshire Constabulary got wind of his nosing about? Would there be repercussions?

But the questions faded to trivialities as Linnet asked if he wanted to meet somewhere to get more information.

"Might be best," he said, ever cautious of overheard phone conversations. "When?" He tried to ignore his mounting heart rate but if he were honest with himself, he'd admit he wanted to be back in the job. However distant it would prove. And, he thought as he looked around his kitchen, if he were excruciatingly honest, he would own up that he was also doing it for the money. Stonewall repair work may be easy to come by, but it didn't pay as much as his police job. So he fought back the rush of adrenalin and jotted down meeting time and place on the pad of paper. "Bring along photos of anyone Marta knew, if you have them," he added, tapping the tip of the pencil on the paper. "It'll help."

He rang off, excitement and dread and a tinge of fear surging through his body. Had he lost his mind? Was he about to step back into the fire?

He shuddered, and his eyes caught sight of the smooth rock he used as a paperweight. It normally brought remembrances of the hike last April with Dena. Yet, now it whispered to him, mocked him. Was he about to trade the stones that formed his career for the stony silence of annoyed acquaintances? The paperweight stone was as different from the sharp-edged rocks comprising his dry stonewalls as his life had become after abandoning his police career. Yet, here he was, about to plunge into detective work again. Was he making a mistake? He felt at ease repairing stonewalls, so why leave his comfort zone for a potential hornet's nest? Because he needed the money?

A glance at the clock told him he had an hour to kill before leaving to meet Linnet. He wandered over to the dining room table to study the map of Derbyshire again. It was purely a time waster; he knew Derbyshire as well as any constable or Royal mail postman. True, Elton was farther south than his village of Somerley, but he had roamed the county in his youth and probationary days, been on holidays to the Manifold, Matlock Bath, Ashbourne, and Hathersage. So why was he consulting the map? To take him back to a less troubled time?

His phone rang and he answered, grabbing it absentmindedly, not looking at the caller ID display, his mind still on Elton, the village where Marta Hughes' body had been found. So the feminine voice that wished him good morning more than destroyed his contemplation; it dragged him out of the room and plunged him into cold water.

"Dena?" He managed to squeak out her name before his throat constricted.

"It's good to hear your voice, too, Michael."

He wiped his hand across his forehead, suddenly damp with sweat. A glance at the calendar confirmed the suspicion burgeoning in the back of his mind. 12 June. One year to the day that he unceremoniously shoved her from his life. Now it sounded as though she were trying to nestle back in.

"You're not outdoors, working on a wall? I didn't know where you'd be, but I thought I'd try your house before I tried your mobile." She hesitated, unsure of what to say or how to say it once the words did come to mind.

In the brief silence Dena's mental image faded, to be replaced by that of Linnet Isherwood. She still unsettled him. Was it her green eyes or the nearly imperceptible pleading in her voice? Or the way she had discovered his whereabouts? He thought himself fairly isolated from the world, from the source of his wounds, but she had tracked him down not only to his village but, more importantly, to the wind-swept hill where he worked. No matter how, she disturbed him. And more than keeping him from his repair work.

McLaren picked up the rock on the table, cradling it in his palm and hefting it several times, judging its weight. A good weapon. If hurled hard enough and accurately enough. Enough to kill a man… He set it back on the table, shaking off the images of death he'd seen during his police career. But the stonewall on which he'd been working stood rock solid in his mind's eye. As did his meeting with Linnet. He had returned a stone to the pile near his feet that morning. It needed trimming; it was too long to fit the spot he had been repairing. The first few top courses of stone fanned out at his feet, pushed from the wall by a sheep or horse struggling to leap over it, probably. He had eyed the length of the wall. Other similar spots needed repair, the usually smooth top jarringly jagged in sections, the stones jumbled against the wall's base or strewn into the field.

He fought the nearly ingrained urge to investigate, to see if clues to the inept jumper's identity could be found. That feeling died quickly when he picked up his stone hammer, reminding him that he was no longer a detective. Just as the images of Linnet and the wall now finally crumbled beneath Dena's voice.

McLaren shook the last impression of that morning's thirst-defying heat from his mind and said, "No. I'm not out. I'm still at home."

"A bit unusual, isn't it, being Friday morning?"

"Good to know your calendar's not slow," he said, trying to think of something to say. He knew it was inane, that he should have been friendly, but a kernel of fear was gaining a toehold in his heart.

"God, you haven't lost your manners. You always did know how to sweet talk me." She let the silence grow between them and McLaren heard her faint breathing in his ear.

"You didn't ring me up just to remind me of the date, Dena. What do you want?"

"I would've thought that was obvious, Michael. If the date isn't significant—"

"It's not exactly the occasion for flowers and chocolate. I repeat: what do you want?"

"You."

A dog barked in his neighbor's back garden, bringing a bit of normalcy to the surreal conversation. McLaren closed his eyes, mentally counted to ten, and said, "It's over, Dena. One year ago it was over. Or don't you remember standing outside my door, crying—"

"You don't need to remind me, Michael. It's all too well engraved on my mind, thank you."

"Then what—"

"As you said, it's been a year. I thought…I hoped enough time had passed that you missed me, that you wanted to get back together. I know how much you've been hurt, Michael. You *know* I do. I was with you through the entire ordeal. I understand. But you can't be bitter all your life, darling. You've got to pick up your life and move on. Just because someone did an unspeakable—"

"Look." McLaren's voice cut through her sympathy like a cleaver slicing through meat. "I appreciate you must still be hurting, too, or you wouldn't have rung me up. I'm sorry for that. Sorry you're in pain and sorry I ended our engagement. *However*—" he said as he heard her intake of breath, "I've no desire to renew our relationship or engagement. Don't take it personally. I'd feel like this about any woman in my life. I'm just not ready to relive that segment or open myself up to those memories." He paused, aware of his racing heart, aware that it was a lie. He *had* opened his heart to memories simply by staring at her photo and the Chief Constable's commendation. And now he was going to be a cop in all but name when he started looking into Marta Hughes' death. He pulled in his bottom lip, his upper teeth pressing into its flesh, as he considered what next to say. He didn't want to hurt her; there was enough pain in both of them to last the rest of their lives. But he didn't want to feed her false hope…

"You needn't change your phone number, Michael. Don't worry that I'll be retaliating by ringing you at two a.m. Have a nice life."

She rang off before McLaren could apologize.

He stood there, staring at the phone receiver, picturing Dena tearing up his photo—if she hadn't done so a year ago.

She was entitled to her anger; he'd been a jerk. But his anger, his sense of justice…

The mantel clock struck the hour and McLaren realized the irritating beeping sound was coming from the phone. He hung up slowly, torn between ringing her back and letting go. His fear won, and he quickly showered, shaved, and dressed. He grabbed a quick cup of tea and downed a slice of toast before heading out of the door. He cleared his car of his work tools and consulted his note once more before treading down on the car's accelerator. The Peugeot's tires squealed as they bit into the roadway and the speedometer continued to keep pace with McLaren's racing mind.

The village fell behind him in a blur of gray and green, giving way to the gray and green of the surrounding countryside. Stonewalls, rock cliffs, hedgerows, and trees melted into an indistinguishable mass as he concentrated on the ribbon of black asphalt and Marta Hughes. He was barely aware of the roadside sign declaring "Castleton" as he turned left onto the A625, so many times he had driven the route. But as he parked opposite the hotel and got out of the car, he was more than aware of the umbrella tables in the outdoor dining section, the person chalking the day's lunch special on the two-sided blackboard by the wrought-iron gate. He felt alive for the first time in a year.

Linnet saluted him with a glass of tomato juice and waited until McLaren joined her at one of the tables before she spoke. She was dressed similarly to the previous day, but had changed to a short, floral-printed silk skirt instead of the ankle-length cotton piece. Her T-shirt was of the same green hue as yesterday's. A silk scarf of the same print was tied loosely around her neck, obscuring most of the silver chain and the ring dangling from it. "What would you like?" she asked as McLaren took the chair opposite her. The chair leg scraped across the pebbled concrete, startling the sparrows attacking a bread crust on the pavement.

"I assume you mean from the menu, which rather limits the options."

"Cuts out world peace, wisdom, and happiness, then. Pity." She returned his smile and pushed aside her handbag.

McLaren sighed deeply and gazed at the hotel's façade. Flower boxes and planters overflowed with red geraniums, a brilliant splash of color against the ash-gray stone of the building. The front door, hung on massive brass hinges, was propped open with a brass kettle filled with books. "Looks like someone's going to do some major reading," he said, nodding toward the volumes. "Not worried about theft, I take it."

"I believe they're free. There's a sign, though you probably can't see it…" She craned her neck to see the door. "Yes. They're donated by various libraries as well as by some locals. It's a nice thought, isn't it, finding a new book you might like? Now, what would you like, other than the aforementioned non-menu items? I'm buying. Part of the investigator's fee—plus expenses I think you said. You might as well begin the Expense bill right now." She watched him as he half turned in his chair to read the chalked menu on the side of the building. "I can recommend the juice, if that has any weight with you." She rocked the glass slightly. The juice caught the sunlight and momentarily looked like a pool of blood.

McLaren shook his head, and the image, if not his headache, vanished. Craning his head to his right, he called to the waiter, "I'll have some coffee, please. Black." The man nodded, left his chalk and sign, and wandered into the hotel.

"Bare coffee, as my sister calls it? No latte? No cappuccino? Nothing like mocha hazelnut?"

"No. Plain and simple, like me."

"Just the essentials. I see." She smiled, holding the glass in her hand as though waiting to toast their collaboration.

McLaren sat back in the chair, feeling the cold metal dig into the soreness of his back. It jolted him awake more than the beer and tea had earlier this morning. More like the water up at the wall repair yesterday. The afternoon had been blisteringly hot, the heat coming off the pasture and rock face like someone had opened an oven door. He had tilted back his head, taking gulp after thirsty gulp of the cool water before tipping some on top of his head. Its coldness had hit his scalp with the sharpness of a rock edge. He had shaken off the excess water, gasping as he ran his fingers through his hair, combing the dark blond locks back into their crew-cut style. That was how the metal chair back bit into him today—sharp, frigid, and jerking him awake. He waited until the waiter had brought his coffee before continuing with his questions.

"Are you always so cautious, Mr. McLaren?" Linnet nodded toward his left hand.

He glanced down at the tabletop, at his hand that covered the small notebook. His fingers curled to lightly run across the opened spine. "I've never been accused of writing legibly, but there's always a first time that someone else can read my scrawl." Pausing with the pen tip on the paper, he reread the notes he had jotted down, then asked for the phone number and address of Marta Hughes' home.

"I haven't said a thing of her husband, Alan," Linnet said, watching McLaren notate the information. "I didn't feel it was my place. Also…" She watched a tourist take a photo of Peveril Castle before continuing. "I thought you decided against taking the case. Yesterday you seemed—"

"A little voice convinced me to change my mind."

"Then I salute the little voice." She raised her glass toward McLaren and finished the last of the juice, then set the glass on the tabletop. He thought how well it complemented her lipstick—dark crimson and catching the light. She brought a folded sheet of paper from her handbag and handed it to him. Paper clipped to it were several photos.

"Key players, I take it," he said, slipping the pictures from the clip and opening the paper.

"In happier times, too." Her voice held a suggestion of regret and sadness. "But most of our youthful days were happier, weren't they?" She had forced a cheerful note into her tone as she watched him examine the faces and scan the typed information. She added, "Alan and Chad…you can figure out. They're the man and teenager. That's Marta with them."

He brought the photo closer to his eyes so he could stare at the woman he was trying to help. She appeared to be in her mid-forties, a brunette with hazel eyes that looked amusingly at the photographer. She came up to her husband's chin, which she clutched with a thin hand. The husband was a graying brunet, and while her son had inherited her eye color, he was blond. McLaren had no time to comment on this, for Linnet said, "The others…" She leaned forward, her left arm bent and supporting her, and tapped each photo as she mentioned their names. "The group shot is Marta, her boss, Derek Fraser, and Emlyn Gregg, who is the vet for the shelter. This—" She skipped over the others in the photograph and pointed to the woman to the extreme left. "That's Verity Dwyer."

"The wrongly suspected coworker." McLaren looked at the woman in the photo. Her auburn hair shone in the sunlight and her blue eyes smiled back at him.

Linnet explained, "Yes. Suspected of killing Marta, though that wasn't proved. But she was convicted of stealing money from the shelter. She's three months into her sentence. She was— Oh, it's extremely involved."

"I've got more time than money. Tell me."

FIVE

McLAREN SETTLED BACK in the chair. The wrought iron had lost its coldness and now just held the unyielding support he needed. He moved the notebook to his lap and eyed Linnet.

She pushed the empty glass to her right, as though considering how best to tell the story, then said, "As I explained yesterday, Verity and Marta worked at the same place."

"An animal shelter. On Blackbeech Road. Noah's Ark, I recall."

Linnet blinked in surprise, then said with a somewhat tremulous voice, "Uh, yes. Quite right. I'm impressed with your research."

"It's included in the price." He allowed himself a quick flash of a smile, took a sip of coffee, then asked her to continue.

"Well, Verity and Marta became friends. Because they considered themselves friends, Marta asked Verity for the loan of two hundred pounds."

It was McLaren's turn to blink. "Why so much? What did she need it for? Did she say?"

"Same thing she always needed money for. Same thing she did on our girls' night out."

"Gambling. She couldn't take money out of her bank account or ask her husband?"

"They're well off, but not dripping rich, if you understand me."

"If that's true, her husband must get a nice pay packet. Marta can't make much, working in a charity shelter."

"She didn't. But Alan does. He's in senior management…
at National Westminster Bank."

"So they live on his money, for the most part."

"Yes. And because he works at National Westminster—"

"Their accounts are with that bank. She couldn't withdraw
cash on her own?"

"Certainly. She often did. But Alan didn't know about her
gambling. Well, that's not exactly true. He knew she went to
the casino—that we both went—but he thought it was just
for fun, a few times a year. She didn't tell him every time
she went or how much she lost."

"He was under the impression, then, that it was just a pas-
time like everything else she did."

"She had become more and more addicted to it. Oh, not
that she played every night or every weekend. But she was
showing the signs of the addict. She tried to keep it from
Alan, so of course she couldn't withdraw the money. He
would have seen the reference to it on their monthly statement and asked her what the money was for."

"And Christmas or a birthday, presumably, was too far
away to furnish her with that story."

"I'd loaned her all the money I could, so she turned to
Verity."

"Was she in the hole to you or anyone? If she asked people for money—"

"She *always* paid it back, Mr. McLaren. That was the
weird thing about it. Marta may have loved to gamble, but
somehow she usually won. Even on the nights she lost heavily, she'd win huge on her return trip."

"So she always had money from her winnings to repay
her debts." He tapped his pen against the notepad as he considered his next question.

Linnet threw the last of her Danish to the sparrows, watching them flock to the offering.

Over the noisy chirping, McLaren said, "You said yesterday that Verity stole some money. I assume this comes into play in the broad picture of what happened to Marta."

"It was last year. Third of May. Verity hadn't any money of her own to loan Marta. That's why this turned so tragic. Verity took some cash from the cash drawer. Yes, I know," she added as McLaren swore, "it was stupid, dangerous, and unethical."

"Besides dishonest."

"Sometimes you do stupid, dangerous, and dishonest things for a friend, not stopping to think how it might turn out."

"Verity got caught in a trap of her own making, I assume."

"Marta swore Verity to secrecy and said she'd pay it back the next day, after she won. Marta went to the casino that night and promptly lost everything—the shelter's money and her own. She was devastated. She didn't know how she was going to tell Verity."

I know the feeling, McLaren thought, phrases of his conversation with Dena welling in his mind. Breaking bad news, especially news that reflects badly on the teller, is always hard. Even as a cop, he'd never found an easy way to tell anyone that their world was about to be knocked out of orbit. He rubbed his forehead and glanced at the sparrows. One grabbed a large crumb and flew away with it to eat in peace. Dena had taken their engagement breakup rather peacefully. At least there had been no screaming. Just tears as she quietly asked questions. McLaren gave his forehead one last vigorous rub and leaned forward, resting his forearms on the edge of the table. "Had this ever happened before? Not her losing; her taking the shelter's money or getting a personal loan from Verity, and then having to explain why she couldn't repay the money promptly?"

"No. As I said, Marta usually won, but on the few times

she had borrowed money from someone, she could always win it back within a few days."

"You said Marta didn't frequent the casino that regularly."

"She did when she owed someone money. She'd go back the next day or so in order to win it back. It preyed on her mind if she couldn't reimburse the person. She felt strongly about her debts."

"So she returned to the casino the next day or so."

Linnet grimaced, shaking her head. "Unfortunately, two days later she became ill. She was out of work for a week."

McLaren paused, as though mulling over the consequences. "Did she get back to the casino then?"

"No. More back luck. The shelter's treasurer appeared on the tenth while Marta will still at home, and—"

"Don't tell me. Discovers the shortage. Ouch. Is that why Verity was suspected of Marta's murder? You told me yesterday that she wasn't charged with it, I recall. But something obviously happened in conjunction with this gambling episode and the theft. What?"

"In a roundabout way, yes. When Verity couldn't explain the discrepancy, she was arrested."

"Why? Had she stolen money before, but they overlooked it for some reason?"

"She was the only person who ran the gift shop. It's in a room off the main reception area. And because she is the only person with access to the cash."

He opened his mouth to say something but Linnet continued, "The register is locked overnight, you see."

"And Verity has the only key."

"Yes. Well, Derek, her boss, and the treasurer have keys. But Derek wasn't even under suspicion of the theft."

"He have an alibi for the time in question?"

"I believe so. Anyway, he wasn't ever seriously considered as a suspect."

McLaren snorted and shook his head.

"Verity works ten to four, Tuesdays to Saturdays. The rest of the time the shop section is closed. Verity took the money from *that* cash drawer, thinking it wouldn't be missed so readily. Sales for the dogs and cats and other animals up for adoption are transacted at the main register in the reception area. That's always busy. Marta knows the money's counted each morning, at the beginning of shift, so the employees know how much change they have for the day's business."

McLaren nodded, his eyes fixed on Linnet's face. "Good news, bad news."

"I suppose so. Anyway, the discrepancy was discovered and Verity was blamed."

"Due to the limited access of the cash drawer."

"Yes."

"Hell of a finger-pointer, that." He picked up his coffee. The cup was cold to his touch. He started to angle in his chair, searching for the waiter. Last time McLaren had seen him, the man was chalking items on the menu near the street. As McLaren grabbed the chair's arms, Linnet said, "Maybe it's nothing, but I think someone's fooling about near your car." She nodded toward McLaren's Peugeot as he stood up. "I could be wrong, but I thought…"

Her voice trailed off as McLaren said, "I'll be right back," and darted across the road.

Of course no one loitered at the off side of the car. He hadn't expected that. And the far side, along the pavement, harbored no one other than the usual tourists consulting guide books or taking photographs, and villagers hurrying to shops for the day's marketing. McLaren paused at the passenger door and squatted as he looked at the door lock and window.

No tell tale pry marks marred the pristine paint job. He tried the door latch. The door remained closed.

If anyone had been tampering with the car, was he farther down the block, waiting until McLaren returned to the hotel café? Unnerving thought.

McLaren jogged to the corner, eyeing everyone as he passed, glancing into alleys and store windows. No one seemed to be watching him. When he got to the end of the block, he jogged back, again passing the same people and stores, again looking for suspicious activity. At the end of the row of shops, he paused, unsure if he should try the opposite side of the street. But what good would that do? If someone had been trying to break into his car, he wouldn't be leaning against a lamppost, advertising his wait. McLaren turned and walked back to the hotel.

"Anything?" Linnet asked as McLaren reclaimed his seat.

"Not even a sparrow," he said as one lone bird landed on the back of a vacant chair.

"Sorry. Guess I was wrong."

"That's all right. I didn't get in my morning jog before I came."

"Then it wasn't in vain." She smiled, her voice taking on a lighter tone.

Jotting something in his notebook, he said, "Always best to be sure. Someone could have been trying for a quick grab, though there's nothing in my car that's visible. Or valuable."

"I would have felt terrible if something had been stolen and I never said."

"I applaud your call to good citizenship, then." He settled back into the chair again. The morning sun had warmed the wrought iron and the heat felt good on his stiff muscles. "So, you were telling me about Verity. She was blamed for the missing money due to the limited access of the cash drawer."

"Yes. It was awful. A farce, in my opinion. The trial began

several months later and she began serving her sentence last year in June."

"So they didn't pin the murder on her, then. Just the cash theft."

"Yes. They knew it wasn't embezzlement because the money had gone missing immediately from the till, in one lump. The prosecution tried to link this to Marta's murder, but they couldn't make a case of it."

McLaren rubbed his eyes, imagining the court proceedings. He could almost hear the prosecution ranting that Verity had hired a hit man to rob Marta after she had won big at the casino. But the robbery had gone wrong and Marta wound up dead. "So Verity is convicted of theft and nothing more."

"Fortunately, yes. It would've been hell to go through the process of overturning a false conviction of murder, the lawsuits for false imprisonment, the retrial. She was lucky in that aspect."

"Her defense council couldn't come up with anything that the jury believed, I take it." He tossed the pen and notebook onto the table and finished his coffee. It had grown cold during the interval but he barely tasted it. The whole story stank, as far as he was concerned. As for circumstantial evidence... He'd seen many cases solved with just this type of reasoning and evidence no more concrete than theories, bad personal histories, and gossip. "Marta never confessed to the theft, then."

"No." She started to reach for McLaren's hand, then thought better of it and laid her hand on her lap. Her voice softened as she searched McLaren's face for his reaction. "Please don't judge her too harshly, Mr. McLaren. She was actually a good person. She was a loyal friend and would do anything for anyone."

"Except tell the truth when it would free them from a prison sentence." He'd said it so bitterly his cheeks flushed immediately afterward. Embarrassed at his outburst, he shifted the blame for his red coloring by fanning his face with the notebook. In a less accusatory tone, he added, "We've all been guilty of transgressions, Miss Isherwood. Some just have more severe penalties than others. I know." He left unsaid the offense leveled against him; Linnet had known of it before she had searched for him.

"You'll still take the case?" She leaned forward slightly as she opened her handbag. "I know it's probably a bit more than you expected, but none of us believe Verity's involved any way in Marta's death. She's not that sort of person. She just had the misfortune that the treasurer showed up when he did. If Marta had lived—" She broke off and avoided McLaren's eyes, feeling the rush of heat to her cheeks. She ran her tongue over her lips and looked at him as she continued. "Marta would have paid back the money. She's not a thief. You'll help us, won't you? You'll take the case?"

McLaren nodded and watched Linnet's pen make out a check for a down payment. When she had signed it and handed it to him, she said, "Her husband, Alan, would certainly be glad to talk to you. He doesn't say so, but I know he's dying inside."

"I better see him immediately, then."

Linnet searched McLaren's eyes for a sign of understanding or sympathy. He merely stared at her, as though he hadn't yet decided on something. Linnet said, "The police couldn't find the killer. Maybe it was because too much time had elapsed before they found her body. But I don't believe everyone they questioned could have proved their alibis, could they? You'll be able to find her killer?"

He stood up, folded the check and slipped it into his pocket, and thanked her before replying, "Slugs aren't always under the first rock you turn over."

SIX

LINNET ISHERWOOD HAD satisfied his curiosity as to why she knew so much about the financial problems with the confession that she'd sat in daily for the duration of the trial. Or, as she actually stated it, when your best friend's been murdered, each fact is branded upon your heart.

McLaren sat in his car, coaxed the check from his pocket, and stuffed it more securely into his wallet. He'd have to wait until Monday to deposit it, but it comforted him knowing a transfusion for his account was less than two days away.

His mobile phone rang; he looked at the caller ID display before answering. Dena wasn't going to catch him again. Though it was nearly as bad, he conceded, answering the ring. It was his sister. He took a deep breath, silently cursed, then forced a cheerfulness that he didn't feel into his voice. Perhaps his sister wouldn't notice the strain. "Hi, Gwen," he said a little too brightly. "Up awfully early, aren't you?"

"You forget about the early bird, Mike." Her voice was strong and laced with the Derbyshire accent of their upbringing.

"Which are you—the bird or the worm?"

"Better not ask. I'm still deciding. You at work?" She didn't have to specify his job; she'd emotionally held his hand through his decision to leave the police and had encouraged him to take up the stonewall repairing, believing he needed time away from people in order to heal.

"Yes, but not what you think." He told her about his decision to look into the cold case.

The silence on the other end of the phone told him she either was surprised or disapproved of his decision.

"You're always encouraging me to get back with people," he said.

"I was thinking more about you and Dena, not a murder victim, however metaphorically you take that."

"Is that why you rang me up?" He had a suspicion she knew the significance of the day's date. "Why aren't you painting something? You run out of canvas or is your easel broken?"

"I'm serious, Mike. You've been alone too long. You need to make an effort to get back with her, with your friends. With Jerry and me," she added almost as an afterthought. "We miss being with you."

"Let me heal in my own way, in my own time, Gwen," he snapped, the calculated cheeriness forgotten, the bitterness creeping back into his voice. "You don't know what I went through or how I feel. You have no right to judge me."

"I'm not judging you. I just want to see you happy again and spending some time with us."

"It'll happen, Gwen. Just don't push me."

"No one is pushing you, Mike. We're just concerned for your health. You've shut us out of your life. We can't get near you. You've distanced yourself from us as surely as if you'd moved to Australia or the moon. You've shut down emotionally and spiritually, like you're barricaded inside your house. You won't share anything with us—your thoughts, your work, your feelings—"

So that was it, his emotions again. "I'll call when I'm ready, Gwen, and not before. I know you mean well, I appreciate your concern, but don't hound me about this. I still need to sort this through." He flipped the phone closed and tossed it onto the passenger seat. She would never understand his hurt and anger. She hadn't the years and the history that made it so crushing.

Suddenly hungry, he searched through the car's glove compartment. Sometimes a Kit Kat or package of trail mix or packet of biscuits lurked between the maps and petrol receipts and tire-pressure gauge. He slammed the compartment door closed. Nothing.

Glancing back at the outdoor dining area, he considered going back and ordering something. Linnet had remained at the table after he left and was now making a call on her mobile phone. He watched her animated hands as she talked, silently emphasizing her conversation. He was still there when she paused several feet from his car, pursing her lips against the phone's mouthpiece. Cooing to her boyfriend, he thought, as he heard the name Sean. Dena and I had been like that, he thought.

A flash of bright red caught his eye and he half turned in his car seat to look. The rear half of a car's back wing shone in the sun for a second, then disappeared behind the edge of a shop. He half leaned out of his car window, trying to see around the building. But the row of shops presented a seamless façade, at least as far as he could see from this viewpoint. He was about to start his car and zip up the side street, when Linnet held up her free hand and mouthed something to him. Exhaling heavily, he removed his hand from the ignition key, promising himself that he'd somehow find out if that had been Dena's red MG, as he suspected. And if she were following him.

Smiling, Linnet held the phone out to McLaren as she stopped opposite his window. "My boyfriend," she explained. "Sean. He'd like to ask you something, if you have a minute."

McLaren shrugged and grabbed the mobile. "This is McLaren." He glanced at Linnet for a hint of why Sean wanted to speak to him.

"Hello, Mr. McLaren. This is Sean FitzSimmons, a friend of Linnet's. Has she mentioned me to you?"

What did the man mean? His life story? McLaren replied that Miss Isherwood had spoken of him.

"I know this will sound positively bonkers, but I'd like to ask if you would answer some police questions for me."

Whatever McLaren had been expecting, it hadn't been this. "Police—"

The voice went on. "Nothing confidential. God, no! Just some procedural things."

McLaren glanced at the photos lying on the car seat next to him. How'd he get into this? What was Sean FitzSimmons on about?

"I'm a writer," Sean explained. "I write thrillers."

McLaren's breathing returned to normal. "Oh, yes. Miss Isherwood mentioned that when we first met. I'm sorry I'd forgotten."

"No harm. I've got a plot I'm working on now for my current book. I have this situation that I'm not sure about. I was hoping that you, being a police detective, could—"

McLaren stopped Sean right there. "No, I'm not a police officer anymore, Mr. FitzSimmons. Besides, I doubt if I'll have time to confer with you. I'm taking on this job just to help out Miss Isherwood. After it's finished I'll return to my other line of work. Sorry I can't help. Ask at any of the larger police stations. They've got officers who do that sort of thing. Best of luck." He handed the phone back to Linnet and shrugged again, as though to say that was all he could do.

"Don't lose any sleep over it," she said, pocketing the phone. "I love him to death but he's basically lazy. He thought you could sort out his plot problem for him. It'll be fine. And, uh, thank you again for taking all this on." She flashed him a smile before continuing down the street.

Thank me when you see how this turns out, he wanted to say. He turned the key in the car's ignition, hesitated as though weighing the odds of finding Dena on the road from Castleton, then eased away from the curb. He'd do a bit of research in the public library before talking to Marta's near and dear.

THE REFERENCE LIBRARIAN furnished McLaren with what press cuttings and reports she had from the murder investigation. The coroner's hearing had been big news in the local newspaper, which gave McLaren a break. He sat at a table, making notes of the medical information, the police findings, and statements from those who knew Marta. The bullet that killed Marta was, as Linnet told him, a .38 caliber, but no extensive ballistic tests had been conducted with known guns; the bullet had been too badly smashed up inside Marta's skull.

He visited the police station that had handled the investigation and read through those files and statements. They corroborated the information from the inquest. At least no one had changed his story. When he closed the last report he sat back in his chair and rubbed his eyes. The reading per se hadn't brought on his headache; his brain thudded from the amount of information he absorbed in so short a time. Like being back in university, cramming for a test, he thought. The constable accepted the returned files with the same wary monotone he had uttered when first handing them over. He glared at McLaren, muttering something about the average citizen playing at Inspector Morse. McLaren felt the familiar race of his heart, the tightening of his throat. Had the officer heard about McLaren and his departure from the Force? Or was it just that someone outside the job requested access to the case notes? He had no way of knowing. And it really didn't matter. McLaren slammed the door behind him as he left to talk to Alan and Chad Hughes.

HE WAS ON THE eastern side of Castleton, having just emerged from the Winnat's Pass, when he noticed a hiker limping toward him along the side of the road. He slowed to glance at the woman—a habit from his cop days. She leaned heavily on a walking stick, took a step, then stopped to rub her ankle. But the thing that held McLaren's attention was the hiker's bloody knee. He stopped the car on the grassy verge and called to her. She looked up, not certain where the voice had come from, then noticed McLaren waving to her.

He let two cars pass before he called again. "You're hurt. Do you need any help? I can phone someone or give you a lift someplace." He eyed her knee, assessing if it were a hospital job.

As though her back hurt, she stood up slowly before replying, "I have no fear that I won't live. Thanks for stopping. Everyone else…" An articulated lorry and motorcycle whizzed past, kicking up a plume of dust, as though illustrating her unfinished remark.

"Yes, I see. Too busy."

"Or too afraid of a hitchhiker."

"You wouldn't be afraid of them, if it came to accepting a lift?" He took in her small, thin frame. Even though she had the well-developed calf muscles of a walker, her biceps didn't impress him. Besides, the area was desolate, more renowned for its heather, lonely moors, and rock outcroppings than for immediate help should anyone try to assault her.

Perhaps sensing his concern, she pulled something from her pocket. She held it up so McLaren could see it—a pocket-knife. "I can hold my own."

"Glad to hear it." Two motorcycles bulleted past, filling the air with exhaust fumes and noise. McLaren sat back in his seat and waited until the sound and stench had dissipated before turning again to the hiker. "Since we don't have to worry about you holding your own, how's your Trust level? Want a lift somewhere? Or does that take the Glory out of your adventure?"

"I've had enough of that for today, thanks. I'd like a lift, if it wouldn't take you out of your way."

"As long as it's in Derbyshire, I think I can manage it." He leaned across the front seat to unlock the passenger-side door as the woman discarded the impromptu walking stick. Ordinarily, he would have got out and opened the car door for her. But he thought that might be considered a threatening movement, knife or no knife; her ankle would have prevented her escape. "I won't be offended if you want to keep your knife at the ready…if it'll ease your mind about accepting the ride."

"I already decided on that." She settled into the seat, fastened the seat belt, and closed the car door before he asked where they were headed. "The Hanoverian, in Hathersage, if that's not too much bother. I've got a room booked for tonight."

"No bother at all. Right on my way, in fact. You…" He paused as he checked his rear-view mirror, then accelerated quickly as the car claimed the road. "You will be all right there? You don't want me to find you a doctor in Hathersage?"

She had bent forward to examine her knee. McLaren glanced at the red patch of skin as she gingerly touched it. "Looks nasty. Is it still bleeding?"

"Not much. Just an occasional ooze, I think, when I bend it. Ouch." She straightened up. "Mum always says I never leave well enough alone."

"Here." He yanked a cotton handkerchief from his shirt pocket and held it out. "Not exactly a sterile gauze pad, but it might help."

She murmured her thanks as she accepted it and wrapped it around her knee. "The only good thing about this is that I didn't rip a pair of jeans." Tugging at the hem of her walking shorts, she added, "Skin heals and is cheap. A ruined pair of jeans would cost me twenty or thirty quid."

"Then again, wearing a pair of jeans might have protected your knee and prevented your cut."

"I guess we'll never know, will we?" She gave the handkerchief one last knot and leaned back.

"I still think you need someone to look at that. You couldn't have washed the wound properly."

"I poured some of my drinking water on it. It'll be fine."

McLaren made a sound like a disgruntled cough and glanced again at her leg. Her sock was damp. "Water won't help your ankle."

"It's not sprained. Just a little sore from my fall. I'll be fine in the morning." She settled her rucksack against her feet before transferring the open knife to her left hand. Holding out her right hand, she said, "I'm Karin Pedersen, by the way. Thanks for stopping."

McLaren glanced at the extended hand, grasped her fingers in what he hoped would pass for a handshake, then concentrated on the road. "Mike McLaren. My pleasure. You on a walking holiday, then?"

Karin returned the knife to her right hand and settled back into the seat. "Yes. I started this past Sunday. I have until this Friday to tramp about."

"Do you walk a lot?"

"You mean, hiking like this? Over the moors?"

"Yes. Or just stroll after tea, down your street."

"I like to walk. It's a great stress reliever. Plus I meet interesting people and get some smashing photos of the land."

"So you're a photographer."

"Not really. Just amateur stuff. But it's fun."

"You're not scared walking about like this on your own? Your boyfriend doesn't mind, doesn't worry about you?" He'd estimated her age to be in the early twenties, but without a wedding or engagement ring on her finger, he could only guess at the boyfriend.

"Not at all. You forget I have great peace of mind." She waved the knife as he said, "I didn't forget."

They lapsed into a brief silence, McLaren occupied with unwanted mental images of Marta Hughes' body sprawled in roadside weeds. Of course he knew hardly anything of Karin Pedersen, but her life was just beginning and he didn't want to read about her premature death.

McLaren stopped his car in The Hanoverian's car park and glanced at the tall inn. Its gray stones were blackened with the soot of decades of coal fires and the exhaust of countless passing cars. But the inn sign, depicting a somber king, showed the effect of its recent cleaning, for the sunlight glanced off the painted surface. "This all right, then?" he asked, looking at the side entrance. "You want my phone number in case you aren't well enough to walk tomorrow morning?"

"You seem a rare type," she said, swinging open the car door.

"I'd ask what type, but I'm afraid of the answer."

"White knight. Gallant. Helpful. Awfully kind of you but I repeat, I'll be fine once I rest up a bit. Besides, I have my mobile. I'm just as capable of calling my boyfriend as you. Or picking up the bedside phone to summon the hotel proprietor. Thanks for the lift."

She got out of the car, then grabbed her rucksack with her free hand. Her weak ankle buckled and, in trying to regain her balance, the rucksack tipped, spilling much of its contents onto the ground.

"Let me help—" McLaren started before Karin held up her hand.

"No big deal. Mea culpa. I didn't latch the flap when I pulled out the bandana to wipe off my knee. It'll only take me a second…" She bent over and moments later had the contents back inside the pack. "There. Sorry about holding you up." Her hand rested on the edge of the upholstered seat as she leaned inside. Again extending her hand, she added, "Thank you again, Mr. McLaren. I don't know when I would've hobbled in if you hadn't come along."

"Glad I could help. I hope the rest of your ramble is uneventful."

"You and me both." She dragged her rucksack out of the way and slammed the car door. As McLaren shifted into first gear, she crossed her fingers and waved them at him. She was still waving as his car regained the main road, rounded the bend, and lost her from sight.

McLaren could never recall later exactly what time it happened, but he did recall it was outside the Longshaw Estate. Blue flashing lights of a police motorcycle swiftly loomed in his rear-view mirror and a yellow-jacketed police officer waved him over. McLaren sighed, confused and curious at once. He hadn't been speeding. He was always conscious of the posted limit signs. Besides, that had been one of his crusades when he was a constable. So why was this officer stopping him?

He turned off the car's engine, placed his hands on the steering wheel, and watched the officer approach his car. McLaren turned slightly toward the officer, his raised eyebrow mirroring his bewilderment. First time he'd ever been on the receiving end of a traffic stop.

"Yes, Officer?" McLaren said, aware of the remembered identical question echoing in his mind. "Did I do something wrong?"

"Name please, sir," the constable replied, flipping open his leather-bound booklet.

"McLaren. Michael. If I did something—"

"Is this your vehicle, sir?"

McLaren glanced around the car's interior, as though expecting it to have changed. He moved his hand to the top of the center console in an effort to shift his body so he could glance into the open hatchback section.

A warning, a clearing of a throat and the words, "Hands on the steering wheel, sir, where I can see them," stopped McLaren's inspection.

He murmured, "Certainly. Sorry," and settled back into his seat.

The constable stepped slightly away from the car door yet kept his eyes on McLaren. He spoke briefly into his shoulder microphone and seemed, to McLaren, to be talking to someone for an eternity. He heard snatches of the conversation, but didn't need the entire dialogue to know that his car was being run through the PNC listings, that it was insured, that it had a current M.O.T. certificate. He also knew it would be verified as not stolen, but that didn't help his anxiety or confusion as to why this was happening in the first place. The officer finally jotted something down in his notebook and returned to his original position at the car door. Staring down at McLaren, the officer said, "You admit this Peugeot 207 is registered in your name, correct?"

The second misgiving that something was wrong kicked him alongside the head. Was his number-plate light burnt out? "If you would tell me what is wrong, Officer—"

"Have you been in continuous possession of this car today, sir?"

"Continuous…"

"From the time you started your journey to this moment?"

McLaren could feel his throat tighten. He fought to keep his breathing even as he replied, "Yes. I've been in the car continuously since I started. Haven't left this seat. What—"

"Where did you begin your trip, sir?"

"Castleton. Mid-morning. I don't know the exact time. Close to eleven o'clock, I should think. If you would tell me—"

"What is your destination?"

"Chesterfield." He hoped that was enough. If he had to give Alan Hughes' home address and explain why he was going there, this would turn into a can of worms.

"Thank you, sir. You have a driving license, I assume." The officer looked at McLaren as though someone in his late thirties should know the law.

"Certainly. I can produce it if it's required. Would you please tell me what this is all about?"

"Yes, sir. Our station received a phone call about a red, three-door Peugeot 207, with plate numbers that match yours."

"*Match* mine! My car…"

"The driver's description also matches you, sir. White male, late thirties, dark blond hair in a crew cut, hazel eyes." The officer paused, perhaps assuming McLaren would deny something. When McLaren merely stared at him, the officer said, "Now, sir, if you would kindly step out of the car for a moment…" His hand was on the door latch and opening the door before McLaren could blink.

As McLaren stepped onto the packed, bare soil of the verge, he stumbled slightly as the toe of his shoe became tangled in a tuft of grass. Steadying himself against the side of the car, he stuttered, "Wh-what's this all about? I…I don't understand."

"Perhaps not, sir. The driver of this car, your car, was just reported as driving erratically, as though he'd been drinking. Have you had anything to drink today, sir?"

McLaren blinked, not believing this was happening.

"Nothing alcoholic, which is what you mean, I assume. Just tea and coffee."

"Would you consent to taking a breath-analyzer test, sir?"

"*Breath-analyzer* test!" My God, I'm about to be given the entire treatment: warning, statement of prescribed limits, declaration of moving-traffic offence… McLaren took a step back and tripped over a rock protruding from the soil.

"Yes, sir." He eyed McLaren, sizing up how much the man had already consumed this morning. "Hands on the car bonnet, if you please, sir. For your safety as well as mine."

McLaren shook his head in disbelief and placed his hands on the front of the car. "But there's no need for a breath-analyzer test! I've not had a thing to drink, other than this morning's tea and coffee. This is all—"

"Ridiculous?" the constable supplied, walking around to the passenger side of the car. He opened the car door and looked inside.

"Yes. I've been—" He stopped abruptly, aware that he had been about to say he'd been a cop. Besides holding no weight, he didn't want his name or history made public.

"You've been…what, sir?"

McLaren tried to think of an answer. What could he say? He'd been framed? Converted through religion? Dry for a decade? A model member of R.A.C.? Ashamed of his relapse? He stared stupidly at the officer, trying to make sense of the situation.

The officer bent forward and searched the car's interior. When he straightened up again, he was holding a beer bottle in his gloved hand. A quarter inch or so of liquid sloshed around inside the bottle as the officer gently shook it. "How do you explain this, sir?"

SEVEN

OF COURSE THERE had never been a question in McLaren's mind that he would fail the breath test. The beer he'd finished off before breakfast would not be enough to register on the breath analyzer. He was completely under the prescribed limit of 35 microgrammes. Still, the realization that someone somewhere knew him, knew his car and registration plate number, and had reported him to the police was sobering. Frightening.

The constable left him with a "Thank you, sir, and drive safely," his motorcycle roaring into the distance. McLaren sat in his car, staring at the man until traffic and the bend in the road obscured him from sight, trying to make sense of what had just happened. The breath-analyzer test had registered nothing; there was nothing wrong with his car registration, license or insurance. A waste of time for the officer; an inkling of some blunder for McLaren. He turned his car and headed back to Hathersage. That hiker, Karin Pedersen, had been in the passenger seat. Perhaps the bottle was hers.

Despite his urge to hurry, McLaren kept the car's speed under or at the limit. A handful of minutes slipped by as he lumbered behind an articulated lorry near Surprise View, unexpected scenery of the Derwent's thickly wooded valley and the boulder-studded slopes of the hills. His fingers drummed on the steering wheel, increasing his agitation. The lorry's motor growled as the driver shifted gears to slow the vehicle's downward pace. As an outcropping of boulders crawled past his window, McLaren shoved a cassette tape into the tape player, and after several seconds of silence, the background sounds of pub patrons filled the car's interior and his strong, baritone voice sailed over the noise of the crowd, followed by three other men's harmonies and the supportive sounds of guitars, viola, and soprano recorder. *My father's walking on the street; my mother the chamber keys do keep; the doors and windows they do creak; I dare not let you in O,* the lovesick lass told her soldier lover. "You're not the only one who's been betrayed," McLaren muttered to the tape player. He let himself finish the verse of "Cold Haily Rainy Night" before he jabbed the player's STOP button. He was in no mood for the song, no matter how much he liked listening to his folk singing group. Keen to get to the hotel and sort out this event, he swung his car around the lorry at the first opportunity, and a minute later parked in The Hanoverian's car park.

His footsteps crunched on the gravel, making indentations as he walked hurriedly to the front of the building. A strip of grass, nearly a foot wide, kept the gravel from spreading onto the main road and immediately deadened the thump of his boots. He stepped onto the pavement curling around to the front door, stopped to let a lady pass, then sprinted up the four steps. His hand gripped the brass door handle and he yanked impatiently at it.

The hotel's front door closed gently behind McLaren as he stepped into the hallway. A runner carpet of an intertwined floral design done in tans, oranges, and greens softened the sound of his steps. He ignored his reflection in the gilt-framed Georgian-style mirror and strode down the hall.

The name suited the inn-turned-hotel; it seemed to have been pulled from an upper-class house of the eighteenth century, with its dark wood paneling and silver sconces. A large reception desk lifted from an ancient pub stood guard in front of a row of wooden cubbyholes for guests' mail. McLaren marched over to the desk and slammed his fist down on the chrome reception bell.

Faint though it was, the bell's "ping" evidently sounded loudly enough. The tone had barely died when a tall, thin man materialized at the far end of the cubbyholes. He seemed to be part of the ancient building, clothes, hair, and eyes the same dark hue as the wood, his skin the tone of the polished brasses over the fireplace. A fireplace large enough to roast oxen, McLaren judged, then turned to the gaunt man as his "May I be of service?" broke the stillness.

"Please," McLaren replied, bracing his left palm on the edge of the desk and leaning forward. "I believe you have a Karin Pedersen registered here."

"The name does not sound familiar, sir."

"Perhaps not, but she arrived here about an hour ago. I wonder if you could ring her room and let her know I'd like to talk to her."

"We've had no one arrive in the last hour, sir."

"Well, maybe it's three-quarters of an hour. I'm not sure of the time. But I know she's here. She had a reservation for the night."

"I can assure you, sir—three-quarters of an hour or one complete hour—we've had no one arrive yet today. There are a number of guests scheduled to arrive later, nearer tea time, but no one has registered any time today."

McLaren stared at the clerk as if the man had lost his mind—or was trying to convince McLaren that he'd lost his. Leaning completely against the counter's edge, he said, "She *has* to be here! She has a reservation! I dropped her off *myself,* just an hour ago, at your car park."

"I assure you, sir, no one has—"

"She entered your side door. I watched her. She walked inside. Maybe she has a different name…" he said, trying to make sense of the clerk's information. "Maybe she's married and registered under her married name. Could that be it?" His fingers gripped the edge of the counter as the room began to tilt.

"Perhaps. What name did you say, sir? I'll look it up."

"Pedersen. Karin Pedersen. I know that's her name. At least, that's what she told me." Why would she lie? McLaren wondered. She didn't seem to be on the run from something. If she were, people hiding from the law or from angry boyfriends didn't take a leisurely hike through the Derbyshire Dales; they take the fastest exit they can and bury themselves in the anonymity of the city.

The clerk flipped slowly through the small stack of registration cards, silently reading them as he said, "These are all from this week. There is no Karin Pedersen registered."

"She *has* to be here! I gave her a lift in my car. We came from the direction of Castleton. She walked into your hotel—"

"I'm sorry, sir. I've looked through the cards and I've informed you there is no one here by that name. I don't know how else to convince you."

"A small, thinly built woman. In her early twenties. Vivid red, curly hair."

"I'm sorry—"

"Her knee was cut pretty bad. It had been bleeding and she had tied a handkerchief around it."

"As I said, sir, no one of that description has registered here."

McLaren threw his head back and exhaled slowly. The plaster grape clusters and cupids on the ceiling shifted in and out of focus. He closed his eyes, trying to think. This was beyond a joke. Then he lowered his head, stared at the clerk, and said slowly, "All right. Could she have registered while you were on break? Do you have another employee who was on duty an hour ago?"

"I am the only front-desk staff during the day. Another

clerk takes over at four o'clock, and someone else is on call during the night. I am the only person here right now. This is my normal working time."

"No one relieves you if you…you know…there's a call of nature?"

The clerk drew himself up to his full height and his voice turned cooler. "There are arrangements, certainly, but that has not happened during the time you say this person supposedly came into the hotel."

The front door opened, causing the long fabric panels at the opening of the reception area to move. An older couple sauntered down the hall, talking about their dinner reservations, then disappeared from McLaren's view. He turned back to the clerk. "Would you at least check your registration book to see if she has a room for tonight? Maybe I've got the time wrong…" That was not possible, but anything to appease the clerk into looking.

Sighing, he opened a large monthly planner. He flipped several pages, consulting dates prior to and after the day's date, then set the open book in front of McLaren. Pointing to the day's column, he said, "This is highly irregular, allowing you to view this book. I assume you won't believe me if you do not see it for yourself. As you can see, sir, there is no reservation for Karin Pedersen. Now, if there is nothing more—"

"She *has* to be staying here! She can't walk anyway. She fell and bloodied her knee. Perhaps she went to a clinic or saw a doctor. Is there one in town?"

The clerk eyed McLaren as though he had just walked into the room nude. "Hathersage is a village, sir. The nearest medical facility—"

"Okay. Fine." He ran his fingers through his hair, trying to stimulate his brain. Closing his eyes for a moment to concentrate, he said slowly, "Maybe she found a local doctor. Is there one in town? Surely someone's name must be on file for a guest who might become ill during the night."

"We keep a supply of medical supplies here, sir. If a guest is truly in need of professional care, we dial 999 or drive them to the Devonshire Royal Hospital in Buxton. I have seen no one of her description, nor have I seen this knee you keep referring to. Now, if you don't mind."

"But she came in here, damn it!" he exploded. "I dropped her off. She entered the hotel by the side door! She told me her name; I talked to her for a quarter of an hour."

"No one has registered."

"She has a reservation for *tonight!* She's got to be here!" He leaned over the counter and grabbed for the cards. The frantic glance of dates and names still failed to reveal Karin Pedersen's name. Silently admitting defeat, he dropped the stack onto the counter and leaned his back against it. "Why would she lie? There's no point in it. Why would she come in here if she has no room…"

The clerk gingerly stepped forward and said in a strained voice, "I'm afraid I can't help you. If you don't leave the premises immediately, I shall have to phone for the police."

"No need to trouble yourself, mate. We already know each other."

Murmuring something unintelligible, the clerk picked up the stack of cards and disappeared into the small inner room behind the cubbyholes.

McLaren nodded and walked into the hall, pausing in front of a painting of King George III. Looking up at the portrait, he said, "Got the name of a good psychiatrist, Georgie? I'm going to need one very soon." The door eased shut on his retreating figure.

Sitting in his car in the hotel car park, McLaren thought over the sequence of events. Nothing made sense other than Karin Pedersen had changed her mind about the overnight

stay and moved on. But her cut knee would necessitate someone driving her. He eyed the hotel sign, a stylized portrait of
George III, and wondered briefly how long the paint lasted
in these harsh Derbyshire winters before he walked over to
the payphone on the side of the hotel. The yellow pages had
one listing for a doctor in the village and the next nearest one
was in Chapel-en-le-Frith, which was more than ten miles
distant. Buxton and Chesterfield were heavily represented
and seemed the most logical choice for care if her knee was
cut deeply. Still, McLaren wanted to be certain. The call
was answered almost immediately, and nearly as immediately McLaren was back to no solution. The doctor had not
treated a Karin Pedersen, the receptionist informed him. He
had treated no one that day with a cut knee—had he tried
the hospital in Buxton?

McLaren sat heavily in his car seat, confused and frus-
trated. His fingers reached for the tape, yet rested on the
cassette's edge. Was this a "message" from Dena? A flex of
her muscles to show she could upset his life? She said this
morning that she wouldn't harass him with phone calls, but
maybe this was her harassment—setting the cops on him, in-
conveniencing him. But the beer bottle… He hadn't seen her
today, hadn't told her that he'd be in Castleton. She couldn't
have done anything.

His gaze drifted over to the passenger seat, then out the
car window toward the direction of Castleton. He imagined
the small lanes of the village, the stone shops, and the castle
ruin perched on the hill overlooking the comings and goings of the residents. He had parked across from the hotel,
sitting in the outdoor dining area with his back toward his
car. Could Dena have planted the beer bottle while he was
speaking with Linnet? Was she the person Linnet believed
she had seen at his car? If Dena had done it so quickly and
casually that she hadn't drawn attention to herself, she could

have bent over, cracked open the door, and jammed the bottle in the floor well between the passenger seat and the door. Maybe he hadn't locked the door after all; maybe she had pushed down the door lock…

He rubbed his forehead, trying to envision the scenario. Could it have happened? Was he imagining enemies at every corner? He shoved the cassette tape back into the dashboard tape player, adjusted the volume to the next song, "The Blacksmith," and leaned his head against the headrest. What was wrong with this supposition? What was he overlooking? Castleton's main street shimmered in his mind's eye. Linnet's face and the waiter at the chalkboard sign and the road lined with cars had seemed normal. But somewhere, at some time, something odd had happened, and he needed to figure it out.

He sat up, leaving the blacksmith's fair lady to ponder her own doubts, and turned the key in the ignition switch. The car engine roared into life but he let it idle. Yes, he thought as he slowly nodded. Dena's red MG. He'd swear in court the car he'd seen had been hers. A burst of applause from the recording drowned his muttered "Damn." Swinging the car onto the main road, he grumbled, "I hope the cheers are prophetic," and headed to Chesterfield.

MARTA HUGHES' HUSBAND, Alan, poured McLaren a second cup of tea before explaining his last statement. They were seated in the kitchen of Alan's house, warm from the mid-afternoon sun and the chicken casserole baking in the oven. Alan, a graying brunet in his late forties, leaned forward, his forearms on the chrome edge of the tabletop, and nodded toward the front room. "Most of the damage was in there," he said, his voice weary with having to relive the event.

McLaren settled the cup back onto the saucer, eyeing the room through the kitchen doorway. Nothing was out of place, but he could imagine the wreckage. He'd seen dozens of such rooms during his police career. "So the coppers never discovered who ransacked your home, then."

"No. But we had our suspicions."

"We?"

"The police, my family, and the neighbors."

"Did you all come to the same conclusion as to the suspect?"

"Yes. Without even having to discuss it. Rick Millington and his group."

"Who's Rick Millington? Have you—family, neighbors, or police—had run-ins with him before?"

"A neighbor kid. And no, not run-ins, but he's brushed up against the law before."

"So he has a reputation, then."

"Unfortunately. Nothing really major. No assaults or car theft or the like."

"What, exactly?"

"Drugs."

"He's a dealer?"

"No. Well," Alan said, picking up his cup and holding it, "at least, I don't think so. But we believe he uses and his mates do, too."

"Is that why so many people believe Rick Millington is your culprit?"

Alan took a sip of tea, then nodded. His fingertips drummed on the table's glass top. "Many of us have smelled marijuana on him. Smell it coming from his back garden, too. In fact, that's how this whole mess started."

"Your home being ransacked."

"Yes. Marta used to see them quite often sitting in front of Rick's house smoking. 'Them' is Rick, his girlfriend, Teresa, and his mate Danny. Marta talked to them several times, in a friendly way, telling them what they were getting involved with, where drugs could lead, but they ignored her."

"How old are Rick and his friends?"

"I don't know exactly, but he's probably fifteen or so. Danny I know is a year or two older. He could be seventeen. Though the whole lot of them act much younger."

"But they didn't take to your wife's friendly advice."

"It was like they never heard her. They continued with the drugs."

"Did Marta or you speak to Rick's parents about this?"

Alan snorted and screwed up the corner of his mouth. "Several times. Deaf ears must be a family trait."

"Or nothing between them. So the parents were not amused, I take it."

"We have our suspicions that they, or at least the father, smoke, too. Or his clothes get their delightful odor from Rick's weed."

"So, if the parents didn't lift a finger to stop the drug use—"

"Marta talked to the police. I don't think that got us anywhere, either. Rick was never jailed."

McLaren was going to say there was such a thing as evidence and catching the suspect in the act, but instead replied, "How did this marijuana use lead to the ransacking of your house?"

"As I said, we don't know if Rick and his mates did it or not. The police couldn't prove a thing. A constable did talk to them, I remember." He pressed his lips together as he sought for the officer's name. In the moments of silence, McLaren heard a lawn-mower engine start up with a long series of coughs. As the motor caught, it settled into a lower pitch.

It was a nice street, McLaren thought, recalling each home's neat front garden, trimmed grass, and swept front steps. Well looked after and quiet, like this kitchen, crisp in its white, green, and blue color scheme. The street held no derelict buildings or litter that silently spoke of urban crime. Perhaps that's why urban crime in such peaceful neighborhoods was so startling. Even behind the most expensive façade, people were criminals. Drug use was just one example.

"Right." Alan relaxed somewhat. "Now I remember. PC Shard. Ian Shard. He talked to the kids. Gave them a warning, too. *That's* how it started."

"From the warning?"

"Yes. When my wife contacted PC Shard a week or so later, telling him that Rick and his mates were still smoking marijuana, the constable talked to their parents. You'd think Danny, at least, would try to be a more upstanding citizen, from all the stories I hear about his grandfather's glorious WWII record, the relics Danny grew up around. You'd think some of that would have—"

"The kids got in trouble with their parents, then," McLaren surmised. "Well, all except Rick, I assume."

"I don't know one way or the other. The constable's talk to the Millingtons might have got Rick in trouble, I suppose."

"But right after that your house was broken into and ransacked."

"Like I said, Mr. McLaren—we all have our suspicions it was Rick, either alone or with Teresa and Danny."

"And, as you said, if they did do it, they're about the right age for it. That's the sort of act that juveniles do."

"Yes. Revenge."

"Was anything damaged?"

"Not really. Just things pulled from drawers, bed linen stripped from the bed, lamps knocked over, food from the fridge and cupboards dumped on the floor. That sort of thing."

"How did whoever it was gain entrance to your house?"

"By the bedroom window. The police told us it was forced open, probably with a crowbar."

"Would you mind showing me?"

"Certainly." Alan sounded surprised and began walking

toward the bedroom when McLaren said, "I'm sorry. I meant outside. Would you show me the window from the exterior?"

"Oh. Yes. It's this way."

The two men went out the back door and McLaren followed Alan to the north side of the house. Holly bushes, cut low to form a three-foot-tall hedge, bordered the property line several feet from the Hughes' residence. A patch of lily of the valley claimed the area beneath the window, while bluebells, columbine, and other woodland flowers fanned out toward the back garden.

"Of course," Alan said as McLaren inspected the windowsill, "we've had it repaired. It was last June, you recall."

"Of course," McLaren replied. "I just wanted to see how far from the ground the window is, its proximity to plants or a storage shed."

"We have one," Alan volunteered and pointed to the six-foot square metal outbuilding in the northwest corner at the back of the garden.

"But not near to the window to afford the vandals a privacy screen. I believe the holly hedge did that."

"Yes. They probably squatted down behind it to wait until no one saw them."

McLaren looked at both corners of the roof. "You've no security light, I see."

"No. We've never felt we needed them. It's been such a quiet neighborhood."

"No alarm system either, then. Or family dog."

Alan shook his head, looking rather embarrassed.

"Well, at least they didn't break into your shed to grab a ladder."

"No. We were spared that further bit of vandalism. The window provides easy entry to the house, the police reckoned."

"Yes. What is it…four feet off the ground? As you say,

easy access. All he or they had to do was hop inside once they'd forced open the window." He bent over slightly, looking at the brickwork. "Did the police find any signs of shoe scuff marks?"

"A white smear or two, yes."

"Trainers." He straightened up. "Was there any suspicion that they chose this room on purpose?"

"What do you mean?"

"Do you or the police believe the vandals were after something in the bedroom and, perhaps not being able to locate it and therefore being angry, vented their anger on the house in general—pulling items from drawers, stripping the sheets from the bed, knocking over lamps."

"Oh, yes, I see. No, we thought at first that they might have been after money or credit cards or my wife's jewelry, but that wasn't taken. Just the general vandalism."

"So no one room was targeted more than another. It's not common knowledge in the neighborhood that you have a priceless collection of stamps, let's say, and they couldn't find it."

"Good Lord, no! Nothing like that. I admit I earn a nice salary, but I've never collected anything as an adult. Nothing expensive, I mean. I do have a rather extensive collection of beer memorabilia—old tin trays, beer mats, advertising posters, pitchers, and the like, in addition to several dozen bottles of different brands from around the world, but nothing in the class of rare stamps or coins. We use our money mainly on plants for the garden—several rather exotic hostas and the like—and for holidays."

"Then they entered your home because this window is lower off the ground than any other, or the holly hedges afforded sufficient cover for their entry."

"I believe so. Would you like to see?" Alan led McLaren through the back garden and to the south side of the house.

There was no hedge to afford cover, nor were there any large bushes or garden furniture. The land held only flowers and a pedestal birdbath.

"Hardly bulky enough to hide behind. The other side does offer the best entry in terms of seclusion."

"Besides, the window is farther off the ground here."

McLaren tilted his head, mentally measuring the window's height from the ground, which sloped toward the south. "What's the elevation here? Do you know?"

"The land is nearly a yard lower on this side of the house. The slope runs like this for the rest of the street, in fact."

"This window, then, is approximately seven feet from the ground here." He screwed up his mouth, picturing the break-in, then walked over to the birdbath. It was brown-painted aluminum, sporting a bowl with fluted edges and a slender, curved base. Placing his hand on its rim, he shook it. "Wouldn't afford much help with a leg-up."

"No. The police thought at first it might have been used as a sort of step ladder, just like you suggest, but the pedestal wouldn't support anyone's weight, let alone someone climbing up on it. Besides, they determined it hadn't been moved."

"Oh, yes?"

"They tipped it over to see if the pedestal base covered a different patch of grass."

"Different blades pressed down."

"Yes. They couldn't determine that it had been moved. Besides," Alan said as they reentered the house, "it simply wouldn't have borne a person's weight. It would have fallen over on the first attempt to climb on it."

They were back in the kitchen. McLaren had looked at the door, trying to understand why it hadn't been used as an entry point. Surely the back of the house afforded more privacy than a side window. But the small light fixture above the door and the double locks answered his question. No one would be foolish enough to stand under a flood light while fighting with two locks. Number twenty Dunstan Terrace had probably seemed invincible to the Hughes family.

"The police tried to make the connection between the bedroom entry and Rick Millington," Alan said as they stood in the kitchen. The aroma of the baking chicken filled the room.

"Because the Millington house borders that side of yours?"

"Yes. They're on our north side, next to that window."

"But the police couldn't place Rick here."

"No. I suppose it was just a coincidence anyway."

"That the intruders chose the window nearest the Millington residence."

"Yes. After all, as you've just seen, it does offer the best and most logical point to enter the house."

"May I impose on your kindness for one more favor?"

Alan's head jerked slightly. His eyes widened as he tried to anticipate what McLaren would ask. He opened his mouth, then merely nodded.

"I'm sorry if it will be painful, but I'd like to see the bedroom."

"Uh, certainly. It's just here." Alan again led the way. He opened the door and stood aside to let McLaren enter the room first, then slowly followed him.

McLaren went to the window, raised the lower half of the casement, and leaned out. Then he closed the window, turned around and asked Alan what items had been disturbed in the room.

Clearly not expecting the question, Alan hesitated for a moment, frowning. He pulled at the collar of his cotton shirt as though he had difficulty breathing, then crossed his arms on his chest. "Why, uh, I believe they pulled the clothes from the dresser drawers."

"All of them?" McLaren asked, his gaze on the large

wooden bureau. It occupied most of the wall at a right angle to the bed.

"Yes. They were pulled out randomly, not lined up…you know." He stopped, embarrassed by the absurdity of his answer. Of course a housebreaker would not stop to line up drawer fronts in a neat line. Avoiding McLaren's eyes, he said, "Only the bottom drawer was pulled all the way out. It was on the floor with the contents dumped beside it. The other drawers had been opened, as you would when you were going to get a pair of socks or a sweater. But the drawers had been rifled; the clothes were disarranged." He glanced at the window as though seeing the intruders entering the room.

"The sheets were off the bed, I believe you said."

"Yes. Everything. Sheets, the duvet, the pillow. Everything on the floor. Even the mattress was partway off. I guess they'd been looking beneath it for something."

"Not necessarily. Could be just plain cussedness." McLaren looked around the room. The queen-sized bed was on the wall opposite the window. A good location to catch the breezes. An upholstered chair angled out from the corner, near the closet. The small bedside cabinet was close to the door and matched the wood of the bed. "That was disturbed, too, I assume."

Alan glanced at the cabinet and self-consciously moved the ginger-jar-style lamp nearer to the bed. "Yes. Everything was opened. They'd gone through the airing cupboard, too. Taken things off the linen shelf, shoved aside our hanging clothes. Nothing broken, though."

"Just disarray. Thanks. I've seen enough." He was glad to leave the room, with its mementos of Marta's life: her photograph still propped on top of the dresser, smiling at Alan; her jewel box and perfume bottle of cut glass; a favorite straw hat, no doubt, topping one of the bed posts; a watercolor of some Mediterranean vista, done by Marta, he noticed, seeing her painted signature.

Alan cut McLaren's burgeoning sadness short as he stopped at the baby grand piano in the front room. Its sleek, ebony side shone in the sunlight. "They did the same sort of thing in here. Cushions from the sofa, some of the pictures off the wall, a lamp knocked over—" He gestured toward a tall wrought-iron lamp with an open filigree pedestal. "That Windsor chair overturned, but not broken, thank God. The ends of the curtains either were stuffed behind the sofa or lay across the back."

"Sounds like they were looking for something. The piano was undamaged?"

"Yes. On first seeing the mess I feared they might have cut the wires or poured water or something onto the soundboard, but it was fine. As I said, Mr. McLaren, we got off fairly lucky. Just things mainly dumped onto the floors and tipped out of drawers. Easy enough to clean up." His gaze shifted to the piano as he recalled the chaos. He swallowed slowly, his eyes nearly overflowing with the pain of that night and with losing his wife.

McLaren trailed his fingers along the piano top before he jammed his hand into his pocket. He nodded, glancing around the room once more. "Well, at least it wasn't too bad."

"No," Alan said, hastily wiping his eyes with the back of his hand. "We got off lucky." He pressed his lips together, and McLaren wondered what constituted "unlucky." Alan picked up the sheet music on the piano top and pinned it against his chest as he crossed his arms. "We phoned the police, of course, and even though they couldn't prove Rick or his cohorts were responsible, privately we believe that they did it so Marta would keep quiet in the future. A little harassment sometimes works wonders."

It was McLaren's turn to press his lips together. Obviously, he wasn't the only one with a helpful acquaintance. Someone else was being taught a lesson.

EIGHT

McLaren sat in his car in front of the Hughes home, fighting the all too familiar anger and sadness that filled his heart and soul. Marta Hughes had been loved; some piece of trash had taken her life, taken her from her husband and son, disposed of her in an obscene way. No one deserved to be tossed away like a sack of rubbish. His fist slammed into the upholstery of the passenger seat in his frustration. Had she died over her casino winnings or was it something else, something connected to her work or her family or friends? And did the stone barn where her body was recovered have any significance? She didn't live in Elton. According to Alan, she didn't know anyone there. Nor had she been born there. McLaren took several deep breaths while he took in the neighboring residences, his mind trying to make sense of Alan's account of their house break-in. The man had seemed surprised to find McLaren on his doorstep. But Alan was helpful, eager to relay anything that might discover Marta's murderer and bring his nightmare to a close.

Leaning his head against the car seat, McLaren rubbed his temples. The simple quest for Marta Hughes' killer was fast turning into a branched road, with nagging questions down each path. Had the ransacking of the Hughes home anything to do with Marta's death? He couldn't believe a group of teenagers would commit murder over a few smoked joints. Was something else behind the vandalism, something Alan Hughes wasn't telling?

McLaren gazed down the road. Hathersage lay in the direction he had come. Beyond that was Castleton. Were either or both of those places linked to Karin Pedersen's disappearance? Had she secreted the beer bottle in his car and then rung up the police? Why? She and he were strangers. But if she was not responsible, was it Dena?

Scratching his head, McLaren leaned forward. The houses beyond Six Mills Road petered out swiftly, giving way to the green-and-gray countryside of dales, mountains, streams, stone house villages and stonewalls. Why had he abandoned, even briefly, his wall work? Was it ego that whispered he could solve a cold case where equally competent police detectives had failed? Or was it something else? Something deeper than ego—a need to be accepted again—to vindicate himself, to yield to the siren song of police work? To remove the blot from his name? He jammed the key into the ignition slot, started the engine, and shot away from the curb in a roar of racing motor, screeching tires, and muttered self-contempt.

VERITY DWYER, Marta Hughes' one-time coworker, was unlocking the front door of her home when McLaren parked his car opposite her house. He called to her as he swung open the door. She remained by the closed door and waited for him to speak, her handbag securely wedged under her arm. When he had introduced himself and explained the reason for his visit, she nodded, unlocked the door, and led him into the house.

"So, you're investigating Marta's murder." Verity seated herself on the sofa across from him, her back to the late-afternoon sun, and studied his eyes. She'd become a master at interpreting the meaning behind uttered words, the subtle shifts in facial expressions or moods that flitted across the eyes. During her time working through her community-service sentence, she'd learned that eye movements and voice inflection told her the truth even when the words were lies. So she took some time scrutinizing McLaren's face and mannerisms, in no rush to tell him anything, not anxious to relive the horror of the past year.

McLaren, too, was content to proceed slowly, to take in her blue eyes and the freckles that splashed across her nose and cheeks, her hands that looked older than her thirty-five years, dry and calloused from rough work. He knew of Verity Dwyer's situation from Linnet and from his recent research. Sometimes printed information was better; it doesn't lie to your face. He nodded toward the wall calendar in the next room. "Your time is almost finished, I see."

Verity nodded, knowing to what McLaren was referring. "I've been X'ing off each day, counting down this sentence. It'll be wonderful to resume my life, as I call it. Though I don't know how many friends I'll have left. But I'll see, won't I?" She tried to smile, to make light of her situation, but only managed to look pathetic. Resettling herself in her chair she said, "What happened to rekindle interest in her case? I thought it had gone cold."

"It has. I've been asked to do some investigation on the side. Entirely as a private concern."

"Meaning you're not a copper."

"No, I'm not."

"But you were."

"You think so?"

"Of course! I can spot one a mile off. Even an ex-cop has an air about him. When you've been around them as much and as long as I have…" She shrugged and fluffed up her shoulder-length auburn hair.

He relented, his eyes locked into her gaze. "You're right, Ms. Dwyer. I was a cop. But now I'm trying to get to the bottom of Marta Hughes' death."

"I see. A highly trained citizen." She tilted her head slightly, as though thinking through something. The refrigerator clicked on in the kitchen before she added, "So you have no authority, then. You can't haul me into the nick for refusing to talk to you."

A smile, so fleeting that it was barely discernible, flashed across McLaren's face. "I can't. But I'm hoping you'll agree to help me."

"For the sake of justice or to help out a mate of yours who botched the case in the first place?"

"Justice is always a concern, Ms. Dwyer. It shouldn't make any difference if the injustice was directed toward a cop or a person connected to the case."

"Justice is blind, in other words, like the statue." She eyed him, trying to discern the cause behind this new probe, the motivation for his involvement. "You weren't connected with the original case, were you? I'd have remembered you."

"Oh, yes?"

"Don't flatter yourself that it's because you're nice to look at. Though I *am* partial to blonds."

He laughed and leaned back in his chair. "Because you've had every one of those marked-off calendar days to recall who worked on your case and who testified in court?"

It was her turn to laugh. "Something like that, yes."

"Just so I'm not one of your nightmares, that's all right."

She picked up the packet of cigarettes on the side table but made no move to slip one from the pack. Instead, she said, "Who hired you? You can't tell me you're doing this because you miss being a copper."

He hesitated, wondering himself if that were true, the questions he had just asked himself minutes ago resonating in his mind.

Verity read his hesitation. "Just want to be back with the boys, then. You need the adrenalin rush, the after-work beer with your mates." Her voice hardened, as though she had lumped him with the stereotypical copper who let off steam with one-too-many beers and affairs.

Feeling the need to defend himself McLaren said, "This isn't about me, Ms. Dwyer. It's about your friend. Should it make a difference who hired me? Isn't my pursuit of Marta Hughes' killer grounds enough for you?"

"Certainly it matters! If you're working for someone I think is guilty of the crime or who Marta hated—"

"You'll refuse to say anything."

"Are you working for someone like that?"

"Who would that be, Ms. Dwyer? I've just met you; I have no way of knowing whom you suspect."

"True. I forgot." She tapped the pack against her index finger and pulled out the cigarette. "I also forgot you're not a cop and might not know all the personnel or pertinent information."

"I do know you and Marta were friends as well as co-workers."

"And, being friends, I should rush to help you."

"I don't know why you shouldn't. If there is a reason," he said as she lit the cigarette and took a puff, "that's as important as anything else you might tell me." He waited in the quiet room, looking at the framed certificates of appreciation and merit that claimed the wall in the adjoining room, studying her face as she had done his, judging her character and her hurt over her treatment at the hands of the English legal system.

A group of young children ran down the street, laughing and calling to an adult to hurry, before Verity replied. The cigarette dangled from her fingers as she once again looked at McLaren. "You're right, Mr. McLaren. Justice shouldn't be dependent on anyone. I was Marta's friend. I'll help you just as I tried to help her. Which, if you haven't heard, is how I ended up convicted of theft."

"What is the length of your sentence? I see it's up in two

weeks." His eyes strayed again to the calendar and the large red, circled date a few days away.

"I received a community order for eleven months. It's been the longest months of my life, Mr. McLaren."

"I believe you." He refrained from saying it was a better sentence than serving time in jail. Verity knew that.

"I'm assigned to a homeless shelter. I do some cooking and cleaning there. Kind of fitting, don't you think?"

"In what way?"

"Marta and I worked in an animal shelter, taking in strays and unwanted pets. I've just moved up a notch in the chain, looking after stray and unwanted people. Though some might call it a step down, I suppose."

"Tough work. And your sentence was due to your conviction of theft from the animal shelter."

"Yes. A stupid mistake, that, stealing the money for Marta."

"Money she didn't pay back."

"She told me she would return the money the following day." Her words came louder and faster now that the painful subject had been opened. Her hand holding the cigarette fell onto the chair's arm and she leaned forward. She practically shook as she screeched, "But she *didn't!* That's how the discrepancy was discovered. The organization's financial officer came by and checked the books."

"You didn't know he was coming?"

"No. It's always unannounced."

"To keep everyone on their toes."

"Or keep us honest." She colored and paused, realizing her verbal slip referred to her. "Anyway, I was caught with my cash drawer short, the money missing and unexplained."

"What are we talking about? How much?" He knew from the case report, but he wanted to hear it from her, to see if she'd try to sugarcoat her guilt.

"One thousand pounds."

"Damn."

Verity smiled and took a drag on her cigarette. "My sentiments exactly, Mr. McLaren. I was damned. In the eyes of the financial examiner, the animal shelter higher-ups, the police, and the court."

"You said you took it—"

"*Stole* it," Verity corrected, sitting up straighter, defying McLaren to challenge the truth. "Marta took it—supposedly for twenty-four hours—so she could go to the casino. Roulette was her weakness. She played fairly frequently but she usually won. She'd make incredible winnings. So when she asked for the money, I really didn't think we'd get into trouble. If she didn't win, she'd go back the following day or so and play again. She'd wind up with enough money to repay everyone's loans."

"*Everyone?* She'd done this before, this taking cash from friends or from the animal shelter's till?"

"From friends, yes. There were three or four she usually touched. But from the shelter? No. That's why I hesitated to give her the money at first. Yet, she had such a good record of winning and prompt repayment. Well, I knew she'd return the money, so I finally gave it to her."

Again he asked a question he could have answered, but he wanted Verity to tell him. "Gave it to her. What does that mean? Did you have access to the office safe?"

"No. Just my own cash register. I work one specific register; the one in the gift shop. That money is my responsibility. I have the key to unlock the register in the morning and when the day is over I relock it. I also count up the day's transactions and balance the drawer at the end of the day."

"So, because you had this particular cash register under your jurisdiction, you could get her the money."

"It *never* dawned on me that we'd be caught! I still can't quite believe it."

"Seems like a huge amount of money to have in a charity agency, if you don't mind me saying so. A thousand pounds. Is that normal, or were you about to deposit it in the company's bank account?"

"It was a lot, which is why Marta knew to ask me. Usually all our tills carry three hundred pounds so there's enough money to make change in the store and for customers who might adopt the animals."

"Where does the other seven hundred come from?" He looked at Verity as though he expected her to say she always carried that amount in her handbag.

"From the back room. We hide that amount back there in case there's some emergency. It's come in handy more than once." Her voice drifted off, as though recalling her court testimony.

"How many people know about the seven hundred? All of the staff or just a few? Did this reserve amount ever vary?"

"I think we all knew about it. Well, all the clerks, I should say. And our boss. But I doubt if the vet knows about it. He really has no need to know. He's just concerned with the health of the animals; he doesn't come out into the main area unless he takes in a sick animal."

"How many clerks are there? Exactly how many people would know about the cache?"

Verity screwed up her lips, mentally ticking off the staff. The ash from her cigarette dangled precariously over the arm of the chair. "Six, I think."

"Including Marta?"

"Yes."

"You all knew about the extra seven hundred in the back."

"Well, we didn't talk about it during our breaks, of course, but I think we all did. Our boss made sure we all would know about it in case something happened and we needed the money. For an emergency," she repeated.

"It is always kept in the same place, I take it. Well, it would be—how else would you know where to find it if you needed it."

"Yes. The boss had debated about the whole thing for rather a long time. He felt uneasy keeping seven hundred in the shelter, but he's a person who likes to be prepared."

McLaren refrained from calling him a Boy Scout and instead asked where the hiding spot was.

Verity looked at him, judging his honesty and need to know.

"I'm not going to burgle the place, Ms. Dwyer," he said. "If there's any hesitation on your part, you needn't tell me."

"Don't take it personally, Mr. McLaren, but I'd rather not."

"That's fine. The place was easy to get to, though."

"Yes, but not obvious."

He thought about people hiding money beneath their bed mattresses or inside biscuit jars and wondered briefly if the back room had an unused teapot.

"So, you see, Mr. McLaren, it all pointed to me. Oh, the back-room money could have been stolen by any of the other clerks there, but the cash from the till—"

"Pointed directly to you, yes. When was all this? I know you said you're serving an eleven-month sentence, but when did you give Marta the money?"

"Third of May last year. The examiner came the tenth of May, as it turned out, and found the discrepancy in the drawer."

"But a week!" McLaren couldn't keep the surprise from his voice. "If Marta had a week to replace the money—"

"She got ill two days after she took the money, on five May. She had said on the third, when she took the money, that she'd go back to the casino in two days to play the wheel again if she didn't win that night. I remember we laughed about that because she hardly ever loses."

"And she became ill before she could return to the casino."

"Yes."

McLaren grimaced, mentally picturing the women's panic. "You were arrested…when?"

She smoothed the wrinkle from the sleeve of her blouse. "Fifteen June. The company's director had given me four weeks to come up with an explanation and to return the money. Of course I couldn't come up with a thousand pounds. Not in four weeks. I barely have anything in the bank, and I'd just spent a large sum on a new roof." She flicked the ash into the ashtray on the coffee table. Some of the ash fell onto the ashtray's lip and over the edge, onto the tabletop. Verity didn't seem to notice. "I could ask anyone for the money. It was tempting, and I toyed with the idea for a while, but it was too embarrassing. What was I to say to them? I couldn't say a friend of mine had taken the money from our workplace and I was covering for her."

"So you took the blame." If it were true, Verity was an exceptional friend.

"I did all the usual stuff people do when they need money. I tried to sell some things—my good silverware, a rare book— but it wouldn't have been enough. I suppose I should have sold my car, but…"

"They're hard to part with once you've become used to independent travel."

"Not that so much, but yes, they are nearly essential. I had a friend who was interested in it, and he came over one evening to look it over. But he took nearly two weeks to give me a definite answer. By the time he refused, it was too late to advertise or find another interested party."

"You didn't tell the company's director about all this? If he had known your efforts, wouldn't he have extended the pay-back period?"

She took another puff on the cigarette. "I honestly don't

think it would have made any difference. He was bound by the board's decision. I do admit I was fairly frantic by then. It felt as though the walls were closing in. I would never survive a prison term. I was more scared of the prisoners than standing trial and the remainder of my life, being branded a criminal and not knowing how friends and acquaintances would greet me once I had finished my time. Part of it's the fear of the unknown, I realize. And seeing what hard prison time has done to people. Many come out bitter and angry, having no faith in anyone or anything, finding no joy in the simple things they once did. Part of it was the complete feeling of being alone that never left me, day or night. I'm a rather timid woman, as you might guess, Mr. McLaren, and I've never been particularly outgoing or joined many groups. As a consequence, my friends number a mere dozen or so. Of those, I have one or two really close friends."

"And they couldn't help you raise the money."

"I didn't ask. They didn't know about any of this until the trial began." She paused, watching McLaren's face as it registered his astonishment and pain. "You think it's funny, I know. Strange that I wouldn't talk to a friend. I learned early in life, Mr. McLaren, to keep my hurts and disappointments to myself. No one likes a whiner."

"Hardly whining, Ms. Dwyer. This was your reputation, the rest of your life."

"Even so, I told no one other than my brother."

"And he didn't help." He said it more harshly than he intended, his voice cracking from the stupidity of the entire episode.

"No, he didn't." She raised her hand, the cigarette smoke curling into the air above her head. It drifted in the faint breeze coming in from the open window, catching the sunlight before fading against the blue-gray backdrop of the room's walls. "I know you're already judging him, Mr. McLaren, but please don't. You're wrong."

"I'm sorry. I didn't mean to pronounce a verdict against your brother, especially when I don't know him."

"It's natural, I know, but as I said, you're wrong. My brother couldn't help simply because he's in prison."

The surprise registered in McLaren's face. He blinked and opened his mouth slightly.

"Wealstun," Verity added.

"In West Yorkshire." He cleared his throat.

"Yes. I won't bore you with his crime, sentencing or history—they're public record and can be looked up—but now perhaps you'll understand why I couldn't ask him."

Or your friends, McLaren thought. The newspapers would have had a feeding frenzy if word had leaked out that a convicted criminal's sister was charged with theft. And from a charity!

"In spite of how this all turned out, the company's director is a kind person. I think he didn't want to go through the arrest and trial rigmarole, but he was being pressured by the board."

"But of course, a thousand is a lot of money to come up with. Not just for you, Ms. Dwyer, but most people."

She nodded and exhaled slowly. "It was a nightmare. I couldn't understand what was going on, what was happening. I knew I was guilty of theft, I assumed the rights as owner of the money when I gave it to Marta, but I couldn't tell my boss or the director." She rotated her cigarette, as though looking for something, then said, "I just remember vividly when the police came and handcuffed me. God!" She avoided his eyes, even now humiliated by the event.

"The date of your trial and sentencing?"

"July. I am grateful for the community order instead of jail time, of course, but…"

"Of which you got eleven months. Yes, it's better than breaking rocks," he said, then realized he broke rocks nearly every day. The difference was that he was a free person and chose to break rocks to repair stonewalls, whereas Verity... He coughed, trying to gloss over the verbal *faux pas,* and said, "Where was Marta through all this? I assume she knew about your arrest and the trial. It must have gone on for a bit. Why didn't she speak up?"

"That was one of the things I had to work through emotionally, Mr. McLaren. I *still* have to work through. I felt betrayed at first. Marta was my friend. She should have spoken up, but she didn't."

"Because..."

"Marta's husband is a big man in the community. He holds some senior management position at National Westminster Bank. She didn't say anything because she didn't want the story to get out."

"Wife of bank vice president, or whatever, involved in stealing money."

"Exactly. It would have ruined his reputation."

McLaren blinked. "Never mind yours, right?"

"I guess husbands are more important than friends."

"Or at least the Truth." He shifted his position in the chair and said, "So where in this timeline is Marta killed...or, at least, disappear?"

"I'll never forget. A Friday night, eleven June."

"You were arrested on fifteen June."

"Yes."

"Damn."

"Exactly. I had four days to get even with Marta for her silence, to kill her and hide her body."

NINE

"WHY WEREN'T YOU arrested for murder, then?" McLaren asked when the tension had relaxed between them. "Seems like you had motive—look what she did to your life." He paused, his eyes again on the calendar in the kitchen. Of all the tales of injustice he'd heard, this was close to the top. His gaze sought her face again and he asked rather hesitantly, "Or did something happen later?"

"No. Besides, I had an unbreakable alibi the night of Marta's death."

"Glad to hear it. What was it, if I may ask?"

"I was in church. Mending hymnals. There were about a dozen of us, I guess. Anyway, the vicar was there, too. They all swore in court that I was there."

"If Marta wasn't found until ten days later, how did your one evening's alibi serve you?"

"Linnet had gone with her to the casino in Nottingham. Oh, do you know Linnet?"

"Yes. I've spoken with her."

Verity nodded and took another drag on her cigarette. She exhaled into the air above McLaren's head. "It took Marta a while to get over her illness. I never did know exactly what she had. But she didn't just bounce back, like you do with a sore throat. So it wasn't until eleven June that Linnet and Marta found the time to go back to the casino. Of course the police were interested in when they both left—they were trying to set up some sort of time schedule for that night. Anyway, Linnet told the police when they both left. The time was confirmed by the CCTV tape in the car park. It shows Marta's and Linnet's cars leaving."

"That establishes she was alive then. But what about the time of her death? If her body wasn't found for ten days."

"She never made it inside her home that night. Her husband rang up the police after he had found the car in their drive. He then rang up Marta's brother-in-law to see if Marta had stopped overnight there, for some reason."

"But the car…"

"I know. But Alan didn't know if Marta went off with someone—"

"Meeting at the house," McLaren suggested.

"—or if someone had followed her and kidnapped her. So Alan called Neal. At least he could start eliminating possible places to check."

"Neal's the brother-in-law who lives in Matlock," McLaren said, getting the timetable and people straight in his head.

"Yes. Of course, Marta wasn't there. That's when Alan got very worried and rang up the police."

"And since the pathologist cannot possibly establish time of death from her body condition, being outside for so long…"

"That's all the police could really go on, having no witnesses. At least none who came forward. We just had that rough timetable of when she was last seen. You see," she said, leaning forward slightly, "they couldn't prove I killed her because they couldn't establish when she died. It could have been eleven June, the night she disappeared, or sixteen June, and by then I'd been arrested."

"Fifteen June."

She leaned back, looking sad. "Exactly."

"And you were mending hymnals during the time she was at the casino."

"The police tried to say I could have met up with Marta

somewhere later that night and killed her, but they had no evidence. It was all just speculation."

"Where was her body found?" McLaren had the information from the inquest report, but he wanted to see if Verity's account was the same.

Her voice timber changed and the words came slower and softer, as though she were again feeling the pain of her friend's death. "Near Elton. In a ditch near the road. It was awful. She was pretty badly decomposed by then. The weather and animals…" She broke off, her face devoid of color.

"Do you know if Marta had friends in Elton?"

"Why she was found there, in other words."

"It would give me a lead if she knew someone in the village."

"Sorry. Haven't a clue. But then, I didn't know a lot of her friends. I didn't mingle with them. She and I were merely friendly at the shelter. I hardly ever go anywhere, in fact, so I'm not the best person to ask about her friends—living in or out of Elton."

"Where were you after the hymnal session was finished? And the rest of the night?"

"We finished up around half past ten, I believe. Close to it, anyway."

"Marta and Linnet left the casino…at what time?"

"Just about eleven on the dot."

"Thirty minutes difference. Have you an alibi for eleven?"

"Just that I was home."

"Anyone see you?"

"No."

"Probably didn't matter to your case."

"I rang up the police to report my neighbor's dog. He was barking loudly, incessantly, and had broken out of their back garden. He was running around in my flowers, chasing a rabbit or something. I tried to catch the dog but I couldn't. My neighbors weren't home, so I couldn't get their help. Some few minutes later, at half past eleven, I think, I heard the dog somewhere down the street, in a fight with some other dog. That's when I rang up police."

"They would have a log of your call. Right. Well, the time constraint and distance work in your favor. You couldn't have driven down to Nottingham at half past ten, found Marta, killed her, and been back by half past eleven to complain about the dog." Even if someone else phoned from your house, he thought, there'd still be a record of it. It would have been played at the inquest and the case would have taken a different turn.

"Do you have any ideas yet, Mr. McLaren? Do you think you know who might have killed Marta?"

He smiled at her enthusiasm. "I've just taken on the case, Ms. Dwyer. I need more than a few hours."

She nodded, suddenly sober.

"Perhaps *you* have an idea. Do you know of anyone who might have held a grudge against her or wished her dead?"

"Oh, yes!"

She said it so quickly, so forcibly, McLaren blinked. "Really?"

"Yes. That neighbor of hers. That kid. Rick Millington. She told me about talking to the constable about the marijuana, which Rick and his group got in trouble over."

"You think Rick killed her? A bit far-fetched, isn't it? If he did ransack her house a bit, it's a long way from—"

"If not him, it was his dad."

"Really?" His voice held both skepticism and astonishment. "Why do you believe that?"

"Because he kept coming on to Marta and she wouldn't

have anything to do with him. She loved Alan deeply; she wouldn't risk her marriage by having an affair with Tom Millington."

"Perhaps not intentionally, but a lot of people believe they'll be faithful for their entire marriage and then suddenly they're involved with someone."

Verity shook her head. Her fingers fumbled with her cigarette, as though she were deciding whether to put it down. "You didn't know Marta. She had an iron will. She wouldn't have done that. Especially not with someone like Tom Millington."

"What's wrong with Tom Millington, then?"

"Have you seen him, talked to him?"

"Not yet."

She shuddered and scrunched up her lips. "When you do, you'll know what I mean." She hunched her shoulders and took a drag on the cigarette.

"So, what you're saying, then, is that Tom Millington killed Marta because she refused his sexual overtures, correct?"

"Could have done. He gets mad, hits her, she falls, hits her head." She angled her head, peering at McLaren through the haze of cigarette smoke. "I realize it's not as good as a written threat or a string of police complaints, but stranger things have happened."

McLaren nodded, trying to picture the fight. If it had taken place in Marta's home, there would have been blood from the head wound. Had Alan found it, cleaned it up, kept it quiet for some reason? Or had the fight taken place in the Millingtons' home, or outside somewhere? It could have happened. He said, "You know this about Tom Millington's sexual advances because you were over at her house once and witnessed it?"

"Not at all. But we were coworkers. We talked a lot."

"About that?"

"Yes. And about other things. You know—girl talk."

McLaren knew what she meant. He'd grown up in a family of women and he'd been engaged. He'd heard enough discussions—serious and comedic—about husbands, boyfriends, girlfriends, jobs, diets, bad hair cuts, actors, kids, school grades, health food, and love to last him until he turned a hundred. He could imagine very well Verity and Marta talking about Tom Millington—pro and con.

"I always wondered if she was killed for her money," Verity said slowly. Her voice had taken on the heavy, slow manner of someone waking from a deep dream and still held in its spell. She rose from her chair, went to the bookcase, and grabbed a photograph. Three women grinned from the confines of a gold-toned metal frame: Marta, Verity, and some other woman. They stood side by side, cheek to cheek, their arms around each other's shoulders. Best friends, sharing a joke. The photo had been sharing part of the shelf with a half-dozen small ceramic animals. They were lifelike, painstakingly detailed. Several books on raptors, European badgers, and wildflowers filled the rest of the shelf. Angling the photo toward McLaren, she said, "Funny, isn't it? I feel closer to Marta now than when we worked together. Why is that? Does it have something to do with guilt?"

"Why should you feel guilty? You've taken the blame for the missing money. Surely you don't wish you had been the murder victim instead of Marta."

"No," she said, staring at the picture. "At least... No, I don't know. At times I'm all right. I go about my day, resigned to my lot and making plans for when this all ends. But there are other times when I think about Marta and how her husband and son must miss her. She had a good many friends, you know. More than I'll ever have. They must miss her dreadfully."

"So to ease or erase their suffering, you think you should have been killed."

Verity gently returned the photo to its spot and rearranged a hedgehog. "Sounds absurd when you talk about it. But no, I wouldn't go that far. I've no death wish."

"What is it, then?"

"I don't know. Maybe it's that she was so young and she was so warm and funny and full of life. Forty-five is awfully young to die, isn't it?"

"Most people leave unfinished dreams, Ms. Dwyer, if that's what you're thinking. Even if you live to be a hundred, there will probably be something you've not done that you wish to. Don't let Marta's brief life and her incomplete works haunt you. You had nothing to do with any of this other than be a pawn. It seems to me that you've been more than giving." Who else would make your sacrifices, he thought. Taking the blame, keeping silent.

"I told Alan I wasn't going to jail for Marta," Verity said, breaking the quiet. "I had taken that money, I admit, but I wasn't going to be saddled with suspicions of Marta's death, no matter how good my motive was. Those suspicions would cling to me the rest of my life. I said I wasn't taking the blame for any of it."

"What did Alan say?"

"Nothing much. He just looked at me with those big brown eyes of his, threw his arm around his son's shoulders like some talisman or bulwark or challenge, and said he was sorry but he couldn't believe Marta had anything to do with the stolen money. What a laugh. Like he couldn't believe Marta was capable of anything like that."

"He didn't know about her gambling, then."

"Sure, he knew, but not about how often she gambled. It was like she was some perfect little saintly statue, perched atop a pedestal. Only her plaster façade had developed cracks he couldn't see. Or he chose to overlook." She took another drag on her cigarette. The cloud of smoke hung in front of her but she ignored it. "I liked Marta; we'd been close friends. Or so I thought until this happened. Until her silence." She flicked the end of her cigarette over the ashtray. "Though I will say in her defense that she didn't agree to my arrest when the money discrepancy was discovered. She was vehement about that."

"But she didn't explain why you'd given her the money," McLaren suggested.

"No. Other than that little squeak, she didn't defend me in any way."

"And, from what you just told me about Alan's response, Marta didn't say a thing to him about the money, either."

"If she did, Alan wouldn't admit in public that his wife was involved in a theft."

"Nice couple."

Verity snorted. "Not as bad as Bonnie and Clyde or Rosemary and Fred West," she said, recalling the serial killers. "But bad enough for me."

"Especially when you considered her a friend."

"Then she repays my friendship that way."

"Hard to take."

"Harder than Alan being momentarily embarrassed at his precious bank, yes, or having to find another job if his boss looks at him funny."

"A slight inconvenience when measured against your situation."

"I guess it just showed their true colors, which hurt me deeply." She crushed out the cigarette. "I've had a lot of time to think about all this. Well, you do, don't you, when you're serving a sentence?" The street had grown quiet. No traffic drove down the road, no dogs barked, no birds twittered at the windowsill or in the trees. The world seemed to be listening for Verity's thoughts. "It's kind of hard to forget. If there hadn't been all that money... Well, maybe none of this would have happened. What do you think?"

"Do you mean the money from the animal shelter?"

"No. The money she won that night at the casino."

"I thought she lost. I thought that was the reason she couldn't put the money back in your cash register, the reason that led to—" He nodded toward the kitchen and the calendar.

"My year of new experiences. Sorry. I didn't make it clear. No, I was talking about the night she won, the night she was murdered."

"Eleven June."

"She'd won a huge amount of money. I know about it because it was brought up at the trial. The croupier testified as to her winning, a player at the table also testified, the cashier testified, and Linnet testified. They all remarked as to the amount. It was the same in each person's telling: two hundred fifty-three thousand, five hundred sixty pounds."

"A lot." McLaren exhaled loudly.

"More than several years' salaries, and earned in a moment with a flick of the croupier's wrist and Marta's positioning of her chips. Must be nice."

"I've heard of big wins before, but rarely of a win that large. She must have been over the moon."

"I suppose so. I never got to ask her." She let the implication hang in the air between them.

"If she was killed that night, what happened to the money she won?"

"Presumably stolen. It wasn't found on her body."

McLaren was nearly home, approaching Somerley from the copse of birch and willow that sheltered the remains of an old stone barn. It'd been a full day and he had a lot to consider—not only with the case but also with Dena and

Karin. Was it coincidence that these two personal segments
had cropped up the moment he'd taken on this cold case? He'd
left his mobile-phone number with Verity, getting her sol-
emn assurance she'd ring him in case she thought of anything
else. Which he hoped she would—she seemed to be a reliable witness and a person who had a stake in what had happened. That she appeared to hold no grudge against Marta,
despite her eleven-month community-service order and lost
job, told him a lot about her character. So yes, he was hoping she would come up with something he could use when
she'd had a chance to think.

He was considering the disappearance of the casino money
when he turned down the main street. Dena's red MG was
parked opposite the pub. He stopped his car behind hers,
locked his car, and strode into the courtyard. She was sitting at a wrought-iron table, writing a letter, but stopped
and looked up at him as he came up to her. "Thirsty? Or
just thought of a good retort from last night's conversation?"
She shoved a strand of her hair behind her ear. It caught the
golden rays of the early-evening sun, bringing out the hints
of chestnut coloring in its brunette hue. It was also fragrant
with the scent of her shampoo—honeysuckle. Like the soap
and perfume she used.

McLaren stared at its beauty, nearly drowning in her scent.

"Well? Am I supposed to be intimidated by your strong,
silent stance, or is this a game of charades and I'm to guess
what you're portraying? Rock of Gibraltar, right? Or a statue
of Adonis. It can't be that you're tongue-tied. I've heard you
rabbit on about cases."

"For God's sake, Dena—"

"Well, that's a start. Maybe not as nice as 'Hi, how are
you?' but it's something. You're probably rusty—no one to
talk to but your pile of rocks. Not that you ever were a smashing conversationalist, but you could always talk about police

work. It was just the personal topics, the unleashing of your emotions, that you couldn't handle. Are you any better at that now? Had any practice standing in front of the bathroom mirror?"

He stared down at her, pain and anger etched on his face. "Why do I—or any copper—get crucified and criticized for the very traits that make us good cops? We're taught from Day One that we must show no emotion on duty, that we must wear a public face in order to be seen to be in control of any situation."

"I've heard your recital, Michael. Your safety and your career are on the line if you lose control. Any control. The damned list is endless! Control of your emotions, the victim's emotions. Control of the traffic, people, the crime scene. Calm down, submit to orders, submit to authority, don't let the suspect know you're scared or repulsed or angry or sad or humiliated. You'll lose your power."

"Those aren't just words, Dena. They're what we have to remember if we're to keep the floodgates closed on our emotions. We experience a wider range of emotions in our shift than most people do in their day. We've seen it all so we've experienced it all: anger, pity, pride, excitement, revulsion, fear, cowardice, envy, hate. But we keep all that bottled up, keep it beneath our public face so we can do our job because the victim is counting on us to handle the situation. We can't cry and effectively do our job, for Christ's sake! Trouble is, you don't understand what we see. You expect us to act like automatons doing our job, then come home spewing out emotions and confiding our souls. It's not that easy! We can't turn our feelings off and on like a water spigot."

"I know, Michael. I've experienced it."

"We've had to suppress our feelings for the safety of our jobs." He paused, aware that he had been implying he was still part of the "we" and "our" he had just mentioned, aware again of the honeysuckle scent of her, the dark eyelashes that cast shadows on her eyes. "We…we live in a world of orders, Dena. If we're not giving an order to someone, we're receiving orders from the top brass. I can't just turn off twenty years of police training the minute I step into the house. My very life depends on my unemotional demeanor on the job."

A phrase of a song slipped outside as a waiter opened the door and entered the pub. When it had grown quiet again, Dena said rather reluctantly, "I understand that, Michael. But it's more than that. I can't get close to you! You've put up a wall around yourself."

"If I have, it's nothing personal. It's left over from my old job."

"So you want me to smile and just take your orders and love your silent, stand-offish attitude."

"Of course not! But you can understand I can't switch it on and off so easily. You should know I'm trying to learn how to do it." He looked at her, wanting her to say she realized his dilemma, that she had been too demanding in wanting him to pour out his feelings to her. But she merely stared at the table, her eyes lowered, her fingers tracing the rim of her glass, as though she were considering something.

A lifetime passed before she spoke. Her voice had not softened in those few moments; the edge was still there, a sign of her frustration and pain. She shifted in her chair so she squarely faced him. "Fine. Smashing. Whatever you say, Michael. I'm tired of it all." She laid down her pen but kept her fingers on top of it. "I repeat, are you thirsty? You want a beer?" She eyed him when he grabbed the back of a chair. "You're awfully dressed up. Trousers, cambric shirt, tie. You quit early from work? Must have. No stone dust in your hair, no work boots. What's the matter?" She eyed him, the concern evident in her brown eyes.

"Mind if I sit down?" He remained standing until she

nodded, then he pulled out the chair. The wrought-iron legs screeched against the flagstone paving. He lifted the chair for the remainder of the way and then set it down, angling it toward Dena. "No, I won't have anything," he answered as he took a seat. "You're drinking wine."

Startled, she said, "Uh, yes. I always do."

"You drank a beer once, I recall."

."Did I?" She screwed up her mouth, clearly puzzled at the subject. "Yes, I did. At your birthday party. But it was a shandy."

"Still, you did have a beer once. The night of my folk group's first appearance. A Bass."

"What a memory! Fine, I had a beer. That once. And I disliked it. Is this why you're here? To see if I've developed a taste for beer?"

"Actually," he said, his voice softer, "I just spotted your MG and thought I'd talk to you."

"Was it something I said last night? I haven't seen you for a year, Michael. Not since you left your job."

"I know. I'm sorry."

"About what? Not seeing me, or leaving your job?" The sheet of stationary rustled in a breath of wind. Dena set her mobile phone on it.

"Both. It's just that—"

"You've been hurt. I *know* that, Michael! So does everyone near to you. Your parents, your sister, your brother-in-law, your friend Jamie. We know what you went through and we feel for you. We always will. You got a rotten deal. But there has to be an end to your wound licking. You have to shake it off and get on with your life. I've waited for a year, hoping for an overture of love."

He pulled in the corner of his mouth and looked past her shoulder, staring at the church tower at the end of the street. The sunlight glanced off the brass cross topping the steeple and tinted the gray stones gold. A magpie floated down from the half-closed bell louvers and settled on a bough of a stately oak.

"If that's too strong a word, an overture of friendship, then. You can't keep your feelings and yourself walled up forever. You can't live like that. You are a warm, caring person. At least, you used to be. I believe you still are, deep inside. That warmth and caring drove you into police work in the first place, Michael. But you can't become stony and unfeeling like those damned stonewalls of yours."

"Were you in Castleton this morning?" He had shifted his gaze so that he now looked at her face, judging the truth in her eyes.

"Pardon?" Her eyebrow arched. "What's Castleton got to do with—"

"A lot. At least, it could. I need to know. Were you in Castleton?"

"Are you serious?"

"Very."

"We were talking about you and your feelings and your life from here on out."

"And my feelings and my life, and our relationship—if it's to continue or improve or get back to where it was—"

"Depends on Castleton this morning. Honestly, Michael!" She picked up the wine glass and took a sip before replying. "I don't know what you want. Will you believe my answer?" Her gaze shifted to his eyes. They were dark and unreadable except for the suggestion of desperation. Setting down the glass, she said, "This really means a lot, doesn't it?"

He nodded, not trusting his voice.

"Well, I don't know what you want—"

"I want the truth, Dena. Just that."

"That's all I've ever given you, Michael. From the first day we met. And when I fell in love with you, I told you so we wouldn't be playing games. It's not fair to play games with someone's emotions."

"About this morning…"

She took a deep breath and leaned forward so that she was closer to him. "No. I wasn't in Castleton." She watched as he slowly let out his breath. "I don't know whether I've helped or hindered my cause with you, but I wasn't in Castleton. Will you tell me why you wanted to know? You weren't involved in a hit and run, were you?" She angled her head, trying to see his car.

"It *was* a hit and run, Dena, but not that sort." He stood up and looked down at her.

"You're going? Just like that, without telling me anything?" She was aware of his great height, of the annoyance building within him. Had she said something to anger him? What had happened in Castleton that mattered so much? Holding out her hand toward him, she said, "Please, Michael. Tell me. I can't help you if I don't know what's troubling you."

"You want to help me?"

"Of course!"

"Even after all this time, after how you felt last night?"

"That was anger talking last night. I wouldn't have called you if I didn't feel something toward you."

"But love turns into hate sometimes. Just pick up a newspaper or listen to a television news program. There are dozens of stories about spousal abuse and murder."

"What happened in Castleton… Should that lead me to murder you? Or you murder me?" she added quickly as he took a deep breath.

"No. That's extreme."

"Then what?"

"Just a little mystery I have to solve, that's all. Good night, Dena."

"This isn't the end, is it?" she called after his retreating figure. "You're not running out on me again…"

"I'll be around." He turned toward her, his hands in his trousers pockets.

"So will I, Michael. At the same phone number and the same street address."

"Just so I don't hit and run again in *your* life, right?" He wished her good night again and left.

Why would she put the beer bottle in my car when I made it plain I didn't want her around? He got into his car. The last rays of sun hit the west-facing roof tiles, ignited a house's brass weather vane in brilliant ochre and red, and shimmered through the tops of the trees. There was at least another hour of sunlight on the hills, but here in the valley the shadows were already forming and it would be dark soon. He turned his car onto the road to his house, just beyond the village proper, the questions and suspicions crowding his mind. Why would she get tangled up with someone who doesn't want her? It made no sense.

McLaren passed the last house in the string of wall-to-wall residences along the road's northern side. A light burned in the front room, ready for the twilight. He entered the smaller lane that led to his house, a narrow strip of black among the greens and browns and grays of the landscape. As he emerged into the clearing, the limestone rock face on his left reflected the sun's light with a near-blinding intensity. It was a relief when his car gained the gloom of the wood again.

He was rounding the bend where the wood was its densest. A sliver of light glanced off the water that fell from the rocky crevice dozens of stories above. The pool where the water collected was deep and cold, inviting to animals and small boys. The memories of summer swims were sharp in his mind, then he quickly jerked the car wheel. A car raced from the leafy darkness, its nearness frightening. McLaren jammed on the brakes, steering the car as far to the left as possible. As he heard the sickening sound of metal scraping against stone, a flash came toward him and he heard the blare of a horn. A moment later a beer bottle slammed into his door and crashed onto the road. He jerked his head to his right. The other car disappeared in a cloud of dust.

He took a deep breath, then slowly got out of his car. Dust hung in the air like the questions crowding his mind. He covered his mouth, trying not to breathe, but the dust seeped into this nose and mouth. Coughing, he pulled open the car door and sat inside with the windows rolled up until the dust had dissipated. He shook his head. He'd braked within inches of a massive oak tree. But the passenger side of the car hadn't escaped so luckily. It was nestled against the cliff face.

He slowly walked to the far side of his car, his head lowered, searching the ground. Near the rear of his car, several yards back, he found what he wanted. He picked up a rock and judged its weight, much as he did when working on stonewalls. The rock eclipsed his hand. Curling his fingers around the rock, he walked several dozen yards farther up the road, in the direction from which the other driver had come. Tracks from his tires showed plainly on the damp patch of earth near the bend. They were the only marks on its otherwise clean surface. The other driver had not even tried to stop or swerve.

McLaren turned and strode back to the center of the road opposite his car. He didn't attempt to cap his anger. He ran several feet, his right hand slightly behind him, his left shoulder leading, as a thrower revving up for the launch of a javelin. Seconds later he threw the rock after the long-departed car. The rock arched into the air, clipped a few leaves from low-hanging tree branches, then dropped onto the tarmac several hundred yards down road.

He drove slowly home, anger at odds with the confusion that tried to make sense of the incident. The accident, he could understand. The road was narrow and curved at that point. It was fairly dark and hard to see. But why throw a beer bottle? Was it related to the beer-bottle incident earlier today?

He parked his car in the wide space off-center of his driveway, put the leftover fish and chips in the microwave to heat, and rang up his mate, police detective Jamie Kydd.

TEN

"THE DAMN THING about this," McLaren said when Jamie answered his phone, "is that I didn't get the registration number on his damned car." Having given his friend the details of the incident he was now releasing his anger and frustration between his gulps of beer.

"I would've thought your car's condition would've been the worst part," Jamie said, laughing. He ran his fingers through his short-cropped black hair and settled back into the upholstered chair. When it looked like this would be a long phone call, he had taken his mobile phone into the lounge. Nothing like comfort to ease difficulties.

"It's scratched," McLaren admitted, setting the bottle down with a thud that even Jamie could hear. "A minor dent to the left front wing, but nothing serious."

"And it's drivable."

"If it weren't, I'd still be running after the berk."

"And you'd smash his face in when you caught up with him, I know."

McLaren's grunt acknowledged his agreement.

"Did you get a look at the car or see any occupants?"

He hesitated, aware he was going to sound like the majority of victims and witnesses he had interviewed during his police career. At Jamie's urging, he finally said, "It was a Mercedes coupe. A dark color. Green, I think. Yeah, a hunter green. I don't think it was navy blue or black. Registration number begins YV. That's all I could get. I think there was someone in the back seat. I think *he* threw the beer bottle."

"The back seat? Implying there were three or more people in the car?"

"Because he was in the back and not in the front passenger seat?"

"You don't think he was deliberately sitting in the back so he could toss the bottle at you?"

"Well…"

"That implies it was premeditated, Mike! The whole thing staged and done on purpose! God, what've you been doing?"

"What do you mean?"

"To warrant this? Have you made an enemy of someone?"

"I've been out of the job for a year now."

"You think those thugs you sent away will forget you just because you're no longer a cop?"

"A year or more's awfully long to hold a grudge and do something about it. Besides, if you don't remember, I was stationed in Staffordshire. I now reside in Derbyshire. That's a hell of a big distance between the station and my house."

"You moved back to Derbyshire on purpose, I know."

"Yeah. For just this sort of thing—so none of those toe rags could find me."

"Well, unless some farmer is upset at the way you mended his stonewall, *someone's* mad! What's with this beer bottle episode, anyway? You still think it's related to that walker you picked up this morning?"

McLaren picked up the beer, looked at it, screwed up his mouth, and set it down again. He needed a clear head to sort out everything. "I don't know, Jamie. That's why I rang you up."

"The impartial outsider looking at this unemotionally."

"I thought perhaps something would stand out."

"Like, you forgot that the hiker was drinking a Duvel when you stopped to assist her."

"Nothing that expensive," McLaren said, recalling the

price of the Belgian ale. "But something like that, yes. I've got a lot on my mind right now."

"Well, unless you haven't told me something, I can't see how this is connected with your cold case. Probably just coincidence."

"Don't give me that, boy. You know my opinion of coincidence."

"Things do happen. And the beer bottle's not part of your cold case."

"Which is another reason I needed to talk." He speared a chip, now barely more than lukewarm, with his fork. He didn't care particularly what he ate, as long as he could fill his stomach. Breakfast was a long time ago.

"I'm all ears."

"I had hoped you'd be part brain, but I'll let that pass."

"Fine. Shoot."

"Good word choice."

"What, shoot? You weren't shot at, too, were you?"

McLaren shook his head. There was no mistaking the anxiety in his friend's voice. "No. I'm referring to the cold case. Marta Hughes murdered and dumped along the roadside."

"Sure. So what do you want? I didn't work on that case, Mike. Derbyshire Constabulary not withstanding, lad, I'm in A Division. Was last year when that happened, too. Elton's in B Division."

"I know. I just thought you could get your hands on some information for me."

The silence at the other end of the phone grew uncomfortable and McLaren was about to apologize when Jamie said, "What kind of information? If it's something about running a car through the police national computer—"

"No. Nothing so risky." He pushed the bottle away from him and forked another chip. He knew that PNC checks were strictly controlled, monitored internally by the Force. He also knew PNC use for anything other than official use resulted in officers being sacked. It was a chance and ramification he would never ask Jamie to take. He laid the fork back on the plate and said, "You've got access to the police reports."

"Yes." His answer sounded wary.

"I'd like to know about the place her body was found—the exact location."

"Are you daft?"

McLaren seemed not to hear Jamie. He continued. "How far out from Elton, on the left or the right side of the road? Where was she found precisely? If you can't get me a copy of the photos—" He held the phone away from his ear as Jamie's yelp boomed over the receiver. "Let me know exactly. I'd like the pathology report. *And* the biologist's, if you can wrangle that, too."

He paused and Jamie snorted. "You'll give me a few minutes to rustle this up, I hope."

"Whenever you get it is fine."

"Thanks." Jamie exhaled loudly, already imagining the swift boot out the door if he got caught looking up the information.

"Just don't lose your job over it."

"I don't intend to. Uh, Mike?"

"Yeah?"

"Be careful, will you?"

"I always am."

Jamie refrained from saying McLaren had not been careful the night of his altercation with Charlie Harvester. He looked up from his notepad and said, "The lads did a thorough search of the area, Mike. I don't know what you'll find there, but I'll ring you back when I've got the info for you."

"I just hope our boys in blue overlooked something."

McLAREN WAS RUNNING, his legs painful to move, his strides agonizingly slow as he struggled his way through the mass of beer bottles that had somehow filled The Hanoverian Hotel's lobby. He had just reached for the driver when his bedside phone rang, jerking him awake.

He groped in the darkness, knocking over the bottle of aspirin and sending a book thudding to the floor. The ringing guided his search and after several seconds his fingers closed around the receiver. He leaned toward the bedside table, throwing off the bed sheet, and answered even before the mouthpiece was against his lips.

There was no answer. The line was dead.

Grumbling that some people should learn to dial more carefully, he hung up the phone and lay down. The sounds of the night seeped into his room—bleats of sheep, the bark of a fox, the faint purr of a car motor, the yowl of a cat. He turned over on his side and went back to sleep.

The moon had not wandered much in its westward path when he was wakened again by the jangling phone. This time he sat up and grabbed the receiver on the third ring. His terse "Yeah?" was followed by silence.

He barked his response again, and again there was no reply.

Slamming the receiver back onto the phone, McLaren cursed the unknown caller and looked around the darkened room for something to throw. The book was on the floor, out of reach. He needed the two pillows, so they weren't considered. Then he glanced at the alarm clock. Its luminous dial stated it was 2:45 a.m. Hell of a time for someone to be up and making calls. He fell back onto the mattress. His head hit the pillows, sending a soft "whoosh" into the room.

Was someone deliberately ringing him up, harassing him? He was ex-directory, so either someone had randomly dialed his number or the person knew him. He would have named Dena, but after today's talk, he was certain she wouldn't do that. So who was calling him? And why?

He rolled onto his side again, punching up the pillow so he could see out of the window. The land lay quiet and dark, devoid of the earlier night noises. Everything beneath heaven was still and slumbering, it seemed, and McLaren shut his eyes, trying to do the same.

Minutes later he gave it up as a bad job and sat up, leaning against the headboard. The caller had to be connected to something currently happening in his life; no one would wait a year for revenge. Unless he'd just been released from prison…

McLaren stared into the blackness outside his window, more dense and real than the gloom inside his house. He had enemies in prison—what copper didn't? But for someone to find out where he lived, what car he drove… That suggested tenacity and intelligence. Or a connection inside the police department.

What copper would turn on another copper like this? Who would betray him to a con? The answer screamed at him with all the certainty of a slamming cell door. Charles Harvester.

McLaren sat up, his body rigid, heart pounding. He pulled the pillow to his chest and wrapped his arms around it, squeezed it, wishing for the first time in a year that it were Dena. The room seemed to pulse in rhythm to the blood pounding in his temples. He fumbled for the glass of water beside the clock, found it, and drank it quickly. Wiping the back of his hand against his mouth, he tried to think. Even Harvester wouldn't do that. They may have hated each other's guts, but to set up something like this, something that smacked of revenge, after more than a year….

He set the glass back on the nightstand and got up. Tossing the pillow onto the bed, he glanced at the clock: 3:03 a.m. Perhaps he could sleep late. If he ever got back to sleep. Funny thing was…he never had trouble sleeping when he worked on stonewalls.

Perhaps because there was nothing threatening about them…or because he knew what to expect. Like the wall he had been working on when Linnet had interrupted him. He had sited down the wall's length, making certain the addition was in keeping with the wall's cant. Not an edge had ruptured the overall symmetry. Except for the absence of lichen wallpapering the stone face or moss wedging into minute recesses between stones, his work was indistinguishable from the original wall, blending into its ancient age. Was that part of the attraction of the work, cherishing the link to the original waller? Perhaps he, too, had been an outsider as McLaren was. Perhaps the ancient craftsman had found his comfort in sun, wind, and kestrels soaring overhead, had shunned other men's company, wanting only to get on with his life and job. Which was what McLaren wanted right now. Not dredging up recollections of injustices until your emotional wounds lay raw once more.

He had thought them buried in the year he'd been here, this desperate attempt to keep his soul and body together when he had left Staffordshire to return to his home village in Derbyshire and to the work of a stonewall builder. He would never want for jobs, he had told himself. Not with the thousands of miles of walls crisscrossing the county. Even if the work was back breaking, it suited his mood. More than suited his personality. A loner, a maverick cop didn't chase after the camaraderie of the workplace office.

The mantel clock struck the quarter hour and McLaren stretched, the faceless builder fading from his gaze, Harvester's face grinning from the darkness.

He walked over to the window and stood there, the cool breeze chilling his feverish body. Charlie Harvester. He hadn't thought of the man in ages; he didn't even know where he was. The first few months after McLaren had left the job, he'd heard snippets of office gossip—humorous cases or who was engaged or the current idiotic police regulation. It had diminished as the weeks of his absence increased, until he rarely heard from anyone in the department anymore.

Taking a deep breath, McLaren leaned against the edge of the window, his eyes on the sliver of moon nestled in the branches of a birch. Was it only a year ago he had left? Dena had reminded him of the dubious anniversary date when she'd called last night. He rubbed his eyes, suddenly exhausted. One year. Twelve short months ago he'd left in response to an injustice dealt him.

It had started years before. When he and Harvester had been in police training school. He, the serious student who always made top marks in class; Harvester, the son of the Chief Constable, sneaky, getting by on instructor favoritism. On completion of their initial training course, their animosity had increased. Working in the same department, they had both attained detective status, though McLaren had one solid year's experience before Harvester finally wormed his way in. It was constant comparisons after that: McLaren, popular, hardworking, and intelligent; Harvester, shunned, not trusted, sliding by on his daddy's name, and a brilliant example of the Peter Principle. He was also jealous of McLaren.

Then one spring night, the years of ill feelings and envy exploded in one fateful event. McLaren had just finished with a case and was back at his desk, attacking the stack of papers menacing the entire office. He'd reached for his coffee when a colleague sauntered into the room and sat down in a chair. McLaren looked up, both grateful for and irritated by the interruption.

"No action tonight?" McLaren eyed the detective from over the rim of his coffee mug. "Or maybe you've cleared up your backlog." He smiled at the shared joke. There were always cases to work. They flooded their department daily, the new file folders placed on top of yesterday's file folders, creating the stacks of miniature towers that threatened to consume their desks, their office, and their lives.

"Just taking a breather. Thought I'd bother you for a bit. What are you working on?"

McLaren shoved the open folder and his notepad away from him and leaned back in his chair. "A pub fight."

"Sounds fun, that."

"Six people involved."

"Bloody hell. Something else besides property damage?"

"One chap's in hospital. He's bad off."

"Damn. Anyone talking?"

"We'll know soon," McLaren said. "We've started interviewing those involved."

"Sounds like a mess."

"Even more of a mess. As our luck would have it, the assault happened just out of the range of the CCTV. We've no more idea right now of who beat up this poor bloke than my dog knows."

"Bloody hell."

"It's more serious than a black eye. The chap's in the IC unit. Stabbing to the abdomen, arm, and neck. Just missed the jugular vein, but…"

"Damn."

McLaren nodded. "Hopefully it won't turn into a murder charge."

"The chap's that bad off, then," the detective said.

"Unfortunately, yes. He keeps wavering. At first, he showed signs of improvement. Then his blood pressure fell and it was looking bad for him. Last time I checked on him, he was improving. The hospital staff is cautiously optimistic."

"Well, they would say that, wouldn't they? Well, I wish him luck."

McLaren pointed with his cup to the electric kettle on top of the metal file cabinet. An assortment of ceramic mugs, a box of tea bags, a canister of coffee, packets of sugar, and a pint bottle of milk crowded the kettle. A beer mug held several metal spoons.

The detective sighed. "No, thanks. I've got to get back."

"Tough case?"

"Not really. Just tedious." The man stretched, throwing his head back. "Isn't it the end of our shift yet?"

"Sorry, mate. It's only three o'clock."

"Damn. Well…" He made no move to leave, sitting there and glancing at McLaren's desk. "Here's luck to that chap in hospital. I know Charlie Harvester's not your favorite subject…"

McLaren's snort cemented the unspoken, shared opinion of the other man.

"…but at least his case of assault sounds easily sorted out."

"Not that I want to hear, particularly, but I suppose you're about to tell—"

"An old man—oh, must be seventy if he's a day—coshed a burglar on the head."

"A round of applause for the old man. Where was this… a home invasion?"

"No, oddly enough. A pub. The old man lives upstairs. Why? What's the matter?"

McLaren's face drained of color and his fingers slowly blanched as he gripped the edge of his desk. "Who? When? What's the address?"

"Bloody hell, man, what's the matter?"

"What pub?" McLaren shouted, halfway getting to his feet. "Who is it?"

"I don't know the bloke's name. I just heard this roundabout."

"When?"

"When did I hear—"

"When did this happen?"

"Now. Quarter of an hour ago. Harvester's still at the scene. Why?"

"Where? What pub?" McLaren was standing now, leaning over his desk, a menacing tower of anger.

"I don't know. Yeah, I do. It's in Tutbury. The Broken Wheel. Hey!" he yelled after McLaren's darting figure. "Where you off to?"

His reply was the slamming of the office door and the stirring of loose papers in the breeze following McLaren's departure.

The drive into Tutbury, past the castle and to the pub, had passed in a dark blur. Road, trees, buildings slipped past his car window as he thought of Charlie Harvester and what had probably happened at The Broken Wheel. McLaren leaned forward, peering into the blackness beyond the reach of the car's headlights, and pressed down on the accelerator pedal. The car shot ahead, took the turn into the village on two wheels, and gained speed on the straight lane. He flashed past a row of houses, barely missed a fox as it crossed the road, then braked in front of the pub and dashed up the front walk. He left his car, headlights on and the door open, sitting squarely in the middle of the road.

Inside he found the usual bustle of police constables and detectives, fingerprint technician and photographer, and the myriad others needed at a scene. But the unusual find alarmed even him, a ten-year veteran of the job. An angry Charlie Harvester was reading Nigel Forester, the pub's owner, his rights.

"What the hell's going on?" McLaren yelled, his gaze darting between Nigel and Harvester. "Nigel, are you all right? Where's Maureen?" He glanced around the room, expecting to see her sitting at one of the pub tables.

"Maureen's in hospital, Mike." Nigel's voice shook and he blinked repeatedly, trying to hold back the tears. He sat in a chair, his face bruised and cut from some physical altercation.

"*Hospital!* Why? What's happened? Are you all right? You need medical attention?" He glanced at Nigel, then at the constables huddled in the background. When no one spoke, he yelled the question again.

"Mrs. Forester has been taken in an ambulance," Charlie Harvester replied, his voice stunningly calm in the sea of agitation.

McLaren turned, focusing his eyes, anger, and energy on the police detective. The man approached McLaren, tapping a pad of paper against his left hand. "Why?" McLaren shifted his gaze back to Nigel. "What happened? Did—" He seemed to see Nigel's wounds for the first time. Turning back to Harvester, he said, "Was Maureen injured in the break-in?"

"You seem to know a lot about this case, McLaren," Harvester said. "How'd you hear about it?"

"I want to know about Maureen. Why did you call an—"

"She's suffered a heart attack."

"God!" He turned his eyes to Nigel, who was silently crying. "How bad is it?"

"I don't know." Nigel raised his head. His cheeks were wet from his tears. "I don't know. She just kind of moaned, clutched her chest, and collapsed."

"You rang 999?"

"Not I. Your mate, here, did it. Maureen just collapsed as he came in. I was going to ring 999 anyway, for the burglar, but—" He paused, the scene too vivid to talk about.

McLaren glanced at Harvester, as though silently confirming what had happened.

"When was that?" McLaren said, returning to Nigel. "The *burglar* needed an ambulance? Why? What went on?"

Nigel pulled in his lips, reluctant to speak. After McLaren repeated his question, Nigel said, "He needed medical attention."

"Euphemistic way of putting it," Harvester grunted, "but

it's adequate. If you need convincing, McLaren…" He indicated the fireplace poker that a Crime Scene Investigator technician was examining. The wrought-iron tool had a definite curve to its otherwise straight length. "What's that tell you?"

"Not bloody much." McLaren snorted.

"Look, McLaren." Harvester grabbed McLaren's shoulder and turned him around.

Shaking off the detective's hand, McLaren scowled. "Let go of me, Harvester." The words were low, barely audible, but remarkably calm.

Harvester shrugged and crossed his arms across his chest. "This is my case, if it's not perfectly clear to you. My case. *I* got the call. *I* interviewed the victim and the assailant. *I* arrested the guilty party—your friend Nigel Forester, as it turns out. So what you're doing here, sticking your nose into something that doesn't concern you—"

"Doesn't concern me!" His bark was a mixture of amusement, disbelief, and anger. "I thought the welfare of any honest citizen was my concern. Every copper's concern. Just because you got the call doesn't preclude me from being concerned."

"Could it be something more than that?" Harvester asked, his eyes narrowing.

"What the hell's that supposed to mean?"

"Seems to me you're a bit over the top with your 'concern' bit."

"When I come to find the pub owner apparently arrested merely for protecting his property against a-a—" he barely glanced at the bent poker "—against a burglar engaged in questionable activities…yes, I am concerned."

"As I said, your concern seems more than a cop would express. Could you be guilty of something else?"

"Harvester, you're full of crap."

"And you're overreacting. You're upset because I've just arrested a friend of yours." He smiled as McLaren reddened. "Score one for me, I think."

Trying to keep his voice in check, McLaren said, "What's Nigel Forester done to warrant this outrage?"

"Assaulted Mr. Tyrone Wade Antony. To be specific, assault with intent to kill."

"Assault! The hell he did. He was defending his property and life. And protecting Maureen, too, if I know Nigel."

"That's where you're wrong, McLaren." He nearly laughed, then recovered himself as the police photographer walked into the room. "Galls, doesn't it? The ace detective, the top cop of the team, and you're wrong. Well, it may surprise you to know that we have proof."

"Like what?" McLaren bit the words off in his growing anger.

"Mr. Forester attacked Mr. Antony with that fireplace poker."

McLaren looked at the pub owner and asked softly, "Is this true, Nigel?"

The older man nodded. He looked older than his seventy years at the moment, his white hair vivid in the light of the police work lamps, his face white from shock. "But just because I was defending myself. He'd broken into the pub by the back door. I heard the door bang open as it hit the cases of empty bottles I'd put inside the door. I rushed downstairs. Maureen and I were in our bedroom, getting ready for bed." He paused, his eyes overflowing with fear at his arrest and his questionable future.

McLaren could envision the upstairs living quarters. He'd been up there many times, ever since he'd been seventeen years old. Nigel Forester had saved him from drowning in a nearby lake, strolling past by chance and hearing McLaren's friend screaming for help. Nigel had swum out to McLaren, got him into a lifesaving hold, and brought him back to shore. Since that day, twenty-one years ago, McLaren had practically cemented himself to the older man's side, mowing his grass, washing his car, painting the walls of their living quarters. Anything and everything to repay for his saved life, especially so because a third boy in their group had drowned before Nigel could help. McLaren knew he could never even the score, but he appeared monthly to do some chore or just sit and chat over a pint or cup of coffee.

McLaren's sense of Right, his need to help others, blossomed. After graduating from university, he joined the police service. When he had completed his initial training, at the top of his class, he had honed his determination to serve where and how he could.

"I could hear him—" Nigel took a deep breath, trying to keep his voice from quaking. "I knew where he was, even in the dark. There's a floorboard that creaks. I snapped on the overhead light and surprised him with the cash-register till in his hand. He was emptying it into a sack he had with him. He'd also put some bottles of liquor or beer into it. I heard the coins hit the bottles as they fell into the sack. I saw a crowbar on the countertop. The tool wasn't mine—I don't own one. He smirked at me and called me a name. I guess the crowbar was too far away from him 'cause he reached into the sack and brought out a bottle. He had hold of it by its neck. He hit it against the edge of the serving counter so the bottom of the bottle broke off. Then he rushed at me. He was holding the jagged bottle edge toward me like he was going to dig it into me. I was scared—for me and for Maureen. As he ran up to me I picked up the fireplace poker and hit him."

ELEVEN

"HEAR THAT, MCLAREN? It's a confession. Mr. Forester hit Mr. Antony." Harvester smiled, the smirk broadening into a grin as though it were a personal triumph.

McLaren glanced around the bar area, expecting to see great pools of blood. The oak-paneled walls, stone floor, and fireplace were as he remembered. The massive beams, nearly black against the white plaster ceiling, had not changed. Yet the room's warmth and intimacy had become cold and menacing from the night's event and Harvester's presence. McLaren doubled up his fist, ready to slam it into Harvester's leer, then shoved his hand behind his back. "Since when are the police so protective of a burglar? You make me sick, Harvester."

Unconcerned with McLaren's opinion, Harvester said, "I've cautioned Mr. Forester and he acknowledged that he understands it. Nothing you can do. We've got the evidence of the assault—"

"What evidence? If you're talking about fingerprints on the poker, that's no evidence. It's his poker! I'm taking this up with the governor."

"What's the matter with you, McLaren? You hard of hearing? Or just so thick skulled that you don't understand? I said it's not your case. Mr. Forester attacked Mr. Antony so severely that the wrought-iron poker bent over his head, for God's sake! That's proof of an assault. That and Mr. Antony's blood on it. It's a clear case of Section 18, causing grievous bodily harm. And, if Mr. Antony dies, it'll become a case of murder."

The years of antagonism seemed to solidify into this exact moment. And now, in his friend's pub, McLaren felt the determination to help others—the need that had sent him into the Force in the first place—growing within him. The anger and frustration at seeing Nigel Forester so wrongly arrested spilled out. He strode over to the CSI officer, grabbed the fireplace poker, and marched into the men's loo. Turning on the cold-water tap, he thrust the poker under the running water and moved the poker back and forth, wiping the blood and hair from the tool. When he had removed all the physical traces, he straightened the poker over his knee. Satisfied, he strode back into the main room and threw the poker onto a table. The poker bounced once as it thudded against the table's wooden surface.

"*Now* where's your evidence?" McLaren barked, hatred in his eyes as he glared at Harvester.

Every eye in the room was fixed to the now-clean poker.

Harvester slowly shifted his gaze from the table to McLaren's face. He stared at McLaren, matching his anger as he snapped, "I'll have you up before the Chief Constable, McLaren! You've just destroyed vital evidence in a case."

"Nigel Forester stays right here." He took a step toward Harvester and brought his fist from behind his back. The two constables who were in attendance exchanged nervous glances but remained where they were.

"I'll have your job, McLaren," Harvester hissed. "Yours and anyone who assists you. You're interfering with a police case." He didn't have to look at the constables to make his meaning clear.

"Hell." McLaren strode over to Nigel, who was leaning his head against the wall. At this angle, with the light falling full on Nigel's face, the bruises and the cut beneath his eye showed up markedly against his pale skin. Turning a chair to face his friend, McLaren sat down and leaned forward, as though having dropped in for a chat. He said quietly but firmly, "You'll be fine, Nigel. You're not going anywhere with Detective Harvester. You've done nothing wrong. You defended your and your wife's life against an armed intruder. Please don't worry. We'll go see Maureen when they've got you patched up, shall we?"

During this conversation, Harvester had stepped out of the room, but he now returned, his face red and a smile playing about the corners of his lips. He walked up to McLaren but stopped several feet from him. "I've just radioed for a superintendent to be turned out, McLaren." He paused, watching McLaren's face for the full effect of his words.

McLaren rose to his feet, the knuckles of his right hand pressing against the tabletop.

Harvester smiled more broadly now that he had McLaren's attention. "I'm making an allegation against you. Perverting the course of justice. We'll see what the superintendent has to say about that." He opened his mouth, whether to add something or to smile, but he didn't get a chance.

McLaren grabbed a handful of Harvester's shirt with his right hand and seized his right upper arm with his left hand. Turning Harvester around, McLaren stepped behind him. As he dragged Harvester outside, the constables rushed to the doorway, wanting to witness history. McLaren dragged Harvester across the flagstone patio, kicking aside chairs and tables as he made for the edge of the garden. The few constables outside stopped their activities and parted like the Red Sea for Moses as McLaren flung Harvester around to face him. Taking a deep breath, McLaren slammed his right fist into Harvester's jaw, sending him backward into the rose bushes.

"You should thank me, Harvester. I've just instigated a family reunion for you." He snapped off a broken rose stem, sniffed it, and threw it at the man. "Harvester's your name.

Now you're with the rest of your kind—the arachnid harvesters, the spindly-legged predators who infest bramble patches. How's it feel to be home?"

As Harvester yelled in pain and tried to stand up, McLaren remained rooted to the spot, his chest rapidly rising and falling, his face flushed. Towering over the sprawled-out man, McLaren growled, "About Nigel Forester—he's going nowhere. Understand?" He waited for a moment, sizing up the man at his feet.

Harvester lay where he was, staring up at McLaren in silence.

McLaren turned abruptly, pushed his way through the coppers who were hesitantly moving toward Harvester, and thundered back into the pub.

THE SCENE FADED from McLaren's eyes as he stood by his bedroom window. The night had darkened while he relived that terrible night more than a year ago. The moon had disappeared behind a bank of clouds and a cool wind had sprung up from the west. In spite of the warmth of the June night, McLaren shivered. He rubbed his forehead, telling himself it had all been for the best. That he was glad to be shut out of a department whose Chief Constable eventually sided with the extremist councilors and a ranting media out for blood. But he knew he was lying to himself. He had loved the job, still loved the job. Regardless of the constables' testimony that the poker had never been bent or bloody, that it was Nigel Forester's word against a known career burglar—all of which left Harvester out on the proverbial limb and madder than ever with McLaren—McLaren had been suspended from duty.

He slammed his fist into the wall. When the Chief Constable had offered him the option of resigning from the Force instead of being prosecuted for assaulting a police officer and perverting the course of justice, McLaren knew a brick wall when he saw one. Knew the handwriting on that wall, too. He'd forever be a marked man, and back in uniform in days.

He had resigned in an overwhelming rush of sadness, the hurt of being torn from the CID branch, which he loved, as painful as a loved one's death. Now, he was reliving that fiasco of justice, that moment of Harvester's triumph. It was something he had no desire to unearth.

A fox barked in the darkness and the moon emerged from its nest of clouds before McLaren wandered over to his bed. He sat on the edge of the mattress, his toes burrowing into the deep pile of the lambskin throw rug, his heels resting on the cool wooden floor. It's been a year, he reminded himself. Surely it's time to get on with my life, to mend the pain. If not for my own good, then for Dena's.

He opened the bottom drawer of his bedside cabinet and rummaged within its depths. His fingers felt the cold metal photo frame and wrapped around a corner as he pulled it from the drawer. He opened the easel stand on the frame's back and set the photo on top of the cabinet, next to the alarm clock. Sitting in the darkness, he stared at the photo. He needed no light to see Dena's brown eyes, envision her smile. Hadn't he conjured up her face countless nights this past year when the nightmares had awakened him, when he had downed too many beers?

Telling her picture that he'd think about the two of them, he lay down. The night closed around him, obscure and soothing. The wind caressed his bare chest, cooling his anger. A flash of lightning crackled beyond the oak. In that second of near-blinding brightness, Dena's face jumped out from the darkness, seemingly alive and blessing him with her smile. Then, as the blackness reclaimed the land and his room, he turned onto his side, facing her portrait. He laid again in the darkness, aware of the storm, the smell of rain approaching downwind. As he drifted off to sleep, he thought that the storm mimicked exactly his life at the moment.

THE RINGING THAT awakened McLaren at half past seven was not from his alarm clock. He hadn't set it the previous night. The obnoxious noise came from his phone on the bedside stand. Forcing his eyelids open, he cautiously sat up, testing his stiff back and his aching head. The phone rang again as he rubbed his hand across the back of his neck and he muttered, "Yeah? What?" to the unknown caller.

His tone and temperament changed when Jamie Kydd's cheerful voice sang into his ear. "Late night, Mike?" The humor was evident in Jamie's voice even if McLaren couldn't see him.

"More like an early morning."

"Storm keep you up?"

"That and…" He glanced at Dena's photo and laid it face down on top of the bedside table. I must've been drunk last night to get that out, he thought, then ran his left hand through his tousled hair.

"The case bothering you, won't let you sleep?"

"Yeah. I've a lot to think about." He pushed the photo frame slightly farther away from him.

"Well, here's another little something to think about." Jamie paused, as though bracing for his friend's explosion of gratitude. "In regards to getting that information you wanted—"

McLaren sighed heavily. "Don't tell me."

"I thought you wanted to know. You rang me up—"

"I meant don't tell me you got caught lifting a file or something."

"What kind of detective do you think I am? No, don't answer that."

"Did you get anything, then?" He ran his fingers through his hair, astonished at Jamie's friendship.

"If you haven't looked at your email yet this morning…"

"Bloody hell."

Jamie grinned. "I'll take that as a 'not yet,' shall I?"

"Get on with it. Did you get anything or not?"

"I emailed those reports to you."

"I must be half asleep. You emailed the reports? How?"

"Simple. I scanned them on the computer, saved them as pdf files, and emailed them as attachments."

"Must've taken you hours."

"Well, it did take a while," Jamie confessed. "I stayed late, after my shift ended. Not too many lads around the station in the wee small hours so I had a better chance of getting the files and scanning them. I, uh…" He hesitated momentarily, wondering how to phrase this bit of news. "I sent the pages I thought were most pertinent. You didn't get the entire report." He pulled a face, steeling himself for McLaren's disappointment.

"That's smashing, Jamie!"

"Thought you'd be well chuffed. I also emailed you a few photos of her body…*in situ* and of the area itself. I just chose a few to send."

"Sure, Jamie. I didn't expect the whole bloody file." That would've taken hours to scan and send. As it is, I hope my damned computer doesn't crash, he thought. "That's super."

"Uh, Mike…I can tell you now, if you'd like, where her body was found."

McLaren withdrew a pad of paper and pen from the drawer in the nightstand. "Yeah?" He wrote swiftly, making no comment as Jamie related the details. When Jamie finished, McLaren sank back against the bed's headboard and stared at his notes. Half mile out…right side of road…in a depression two yards from the road's edge…stone barn searched…

victim's right shoe missing. "This is first rate, Jamie. Thanks. I'll get to those emails right away and let you know what I find at the barn."

"I just hope it's more than straw and stones."

THE BALLISTICS REPORT stated that the bullet that killed Marta was a .38 caliber fired from a revolver. Most likely a Webley. The pathologist reported that although it was evident Marta had been drinking that evening there wasn't enough alcohol in her blood to register as over the limit. Marta had been shot at close proximity, perhaps six to ten inches. Gunpowder markings were consistent with that distance, the particles imbedded into the skin. Death was instantaneous, or close to it. This was the only evidence of a gunshot on the body. Fixed lividity and other usual indicators that help pinpoint a time of death could not be used, due to the advanced decomposition of the body. The entomologist established the presence of ticks, spiders, and several species of flies, as well as maggots, on the remains.

McLaren looked up from the computer monitor. Insects, especially flies, went through life cycles that could be clocked, from laying eggs, to developing larvae, to adulthood. Knowing the type of insects on and under the body, the quantity of a specific insect, and the stage of the life cycle pointed the finger at the time of death. Insects were a witness more reliable and unvarying than the human kind. Especially in this case, McLaren thought, with Marta's body lying for over a week in the open, in the summer heat. He went back to the report. Although not conclusive, death probably occurred the night of her last casino outing. The insects' activities were consistent with the time.

He next looked at the photos of the stone barn, the immediate vicinity, and Marta's body *in situ,* and printed them out.

After logging off, he laid the photos on the kitchen worktop, next to his keys. Then, whistling, he went to take his shower.

THE STORM OF early morning left a blanket of mist that still hugged the valley and wallowed in depressions in fields and gardens when McLaren left his house at nine o'clock. A chill laced the air and condensation coated the cooler surfaces such as outdoor water-pump handles, farm machinery, and ungaraged cars. The small willow at the edge of his garden took on a phantom-like quality, its leaves a green smear beneath a wash of gray. There was a stealthy movement as a bough waved faintly at McLaren and a tendril of mist swirled past the dark lump of the cypress. A bird chirped somewhere in the obscurity, then everything was still.

Except for McLaren's whispered, "Damn."

As he approached his car, he saw it. Eleven empty beer bottles set up like a frame for tenpin bowling. The extra bottle was placed in front of the bottle at the triangle's apex, which pointed toward the car's windscreen. A twelfth bottle lay on its side, pinned beneath one of the windscreen wipers. Deliberate. A mute message.

He returned to his kitchen, dug around in the closet, and located a pair of rubber washing-up gloves and a large paper sack. Back outside, he pulled on the gloves and put the bottles inside the sack. Perhaps Jamie could work on them off duty, he thought, then folded the top of the sack closed. He stood there for several seconds, staring at his car, aware of the weight of the bottles. Again he asked himself the unanswerable question: what was going on and who was doing this?

The gravel area where the car was parked held no hints. No footprints, no castoff shirt button, no blood splatter. Still, the detective in him was too strong to ignore, and he carefully stepped away from his car and walked around it in a wide circle. Nothing.

He set the bag on the car's passenger seat, intending to drop it by Jamie's house later in the day, then got into his car and drove to Noah's Ark. The bottles haunted him all the way to Chesterfield. Was he the trapped, fallen beer bottle?

THE ANIMAL SHELTER was a modern one-story building of white-painted cement blocks and steel. A row of windows near the roofline encircled the structure as a strand of pearls claimed a woman's neck. McLaren parked beside a panel van that declared "Noah's Ark" along its side in brilliant green paint, took another sip of coffee before settling the travel mug into the car's cup holder, and opened the car door.

The mist had burned off in the thirty-minute drive to Chesterfield, leaving the air warmer and hinting at a still-warmer day. Blackbeech Drive, on which the animal shelter was located, hummed with traffic this Saturday morning, and McLaren wondered if the neighboring businesses saw enough customers to keep them going. He locked his car and wandered up to the shelter's front door. An electronic tone, like a doorbell, sounded toward the back of the reception area as he entered.

A young woman barely out of her teens straightened up from her bent-over position behind the front desk. Giving McLaren a smile, she asked if she could help him.

The sunlight slanted through the glass insets bookending the front door and the row of windows near the ceiling. Nice, he thought, noticing the pale blue walls and white ceramic floor tile. Bright, airy, cheery. Nice for the animals, too, if the upper windows circled around toward the pen area. Then, he suddenly knew they did. Any place touting itself as an ark and shelter would see to the comfort of its animal residents. That included a light, cheerful spot for the cages. He took in the pamphlet stands and signage for dog-training classes before focusing on the woman's face.

"We're offering a discount," she said, her voice eager and friendly, seeing what had held his interest. "Good until Saturday week on spaying and neutering of your animal if you adopt them through us and have our veterinary staff perform the procedure." There was an accent to her voice that McLaren couldn't pinpoint. "Plus," she added, getting no response from him, "we're giving coupons for twenty-five-pounds worth of pet food—good for cat, dog, or rabbit—upon adoption. They're redeemable at most supermarkets, pet supply stores, or here at the shelter. Does that interest you?" She smiled again, this time showing perfect, white teeth.

"Ordinarily, yes," McLaren said, smiling back. "But I'm never home to let a dog out. I'm allergic to cats, and I still have nightmares about Harvey."

She looked blank.

"The six-foot-tall invisible rabbit. James Stewart starred in the film."

She shook her head.

Too young, McLaren thought. Still, there are the classic flicks on the telly.

"We have several nice birds," she continued. "An African gray parrot, several budgies, a cockatiel…"

"I appreciate your assistance, but I'd like to talk to your vet, if he's not too busy at the moment."

"If it's a matter of your pet's health—" she began before McLaren interrupted her.

"I'd just like to ask him a few questions. If you would be so kind as to get him." He pulled a business card from the counter display announcing the shelter's variety of veterinary services. He tapped the card with his index finger. "I assume this is he? Emlyn Gregg?"

"Yes, it is. *Doctor Gregg*," she offered, a tinge of formality in her voice.

"Well, if Dr. Gregg, DVM, can spare me five minutes—" he added the medical initials in a one-upmanship display "—I'd appreciate it."

Picking up the phone receiver, she said, "I'll call him for you."

McLaren nodded and took a blue poker chip from the supply in the Plexiglas cube on the countertop. A clever bit of marketing, he thought, reading the advertising printed on the chip. "Don't gamble with your pet's health. Noah's Ark." The other side gave the shelter's name, address, and phone numbers. Other colors of chips mixed with the blues in the cube. He pulled out a red chip. "When the chips are down, call Noah's Ark." The emergency phone number ran in bold print beneath the slogan. The black chip announced "Stack the odds in your pet's favor. Noah's Ark health care." All three chips gave the same shelter information on the back. He smiled again at the slogans, stuck the chips in his trousers pocket, and leaned against the edge of the counter to await Emlyn Gregg's arrival.

"Dr. Gregg, you're wanted in Reception. Dr. Gregg, please come to Reception." She replaced the receiver and watched McLaren turn over the brochure before she said, "He'll be right out."

"Thank you. You've been in business quite a while." He held up the brochure. "Seventeen years."

"There's a great need for animal shelters. Pets currently seem to be reduced to a throwaway item. People are too busy to spend the time required for complete care of a dog or cat. When their job or schooling gets in the way, they leave the animal in the countryside."

"Borders on cruelty, in my book. Do you live in a village, somewhere like Elton?" he asked, eyeing the girl. "I just wondered if you saw many animals left like that."

She smiled shyly, her exasperation with him forgotten. "No, I live in Chesterfield. But of course I know about it, dropping off animals like that. It's unconscionable. And of course there's the overpopulation problem."

"Which is why you're running the special on spaying and neutering."

"Actually, we aren't—"

"You wished to speak to me, I believe?" A male voice sounded behind McLaren and he turned to find a fifty-ish-year-old man with brown eyes and hair, extending his right hand. His white medical coat gaped open, revealing his blue printed shirt. It complemented the jeans he wore.

"Thank you, yes." McLaren stuffed the brochure into his pocket and shook the vet's hand. "If you have a minute or two."

"Of course. What's this in regard to—an animal of yours?"

McLaren had begun walking slowly to a corner of the reception area and Emlyn Gregg had followed, replying that he could give McLaren fifteen minutes or so. They stopped beside a shoulder-high cardboard display stand offering sample packets of various dry pet foods. McLaren turned so his back was toward the corner and he could see the receptionist and the front door. Old habits die hard, he thought before turning his attention to Emlyn Gregg.

After introducing himself, he explained succinctly why he needed to talk to the vet. Emlyn frowned and pressed his lips together, and for a moment McLaren feared the man would refuse to help. A dog barked from the kennel area behind them, enticing several more dogs to answer before Emlyn shook his head.

"Bad business, that." He plunged his hands into his coat. He stood in a shaft of sunlight that illuminated the top of his head. Dyed, McLaren thought, glancing at the dark brown hair. What's he afraid of—losing his youth or business competition?

"Were you here when the money was stolen? That was last—"

"A year ago this past May," he said, shaking his head again. "Bad."

"So you were here then. You knew Verity Dwyer?"

"Yes to both questions. I've been here since the shelter opened. 'Course, I was an assistant vet when I first began. Not that I was just out of school. Well, I wouldn't be, would I, at my age?" He smiled hesitantly before continuing. "When the senior vet left, I moved into his slot."

"That must have been nice. Not only the promotion, but the salary increase and all the things that go with it."

"Things that go…"

"The usual perks from a larger salary. Newer car, exotic holidays, bigger house. I like a big house in the country… in a village. So quiet." He smiled, his voice light. "You live in a village?"

"No, I don't. I live here in town, near to the shelter, if you must know."

"Just wondered. When I make my first million that's what I'll buy—a house in a village."

"Yes, well, I can't afford that luxury. I have to be near work in case of an emergency. I bought the former vet's home, by the way."

"He left after…how long?"

"I'd been here five years by that time. Dr. Doyle was the lead man. Don't know where he's got to."

"Back to Verity—"

"Right. Yes, I knew her. A splendid worker and an equally splendid person. That's why this was all such a shock, you know. I would have sworn she was honest. Stealing like that—" He pulled in his lips and shook his head. "Well, you never know, do you? No such thing as a criminal face, is there?"

"You didn't hear her explanation about the missing money, then?"

"Yes. Both from her when the financial officer discovered the discrepancy and during the court trial. I wanted to believe her, but…"

"Why didn't you? If you believed initially that she was an honest person—"

"The story was absurd! I also knew Marta. She hadn't any more of a gambling problem than I'm the Lost Dauphin."

"She evidently kept her gambling secret from many people, Dr. Gregg."

"That may be, but it still doesn't replace the money that Verity took from the cash register. Since it was her register, she was responsible for it."

"So her sentence doesn't bother you in the least, then."

"You're making me out to be a cold-hearted clot!" he snapped.

"Aren't you?"

Emlyn's face flooded with color. Taking a step toward McLaren, he barked, "The hell I'm not! I like Verity. I stop by her house every month or so to see how she's faring, take her a little something to cheer her up. That's a rough sentence, doing community work."

"Isn't this rather a contradiction? First you state she's responsible for the money in her till and therefore, since it's missing, it's her fault. Then you tell me you ease your conscience by bringing her gifts. Which is it? How do you feel?"

"Look, McLaren. I don't know who put you up to this. Probably Verity, wanting to clear her reputation. But you're a bloody amateur in your technique."

"Really?"

"I hate to see anyone doing time if he's wrongly convicted,

but Verity's the only one who had access to that money. I know, I know," he rushed on as McLaren opened his mouth, "the Great Explanation. That Marta was going to repay the money but she was ill. That still doesn't excuse the fact that Verity stole the money from the shelter in the first place. It's too bad she did it and too bad she got caught, but facts are facts. We can't change the past."

"I agree." He exhaled slowly, as if considering another idea. "All that brought a bit of a scandal to the shelter, didn't it?"

Emlyn nodded. "Unfortunately, yes. We were in the newspapers and on television for weeks. People were reluctant to patronize us."

"How long did that last? Did the shelter suffer, either financially or with fewer animal adoptions?"

"It was difficult for a few months, yes. Not only weren't the animals adopted out but donations slacked off. We depend on monetary donations for about one-third of our operating costs," he explained, his voice calmer. "With no animals going to people's homes, we had more animals to provide for and less money coming in to buy food."

"Plus, the shelter was minus the missing thousand pounds. That must have hurt."

Emlyn frowned and stared at McLaren, wondering how he knew about the missing reserve cash. Probably followed the trial, he thought, and crossed his arms. "That wasn't the half of it. The board and a few of our staff were furious at the position Verity and Marta had put us in. If things hadn't ended as they did, they would've been asked for resignations. Or firings," he added, his voice hardening.

"Sounds like a bad time for everyone."

"As they say, if looks could kill."

"Including yours?"

Emlyn hesitated, then said, "Yes. I admit it. I was furious.

The missing money tainted all of us here. I could've been involved, but I wasn't. I could've been fired, too."

"But you weren't. Know anyone who was mad enough to kill Marta, then?"

McLaren got the same negative response from the receptionist when Emlyn retreated to the back-room surgery. He thought she was telling the truth, for she didn't seem bright enough to fabricate anything as complicated as a name and a motive. Especially when it came to thinking on her feet. He took another business card—for the shelter's owner, Derek Fraser—and left. It wasn't until he unlocked his car and got inside that he noticed the bag of beer bottles was gone.

TWELVE

McLAREN STOOD IN the car's open doorway, his hands propped against the doorframe, his arms stiff and holding him upright. He leaned slightly into the car's interior, as though a closer proximity to the car seat would clear his vision. And mounting confusion. The extra inches did not help; the seat was still empty.

His hands slid off the car body, making small squeals as they rubbed against the metal, and he slowly sank onto the driver's seat. He stared, disbelieving, at the closed passenger door. It was shut. And locked. He had unlocked his door to get into the car. He exhaled slowly as his head hit the headrest. He wallowed against the upholstery, thinking, replaying the scenario in his mind. It didn't make sense. How could his car have been burgled?

He closed his eyes, going through every minute of his morning. There'd been Jamie's phone call, the details of the area where Marta's body had been found, then McLaren's hasty shower and dressing prior to his grabbed breakfast and leaving his house. Twelve beer bottles had been placed on his car sometime during the night. He bagged those bottles carefully to take to Jamie later on today. Rubbing his forehead, he turned his head and looked once more at the car seat. *Am I losing my mind?* He ran the tip of his tongue across his lower lip. The skin was dry and cracked from too many hours mending stonewalls in the sun and wind. His tongue had no moisture either, to remedy the roughness.

Sitting up, McLaren glanced at his watch, then at the clock

on the dashboard. Both registered the same time. Good. At least I'm not in some strange time warp. Unless the aliens have fiddled with the watch and clock. Across the street, a road sweeper was brushing up a bit of litter with his broom; a police officer was directing traffic around two cars that were involved in an accident.

McLaren got out of his car and crossed the road. As he stopped on the curb, the road sweeper looked up. When McLaren made no attempt to move on, the man leaned against his broom and asked, "Lose something, mate?"

McLaren fought back the urge to say, "My mind," and replied, "No. I was just wondering if you saw anyone in the car park across the road."

The man squinted into the sun, shielding his eyes with his hand. The parking area was barely visible beyond the constant stream of vehicles crowding the road. "What? At the animal place?"

"Yes."

"When?"

"Just now. Well, a few minutes ago."

"What's your game, mate?" The man eyed McLaren with suspicion, as if expecting a man-on-the-street interview complete with video camera and microphone.

"I just need to know if you saw anybody over there, possibly near that red Peugeot."

The man sniffed without giving the shelter another glance and went back to sweeping. "Not likely to, am I? I've got me work to do. I don't have time to gawk at the landscape." He made a vigorous jab with his broom at a piece of paper stuck to the tarmac.

"This was just a few minutes ago," McLaren insisted, following the man's progress down the street. "Not more than ten, probably."

"Here, now." The man turned to face McLaren, his broom

held upright like a rifle at attention. "I don't know why you're so interested in that car. If you want to know something, go ask that copper." He pointed the end of the broom handle at the officer standing in the center of the road. "I've just got here myself. So you ask that cop. I don't know nothin' about no car. And I don't like your nosiness. Now, bugger off!" His turned back dismissed McLaren as clearly as if he'd waved goodbye.

The police officer directing traffic had no time to talk to McLaren. Or inclination. He viewed McLaren's question with the same suspicion as the road sweeper had, except that the officer stared at McLaren—probably getting a lasting mental image of his face—before telling him to file a police report if his car had been damaged.

Sighing heavily, McLaren returned to his car and drove to the house of Marta Hughes' neighbor.

TOM MILLINGTON WAS outside, washing his car, when McLaren walked up to him. The Millington house was much like its neighbors—a detached dwelling of brick and wood, built years ago as Chesterfield grew beyond its status as a 13th-century market town and 19th-century industrial center. Suburbs had stretched the town's boundaries, yet unspoiled countryside still flourished just outside its thoroughfares. The town's residents had the best of both worlds, McLaren thought, stepping over the water running down the Millington driveway. A town with modern conveniences, yet the Derbyshire countryside minutes outside its confines.

Tom turned off the water at the outside tap, lay down the hose, and watched McLaren walk up the driveway. Drying his hands on his jeans, Tom asked, "Anything I can do for you?"

"I hope so." McLaren stopped several feet from Tom. He introduced himself, then stated that he was investigating Marta Hughes' death.

Tom bent down to straighten one of his socks, then slowly straightened up before he said, "Marta! Aren't you a bit late with all that? That happened a year ago." He eyed McLaren, assessing who he really was, and jammed his right hand into his front jeans pocket. "Who you say you are again? Police?"

"I'm retired."

"Retired, eh? Then you've really no authority—"

"I've been retained by someone to look into the case."

"Well, you would say that even if you're poking about on your own." He squinted against the sunlight on the car's body. "I suppose it's her family who want answers." His gaze shifted to the Hughes family home. He cracked his knuckles, then flexed his fingers. "Alan's still grieving."

McLaren took in Tom's slicked-down hair, muscular build, and combatant stand, sizing up the man in one word. Arrogant.

"They never figured out who killed her, did they?" He dried the back of his hand on his shorts. "The cops, I mean. That why you're talking to people?" He stared at McLaren through slightly lowered eyelids.

"It's an instance of a killer getting away without coming to justice," McLaren said, suddenly feeling the rage of his own injustice at the hands of Harvester. Taking a deep breath, he mentally counted to ten before adding, "I would think most anyone would feel the same."

"Oh, sure, sure." Tom pulled his shoulders backward, as though they were stiff from washing the car. They were muscular, McLaren noted. And broad. The man did more than wash his car to stay in shape. "Didn't mean nothing by it. Just curious. You know—talking about Marta again after this long."

"Did you see her leave that evening?"

"Naw. I don't stand at the front windows and watch people's comings and goings. Though," he said, winking, "she's the exception I'd make if I did. Ya know?" He winked again and grinned.

"You found her attractive, then." This wasn't McLaren's intended line of questioning. He found it distasteful, especially about a deceased person, but he pursued it.

"Sure! Who didn't? A good-lookin' woman—brunette, hazel eyes, thin. Not too thin, though. She had enough padding where it counted, if you get my drift." He patted a lock of his sun-streaked brown hair back into place.

What a jerk. First class nit. He suddenly felt very sorry for Marta if she had been subjected to this salivating nerd. He said with great restraint, "Were you on friendly terms with the Hughes family? I understand you have a son. Do he and the Hughes lad get on well? Hang around together, play football, perhaps?"

"Not particularly what you'd call mates. My boy's got his own friends. Besides, he considers Chad Hughes a bit of a wimp."

"Why is that?"

"The kid won't join my boy and his mates on anything."

"Like what, for instance?"

"Oh, different stuff." He bent over and started coiling the hose into a neat circle.

"Are you referring to smoking marijuana?"

Tom slowly let the hose sag to the ground. He straightened up and took a step toward McLaren. "Where the hell did you hear that? Hughes been talking?" He nodded toward the Hughes house.

"Why does it matter where I heard it? Is that what you're referring to?"

"What the hell difference does that make in finding Marta's killer?"

"Because I heard that your son and his pals got in a bit of trouble with the police. Because if it's true, and your son suffered for it—either from parental punishment or police keeping him under watch—he could have been angry at Marta Hughes for *supposedly* tipping off the coppers. And, if he did," McLaren rushed on as Tom opened his mouth, "it gives him some degree of motive."

Tom held up his index finger and tried again. "Now, wait just a minute. You can't come around here accusing my son of anything. That's as far as that incident went. Rick's been clean ever since then."

"Clean, or just not caught?"

A minute passed as Tom seemed to consider something. His hand returned to his pocket and he forced a smile. "Well, I guess a parent never knows for sure, does he? I'd swear Rick gave it up when he broke from Danny. That's Danny Mercer, his former mate. But, like I said…"

"So you or your son harbor no ill feelings toward Marta or her son."

"Like I said, she was a real eyeful. Kind of hard to stay mad at something so gorgeous."

"Did your wife like Marta?"

Tom shrugged and went back to rounding up the garden hose. "She never came straight out and said, 'Gosh, I sure like Marta,' but I think she did. They didn't chat over coffee in the morning, but they talked when they met on the street. Talked about spring flowers and such. You know—women talk."

"Did your wife or you see anyone at the Hughes' house the night it was broken into?"

"Nope. We were either asleep or I was in my workshop in the garage and my wife was in the back room watching a film on the telly. This all came out in the trial, you know. No reason to rehash it."

"Your son…where was he?"

Tom stood up and turned toward McLaren. "You intimating he did the break-in?"

"I'd merely like to know if he was out. Perhaps he saw a light on in the house where one normally isn't. That sort of thing."

"Yeah?" Tom eyed him as though he wasn't sure McLaren was telling the truth. He said, "Rick had been out earlier, at Danny's house, but he was home by seven."

"You're sure of the time?"

"Sure I'm sure! We had our tea when he got back."

"And the break-in was later."

"Don't know when, exactly, but later that night."

"I understand Marta found the mess herself, that her husband wasn't home."

Tom winked and tilted his head toward the house. "Usually it's 'while the cat's away' with me, but my wife was home that evening."

"Meaning—"

He shrugged. "You know how it is. You try for a bit of action on the side, but it doesn't always work."

"Not with Marta Hughes, at any rate."

Tom spread his hands out, as though he were a helpless pawn in the Whims of Life. "Let's say, I know where her son gets that wimp quality."

"She wasn't interested in you, evidently."

"A real square. I couldn't even get past the neighborly hello with her."

McLaren left with a noncommittal "Thanks" on his lips and in agreement with Verity Dwyer that Tom Millington was a jerk.

He was headed toward his car when he saw a young man working in the front garden of the Hughes house. McLaren jogged over as the boy threw a weed onto the small pile beside him. Looking at McLaren, he stood up. "Do you want something?"

"Are you Chad Hughes?" McLaren said, thinking the boy

had to be. He'd seen Marta's photograph, and even if Marta had been a brunette and this boy was blond, there was no mistaking the same hazel-colored eyes. Or the expression that stared at McLaren.

"Yeah. I'm Chad."

McLaren introduced himself in the way that was quickly becoming a rote rendition. When he'd finished, he asked Chad how he was getting on.

"What you really mean," Chad said, tossing his trowel onto the stack of weeds, "is how I'm coping with Mum's death. What it's been like this past year. What am I supposed to say besides rotten? It's been hard for me, sure, but especially for my dad."

McLaren nodded, knowing Chad and Alan were constantly reminded of Marta; she was everywhere in the house.

"And you're also wanting to know if I've got any ideas about the whole thing." Chad tilted his head so he could see McLaren's eyes. "You are, aren't you, or you wouldn't be chatting to me? Nice as you might be, you're a stranger, and strangers just don't pop over to talk. So you want to ask about her death, who could've done it or a motive."

"Yes, I suppose so." McLaren smiled, warming to the young man.

"Besides the obvious suspect, you mean."

McLaren glanced at the Millington house. Tom had carried the hose into his garage and was now walking back to the front door. He waved at Chad and McLaren before calling, "Good luck," and going inside.

"Slimy bastard." Chad's face flooded with color.

McLaren wanted to agree but instead said, "Why do you say that? Do you suspect Mr. Millington of killing your mother?"

"Him or Rick."

Tom came back outside with a broom and began sweeping the front path, whistling.

McLaren watched Tom make his way down the flagstones for several seconds before saying, "Why do you think it's one of them?"

"Because it's their style."

"What—murder?"

"Not intentionally, no. But they're both hooligans. Only difference is their age."

"You say this because—"

"I got into it with Mr. Millington shortly before my mum died."

"A fight?"

"Yeah. He'd made some indecent remarks about my mum and I couldn't take it anymore. I came after him. A bit later, my mum was dead. I think he came after her."

THIRTEEN

"YOU DON'T KNOW HOW I've blamed myself," Chad said, blotting his eyes with the side of his hand. It was a large hand, as befitted his tall, powerful build. The skin was tanned and roughened from yard work, contrasting greatly with the paler, smoother skin that played around the edges of his T-shirt sleeves and neckline. Chad tilted his head back, looking skyward, and his voice matched his inner anguish. "God, if I'd just kept quiet. If I'd just ignored it, Mum would still be alive."

"Perhaps not," McLaren said as Chad lowered his head and looked at him with tear-moistened eyes. "Not if someone else killed her." He spoke lowly, choosing his words carefully, aware of the pain deep within the teenager's eyes.

"What? Like, who?" Chad's voice was hopeful, yet challenging, defying McLaren to produce a more likely suspect, or to relieve him of his guilt.

"I've just begun investigating, Chad. I don't know yet."

"At least you're honest." He ran the back of his hand across his nose, then pressed it against his khaki shorts.

"I try to be."

Chad stared at McLaren, trying to make him out, then smiled. "I think you are. You wouldn't admit it if you weren't. You'd be all bluff and swagger, coming on like some of those super tough telly cops."

"I never was a Dirty Harry."

Again Chad smiled. He leaned against the corner of the house, near the front door, and said, "Mr. Millington was always making cracks about Mum. It got to the point where

I just couldn't stand it anymore so one day I punched his lights out."

"This was over what?"

"He always did hint stuff. This time he flat came out and said it."

"Hint stuff…like what? Sexual innuendoes?"

Chad avoided McLaren's eyes, as though embarrassed by the subject. He said rather lowly, "Yeah. He always made remarks about how smashing Mum looked—well, 'always' being several months, I guess. At least it was several months that I knew about it so I guess it went on for a while. He'd say how she should be a model…or something else." He paused, his face reddening.

"I've found that those types of people are usually all talk, Chad. It takes two to tango."

"Sure, I realize he was probably all mouth and no trousers, just acting macho, but it hurt. My mum never did a thing to deserve it. She never flirted back; she never dressed… indecently. She never went over to his house alone. She was a decent lady and I got sick and tired of him suggesting improper stuff."

"Like what?"

"You know. Like, sleeping together." Chad mumbled this last statement so softly that McLaren could barely hear it.

"That's what caused the fight?"

"Yeah. Mum and I were outside and as she started to go in the house, Millington calls after her that he had a few minutes free, and since both of their spouses weren't home…well, you get the idea." Again he blushed, but he doubled his hand into a fist and slammed it into the door.

"That's when the fight started."

"I couldn't let that go, could I?" He searched McLaren's eyes for a sign of approval or exoneration.

"I don't think most sons, brothers, or husbands would."

"He's had it coming to him for ages. This was just the last straw. He's got a dirty mind and a dirty mouth, and I had to stop his abuse of my mum."

McLaren nodded, his eyes on the Millington house. Was Millington's wife the target of Tom's verbal abuse? Worse yet, was it also physical abuse? "Did your father know about this?"

"About Millington's talk, you mean?"

"That or how she felt about it?"

"I guess he would have done. That's hard to keep quiet, isn't it? I mean, Millington wasn't exactly secretive about it. He'd stand in his front garden and yell stuff at Mum. I guess Dad could've heard it."

"Had your father ever said anything to Millington or to your mother? Did you ever see your father mad?"

Chad chewed his bottom lip while he considered McLaren's questions. Finally, he shook his head. "I think I would've heard if Dad had known. He's a pretty quiet guy on the whole, though he does explode if he's pushed too far. But really, nothing much rattles him. Good bank material, if you know what I mean."

"Steady in a crisis." But maybe not in his personal life.

"Yeah. I think if Dad had known about all this he would've said something to Millington 'cause he'd be madder than hell at Millington. Dad wouldn't have let it go on so that Mum was continually harassed like that."

Or let his son play the husband's part by telling Millington to leg it. "So you think Tom Millington got back at your mother because you defended her."

"I know it probably sounds far-fetched, Mr. McLaren, and I don't think he planned it. I mean, he didn't sit at the table plotting to kill her. Well, he wouldn't, would he? That's a bit over the top! But if he got mad at her…like, one night he came up to her and said something about me and him getting into a fight, and he was mad at me because I knocked him out flat and he was mad at Mum for not…well, with all the stuff that happened—"

"He pushed her, perhaps, but a little too hard, and she fell, hit her head, he saw that she had died accidentally."

"Yeah. Something like that. You've seen him. He's a mass of muscles. He could easily have knocked her down." He kicked the bottom of the door. "I don't think he hid in the bushes and ambushed her. But he's got a temper. He might've got into a shouting match with her and things got out of hand, like you said."

"What about his son? You said he might have committed murder."

"Rick?" He screwed up his mouth. "That piece of trash?"

"He had a run-in with the cops, I understand, and your mother instigated it."

"He could have done, sure. He's got his dad's temper. He also hangs out with a piece of garbage called Danny Mercer. They all smoke pot. Mum talked to them, told them the dangers of that stuff, and everything else. When they just ignored her, she finally talked to the police about it. She—" He paused, his gaze shifting back to McLaren. "She felt very strongly about that sort of thing. About stopping abuse and keeping the neighborhood free from problems."

"Were Rick or Danny angry about that?"

"Yeah. They got it from both sides—their parents evidently came down hard on them, and some police constable talked to them. It didn't sit well with Rick, I know, 'cause he yelled over to me one day that me and my mum better watch our backs."

"Is he the sort who makes good on his threats?"

"He does to some extent. I've seen the results of his anger at school and around the neighborhood. He's not afraid to use his fists; there are a bunch of kids who know what it's like to be on the receiving end of his kicks and punches."

"Is he a bully?"

Chad considered the question for a moment before replying, "All the kids he's beat up, at least the ones I've seen, are smaller than he is, so yeah, he's a bully. But Rick's not above lying in wait for someone if the bloke is bigger than him. That's how he works, Mr. McLaren. He slinks around, planning how to get even. But yeah, I think he could've attacked my mum if he ambushed her one night."

"So it wouldn't take much to overpower a woman as tiny as your mother if her attacker was as big and sly as Rick Millington."

"That's the gist of it."

McLAREN GOT THE GIST of Alan Hughes' temper thirty minutes later. They were in Alan's office, a wood-paneled room with large windows that looked onto the bank's lobby. The Venetian blinds had been drawn up—presumably so Alan could keep an eye on the morning's activities or the employees could see he also worked part of his weekend—and Alan was standing behind his desk, facing McLaren. Perhaps the blinds should have been down; Alan's crimson face would not be visible to customer and clerk alike.

"You've got a nerve even suggesting that," Alan exploded, his fist hitting the top of his desk. "My wife was killed. Her body was dumped by the roadside like she was a bag of rubbish. And you ask if I knew about Tom Millington and her."

"I'm not saying they had an affair, Mr. Hughes." McLaren kept his voice low. He was all too conscious of a few looks they were getting from curious customers and employees. "I just wanted to know if you think Millington could have actually forced your wife—"

"To do what—have the affair?"

"I was thinking more of accosting her one afternoon or evening."

"God, this sounds like some Victorian melodrama. No, I don't think so."

"You knew about the harassment, however."

"Yes."

"Did you do anything about it?"

"Like what—go over there with a gun and threaten him to stop it?"

"I hope not. Maybe talk to him, tell him that his advances weren't appreciated."

"Yeah, I talked to him. Once. When Marta came into the house with her face red and crying. She didn't want to tell me what had happened but she finally did."

"And you went outside then to confront Millington?"

"You're damned right I did. He was in his garage. I told him he had better stop his foul suggestions or I'd beat him to within an inch of his life."

"Is that all?"

"Is that *all?* What the hell more do you want me to do? Choke him? Punch him in the stomach? Kick him in the groin? Yes, that was all."

"That stopped the harassment?"

Alan opened his mouth, took a breath, then blushed. He grabbed the back of his leather chair and said more quietly, "Well, no. At least, not right away."

McLaren frowned. "Oh? When did it stop, then?"

"Well, it didn't." His voice had dropped to barely more than a whisper and his face suddenly drained of color. "It went on right up to her death."

"How long was this? From the time of your confrontation to the night of your wife's disappearance?"

"A month. I talked to Millington in May."

"Why didn't you say anything more to him if his attentions continued? Didn't you know what was happening? Did your wife not tell you Millington was still bothering her?"

"I— She didn't tell me. I didn't hear anything more from her after I talked to Millington, so I assumed it was a thing of the past. I didn't know he was still harassing her until I overheard one of his remarks some weeks later. The evening before she and Linnet went to the casino." He turned the swivel chair toward him and slowly sat down.

"When you heard him talking to your wife, did you confront him again, tell him to leave Marta alone?"

Alan riffled the corner pages of his appointment diary, staring at the desktop. A tea trolley rumbled past the office door and into the open reception area before he said, "I was going to, but I didn't have time that night. Marta and I met some friends for dinner and went to see a play at the theater. *The Twisted Plot,* if you need to check up on my whereabouts. It was past midnight when we got home. I promised myself I'd talk to Millington the following day."

"But you didn't."

"No. Marta left work, Friday, at noon, went to her brother-in-law's, and then met Linnet at the casino."

"Why did that stop you from talking to Millington? You were home that evening, weren't you?"

"Later I was. Chad and I went out to eat, then I helped him with his homework. By the time I thought of Millington again, it was late. I figured it would wait until Saturday morning. Then, that night, when she didn't come home, I forgot about it."

What kind of husband would forget about speaking to his wife's tormentor? McLaren wondered as he left the office. A coward? A man no longer in love? A man suspicious that his wife and neighbor actually had the affair? McLaren crossed the spacious lobby, aware of Alan's stare and the whispered conjectures of the cashiers, aware of his hard-soled shoes

clacking on the terrazzo floor. Aware of the suspicions and
questions shouting in his brain, reminding him that Alan had
no alibi for that questionable period of time. Had there come
a point when Tom Millington's innuendoes became actuality
or imagined actuality, and Alan finally snapped, taking out
his anger on Marta in one gunshot to her head?

THE CASINO IN Nottingham was not particularly busy, but it
was only late Saturday morning; it would see its bulk of customers later that night. He parked away from the majority of
cars clustered as near to the entrance as they could get and
walked up to the canopied main entrance. The lights declaring the casino name were blaringly bright even in the daylight, and McLaren wondered how much of their profit went
to pay for the electricity bill. About as much as they spent on
their landscaping maintenance, he thought, watching several
gardeners weeding a perennial border. Clumps of ornamental evergreens, pruned into a smooth geometric form bely-
ing their realness, created a backdrop for terra-cotta pots
overflowing with annuals and signs proudly proclaiming
the casino's round-the-clock accessibility. No leaf littered
the grass; no cigarette butt marred the pavement. The entire
place was immaculate and artificial.

The interior was, too. He nodded to the doorman stationed
at the large glass-and-brass double door and walked into the
gaming room. It was a blaze of red, gold, and white, with
chrome furniture and recessed ceiling lighting that pinpointed
specific areas: blackjack, craps, baccarat, and roulette. The
slot machines, with their lights and noise, lined the perimeter
of the room like pagan gods that the players placated with
coins and prayers. The poker tables were isolated from the
commotion, probably in that next room, he thought, giving
the players quiet in which to think.

McLaren walked over to the nearest roulette table. Several

people were seated around it, talking and drinking and moving their chips. Columns of red, white and black dotted the green cloth like confetti left over from someone's win. The croupier's voice floated over the conversation at the table. "No more bets, please. No more bets." The wheel spun and he flipped the ball onto the bowl again. The roulette ball clacked around the roulette bowl as the croupier looked at the table patrons. "Twenty-nine noir. Twenty-nine noir wins. Thank you, sir." He accepted the tip from the winning player as he pushed the chips toward him, then started the process over again, calling for bets.

McLaren strolled into the manager's office, introduced himself, and asked to speak to the croupiers who were on duty when Marta was at the casino. The man consulted last year's work schedule, compared it to who was working now, and told McLaren that of the four croupiers on duty then, two had quit, one was on holiday, and the other man was due in on the hour. "If you'd care to wait…" He indicated a leather sofa along the far wall, facing his desk.

"I'll stroll around, thanks just the same," McLaren said. "Maybe play a hand of twenty-one while I wait. What's the croupier's name who I'll be talking to?"

The manager told him and added that he'd be coming in the employee entrance in the rear of the building. "He'll be at the first table, closest to the main door, if you miss him."

McLaren thanked him and left the office. He was halfway through his beer when he decided to try to meet the employee outside. Besides being less noisy, the outdoors afforded less temptation to hurry to his table, less nervousness at being overheard. He paid for his drink, left by the main door, and hurried around to the back of the building. Deck chairs, garden tables, and clusters of tub plants dotted the lawn, creating restful areas for staff breaks. McLaren eased into a canvas chair, found it sturdy and comfortable, and waited. Ten minutes later his man showed up.

"I wonder if you might remember a particular customer," McLaren said after explaining why he wanted to talk to the man.

The croupier eyed McLaren, perhaps wondering if this was legal.

Sensing the man's hesitation, McLaren added, "The manager, Mr. Pollard, said you were working that night."

Anyone could call the casino and find out Pollard's name, but why go to so much trouble just to find out about an old win, the croupier reasoned. He glanced at his watch. He had time. Slowly, he said, "Perhaps. Which customer would that be, sir? June of last year?"

"Yes. She was with another lady. Perhaps at your table."

"You expect me to remember one person out of the thousands that play at my table?"

"You'd remember her."

"Looker, was she?"

"She won big."

"How big?"

"Over two hundred fifty thousand."

The man smiled, as if enjoying a private joke or seeing Marta in his mind's eye. "Oh, that one. Made a bit of history, she did. She wasn't at my table that night, but I heard about it. Talk to the cashier—she talked to the woman. *Still* talks about it. She's on duty now, probably. I've got to get to work, mate."

McLaren thanked him and walked back to the front of the casino. After asking at several stations, he found her.

Yes, she'd been on duty that night. Yes, she still remembered it. How could she not? It had been a huge win; one of the casino's largest payouts for roulette.

"Do you remember anyone watching her or following her from the casino?"

"I heard she was killed." The cashier shook her head. "Real pity, that. Excuse me."

McLaren stepped aside as a customer came up to the cashier to change her chips into cash.

"Thank you, sir. Sorry about the interruption. Yes, I remember her. She was pretty and was so excited about her win. I don't mean I lack feelings for any other murder victim, but this lady seemed to be going through a hard time. Marta, her name was. She was a regular. You get to know their names, you know."

"What do you mean hard time? Did she talk to you about something specific?"

"No. But I heard a bit of her conversation with her friend. What is her name…"

"Were they talking very loudly? Could someone have overheard them?"

"I don't think it was overly loud. At least, no one hung around them or loitered near the Ladies'. They'd gone in there to count their chips. I just heard a bit of their chatter when they came up to me to cash it in. They were talking about buying back something. The other woman said Marta could then sleep easier, so I guess it was a big purchase or maybe getting something out of hock."

Buying back her conscience, McLaren thought. Or her friendship from Verity. A cheer rose from a group of people standing around a slot machine and a man jumped up, yelling excitedly. "No one seemed overtly interested in her or followed her?"

"No. I was watching because, as I said, it was a huge payoff. They talked about her bet, which was straight up on one. Her friend laughed and said wasn't Marta glad she had switched from her corner bet of nineteen, twenty, twenty-two, and twenty-three—she'd evidently been betting that combination quite a while. Anyway, as I said, I was a bit concerned about them being alone, without some man with them to protect all that money, but she had her friend with her, and they did look around the room. I guess they were making sure no one was following them."

McLaren nodded, considering something.

"I don't think they had any trouble in the car park, if that's what you're thinking," she added.

"Pardon?"

"You thinking someone could've gone out another exit and killed her in the car park?" She shook her head. "The police had the same idea. They took the CCTV tape. They couldn't find anybody on it. Just the two women leaving and a few people arriving. No one came up to them."

"I guess they'd be able to see that," McLaren agreed.

"They've still got it."

"What—the tape?"

"They've not released it yet because they haven't found her killer. I guess they still want it for evidence. You know, in case they find somebody and they need to refer to the tape."

"Was there any suspicion the two women met someone in the car park?"

"You'll have to ask the coppers, sir. But I testified at the trial as to what happened inside. About anyone seeming interested in them—that sort of thing."

"Which there weren't."

"No, not apart from when they first won. You know—their cheering and the people at their table being excited."

"Only natural."

"I watched them as they left, as I said, and no one tailed them. They left in separate cars, I believe, so it would've been harder to go after them, if that was some bloke's intention. How would he know whom to follow? Maybe the other lady took the money as a precaution. You know," she said when McLaren looked blank. "Confounding the would-be robber."

The police are confounded, too, McLaren thought as he thanked the cashier and left.

McLAREN DIDN'T LEAVE the area immediately. He walked around the building, studying the exits, the plantings of shrubbery, the locations of the CCTV cameras. Was it possible someone slipped out another door, waited for Màrta, and kidnapped her? But the cashier said nothing like that appeared on the security tape. He drew a notebook from his pocket and circled the building again, sketching it and the positions of the cameras and security guards. Was it possible the cameras hadn't caught everything? Could someone, perhaps knowledgeable with the casino set-up, have waited beyond the camera's view on purpose?

He wandered over to a guard stationed at the car park and asked.

The guard viewed McLaren as though he were planning the heist of the century. "Why do you ask?"

McLaren explained that he was investigating the Hughes murder.

"Well, the coppers have already been over this," he said briskly, turning back to the CCTV screen in his small booth. "If you want to know something, ask them."

"I'm here and I'd like to know your opinion. After all, you work with the security system. I thought you'd know if there were areas that weren't covered, if it needed improving. You do an important service to your clientele, but if the cameras miss some area, like just outside casino property—"

"Look." The guard exhaled heavily and turned again toward McLaren. He was as bulky as a slot machine, with narrow eyes that seemed to weigh everything they saw before filtering it to his mind. Which probably spun with the rapidity of the machine and came up three lemons just as often. The guard leaned his arm against the hut's windowsill. "I don't install the things, pal. I just watch the monitor. There was nothing to see that night."

"Really? No one followed her outside the casino, stopped to congratulate her, even from several yards distant?"

"A few people did that, sure, but they were cleared in court. There was one bloke who spoke to her, but he kept his distance and walked off as she got into her car. I saw her drive off."

"No one else, no one who you or the police would term 'suspicious,' then."

"No. I was asked by the cops here, and I was asked again at the cop shop. The cops even looked at the tape themselves. Nothing like that showed up on the cameras. Not even walking out of camera range."

"I realize that, but I thought that if you could tell me how *far* the cameras record the scene, I could get an idea of where Mrs. Hughes' killer—"

"You hard of hearing or just obnoxious? I told you I didn't see nothing. I got nothing to do with how the cameras are set up. I didn't hear a thing that night. No one could've conked her in the car park. I would've seen that on the monitor. If someone needs aid, I get involved. If they need the RAC to fix a flat tire, I ring 'em up. But other than that—"

"Sure. Coffee and donuts till it's time to leave."

The man stood up, his eyes mere slits, his lips drawn back. "You bloody—"

"A woman was *murdered*," McLaren snapped, matching the guard's voice tone and volume. "If you don't care about that, about helping find her killer, you're as pathetic as the scum who topped her." He stood there, his feet apart, waiting for the man to charge out of his booth, ready for a fight.

Instead, the guard grabbed a pad of paper and his pen and said, "What's your name again?"

"McLaren. Do you need me to spell it?"

"I can spell it. B-A-S-T-A-R-D."

"Funny."

"I've got something else that'll make you die laughing, matey. You're barred from coming back here, understand?"

"You can try, but frankly, I don't think you'll succeed. Thanks for your time. You've renewed my faith in bouncers—all brawn and no brains." He walked to his car, the guard's opinion of McLaren heard far beyond the walls of his booth.

McLaren LEFT THE CASINO and stopped in a lay-by to put a mobile call through to Ian Shard, the police constable who had talked to Rick Millington. As the phone rang, McLaren considered the possibility of someone waiting outside the range of casino cameras and confronting Marta. A winning that large would tempt many people. But if the police hadn't seemed concerned about that, and Marta's friend Linnet hadn't seen anyone following them… He rubbed the back of his neck. Perhaps there was another angle.

If there was, PC Shard couldn't supply it other than reiterate that Rick Millington and his mate Danny Mercer had evidently been read the riot act by their parents. "Other than one of them getting into it with Mrs. Hughes," the constable said, sounding tired, "I haven't any other ideas."

"Can you tell me exactly where Marta Hughes was found?" McLaren would never tell Chard, but he was testing the constable. And the investigating team in general. How thorough a search had they done?

"You going to look that over?"

He would ask that. Every good detective worth his salt viewed the crime scene. Charts, videos, and photos were as good as they went, but they didn't replace actually viewing the area. "I'd like to see it," he insisted. "It may suggest something to me."

The constable hesitated, unsure if he'd be injuring his career if his Superintendent found out. After McLaren's repeated request, the constable finally said, "Just outside Elton. On the western end. Before the road splits for Youlgreave and Middleton."

"Where? Anything you can point me to?"

There was a grunted, "One second." There came the squeak of a metal file drawer opening, a rustle of papers, and a mild oath quickly following several heavy thuds. A chair squeaked and a rattle of metal against something ceramic seeped into McLaren's ear. Another second or two of silence, then moments later, PC Shard sighed and said, "Got it. Just don't let on you got it from me, understand?"

"Your name won't come up."

"Yeah, well, it better not, mate, or I'll get the sticky end."

"Nothing will mar your perfect career, Shard."

"Well, it better not. My wife's got used to a roof over her head."

"I wouldn't dream of moving her. Let's have it."

"Like I said, it's just before the road branches. It's on the Elton side. You know where that ruined barn is? On the western side of that. Between the edge of the barn and the road."

"In that depression." McLaren nodded as he visualized the spot.

"Right. I don't think you'll find anything, but I hope you do."

"Thanks, Shard. That's at least two of us."

THE TOWN OF Matlock lay between Nottingham and Elton, practically in a straight line on a map. The roads were nearly as accommodating, for the A6 ran into and west of it before it snaked northwest into Bakewell. From the A6 at Matlock,

Marta could have cut over to Elton using the small road out of Brightgate or gone slightly north to get on the B5057. Either route would have taken her into Elton quite easily and quickly. *If* she had driven back to Matlock on the night of her disappearance. McLaren hoped he was about to find out.

He had the address of Marta's brother-in-law—provided by Alan Hughes—and decided this was the perfect time to question the relative.

He followed the A6 into the town, turned left onto a major connecting street, and wound around the western end of town until he turned down the sought-after road. The brother-in-law's residence was at the bottom of the cul-de-sac.

Neal Clark was probably forty, McLaren judged as he sat in the front room and looked at the man. Of medium height, he had a superb physique. Not bulging with muscles, but his arms and thighs were well toned, in keeping with his flat abdomen. Works out, McLaren thought. Or heaves car bodies for a living.

"So you want to talk about Marta," Neal said after McLaren stated the reason for his call.

"If you've no objections." McLaren eyed the man, judging if he still hurt from his sister-in-law's death. "If it's not too painful a subject."

"Not my topic of choice, but I'm okay with it. What do you want to know?"

"I'm trying to ascertain her movements that night."

"The night she died."

"We assume she did, but without a witness—"

"You don't know exactly when it happened."

"Had she ever talked to you about any problems she was having or anyone who might be bothering her?"

"Like, did she have any enemies?" His blue eyes, vivid and nearly mesmerizing in their gaze, seemed to hold the pain of losing Marta, registering what his face did not betray.

The thin lips were set in a straight, firm line; the eyebrows neither arched in surprise nor lowered in sadness. The face was a mask, shielding the world from his thoughts and ache.

"Something like that, yes. Had she talked to you about a particular person she was concerned about or any troubles she had? I understand you and she saw each other that day."

"Yes, for lunch. Here. I don't mean here in my house. We met in town. We do that fairly frequently. Well, more so after my wife's—her sister's—death a few years ago. Hit-and-run car accident," he said, slightly slower. "Marta spent the afternoon with me until she left to meet a friend in Nottingham. They were going to the casino." He picked up a chip from the side table and handed it to McLaren. The casino's logo and name were printed on the chip.

"Did she patronize the place frequently?" He flipped the chip across his knuckles, as many poker players do while they are waiting for their turn.

"I know she went often, but I don't know to what extent. We didn't talk about that—either that day or any day."

"What did you talk about that day, if you don't mind telling me."

Neal sighed and slumped back in his chair. "I don't know." He ran his fingers through his short red hair, as though kneading his brain. "Yes, I do. We talked about her neighbor and her coworker. We also talked about Alan's birthday and would he prefer a small family gathering at their place or should we go someplace for the afternoon and evening, like the racetrack or maybe biking along the Tissington Trail. I even suggested we try rock climbing at Windgather Rocks near Whaley Bridge, but I think Marta was a bit nervous about that."

"Alan's a bit of an adventurer, then."

"Don't know how adventuresome he is, but he likes sports and activities like this. I always thought it odd that he wound up as a banker."

"Not the type to sit behind a desk?"

"I suppose he's had to, for the sake of his career. But I always thought he'd be more suited to something more active. They should've lived in a village, I thought. He's that sort of person."

"Did you and your sister grow up in a village?"

"No. In Buxton. We had summer jobs in Buxton, too. I always envied the kids who were camp counselors, but we were confined in town."

"I sometimes think that many of us never get to live where we'd be most happy. It puts a damper on our urge for kayaking, for example, if we're trapped in a town."

"That's why we were thinking about doing something like this for Alan's birthday, which was June twenty. He liked a bit of outdoor excitement now and then."

McLaren made no comment about the date, but thought again what a tragedy Marta's death was for those who loved her.

"He came to my studio on one of his birthdays and gave wire sculpture a try, but I don't think it had enough action for him."

"Your studio?"

"Yeah. I'm a silversmith, though I concentrate on art objects like that." He gestured toward the sculpture on his fireplace mantel.

"It's nice."

"Oh, ta. One of my earlier creations. It's supposed to represent Persephone returning to the world after her six-month sojourn with Hades. I've titled it 'Spring's Renewal.' First one I cast. Usually I work in wire, but…" He shrugged as if to say a person had to broaden his talents. "Anyway, as I said, I work mainly on art objects and jewelry. I've got a few pieces in galleries but the main portion are made on consignment."

"Congratulations."

Neal flashed a quick smile, his eyes on the sculpture.

"So you tried the silversmith lesson and Alan didn't wax enthusiastic."

"He didn't complain, but I think once was enough."

"And did you decide on something?"

"I believe Marta opted for going to a gun club and doing some target shooting."

"Alan likes to do that?"

"I don't know. He's never done it, as far as I know."

"They why did Marta suggest it? Had Alan expressed a desire to learn?"

"Probably because he'd never done it before. Or because it's one of my hobbies. She knew how much I enjoy it."

"So you talked about the birthday that afternoon. You said you also talked about her neighbor and coworker. Would that be Verity Dwyer from the animal shelter and Tom Millington, her neighbor?"

"Yes." Neal sat up and leaned forward, his elbows on the tops of his thighs. He pressed the tips of his fingers together and looked at McLaren with the same pain-filled eyes, yet his voice had tightened, as though holding back anger or disgust, and his words came lower and faster, nearly clipped in his desire to finish the subject. "I told her she needed to tell Alan about that sleaze bag Millington. That would stop the harassment. Or let me come over there and beat the bastard to within an inch of his life, but she didn't want me to get involved. Said she'd handle it."

"And Verity?"

"Her conscience was bothering her and she didn't know what to do."

"What bothered her?"

He grabbed another poker chip from the small bowl on the table and ran his thumb over its ridged edge. "About the money. I suppose you know about it."

"The money from the shelter."

"Yes." Neal's fingers closed around the chip, pressing against it until his fingers blanched. He nodded as he considered something.

McLaren didn't rush the man, but looked around the room. It was uncomplicated, simple, straightforward in its façade, as Neal was. Furniture of simple wood or chrome frames held solid colored fabric. A brown carpet stretched into the adjoining room—the dining room—where the same hue was picked up in the large, burlap-matted watercolor above the table. Another watercolor, smaller and matted in pale blue mat board, hung over the sofa. No knickknacks other than a small silver sculpture, metal-cased clock, and a box of matches occupied the fireplace mantel. There seemed to be nothing to dust or conjure up memories.

As though sensing he was wasting McLaren's time, Neal finally said, "She'd not hesitated in loaning the money to Verity, but now she was having second thoughts that Verity would ever repay it."

The small clock chimed the hour, its tone so soft it would have been lost if Neal had still been talking. McLaren grabbed the poker chip he'd been flipping with all the tenacity of a man holding onto the edge of a cliff. The sun seemed to sink immediately below the horizon and he strained his eyes to make out Neal's face in the haze that threatened to engulf him.

"*Marta* loaned Verity money?" He tried to speak calmly, keeping the astonishment from his voice, but his voice had cracked after uttering the first word. He covered up his shock by coughing.

Neal jerked his head up, seeing McLaren's raised eyebrow. "Why…yes. I thought you knew."

"I'd heard something about the money," he said, not untruthfully, "but not the full details."

"There's really not much to it. Verity needed several hundred quid for some bills that had piled up. She didn't want to borrow from the bank, which would have added to her financial problem, and she was desperate to get it taken care of. I guess her creditors were applying pressure." He slumped back in his chair and relaxed his hold on the chip in his hand. "Anyway, Marta loaned her the money. I don't know how much, but it was a sizable chunk. That's why she was headed to the casino that night. She wanted to win big so she could replace the money she'd loaned Verity before Alan found out. He's a real stickler about that sort of thing. Don't lend money to friends or relatives." He tossed the chip back into the bowl and crossed his legs. "Seems to me there are times to make exceptions."

McLaren stared at the watercolor above the mantle. It had been painted by Marta and depicted another probable holiday spot. Switzerland, he guessed, scrutinizing the snow-capped mountains and herder's hut. A car horn sounded on the street, bringing McLaren back from the depths of the painting. "And the casino…did she come back here after she finished that night?"

"That timeline of yours again?"

"Yes. I'd like to find out where she went and when. It could help pinpoint who was with her."

"As to that, I've no clue. She didn't come back here. Sorry."

I am, too, McLaren thought, walking back to his car. Just who the hell is telling the truth about the missing money?

FOURTEEN

McLAREN GOT to the stone barn late afternoon. He had left Nottingham by the A610, continued up the A6, and stopped for lunch in the village of Cromford. Traffic was heavy, being the height of the tourist season and a Saturday, so he was later leaving than he had wanted. At Grangemill he took the B506 north before turning west for Elton. The village never failed to fascinate him, from the stone church and churchyard several steps above road level, to the pub of sporadic business hours, to the ancient stone circle on the nearby moor. I should live here, McLaren thought as he drove past the centuries-old inn now accommodating a bed-and-breakfast. It's a paradise of stone farm buildings and fields, enough to keep me in cold, hard cash for years.

He turned off the main road, poked along behind a tractor, then spotted the stone barn. It matched the image in the emailed photo. He glanced at his notes from Jamie's phone call. West of the village, a half-mile out, on the right side of the road. He smiled, hoping good luck would be with him.

The building was remarkably preserved, its walls upright and solid. The roof had lost some tiles, but it was sturdier than similar structures McLaren had seen. Near the roof's peak, a large hole permitted sunlight, rain, and birds into the loft, the heavy bough of the overhanging oak still cradled in the opening. A few sunflowers poked from this void, where their seeds had taken a foothold. On to the eastern side of the barn, the years hadn't treated the lean-to as kindly, for the two adjoining walls were little more than piles of stone, moss-and-lichen-covered where they wallowed in the shade. Of the two remaining walls, birds had built nests and weeds had wrapped their tendrils around the window frames.

McLaren parked on the left side of the road, half amused at the remnants of his detective skills, and walked over to the barn. The weeds and grass were high in the open space, higher still near the building's foundation and in the ditch bordering the road. He jumped the ditch, hoping he was not treading on something hidden in the grass, and wandered over to the barn.

The wooden door stood solid and grim, its exterior battered from decades of abusive weather. But the door held firm even if its paint had faded and cracked, the wood where it was exposed to the elements dull and rough. Splinters at the doorjamb, opposite the door's dead bolt, spoke of someone's attempt to enter the building—kids bent on mischief, or the farmer, who had misplaced his key? The door stood slightly ajar now, revealing a black-as-night interior. McLaren stood to one side of the door, his cop's instincts on edge as he placed his open palm on the wooden panel and eased the door open. The hinges complained fiercely, squealing into the stillness with the intensity of a suspect yelling for his lawyer.

McLaren remained where he was, staring into the interior, letting his eyes adjust to the darkness. Great place for a murder.

Why had she ended up here? Had whoever picked her up at her house driven her here for a meeting? If so, did they talk inside the barn? The building had to have some significance. Otherwise they could have talked outside most anywhere. McLaren looked again at the ground leading to the barn door. Maybe her body had simply been thrown here.

McLaren snapped on his torch and played its brilliant beam around the barn's interior. The dirt floor was spotted with cigarette butts and crumpled packs, beer bottles, and discarded crisps packets. A teenager's rendezvous.

He went inside, cautiously shining the light on the floor, and picked his way over the rubbish. The torchlight revealed nothing unusual, nothing that looked as though it had been there for a year. Shifting the torch beam from side to side, he walked around, peered into the corners, gazed up at the rafters, tipped over the old buckets and wooden crates and bales of straw. Nothing.

The wooden steps leading up to the loft were dust-covered and cobweb-strewn. But dust settles and cobwebs gather in a year, McLaren thought as he angled the torch beam along the stonewall and up to the landing, then back onto the step nearest his feet. It seemed solid enough. He pressed his right shoulder against the wall and carefully climbed the stairs.

His right hand held the torch, and though it accented the backless steps and showed where to place his feet, he felt ill at ease. No handrail kept him safely on the staircase; it must have fallen or been yanked off years ago. He groped for the reassuring coldness of the stones behind him. The blackness closed around him, thick and still except for his labored breathing and shuffling gait. A wooden plank groaned as he put his weight on it and birds above in the loft chatted excitedly, yet silence quickly descended and in that abrupt quiet he felt as much alone as he had ever felt in his life.

A mouse scurried across the step, its tail carving a thin trail in the dust. McLaren stopped, pushing his back against the wall. The beam of the torch threw the rodent into exaggerated relief, a monster of light tan fur startlingly bright against the darkness beyond. He watched the mouse scuttle across the plank and jump onto the floor before he let out his breath. Dark spaces did that to him—pushed memories into the open and unleashed demons from their locked cages. He stood there for a moment, taking a deep breath and slowly exhaling, listening for the faint rustle of cellophane or dry leaves as the mouse dove for cover, waiting for the rest of the pack to high-tail it to safer quarters. But the only sound was the caw of a rook somewhere overhead and his heart-beat in his ear.

He slowly panned the torch's beam across the remainder of the steps, hoping he would see no other mouse. The steps were vacant except for wisps of hay, dust, and dried clumps of mud. McLaren aimed the light back at his feet and climbed, the methodical, measured thump of his footsteps thudding into the interior space. The light angled against the wall, revealing chinks where the mortar had cracked and fallen, fingerholds of moss, and a seedling wedged into a crevice and holding on with all the tenacity of its roots. He brushed off a strand of cobweb and felt along the wall with his free hand, as Braille writing slides beneath reading fingers, the stones slipping beneath him as he ascended. Step by cautious step he climbed, dislodging the hay strands and dust.

Occasionally a stone's rough edge caught his shirt or dug into his flesh, and he silently berated the stonemason for his hurry or clumsiness. By the time McLaren reached the landing, his shoulder was sore and bruised from the pressure of his body leaning and rubbing against the stones. But the stability of the wall had saved him from a fall—and had kept the memories at bay. He shone his light around the loft.

It was brighter up here. Sunlight seeped through the jagged hole in the roof and illuminated sections of the enclosure. A large barrel crowded into one corner and some old farm tools leaned lazily against the wall. A coil of rope, its ends frayed and probably chewed by mice, sagged over the barrel top. A dirt-covered padded horse collar hung around the newel post on the landing. McLaren walked into the room.

The straw was thick in places, barely covering the wooden floor in others. It smelt of dust and mold and there were tun-

nels near the far wall—probably where animals had hollowed
out nests or warrens. He kicked apart the burrows, the old
fear taking hold of his mind and heart. The disturbed straw
laced the air with dust that turned a golden tan in the shaft
of sunlight. It fell heavily, rather than floating, to the floor.
He shook his head, holding his breath until he stepped away
from the clumps, and coughed.

A stump of candle and a box of matches lay on the windowsill nearest the road. A chipped china saucer bearing
clumps of candle wax sat on the floor. Damned kids. They
want to burn down the place? He strode over to the window,
picked up the candle and matches, and shoved them into his
back pocket. He took a slow look around the area. As he
turned back toward the landing, he saw the glint.

An empty beer bottle snuggled half in, half out of the
straw, the sunlight glancing off the smooth, amber glass. It
seemed to wink at McLaren, the golden gleam fading and
glowing as a tree branch waved outside in the breeze, its
leaves sporadically masking the sunlight. He watched it for
several seconds, mesmerized by the trick of the light until
the glint faded. More rubbish, he thought, leaving the bottle
where it lay and clumping down the steps.

The ground outside the barn had grown over in the year
since the cops' fingertip search. McLaren stood in a patch
of sunlight, envisioning the line of constables crawling over
the ground shoulder to shoulder, pulling up grass and weeds,
clearing the area down to the bare earth. They would bag
everything they found: cigarette ends, pull tabs from bev-
erage cans, cellophane package wrapping, scraps of paper,
broken lipsticks, broken combs, earrings, coins, keys, inkless
pens, plastic straws, paperclips… Anything and everything.
There was no indication at the outset of a case what way
it would turn and what may prove important. So it was
all bagged and preserved. Which was why, one year later,

McLaren was surprised to see that the land had recovered so well, swathed in a healthy mix of grasses and flowering plants. And why he walked over to the large oak tree to the north of the barn, several yards away. He'd find nothing where the police had searched.

The grass was flat at the tree's trunk, as though it were a popular spot for picnickers. A crushed lemonade carton and a small notebook suggested someone had left in haste not too long ago. As he bent over to pick them up, he noticed a large stone, approximately a foot tall and rounded, barely visible among the mass of tall weeds and ivy. A nice spot to sit and sketch. Or write. Pocketing the notebook, he walked over to the stone and began yanking up the plants in a yard-wide circle. He had nearly cleared the ground when he discovered a silver charm of a downhill skier tangled in the dense stems near the roots. Probably from a bracelet. He picked it up, blew off the soil and dust, and slipped it into his pocket.

The remainder of the area yielded nothing unusual.

This spot, farther away from the stone building, had not been subjected to the ruthless search of the previous year, for the grass grew even and thick between the gravel side of the road and the edge of the wood. Clumps of Queen Anne's lace and wood dock dotted the patch of green, waist-high and impenetrable in its exuberant growth. Several large boughs from the trees fringing the glade had crashed to earth at one time. A large tree trunk angled out from the forest's border. Bramble and creeping thistle, tall and reaching for the sun, seemed to explode from the ground around the trunk. McLaren abandoned his casual search of the low depression alongside the road and lifted the boughs. Nothing but matted grass met his eye. He poked through the growth with the broken branch, then with his fingers, feeling the wet earth beneath. Still nothing. He stood up and gazed at the trunk. Tiers of many-zoned polypore fungi enveloped one end of the trunk. The sunlight played upon the half-circled brackets, enhancing the browns, grays, and tans that radiated out in wavy rings. The top of the trunk had splintered, possibly from its fall, but the mid section of the dead wood looked solid. Had it been here last year?

He waded through the stinging plants, the prickly leaves and thorns tearing at his flesh and clothing. Ignoring the angry red welts and drops of blood, he pushed aside the plants with his feet, then stepped on the stems to crack them and keep them from springing up again. After clearing the entire length of the trunk, he got on his hands and knees. The exposed earth beneath the edges of the trunk was damp. No yellowish grass or wildflowers stretched outward into the clearing. The wood had been there a while, McLaren reasoned, but had the search crew moved it? He needed to see if anything was trapped beneath it.

Thrusting his left hand under a large bough, he pulled at the branches with his right. His fingers touched something smooth. Trying to determine the object's identity, he felt along the flat surface. It tapered slightly. McLaren yanked harder at the branches but the bough did not shift. He stood up, ignoring the dampness of his trousers. Tugging and kicking the trunk did not budge it from its position. He picked up a fallen branch and used it against the trunk as a lever. It snapped in two at the first hint of pressure. He turned toward the barn, exasperated, his eyes moving toward the upper story. A long-handled rake and shovel leaned against the wall in the loft. They would make acceptable levers. But to get them he would have to enter the barn again, mount the stairs, confront the dark and the nightmares. That was not an option. Not now. One time was enough to flirt with the memories he'd shoved into the recesses of his mind. He could not face them again so soon.

He threw down the branch and strode to his car. Getting

in, he told himself the car needed a wash anyway. The engine started with a purr and he eased the vehicle off the road. The depression paralleling the tarmac was not long, slanting upward and flattening out to meet the general lay of the land. Yet, the grass and wood dock were thick in patches, perhaps hiding holes or broken bottles. He set the parking brake, got out, picked up a dead branch, and jabbed into the vegetation. The soil was solid, yielding no surprises. He tossed away the stick and got back into his car. The hell with Proper Procedure.

The earth was firm, erasing the question of getting stuck. He steered around one of the large, fallen boughs and stopped in front of the trunk. It looked larger when viewed from within his car. Yet, he reminded himself, the top part was rotten and would probably break off when the trunk started rolling. With that thought to cheer him, he backed up and aimed the car's front bumper directly at the trunk's midsection. He stopped the car when he felt the bumper nudge the wood. He took a deep breath as his foot pressed down slowly on the accelerator pedal.

Nothing happened. For all the engine's groan, the downed tree remained where it was. McLaren applied more pressure to the pedal. The car crept forward, the tires digging into the earth. The trunk stirred, finally inched forward hesitantly as it came against bumps of packed soil and tufts of grass. Chunks of bark slid off beneath the bumper as the dead wood rolled. When McLaren judged he had cleared the site, he braked, letting the trunk come to rest against a small birch. He backed the car, angling sharply to the right, and drove back onto the grassy verge of the road.

When he walked back to the trunk, he saw that he had shifted it a good half-dozen feet from its original spot. The exposed ground for the length of the trunk stretched pale tan and brown; no plants struggled toward the sunlight. McLaren smiled. Maybe the search team hadn't bothered to shift the piece of dead wood; maybe they'd been too rushed or considered it too far from the body, which had been near the barn.

He saw the silvery object immediately, where he judged he had touched it beneath the large bough. He squatted and pulled it from its imprisonment in the damp soil. Flicking off the mud, he rotated it slowly, looking at it with a growing sense of excitement. It was a heel from a woman's shoe, a high-heeled shoe. A dress shoe. The sunlight glanced off the silvery patina and he blinked. Jamie's words sounded in his mind: victim's right shoe missing.

Feeling clever, he laid the heel on the grass and continued prodding the rest of the soggy earth where the trunk had lain. The area was large and his fingertips soon became sore and dirty, but he had no thought of stopping until he searched it thoroughly. He started his hunt at the tree's midsection, where the shoe heel had been buried, and worked his way steadily, slowly toward the larger end of the trunk depression. He found nothing. Returning to the midsection, he searched toward the crown. Quarter of an hour later he was rewarded for his meticulous work. His fingers closed around something hard.

He drew it from its near imprisonment of the earth and flicked off the globs of mud. It was circular—or had been before it had broken—about the size of a walnut shell and black or dark blue. He got up and walked to a dry patch of soil, where he wiped the object across the grass. Holding it up, he slowly rotated it, trying to make out what it was. He pulled his handkerchief from his back trousers pocket, spat repeatedly on the object, and cleaned off the major portion of mud with the linen. It still had mud wedged into the ridged rim, but he knew what it was. A poker chip. A fragment of a chip, actually. He angled it so the sun slanted across its surface. Was there printing on it or just the usual design found on most commercial chips? Was it from Noah's Ark or a custom-printed chip from a casino? Either way, he smiled as he picked up the shoe heel and carried them gingerly back to his car. It was prophetic. Hadn't he always been called in to clear up messes when the chips were down?

FIFTEEN

IN OTHER CIRCUMSTANCES, McLaren would have hesitated about getting into his car wearing wet, muddy clothing. The car's exterior was also wet and muddy from the trunk rolling, and—perhaps even more important—he was tired and wanted to wrap up his day.

He leaned slightly to his left as he looked at the fragment of the poker chip. His makeshift cleansing had removed most of the mud and he could now see a bit of writing on the chip's face. Part of the paint was scratched but he could make out the first two letters: ON. Could be part of a word, like "one," he thought, recalling a slogan on one of the animal shelter's chips: "One pet, one heart of unconditional love." Of course, it could also stand for the amount of the casino chip's worth: One hundred. He sighed heavily. The edge of the chip also seemed to have a band of white on it, like the usual chips found at a casino. But the Noah's Ark chips had also had that, so he was really no closer to a solution.

He laid the chip fragment and the high heel on the car seat, yanked his mobile phone from his pocket, and called Neal Clark, Marta's brother-in-law. "When Marta met you before she went to the casino," McLaren said when Neal answered the phone, "how was she dressed?"

Several seconds passed before Neal recovered from his surprise to answer the question. "How? You mean, evening clothes or jeans? That sort of thing?"

"Yes. Do you remember the shoes she was wearing?"

Again a lapse of silence fell between them. A rook shrieked

to an unseen companion before flying to another tree. Neal said slowly, "I think she wore high heels. Yes." His voice grew stronger as her image cemented in his mind. "A blue-and-silver dress with silver-toned high heels. Is that what you want?"

McLaren rang off, thinking it was perfect.

Linnet Isherwood echoed the dress and shoes color when McLaren rang her up, but added that the dress had cap-sleeves and had been knee-length. "She wore a silver bangle brace-let—a Möbius strip design with some phrase engraved on it—and a necklace of blue beads. Does that help?"

McLaren assured Linnet it did and asked one more ques-tion. "Did she ever wear a charm of a skier—either on a brace-let or necklace?"

"No…not that I recall. Not that we were the greatest of friends, so I can't swear. I never saw one. Sorry."

He assured her it didn't matter and thanked her before hanging up.

Asking Marta's husband, coworker Verity Dwyer, and three other friends about the silver charm produced nothing but verbal head scratching, confusion, and strong denials that she ever owned it. Alan flatly denied Marta had such a piece. "I saw her every day, in all situations," he said rather hesi-tantly, leaving Marta's state of undress to McLaren's imagina-tion. "She didn't have anything remotely like that. She went in for finer jewelry, like silver chains and bangle bracelets, semi-precious gems. Charms were too…" He tried to find the right word. "Too cute."

"You knew every piece she had, then."

"Certainly. Her jewel box sits next to my tray where I keep my cufflinks, tie tacks, and such. I've seen the box's contents thousands of time. She never owned a charm like that—or any charm."

Which just about closed that subject.

McLaren frowned, trying to recall if the computer reports he printed out had mentioned clothes or jewelry. He had no recollection of it, if there had been. Maybe Jamie had not emailed that. He punched Jamie's phone number into his mobile.

"You find anything at the barn, then?" Jamie said.

"You free for a drink?"

"Yeah. Always. When? Now?"

"No. I need to get home, shower, and change out of these muddy clothes."

"Muddy… What the hell have you been into, Mike?"

McLaren related the tree trunk adventure, giving only the broad scenario, before saying, "I'd like your opinion on this. If you've got time tonight."

"How can I refuse? My cop's curiosity is up."

McLaren rang off, revved the car engine into life, and drove home.

IT'S A MEASURE OF our friendship that Jamie hadn't hesitated to meet me, McLaren thought as he toweled off after his quick shower. He had left his muddy clothes in the middle of the kitchen floor, not wanting to trail the dirt through the house, and now changed into jeans and a tee shirt. And, he admitted as he combed his hair, that Jamie didn't need to ask *where* to meet. The Split Oak, in Somerley, had become their standard meeting place. Not because the food or drink was outstanding—though both were very good—but because it was convenient to both men. McLaren lived in Somerley; Jamie lived five minutes down the road, in Castleton.

The car park at The Split Oak was full that night. McLaren had to leave his car opposite the grocery shop. It had closed hours ago but a small security light shone from the shop's interior. He walked along the pavement, passing the newsagent's, a clothes shop, bakery, and combination gift shop/

tearoom. The space between the bakery and gift shop housed a small park where one of the shops in the row had been demolished. It was more of a rest spot, McLaren thought, passing the grassy rectangle that had been filled with a few small trees, some park benches, and a sundial. Nothing more than an environmental use of space. He crossed in front of the streetlight throwing a yellow glow onto the grass and pavement. His shadow, black and thick, stretched across the road, losing itself in the darkness lying at the foot of the buildings. He quickened his step, conscious of the guitar music filtering from the pub's open door and the rumbling in his stomach. He passed Jamie's car, parked along the curb, and entered the pub.

As many others of its era, it had been a coaching inn during the days of Elizabeth I and King James VI. A refuge from the night and storm. And from highwaymen. It had offered a slice of comfort in the wilds of Derbyshire's mountains and moors, a spot of civilization for which travelers were only too glad to pay. The slate roof sagged across the oak-beam ceiling and the casement windows let in blasts of winter when the wind blew westerly across the moor, but it held History and Charm and ghosts, perhaps, within its thick-set walls. And a good acoustic band on Saturday nights, McLaren mentally added as he joined Jamie at his table.

McLaren finished the last of his dinner—soused mackerel, glazed carrots, leeks with brown butter, and a bowl of fruit. He bypassed his usual favorite, soles in coffins, and opted tonight for the lighter fare. The mackerel had been extraordinarily good and he was thinking of ordering something else, but felt content for the moment to work on his pint. The pub was noisy with the laughter of weekend fun and the competition of a darts game. Which suited McLaren fine. There was less chance of being overheard. He leaned back, balancing the glass beer mug on his knee, and watched his friend down a forkful of cider cake before he told about finding the silver charm and shoe heel. When Jamie was duly impressed, McLaren explained why he wanted Jamie's help.

"What bothers me," McLaren said as a cheer erupted from the direction of the darts game, "is that Marta Hughes' body was dumped. Not so much the physical dumping, because you have to get rid of the body somehow, but that it would require some amount of strength to drag it out of a car."

"Unless she was killed there."

"Which might just be correct. Look, her car is sitting prettily at her house; there's no evidence of blood; no hair or fingerprints were found that couldn't be accounted for. I can't see someone waylaying her on the road, dumping her at the stone barn, going back to get her car, and then leaving it at her house. Besides the question of logistics—like how the hell did he get away from Marta's house if he drove her car there—it doesn't make sense! First of all, why risk all that maneuvering? Someone might see you either as you got into her car or drove her car or parked it at her house. Second, why even bother to do that? If she was waylaid, why not leave the car where it was? And third, since the lab boys found nothing foreign in her car, I can't see some bloke cocooned in a macintosh or sweats, gloved, and wearing a plastic bag over his head to keep his DNA out of the car. Even gloves and clothes will leave trace evidence. No, she was alive when she got home, Jamie, but *she* got into someone's car, was driven to the barn outside Elton, and was probably killed there."

Jamie laid his fork on the plate and nodded. "From what you've told me, Mike, for all that Rick Millington seems a somewhat likely suspect, he's only fifteen years old and can't drive."

"But his mate Danny is seventeen."

"And being a helpful bloke and friend, he could have driven *his* car and helped Rick with the body."

"That's what's bothering me. If father Tom did it, that eliminates the car-driving problem."

"Why would she get into either Danny's or the Millingtons' car? Was she that friendly with them?"

"I thought maybe I was too close to it or had lost my edge. I've been out of the job for a year," he reminded Jamie.

"If you've lost your edge, I'm the Chief Constable."

McLaren eyed his friend's physique. "You'll have to add a few stone." He lapsed into silence while Jamie tapped his foot in time to the music. Moments later, he snapped his fingers.

"What?" Jamie shifted his attention back to his friend.

"Why does it have to be Danny's or the Millingtons' cars? Maybe she got into *someone else's* car." He cocked his right eyebrow and watched the astonishment grow on Jamie's face. "Well?" He smiled as he grabbed his beer.

"Certainly makes more sense if she got into Verity's car, for instance." He saluted McLaren with his mug before adding, "Speaking of driving…I've done some digging around and I came across a speeding ticket."

"Must be more remarkable than issued to A.N. Other, I take it."

"You'll be interested." Jamie took a swallow of ale.

"You sound confident."

"You *will* be interested," he repeated. "I know you."

McLaren smiled. "That's why we're here."

"You ready for this, or do you want to keep making smart comments all night?"

"I'm ready to be awed."

Jamie looked around and leaned forward a bit, as though sharing a conspiracy. The band started singing about lost love. "I don't know why I'm doing you this favor, after your last comment, but—" He rushed onward, giving McLaren no time to reply. "I did a bit of digging around for you. Limited use, I know, since I can't get into the police files on this one."

He grimaced, silently apologizing, but McLaren shook his head. It would be worth Jamie's job if he were caught doing unauthorized work such as that, even on his time off. Jamie nodded at McLaren's meaning and continued. "Anyway, I *do* know that your victim, Marta Hughes, received a speeding ticket the night of her murder."

"Marta..."

"The driver tripped the speed camera, which took the photo. The registration plate number showed up nice and clear."

"Linnet Isherwood didn't mention that."

"The woman who started you back on your illustrious career."

"Don't know how illustrious or starting me back, but she came to me, asking me to reinvestigate the case."

"Which you rushed into."

"I didn't rush into anything," McLaren said, slightly annoyed. "I gave it some thought."

"While she was talking, I expect."

"I gave it a good deal of thought, Jamie. I wasn't eager to plunge back into all this. You ought to understand that."

Jamie nodded. He knew what McLaren had suffered. Stepping back into detective mode, even privately, took deliberation. "I know you, Mike. You love police work. You couldn't have said no to Linnet Isherwood even if it meant your life. It's in your blood. It's like a siren song, calling to you from a great distance, luring you back to the job."

"Always did like the sound of fire-engine bells and cop-car sirens. Nothing beats a good adrenalin rush," he said, half jokingly, then sobered. He did love the job. Helping people, solving puzzles, righting injustices. It was a siren song, beckoning him to pick up those unrighted injustices, but if there would be any adverse effects from his now-amateur meddling... He stared into his beer, then asked where the ticket had been originated.

"Just south of Elton," Jamie said. "Twenty-three forty-seven hours."

"And we know she left the casino at twenty-three-hundred hours," McLaren said. "Or close enough to call it that. Heading toward Elton or from Elton?"

"Toward," Jamie said. "Heading north."

"So we know she was alive at that time."

"Or someone else was speeding, anxious to dump her body."

McLaren snorted, still convinced Marta had been killed at the barn. "What road was this?"

"Along the A61, north side of Ripley."

"Not the A615 going into Matlock, then, or the B5057 going into Elton where her body was found."

"Sounds as though she was going home after all, heading north toward Chesterfield." Jamie picked up his glass and took a drink. The singers finished their song and those people listening applauded.

"I read the reports you sent, Jamie. Thanks."

"Get any ideas from them?"

"Don't know about ideas, but it's interesting that Linnet Isherwood was briefly under suspicion."

Jamie set down his glass, his face grim. "Because her husband left her and the kids prior to all this financial trouble of Marta's, you mean?"

"Isn't that good enough motive?"

"They ruled her out because she didn't leave the casino in Marta's car."

"Yeah. My friend, the goon at the casino car park, admitted Marta and Linnet left in their own cars. The casino cashier confirmed that, too. Told me the cops had seen the two women leaving separately on the CCTV tape."

"And there is no photo of Linnet Isherwood's car, as there is of Marta's as she tripped the speed camera. You know, Mike, if Linnet had been following Marta home, about to take Marta for another ride after Marta had parked her car, *Linnet* would've been speeding, too! She'd be going just as fast in order to keep up with Marta. Linnet couldn't let Marta get out of her sight. After all, Marta might not have been going straight home, and Linnet wouldn't have known that."

"Spoiling some kidnapping plan or such." McLaren's fingers drummed against the side of his empty beer mug.

Jamie eyed his friend's glass. "You need another? My round, I think."

McLaren shook his head. "No. Just that…talking about cars… You got another few minutes or so?" McLaren asked without glancing at his watch.

"Sure. I'm a grass widower this weekend. Paula's at her folks'—"

"I've got a couple mysteries of my own—personal—I'd like your opinion of." He told Jamie about the beer bottles—the ones found in and on his car, the missing bag at Noah's Ark, the bottle thrown at him when he was forced off the road—and about the disappearance of Karin Pedersen. "Normally, I'd let all this go," he said, his fingertips stroking the lip of his glass. "I'm beginning to think I'm losing my mind. I saw Karin enter the hotel but the clerk denies she was there. I saw all those bottles on my car, bagged them to bring to you—"

"Thinking I could get them printed for you."

"—but they disappeared from my car! I swear they were there, Jamie. I *know* I locked my car before I went into the animal shelter. I *always* lock my car. It's a habit."

"You couldn't have forgotten just this once, Mike?"

McLaren frowned, staring at his friend. "No! It's a habit.

You think that just because I'm not a copper anymore, I ignore a basic safety—"

Jamie waved away McLaren's argument. "I know it's hardly likely, but you had your mind on the case, on questioning the shelter employees."

"I wasn't thinking about the case *that* hard! Anyway, why would anyone steal a bag of empty beer bottles? It's absurd."

"Suppose the bloke didn't know it was empty bottles? Suppose strolling past your car he glances inside, sees a big paper bag, thinks it's something expensive, something he can sell, so he reaches in and grabs the bag, only to find out later when he opens it in a nice, safe alley that it's just rubbish."

"Because," McLaren said, his voice growing tired, "the bag was open, so this accommodating thief could see what was in the bag before he snatched it. Because he couldn't just reach into my car since—"

"I know, I know. The car was locked."

"Plus, I don't recall there being anyplace especially close where he could stop to examine his ill-gotten gain. I parked so that the passenger side, where the bag sat, was parallel to the street. It's a busy thoroughfare, Jamie. Besides the cop working the traffic accident, there was a street cleaner. There were pedestrians, shopkeepers, drivers. All these people passing by that damned animal shelter. I can't see the chap taking such a risk."

"Maybe he looked the part so no one paid him any mind."

McLaren rubbed his head, excruciatingly tired. "Meaning?"

"Meaning that if he wasn't dressed as a rag-and-bone man, and if he strolled up to your car from a believable direction—"

"Like, he looked as though he came from the shelter, where the car was parked."

"—so no one happening to see this would question his proximity to your car, and he looked as though he were unlocking your car door with a key, except that he was reaching into your car through the open window."

"The damned car *was locked!*" McLaren reiterated.

"Could or could not be correct. But if he jimmied the car open…" His eyebrow went up as he left the inference unsaid. "Not everyone uses a sticky jam knife to open letters, Mike."

McLaren exhaled slowly as he considered the possibility. "Could do, I suppose. I hadn't considered a professional thief with proper tools. Still, it's a hell of a chance to take, breaking into a car in broad daylight."

"Murder's *also* a hell of a chance to take, but *someone* did."

ON THE DRIVE HOME, McLaren considered all the angles of his two personal cases, as he called them. Jamie had suggested that the hotel clerk might just have been protecting his guests when he denied Karin Pedersen was staying there. "Doesn't want to get involved" was how Jamie had phrased it. "You've been a copper long enough to know about reluctant witnesses." The beer-bottle episodes were a bit more puzzling, and he promised McLaren that he'd think about it.

The trip back wasn't long, perhaps five minutes, but McLaren slowed on approaching the sharp bend where he'd had the near collision with the bottle-throwing driver. The car headlights threw brilliantly bright patches of light onto the road and into the canopy of leaves overhead. Tree boughs jumped out of the darkness in the headlights' glare, seeming bigger and more threatening than in daylight. McLaren passed the rock cliff, a sheet of light grayness, and then the great oak that marked the road to his house. He turned off. Immediately the crunch of gravel replaced the lullabying hum of car tires on tarmac, and he slowed as the tires sought more traction in the loose base.

A perfume of honeysuckle announced his arrival at the widened spot in his drive, and he steered the car over to the place where he always parked. He turned off the engine but sat in the car for a half minute, letting the scents and sounds of the June night wash over him. Roses, early blooming lilies, and hesperus cast off their intoxicating aromas with the abandonment of a woman; a nightjar and barn owl called out to some unseen mate. Downwind, a fox yapped, then the land fell quiet.

Last time I'd sat in the car on a June night, he thought, inhaling deeply of the scene of honeysuckle, was last year with Dena. He bent his head, leaning it against the steering wheel, recalling the kisses and conversation, the plans for their shared future. Then he had left the job and all that had ended. His happiness had also ended and Dena's departure created a wound in his soul that he thought would never heal.

McLaren eased out of his car, suddenly tired from the day's pursuits and acrobatics. He slammed the door, making certain it was closed, and turned the key in the lock. Despite his belief that it was a regular habit, he paused and turned back toward the car as he clicked the remote lock device. The yellow parking lights blinked on and off and the car horn beeped into the quiet of the night. He tried the door latch, making sure the automatic locking system was working. The car was secure. He turned and made for the kitchen door.

Trying to recall it later, he couldn't decide if he'd heard anything prior to the event or if it'd just not registered. Like sounds or sights too common to be memorable.

In a rush of power and near silence, an arm shot out of the darkness as he unlocked the back door. Fingers gripped his throat and a hand grabbed his upper arm and twisted him around. A knee slammed into his stomach and something solid and heavy smashed into his head. His hand groped at the air, at anything solid, to keep himself from falling.

Laughter...or the owl's hoot...bounced in his ears. A blinding pain caused his stomach to tighten...echoes of crunching gravel...then darkness and oblivion.

SIXTEEN

JAMIE KYDD DID MORE than think about it, as he had phrased
it to McLaren before going home that night from the pub. He
rose uncharacteristically early Sunday morning. Uncharac-
teristic because when his wife was out of town, Jamie usually
slept until eight or so. But McLaren's stories of the disappearing hiker and the reappearing beer bottles invaded Jamie's
dreams. So he disregarded his regular grass-widower routine
and was showered, shaved, dressed, and out of the house as
the first slants of sunlight hit the chimney pot.

For all his kidding last night, Jamie believed McLaren's
statement. Habit aside, no cop would walk away from his
unlocked vehicle. So what was the answer? That the car had
been broken into was obvious. And by a professional, for they
had found no chipped paint or torn weatherstripping around
the door when they examined the window last night. Would
a professional risk breaking into a car, in daylight, for a bag
of empty bottles?

Jamie turned the question over in his mind as he drove
to The Hanoverian Hotel in Hathersage. The bottles episode
seemed to have begun with McLaren's rescue of the injured
hiker. But again, why? Jamie glanced at his watch, determined to find out the answer to that and to Karin Pedersen's
disappearance before he was much older.

The hotel was stirring by the time Jamie left his car in the
hotel car park. The village bakery was doing a brisk business,
as was the newsagent's. Already cars were parked along the
main road. And probably winding up the hill to Little John's

grave, Jamie thought as he glanced at the church tower just peeking out of the blanket of trees. He watched a couple—obviously tourists—stop on the pavement and consult a map before he entered the hotel.

The aromas of fried eggs and ham, grilled tomatoes, and brewing coffee hit his nose as he closed the front door. It also reminded him of the inadequacy of his own breakfast, a day-old scone and a hurriedly consumed cup of tea. He pretended that the smells weren't there and walked into the reception area.

Even at this early hour, a clerk was on duty, freshly scrubbed and dressed immaculately. He looked up as Jamie came up to the front desk, smiled, and wished him good morning.

"Good morning to you," Jamie responded, flashing his brightest smile. He didn't feel particularly cheery, having slept only a few hours, but he put on a good show. His police training was good for more things than handing out speeding tickets.

"May I help you, sir?" the clerk asked, setting down a stack of letters. "Do you wish a room?"

"Actually, I was hoping you could help me in another capacity."

The clerk's smile remained plastered to his face, but a doubtful look crept into his eye. "Certainly. If I can, sir."

"I'm trying to find a friend of mine. Karin Pedersen. I'm concerned about her whereabouts because she was supposed to have phoned me last night and I haven't heard from her. She'd mentioned she was staying here, so I'm hoping you might know something about her. She's a small woman, in her twenties, with red curly hair—"

"The woman is known to me."

"Wonderful! Is she staying here?"

"But not in the capacity you believe."

"Oh, yes? She's changed her plans, then?"

"I know nothing of her plans." The clerk picked up the letters. "Nor do I know anything of her."

"But you just said—"

"I know *of* her, that is all. I do not *know* her. She is not a guest of The Hanoverian."

"If she's not a guest, how do you know of her?"

"Because," he said, already exasperated, "yours is not the first inquiry about this woman. There was another gentleman Friday. He was quite insistent that this person was lodged here. I had a rather difficult time persuading him she was not. In fact," he said, squaring up the stack by tapping the envelope edges on the desktop, "I really do not believe I convinced him. He left muttering. I fully expect him to return. And when he does…" He nudged the phone a bit closer to his right hand.

"This is extraordinary! Karin distinctly told me she was spending the night here. I can't believe it!" Jamie turned slightly so he could see the side door that led to the car park. "I hope nothing happened to her. Though I expect she would have rung me up if she'd been delayed. She's hiking," he added, turning back to the clerk. "You don't think she could have fallen, do you? Have you heard anything on the news?"

"I heard nothing on the news or from any other source. In fact, the other man inquiring for this person mentioned something about her having a scraped knee, I believe it was. I seriously doubt that had your friend suffered from such an injury, it would have detained her. Now, if you don't have anything further, I have a lot of work to do." He placed the letters in the Out tray on the desk and walked over to the postal card display rack.

Jamie walked slowly toward the door. From the depths of the hotel he could hear a vacuum cleaner being run. Across the hall, behind the closed doors, the softer sounds of conversations and the rattle of china plates drifted over to him. He turned toward the clerk, who was inserting new cards into the stand. "There couldn't be a mistake, could there?"

The man looked up, a card in his hand. "A mistake?"

"My friend couldn't have registered with someone else, while you were at tea, perhaps?"

"There is no such person registered at this hotel. If you do not believe me, perhaps you will believe our reservation cards." He strode over to the desk and produced the same stack of cards he had shown earlier to McLaren. Jamie glanced at each card as the clerk flipped through them, nodding at the obvious conclusion. When the clerk had returned them to the box, he said, "I trust you are satisfied your friend is not here, has not been here, and has no reservation to stay here. Now, if you don't mind, as I said, I have work to do. Good day, sir." The clerk returned to the card stand as Jamie walked from the room.

He paused by the front door, his mind trying to make sense of the situation. McLaren had jested that he was going insane, and now Jamie nearly believed him. But if he had seen Karin enter the hotel, Jamie wasn't going to doubt him. Something had the stench of week-old fish.

He half turned, bent on questioning a staff member, and had taken a step toward the rear of the building, when he abandoned the idea. If something odd was going on at the hotel, surely the staff had been instructed not to say anything. Even if a maid had seen someone fitting Karin Pedersen's description, it didn't prove it was Karin. There could be another red-haired guest. He decided to catch one of the staff on a cigarette break, outside the hotel, and walked across the road to the bakery.

A woman placing croissants in the large glass display case looked up when Jamie entered the shop. He nodded at her and glanced around the main room as he approached her. The shop's age was immediately apparent in its blackened oak timbers, white plaster walls, and sloping ceiling. But certainly not in its fare, Jamie thought as the scents of warm bread, pastries, and tarts beckoned to him. He felt the same response from his stomach that he had at the hotel, but this time he didn't ignore it. He bought a cinnamon scone and a pot of tea and sat at one of the small tables overlooking the street.

The village was fully awake by now, tourists snapping photos, traffic building on the main road, shops open and their daily sales or specials declared in bold signs. Several people were hurrying toward the church as the peal of bells called through the warm air. Jamie stared at the street, trying to imagine Karin Pedersen's destination once she left the hotel. Her reason for pretending to have a reservation at The Hanoverian—if that was the correct word—was still a mystery, but Jamie was convinced she had been there.

Finished with his meal, Jamie walked up to the shop assistant, who was ringing up a sale. She waited until the customer collected her purchase before asking if Jamie wished something further.

"A French loaf, please," he said, eyeing the long, crusty loaves standing in a wicker basket behind the counter. He could always use a loaf of bread. Plus, it never hurt to pay for potential information—and good relations. "Ta." He paid for the bread, then asked, "I don't suppose you remember seeing a friend of mine Friday. Or perhaps yesterday."

The woman shrugged. "Can't say, can I? What's your friend look like? Why are you asking? If she has a complaint about something she bought here…"

"No, no, nothing like that," he hastily said. "I was supposed to meet her in Hathersage Friday and she didn't show. I was wondering about her, that's all."

"If you think she's gone missing, why not ask the police?"

"Oh, I don't think it's anything like that. She's hiking down from Howden Moor. Probably delayed for a day or two."

"Blimey. Bloody awful long way, that. Why not ring her up and ask when she'll be coming?"

"I'm afraid it's not that simple. She has no mobile."

The clerk blinked. "No phone? Why not?"

"She broke it in a fall," Jamie said, saying the first thing that occurred to him. "She rang me up on a mobile she borrowed from another hiker she met. She wanted me to know she'd be out of touch for a bit. That's why I can't contact her right now. So I have no idea if she's still walking or I missed her."

The shop assistant frowned. She waved to a customer leaving the shop, then said, "I still think it's a job for the police, but what's your friend look like?"

"She's small and thin, with curly red hair. Early twenties. Her name's Karin. Karin Pedersen."

"No, 'fraid not. No one like that's been in Friday. Or Saturday. No red-haired hikers. I'd have remembered. My sis has red hair and I'm always looking at other redheads to compare hair color." She returned to wiping down the countertop.

"Perhaps someone else was on duty Friday and saw my friend." A suggestion of authority underlined the hopeful suggestion.

The woman paused in her cleaning and considered the idea. Outside the shop, a woman comforted a crying child with a hug and an elderly man instructed his Labrador dog to "stay" while he went into a neighboring shop. Shaking her head, the assistant returned to her cleaning. "We're open only from seven in the morning till five in the afternoon. I was on all day. Like I'm on today." She attacked a smear of sticky fingerprints with a renewed application of spray cleaner and more muscle.

"Perhaps when you went on break or stopped for your tea…"

Without looking up from her cleaning, she said, "I worked straight through. I always do. If your friend shows up today, I can let her know you're looking for her. Where shall I tell her you'll be?"

"Thanks, but I'll just hang around The Hanoverian. That's where we're supposed to meet." He grabbed the bread and left the shop.

Thinking Karin might have been hungry and needed to eat before she left Hathersage, Jamie tried three more businesses—a teashop, a small restaurant, and a smaller grocery. His account was the same and the responses were the same: no woman of Karin's description had been in the establishment on the day in question. Or recently. They were sorry, but perhaps his friend had eaten in the hotel restaurant. Or stayed at one of the bed-and-breakfasts in the village. Which just might explain everything, if Karin had walked into The Hanoverian and decided to bed down elsewhere if the hotel's price was too high for her budget. Jamie thanked them and returned to the hotel.

A couple probably in their early twenties was packing up their car. Three suitcases waited on the ground as the man unlocked the car's boot. The woman cooed to an infant and rearranged the blanket enveloping the child. Jamie picked up the baby bottle that had dropped onto the ground, handed it to the woman, and headed toward the back of the hotel. A maid and waiter stood near the back door, taking a smoking break. He walked up to them and rattled off the now-familiar lines.

The maid shook her head and said she'd seen no such guest. "I've done up most of the rooms already this morning, sir, and seen most of the occupants. Not a red-haired woman in the group."

"She couldn't be still here, perhaps sleeping late... Someone you haven't seen..."

"Could be, of course. But I know who's registered in each room."

"Oh?"

"Yes, sir. I don't snoop! Heavens, I don't mean that! But I know by the hotel registration. I need to know when I go to each room if I'm serving a single occupant in a double room or a family—"

"Or course. Helps you with the towels and sheets," he said, not unkindly.

"Yes, sir. So I don't believe your friend is staying with us. Not that I'm one-hundred-percent certain, but I don't think so." She chewed her bottom lip and frowned slightly. "Unless..."

"Yes?"

"There is one lady that could be her, I guess. All depends on your definition of red hair, though."

"Hers is very red. Almost a fiery red."

The maid shook her head. "No. Can't be her, then. This woman's hair is more carroty. And she's old. You said your friend's in her twenties?" Her eyebrow went up, as though silently commenting on the ten or twelve years' difference in his and Karin's ages.

"Yes. Perhaps her hair looks duller because she's indoors," he added hopefully.

"Can't be her. Sorry. Our guest is a lot older than that. Probably fifty. Walks with a cane, too. Can't see your friend hobbling all this way on a cane."

"Not her, then. Thanks anyway."

The maid crossed her arms over her chest, her cigarette dangling from her fingers. "You seen her, Robbie?"

The waiter took a last puff on his cigarette, then crushed it in the sand-filled stand near the back entrance. He was short, dark and muscular, and had the appearance of always being ready for a fight. But he was courteous to Jamie, perhaps unsure if Jamie were a guest. Didn't pay to jeopardize one's job. He barely glanced at the maid before looking at Jamie and replying, "No. Doesn't sound familiar."

"If she had dinner somewhere else Friday night and was out all day yesterday," Jamie said, "and hasn't come down yet for breakfast, you mightn't have seen her yet."

"Could be, sure. But I've not seen her in the hotel at all. Usually a guest will call down for tea or coffee of an afternoon or evening, or even ask one of us about something in the area. Tourist stuff, you know?"

"No one like Karin has done that."

"Not to my knowledge. 'Course, I wasn't on Friday night. I work mornings and afternoons mostly. So I wouldn't know about any room-service requests that night. But I haven't seen her this morning." He stopped, his mouth open, then said, "'Course, she could be in the dining room right now. Want to see?"

The waiter led Jamie and the maid down the hall and opened the double doors of the dining room. They lingered in the doorway, eyeing everyone in the room. After several seconds, the waiter asked, "She there?"

Jamie shook his head and turned to the two people peering over his shoulder. "She could still be in her room, but it's pointless to wait. Or waste any more of your time."

They walked back outside and the waiter consulted his watch. He drew another cigarette from the pack in his pocket while the maid said, "If we see her, we can ring you up, if you like." She smiled, the sunlight on her brunette hair lightening its dark shade.

"Thank you. If it wouldn't be too much trouble for you."

"Not at all, sir. You're worried about your friend. If she shows up I'll let you know. I'll ask the waiter who was on duty last night. Perhaps he's seen her or taken her tea in her room. Ta." She put the piece of paper with Jamie's phone number into the pocket of her work trousers and left him with "Hope you find her."

So do I, Jamie thought, but not for the reason you think. He strolled back to the hotel car park and stopped opposite the side door. There was no mistaking that it was a side entrance for the convenience of guests arriving by car. The hotel name sprawled over the doorway in large, well-lit lettering. There also were no container plants or shrubs that she could have ducked behind, giving McLaren the impression that Karin had entered the building but had actually afforded her cover. No, if McLaren saw her walk inside, she went inside. But that didn't explain the clerk's unwavering statement that no Karin Pedersen was a guest at the hotel.

Jamie repocketed his car key, grabbed the side-entrance door handle, and slowly opened the door. It was heavy, probably made of steel, but swung open easily. He eased it shut, nervous for some inexplicable reason that the desk clerk would hear him and investigate, and stood with his back to the door.

The entry area was small, holding the odors of tobacco smoke and fried foods. Yet it hadn't the claustrophobic feel Jamie associated with minute spaces, for it was painted in white and apple green. A helpful sign declaring "Guests' Rooms and Reception" pointed to the two destinations, its background whiteness tainted red from the glow cast by the EXIT sign over the door. To Jamie's left a narrow hallway, brightly lit by a row of recessed canister lights, stretched toward the back of the building; ahead was another door with a glass insert. Beyond that he could see the reception area and part of the clerk's desk. He turned left and walked down the hallway.

A flight of thickly carpeted stairs extended to the next

floor and Jamie climbed the steps two at a time. The passage smelled of carpet cleaner and lilacs and the walls were papered in a muted floral print. The polished wooden handrail slid beneath his hand as he sprinted up the steps, his heavy gold wedding band making faint rubbing sounds along the rail's slick surface. At the landing, to his right, the hall stretched toward the front of the hotel. Guest rooms lay along the length as far as he could see. He ran lightly down the hall, looking at each door as he passed. Nothing seemed irregular. The main staircase opened up to the ground floor at the end of the corridor. A large potted palm squatting on the landing nodded in the draft from the air-conditioning unit wedged into the front window. Jamie jogged back down the hall, then ascended to the top floor.

It was identical to the floor he'd just left, housing only rooms and a maid's closet. A small boy stood beside the partially opened window at the front of the building, offering breadcrumbs to the pigeons cooing and crowding together on the narrow outside ledge. Noises from the street below rushed in through the window—conversations, laughter, dogs barking, a police car siren. The boy seemed oblivious to the world beyond the pigeons. He tore up the bread and placed each piece in a specific spot, covering the ledge in systematic order, like a row of checkers. As fast as he put down a piece of bread, a bird would grab it. Other birds not yet fed or wanting more pecked at his hand and fingers. The boy shook them off, scolding them for their gluttony and impatience. When he had finished, he dusted his hands over the ledge, knocking off any remaining crumbs, and turned. It was then that he saw Jamie. A grin broke as he said, "We're going to see Little John's grave now. Do you know about him?"

"He's Robin Hood's trusted friend."

"One of his Merry Men. They lived in Sherwood Forest, but they're not real. I have to be going now. Mum doesn't like it when I'm late." He ran a few feet down the hall, stopped, then turned back toward Jamie. "I made a poem for Little John. I'm going to put it and a flower on his grave so he can read it. I want to be like Robin when I grow up." He ran to his room and banged the door closed.

So much for fame, Jamie thought. He went up to the window and glanced outside as he closed it. From this height he could see the bakery, teashop, and post office across the street, their roof tiles glistening from the morning's heavy dew. He turned as the door to the main stairway opened and an older couple stepped into the hallway. Nodding to Jamie, they continued with their conversation and entered their room. Jamie waited until their door was closed before he scampered back the way he had come, taking the steps downstairs and returning to the side entryway.

He stood near the side entrance, wondering what his reconnoitering trip had proven. At least he could report to McLaren that he'd found nothing sinister in the hotel, no remnants of a fight with enemy agents. Though if there were anything sinister going on, he reasoned, it was probably on Karin Pedersen's part and not the hotel's. Still, he needed to check as thoroughly as he could; he wouldn't be able to sleep if he didn't. He eased up to the inner door and peeked through the small glass inset. The clerk was not in sight. Jamie angled his head so he could see the entire desk. Still no clerk. He said a quiet, silent prayer, eased open the door, and tiptoed into the reception area.

No one was at the desk or small table holding pamphlets and flyers of area attractions. Jamie paused for several seconds, thinking perhaps the opening door had triggered a beep in the clerk's retreat behind the front desk. No one appeared. He repeated his prayer and slipped behind the desk.

The wooden box that held the registration cards sat where he'd seen it earlier, beside the phone. He leafed through the cards but found no Pedersen. He scanned the hotel guest book for the previous two days but again found no Karin Pedersen signed in. He was reaching for the large calendar on which reservations were noted when he heard the sound of footsteps. A masculine voice called to someone either in the main hallway or dining area. Jamie rushed into the back corridor as the front door slowly opened. He crouched low and pressed lightly against the door to keep it from swinging. No footsteps followed him to the back hallway. He let out his breath as the phone rang and the clerk's voice answered with a formal "The Hanoverian. How may I assist you?" Then, still hunched over, Jamie crept outside.

SEVENTEEN

JAMIE'S OTHER HUNCH—that Karin had changed her overnight plans and was safely ensconced in a local bed-and-breakfast—proved to be as much of a dead end as everything else he tried that morning. The area's handful of B-and-Bs and the medieval hall-turned-guest-house had no guest of Karin's ilk. Nor had a Karin Pedersen registered in any of them in the past week, the day of McLaren's misadventure, or for the upcoming week. Karin Pedersen, evidently, was a hallucination of Michael McLaren's mind.

At noon, Jamie paused for lunch. He returned to the tearoom, not because he was enamored with such places, but because it was one of the few places where he could sit over an inexpensive meal. He made out a list of people McLaren had talked to, then a list of the odd occurrences happening since he had taken the case. Jamie stared at the two lists for many minutes. Besides the broken poker chip, which could signify Noah's Ark or the casino Marta had patronized, he could determine nothing linking people from Marta's life to McLaren's trouble. Jamie stuck the sheet of paper into his jeans pocket, paid his bill, and left.

He sat in his car, the windows down, and rang up McLaren. He leaned back, the car-seat upholstery smelling faintly of fast food meals, cigarette smoke, and perfume. Funny how this defines my life, he thought. Fast food and cigarettes characterizing the hectic schedule of my job, the perfume a lingering remembrance of my wife, my private life. He shook his head. He kept them separate, fiercely protective of the time with Paula and his off hours, making it a point not to bring home work, even the emotional dregs, that would infringe upon their time together. Yet the two worlds were here, tied together like some eternal knot.

Jamie shook himself from his reverie and, glancing at the time, realized the phone had been ringing for quite a while. He punched in McLaren's mobile-phone number and stared again at the lists as he waited for McLaren to answer.

After thirty seconds, Jamie rang off. Must be struggling with another log, he thought, half smiling. Or left the phone in his car. He pocketed his mobile and drove to the local doctor's house.

A SOUND—URGENT, harsh, and relentless—broke through the dark morass of confused images. McLaren moved his head slowly as he tried to open his eyes. A beer bottle hurled at him and he ducked. The movement brought instant pain and more confusion as he cracked his eyes open and saw linoleum floor, a base unit, and a splash of shiny whiteness. Wooden spindles near his right hand seemed non-threatening and supportive of his weight. He grabbed the closest one just above a horizontal piece of wood and pulled himself over on his right side. His universe tilted and spun, a turmoil of black, silver, and red, the colors deepening in hue as the whirlpool enlarged and swirled faster. Yet, the unceasing sound called to him, adding to the buzzing in his head. He tried to sit up, pulling himself mentally from the spiral that churned at his feet. A bottle bobbed in the spinning mass and a poker chip rushed at him. He reached for it as the wave of sound rang louder, but the chip spun away to sink into the center of the whirlpool. Again he sought the firmness of the polished wood, somehow knowing it would rescue him from the spinning madness. His fingers closed tightly around the slender wood and he pulled himself upright. Opening his eyes, he could see a flat piece of wood attached horizontally to the spindle, and an even larger and longer slab of wood slightly above that one that seemed to support a length of dark blue fabric. Was it his police uniform? Was the unending sound the siren of his patrol car? Was he calling himself to work? He grabbed the edge of the fabric and pulled. The cloth and several hard items flew at him. His head seemed to explode from the pain, and he fell back onto the floor, surrendering to the whirlpool and the siren song.

JAMIE'S AFTERNOON matched his morning as far as gathering useful information was concerned. The local doctor was adamant that he had treated no one of Karin Pedersen's description, nor had his receptionist received a call from such a person. However, to appease what he diagnosed as Jamie's anxiety, he consulted his appointment diary. No, he informed Jamie, sitting back in his desk chair, he had not seen anyone with a cut on that day. Or the day prior or afterward, he added, flipping the pages. Was Jamie certain he had the correct village? he suggested, blinking behind his round spectacles. Perhaps his friend was in Hatton. Perhaps Jamie had misunderstood.

Jamie assured the man he had not misunderstood and stood up.

"If the wound was only superficial," the doctor continued as Jamie was about to thank him for his time, "perhaps she merely cleansed it herself. Nothing wrong with soap and water."

"That's a possibility, I'm sure. But I think the cut required something more extensive. It bled rather profusely."

"Of course, there are the hospitals, if the wound required stitching up. Have you inquired at Buxton or Chesterfield?"

"No, sir. I thought I'd ask around this area first."

"And there's always the chemist's."

Jamie drew back his hand and blinked. "Pardon?"

"Here in the village. Just down the street. You've not inquired in there, I assume."

"No, sir. Frankly, I hadn't thought that far."

"Could be your friend purchased an antibiotic ointment and some sort of first-aid dressing. You know, sterile gauze, adhesive plaster, or those pre-medicated cloths. If her knee needed attention but she didn't want to have it properly attended to, she might have looked after it herself." He smiled as Jamie thanked him and hurried from the office.

The chemist's shop was on the edge of the business district, up the road from the establishments Jamie had called at that morning. It was a small building, squeezed between a mountain bike/camping centre and the pub, its façade the same gray stone that comprised every building in the village. Health and beauty products sprawled across the interior, extended ledge. The placard above the door proclaimed "Hathersage Chemist Shop" in white lettering against a black background. Jamie said a mental prayer, took a deep breath, and walked inside.

The aroma inside the shop was a heady mixture of perfume, soap, sachet, hand lotions, and chocolate. His second observation was the shop's orderliness, from the straightness of the head-tall sales shelves to the white-and-black-checkered ceramic floor. He pushed the triangular gate on the waist-high railing that separated the shop proper from the entry, passed the tower of stacked plastic carrier baskets, and sought out the shop assistant.

He had finished his recital and was preparing to be disappointed again when the clerk said, "Yes, your friend was in here."

"You're sure?" He replied more slowly than usual, forcing the excitement from his voice, hoping he sounded mildly interested. "Friday."

"Oh, yes." The woman nodded. She removed her glasses and wiped the lenses before putting them on again. "I recall her quite well. A cute girl, though rather thin, with a mass of curly hair. Red as fire. You couldn't help but notice her, even without the wound to her knee. I thought it should be seen to properly—you know, by our doctor—but she insisted it looked worse than it was. I suppose she knew what was best for her."

The buzzer above the door alerted the clerk to a woman entering the shop.

Jamie let the clerk answer the woman's question about the location of the cough medicine and move on before he asked, "She bought items for her cut knee, then?"

The woman looked at Jamie as though it were obvious. "Certainly! Some astringent, a large sterile gauze, and some adhesive plaster. She had a few scrapes on her palms—probably from bracing herself when she fell—but they were quite minor. She also bought some energy bars and a bottle of fruit juice. I guess she was going to continue with her hiking."

"She *said* that?"

"Well, no. But she had her rucksack with her and she was dressed for hiking. You know, shorts and cotton top and hiking boots. I just assumed that she would do, seeing as how she bought what a lot of hikers buy. Food, I mean."

Jamie nodded slowly, running his index finger across his chin. Mike will be glad to know he's not going insane. But what's this hide-and-seek game really mean? He considered his earlier question, that Karin had changed her accommodation plans purely as an economic measure, then tossed it out. If she had, why hadn't the bed-and-breakfasts in the area any record of her stay?

Taking Jamie's silence for concern, the clerk said, "I shouldn't be alarmed, sir. She suffered a cut knee. It wasn't life threatening."

As though not hearing, he said, "What time was she in here? Do you remember?" That would answer his question. If it was soon after McLaren delivered her to The Hanoverian's door, she could have continued her trek, perhaps stopping the night at Bamford or Nether Padley. But they were a good several hours' walk from Hathersage, never mind they were the village's closest neighbors. And if she were headed for another village, why not ask McLaren to drop her there? Unless she changed her mind after he left, having seen the hotel's price list. But what would it mean if she had left hours later...

The clerk smiled, as though giving assurance and proclaiming it was the easiest answer in the world. "That I do recollect. It was nearly five o'clock."

"You're certain?" McLaren said he'd dropped Karin at the hotel just after noon.

"Yes, sir. I remember because we close at five on Fridays. Pardon me." She checked out the woman with the cough syrup, paperback novel, shampoo, and box of facial tissues.

Jamie waited impatiently, arms folded across his chest, and read the weekly specials posted on the display board near the stack of carrier baskets.

The clerk thanked the woman for her patronage as Jamie turned back to her. The buzzer sounded once more, this time announcing the customer's departure. The clerk moved a stack of advertisements to the side of the counter, took a deep breath, and patted her graying hair into place. "Now, then. About your friend...I thought, when she came in, that she'd probably be the last sale of the day."

"Was she limping?"

"Pardon?"

"Like she had sprained her ankle. Or did she seem fit, other than her cut knee?" Jamie was afraid of the answer but needed to know Karin's physical state. McLaren had mentioned her injured ankle. If it had really been hurt, Karin wouldn't have hiked any farther that day. She should still be here in Hathersage.

"No, sir. At least, not that I recall. I think I should have noticed, though. And if the ankle had really bothered her, wouldn't she have bought an elastic bandage or small splint or something to bind her ankle? She bought the other items for her knee…"

Jamie agreed that made sense. Still, the entire episode seemed bizarre. "This was at five o'clock," he said woodenly, trying to understand the timing.

"This is important, isn't it?" The woman angled her head, studying Jamie's expression. He was frowning, but it was through puzzlement, not fear.

"Yes, it is." He took a deep breath, mentally flipped a coin, then said, "She's missing. I'm trying to find her."

"In that case…" She snapped her fingers and beckoned Jamie to follow her. "Just back here. Won't take us more than a few minutes. Oh, Chris…" She called to a young man who was stocking the shelf with plastic combs and hair-coloring dye. "Watch the register for a few minutes, will you? Ta. There's a dear."

"Where are we going?" he said as the woman walked to a small room that jutted out into the main floor area. One side of the room had a wall-to-wall window, the glass of which was dark. Probably one-way viewing, Jamie thought as the woman unlocked the door and flipped on the interior light.

"We may look eighteen hundreds on the outside," she said as Jamie entered the office, "but we're twenty-first century in here." She indicated the small console that held a wood-encased panel of buttons, small lights, and a toggle switch. Above the panel a half-dozen small TV monitors, each one displaying a different image, showed bright against the wall on which they were mounted. A telephone receiver was affixed to the wall, affording instant communication.

Jamie glanced at the monitors showing the store's aisles and customers, then eyed the screen revealing the pavement outside the front door. A man stopped to light a cigarette before crossing the road. A cyclist came into view then rapidly shot out of the frame as he pedaled down the street. "Impressive." Jamie shifted his eyes from the monitor to the clerk's face. "Have a lot of trouble with shoplifting?"

"Not now. I know many of the bigger stores, as well as most town centers, have a security guard monitoring the cameras. We do during the busy times. But when we don't, there's always the videotape for the court trial." Smiling, she patted the small countertop on which the control console sat. "It's paid for its cost many times over."

"I don't doubt it." Besides recording shoplifters in the act, these closed-circuit television cameras also were powerful tools as preventive surveillance such as at sports events and in locating missing persons. If Karin had passed enough of these CCTV cameras, he'd have a nice record of her journey.

The shop clerk pulled out Friday's tape recording and had slipped the cassette into a recorder. As she rewound it, she said, "Not only do I know your friend was in here at five o'clock, the date and time are displayed on the tape. Now, then." She stopped the tape and she and Jamie watched the next few minutes of footage in silence.

Karin's bright red hair was immediately identifiable as she entered the shop. The clerk was correct in her memory of Karin's purchases, but it was after she left the shop that Karin proved most interesting to Jamie. He leaned closer to the monitor. The clerk, sensing Jamie needed to see something, enlarged the image showing the exterior scene.

Karin stood outside the shop, to the right of the door, still in the CCTR camera's range. She lodged the bag of purchases under her left arm and withdrew her mobile phone from her rucksack. After punching in a number, she waited for several seconds, then talked into the phone. The call lasted only ten seconds or so before Karin rang off and slipped her phone back into her sack.

His eyes still on the tape recording, Jamie asked, "Is that it? Does she leave?"

"No. She was still there when I closed down. I don't know when she left, though. I lock up and leave by the back door." She nodded toward the screen but Jamie didn't notice, his attention on Karin.

Pedestrians and cars passed Karin, shadows on the pavement and on the storefronts across the street shifted positions slightly, and still she remained in front of the chemist's. Jamie was beginning to wonder if she had stood there all night when a car slowed, angled into the open space along the curb, and waited while Karin walked up to the passenger door. An indistinguishable form leaned across the front seat and opened the door. Karin dumped her rucksack and purchases from the chemist's into the back seat before getting into the car. Seconds later, the car drove off.

Jamie stood up, hardly believing what he'd seen. If Karin had a friend with a car, why hadn't the friend been summoned to drop her in Hathersage? And if McLaren had deposited her on the hotel's doorstep just after twelve o'clock, what had Karin been doing for four, five hours before this friend had arrived? Where was she now?

The clerk was taking the tape out of the recorder as Jamie turned and leaned against the counter. Shoving the cassette back into its box, she said, "Was that any help to you?"

Jamie assured her it was, thanked her, and left the store, more optimistic than he had been in hours. But what really made him whistle as he slid behind the wheel of his

car was that he had the mysterious car's make and model—
a gray Mercedes CLC coupe, with a registration number
that began YV59.

EIGHTEEN

LATE-AFTERNOON sunlight slanted through the western windows of McLaren's house when he finally regained consciousness. The kitchen floor was hard and cold, an alien bed for him, but he hadn't been aware of any surroundings other than the strange blackness that engulfed him and the cacophony of sirens and screeching car tires. He lay as he was, on his back, staring at the white ceiling, trying to understand why every one of his bones and muscles raged with pain. He carefully lifted his right arm and held it up so he could see it without moving his neck. It was fresh agony to move it, to hold it steady so that he could focus on it. His muscles screamed to be free of their burden, but he forced himself to keep it there. He shifted his head downward, bringing his chin closer to his chest so that he could better see this arm. He winced. His bare flesh and shirtsleeve were caked in smears of dried blood. Same with his left arm. He dropped his arm, lying still, his eyes closed, forcing himself to remember what had happened. He had returned home late Saturday night. He and Jamie had met at the pub, he had driven home, got out of his car...

A wave of pain coursed through his right arm and shoulder as he turned over, pressing his palm against the linoleum. His elbow buckled in his agony and his side hit the floor. He remained how he had fallen, amazed at the intensity of the pain, closing his eyes and losing track of time.

THE SHADOWS HAD BEGUN their slow creep into the kitchen when McLaren finally managed to sit up. He had grabbed onto a table leg and hauled himself upright. Now, sagging against the leg, he could see the wall clock: 7:17. In the evening? He turned his head, making sure the sun was not playing tricks. It hovered above the western line of horse chestnuts, poplars, and oaks claiming the crest of the hill. The top of the near stonewall glowed in the heavy golden light and already cast a purple shadow that sought the eastern rim of the field. No, McLaren conceded, the sun was not crazy. I am. What had happened to the morning? What day was it?

The annoying sound, faintly remembered from his nightmare, returned, jarring him fully awake. He glanced outside again, nearly expecting to see a police car parked outside on the patio. It wasn't until the third or fourth ring that he realized the sound was the ringing of his home phone.

He tried leaning forward and getting onto his knee in an attempt to stand, but surges of nausea engulfed him. He fell back to his sitting position and slumped to his stomach. The light rocked wildly between piercing brightness and smothering blackness as McLaren pulled himself toward the phone, bracing his elbows and knees against the floor and scooting ahead inches at a time. The worktop looked to be a mile above his head as he stopped at the counter's base; he knew he could never stand in time to answer the insistent ringing. He reached above his head, fumbled for the long, coiled cord, and pulled. The phone crashed to the floor. He righted the phone base and grabbed the receiver in a none too steady hand. "Hello? Yes?"

"So, you're finally home." Jamie's voice poured over the phone like a lifejacket flung to a drowning man.

McLaren nodded. His jaw, he discovered, hurt like hell and was difficult to move.

"You there?" Jamie asked, concern replacing his jest.

"Yeah. Barely."

"Why? Where've you been? I've been ringing all day. You been busy?"

"Not in the way you mean."

"You take a day off from the Marta Hughes case? What'd you do—spend the day with Dena or do some urgent stone-wall work?"

"I'd feel better if I had, but no. I've been right here, evidently."

"Evidently? What's the matter, Mike? Someone there? Can't you talk? Say something about the weather if some-one's there and you're in trouble."

"Now you sound like a bloody spy movie, Jamie."

"Well, at least you're all right."

"No, but I'll let that pass right now. You doing anything tonight?"

"Why? Want to meet at the pub again?"

"I'd rather you come here. Bring something for dinner, if you can. Chinese take-away or fish and chips. I've got stuff to drink." He winced at the thought of beer.

"Sure, Mike. Only, you sound strange. You ill? I still don't believe you're not being held hostage or something. Say some-thing about Dena if you need me to call the cops."

"Just bring the bloody food, if you would. Hurry up." He replaced the receiver on the phone, pushed it aside, then sat there for a moment, breathing deeply. His neck hurt like hell, hurt more than merely sleeping on it wrong would produce. Or straining the muscle when he'd tried getting up. The area throbbed and burned, a deep pain that came from the mus-cle. He got to his knees, then pulled himself to his feet and, holding onto furniture as though he were walking on a storm-tossed boat deck, stumbled into the bathroom.

He pulled off his shirt, torn and blood-streaked below the site of the throbbing flesh, and dropped it onto the floor. He flipped on the fluorescent light fixture and stared into the mirror above the sink. A patch of broken, red skin stared back. He winced as he leaned closer to the mirror. The edges of the wound were jagged, as though the skin had been jabbed and the weapon then twisted. It had bled profusely, McLaren thought, for not only was his shirt bloodstained but the wound was also a mass of dried blood and raw flesh. It wasn't as deep as a knife wound, but it was deep enough, situated at the side of his neck just behind the jugular blood vein.

He stood upright, exhaling slowly, his eyes still on the wound. God, if he'd been hit an inch more toward his throat... He closed his eyes, sickened by the thought of bleeding to death, of the narrow escape. Staring again into the mirror, he could easily and vividly see the lesser wounds to his arms and hands. Dried blood probably makes it look worse than it is, he told himself. Still, he'd evidently fought hard, judging by the numerous smaller cuts and scrapes covering his arms and hands, and the bruises that were changing colors from deep violet to green.

After washing and drying the wound, he pulled a bottle of astringent, a sterile gauze, and some adhesive plaster from the bathroom cabinet. He swore as the liquid touched his raw flesh but vigorously dabbed the wound with another dose. He then covered the wound with the gauze, sticking it to his neck with long strips of the adhesive. When he had finished with his neck, he washed his arms and hands, and rubbed more of the antiseptic over the cuts.

He shed the rest of his clothes in the bathroom, leaving them on the floor, and walked into his bedroom where he slowly dressed in shorts and an oversized tee shirt. Then he walked barefoot into the front room, switched on a table lamp, unlocked the front door, and eased down onto the couch.

While he waited for Jamie, he tried to remember the fight, tried to recall anything about his attacker. He sank back into the cushions, letting his head rest against the back of the

couch, and stared at the wall, seeing only the short walk from
his car to the kitchen door.

It had been dark, with no light coming from the house except the table lamp in the front room and a smaller lamp on
the kitchen table. But even the kitchen light had not illuminated his attacker, who must have hidden behind the large
shrub rose near the door. There was no other place. He'd
transplanted or uprooted the boxwoods and peonies shortly
after moving into the house, thinking he was one up on crime
prevention, eliminating favorite ambush spots. He had left
the rose because it had been a small bush. And because he
couldn't fathom any burglar willingly lurking behind such
a jumble of thorns.

Despite the pain of his jaw, McLaren smiled, thinking his
attacker was tending to his own scratched skin. He had to
have been marked. The rose had grown nearly to the roof's
gutters, a dense shrub leaving little space between it and the
house wall. Yes, the bastard had to have scratches on him.

But what had he used for a weapon?

McLaren closed his eyes, focusing his mind on the appearance of his wound. As a copper, he'd seen drunken fights
with broken beer bottles, seen the injuries those weapons had
inflicted. His wound looked like those.

His throat and stomach muscles tightened and he stared
at his shaky hands. What was happening? Was he imagining
all these beer-bottle episodes, or did they have a meaning?

The house was uncomfortably warm in the early evening,
having trapped the heat of the day. McLaren was too tired and
hurt too much to get up and open windows. So he lounged
on the couch, listening to the caw of the rooks in the oak tree
near his front door, and tried to think.

Beer had to be the link, the clue to his attacks and the
police stop and the theft of the bottles in his car. If it were
just bottle-related, any type of bottles would have been used.

Yet every one of these episodes included beer bottles. What was the significance?

The rooks took flight in a squawking, dark mass as McLaren thought through every confrontation, every fight he had ever had. Most of the episodes had been while he was in the job, and the majority of those had been drunken brawls in countless pubs. No one fight stood out from the hundreds he'd been involved in. Even then, he'd been included merely as an outsider, as a copper doing his job. He'd lectured no one; he'd taken no one's side. He didn't remember the parties' names or faces and he'd received no threats before or after seeing them into jail cells. No, these beer-bottle incidents were personal, as though he should know a name or recall a major incident.

His eyes strayed to a tiny photo on the wall. It hung between the bookcase and a large antique map of Derbyshire. It was a photo of Dena, encased in an oval wooden frame. Funny he hadn't seen it when he'd removed the other traces of his life before he left the job. Maybe the light from the table lamp brought it out of the shadowy recess. *I hardly ever sit here...* He muttered something beneath his breath as he stared at the oval shape. The photograph was too small to make out facial features at this distance but he knew her expression, knew the tint of her eyes and the way his camera had caught on the light on her cheek and the wind-blown hair. He cursed his forgetfulness from his house cleansing. When he felt better he would box it up with the rest of the remnants from that life. He had no desire to remember last spring.

Last spring. Last May. There was something else about that time. He struggled into a sitting position, his heart pounding in his chest. A name and scene flashed across his mind's eye. He slowly leaned forward, forearms on his thighs, breathing coming faster as the face of Charles Harvester danced before him. Charlie Harvester. The colleague who had tried to arrest McLaren's friend Nigel for attacking the burglar invading his pub. The burglar had lunged at Nigel with a broken beer bottle before Nigel fought back with a fireplace poker. Defended himself and his wife, McLaren remembered, the anger he thought he'd buried now filling his heart. Was the burglar out of prison? Was this some nasty taunt to tell McLaren he was free and had revenged himself? Some sick warning? Or had he enlisted the aid of one of his toe-rag mates to harass McLaren?

Or had someone overheard him and Jamie talking in the pub last night? Was Marta Hughes' killer telling him, not too subtly, to back off the case? But had beer anything to do with her murder? For, as McLaren reasoned again, sinking back against the couch cushions, a beer bottle had to mean something, had to be associated with his recent attacker or with someone he had wronged in the past.

Neither Linnet nor the cashier at the casino had mentioned that alcohol had been a concern the night of Marta's win. Had there been an altercation at the casino, possibly between a drunken roulette player and Marta, and this was the man's revenge for McLaren taking the case? But that suggested the casino customer knew McLaren was working on the case. And knew where McLaren lived.

He exhaled slowly, the back of his hand massaging his forehead. There were several possibilities, but which was the correct one? He got to his feet and, again using the furniture as handrails, lumbered into the kitchen. Standing at the end of the worktop, he stared at the fridge. How badly did he want a drink?

The ringing doorbell interrupted his mental debate. Yelling that the door was unlocked and for Jamie to come in, McLaren trudged back into the front room.

"Come and get it while it's hot." Jamie set the bags of fish and chips on a magazine lying on the coffee table. "No mushy peas. They were out of them. I know you won't mind. Hey, you here? You really should lock your door, Mike. Any hooligan could barge in. You could be— God! What the bloody hell happened to you?" He stared open-mouthed at McLaren as he inched up to the table.

"*Now* you give me advice about that hooligan. Some friend."

One of the bags of food fell onto its side but Jamie didn't notice. "You want a doctor? You okay? God, you look like hell. Those bruises... *What happened?*"

McLaren turned toward the kitchen. "You want a beer?"

"Sit down. I'll get it. You look like you shouldn't even be walking." He stayed until McLaren was seated in a straight-back chair, then darted into the kitchen. Minutes later, he returned with a tray loaded with plates, utensils, beer, and glasses. When he'd poured out the beer and handed the glass and a plate of fish and chips to McLaren, he sat on the couch. "Now." He swallowed a few chips, then said, "Let's have it. What the hell happened?"

McLaren rested the glass on his thigh. "You won't believe it. Even I can barely believe it."

"I won't know if I believe it or not until I hear it. Give."

"There's not much to tell, actually. It happened too fast."

"You sound like a ruddy victim in a police report."

"I feel like one."

"Fine. I sympathize. What happened?"

"When I left you at the pub and drove home I parked the car in my usual spot—"

"Where it is now?"

"Yeah. I got out, locked it, and walked up to the kitchen door. I don't recall being aware of anything unusual. I had no sixth sense that something wasn't right. I got my key out to unlock the door and that's it."

"What does that mean?"

"All I remember is walking up to the door and then waking up on the kitchen floor." He flexed his jaw. "I'm a mess, aren't I?"

"You must have unlocked the door before you were jumped," Jamie said, ignoring the question, "and crawled inside sometime later. I can't see your assailant graciously carrying you inside. From the looks of you, he wanted to kill you."

"Bloody nice thought. Thanks." He chewed on a chip as Jamie rambled on.

"You probably blacked out from the exertion of getting to the kitchen. When did you regain consciousness?"

"Not long ago. When you rang."

"What time? I've called a few times today. Wanted to astound you with my sleuthing."

"I don't know what time. Yeah, I do. Seven something. The last time you called. When I asked you to come over with dinner."

"Little after seven, then. So you were out nearly twenty-four hours. God, I'd hate to see the bloke you tangled with."

"I probably got the worst of it. He wasn't lying on the ground outside, was he?"

"I came in the front door."

"Right."

"I'll ease our minds." Jamie jogged to the back door, opened it, looked around, then closed it, and returned to the front room. "No one outside."

"I didn't think so, but thanks for checking."

They sat, eating their dinner, each trying to make sense of McLaren's attack. As McLaren took a swallow of beer, Jamie said, "Do you know what he hit you with? Had to have been more than his fists. You're cut." He nodded at McLaren's arms.

"I've my theory, but give me your opinion—*if* you've the stomach for it. Or perhaps it's bad timing." His fingers went up to his bandaging as he waited for Jamie's answer.

Jamie put his plate and glass on the table and came over to McLaren as he pulled off the gauze. Angling his head slightly to get a better look at the wound, Jamie said, "Beer bottle. Or something round and that size. But I'd say beer bottle. Nice jagged rim to gouge you with." He sat back down and picked up the beer glass. "Do we agree?"

"Yeah, but there's no prize for guessing correctly."

"Don't need one, Mike. Just having you still in the Land of the Living is my prize."

McLaren avoided his friend's eyes, suddenly embarrassed. He flashed Jamie a quick smile before relaying his theory.

"Do you know if Tyrone Wade Antony is still in the nick?" Jamie asked on hearing McLaren's idea of the pub burglar.

"Haven't had time to check. This only occurred to me a half hour or so ago."

"I can find out. Did you look outside to see if this yobo left anything? You know," he added as McLaren frowned. "Torn off button, house key, wallet, blood spotting."

"My blood's probably the only thing out there, but have a look if you want to play detective. I'm not up to crawling around. Especially not in the rose bush. I think that's where he hid."

"Right. Just give me half a tick." He jogged into the kitchen, grabbed the torch that was plugged into an electrical socket, and trotted outside.

McLaren had finished his fish and was downing the last of his beer when the kitchen door banged shut. A few stamps on the floor told him Jamie was knocking bits of grass, rose leaves, and twigs off his shoes. There was a dull click as he evidently plugged the torch back into the outlet, and a metallic clatter as his latchkey fell onto the tabletop.

"Bloody rose," Jamie said, dabbing his fingertip on his tongue and then applying his saliva to the scratches on his arm. "I should send you the bill for a new shirt."

"Find anything?"

"Besides finding out how low my tolerance of pain is? Sorry, old man. Neither hide nor hair."

"I'd have liked you to find something a bit more concrete, like a driving license, but I'll pretend I'm content."

"Written documents are rather nice, aren't they? Now what's the matter? What did I say?"

McLaren snapped his fingers and held up his hand. "God, what a complete berk I am. I forgot about the notebook."

"What *are* you on about?"

"Yesterday when I was poking around the site where they found Marta's body, I found a notebook. It was at this little picnic area, near that rundown barn."

"Yeah, I know the spot."

"I grabbed it, intending to leaf through it to see if it had any bearing on her case, and I forgot about it. You don't think *that's* what my attacker was after?" He looked as though he would be sick.

"Could be, I suppose, but that would imply that he was there and saw you take it, Mike. You didn't see anyone there, did you? Any happy picnickers or birders tramping through the wood?"

"No. I'd swear I was the only one there, and I'd been inside the barn and across the road at that clearing." He caught his breath as he envisioned the scene. "He could have been *in* the wood."

"Like several yards in, so he was hidden yet could see you in the clearing?"

"Yeah."

"How far is that clearing from where you found the notebook?"

McLaren stared at the ceiling, trying to estimate the distance. "Probably too far away. Maybe several hundred yards."

"Did you have the notebook in your hand when you placed it in your car, or had you stuck it in your trousers pocket?"

"Uh, I had it in my pocket."

"You don't sound like you could swear to that in court."

"Yeah, I put it in my pocket. I saw it on the ground, picked it up, pocketed it, and did a fingertip search of the area. I took it out and laid it on the car seat when I got back into the car after looking at the tree-trunk site."

"So the notebook should be in your car now."

"Would you mind?"

"Why not? The night's young. Be right back." He left the room, grabbed the torch and door key, and ran out to McLaren's car. Seconds later he had locked up and strode into the front room. "This what you're worried about?" He dangled the small notebook in front of McLaren's eyes before dropping it on his lap.

"At least I didn't dream that." He flipped open the cover. "Thanks." He scanned through the pages but soon gave up. He closed the book and tossed it onto the coffee table.

"No good?"

"Somebody's nature journal."

"Waxing lyrical over fungi and bird's eggs and first crocus of the spring, no doubt."

"It could have been something. Ow! Damn." He grabbed his upper arm and pressed his fingertips into his aching flesh.

Jamie picked up his beer and relocated to the couch. "You know, Mike, when you first took on this case, I didn't give it much thought. I mean, it seemed straight forward enough. But now…"

"I've tried to figure out what Marta's case has to do with beer, but unless there's something in her past that I don't know, I can't see it."

"You know what I think?" Jamie said, sitting forward. "I think it's connected to your disappearing friend, Karin Pedersen. Didn't this all start with the beer bottle in your car, when the cop stopped you?"

McLaren nodded and picked up his glass. He held it up to the light, as though he were going to salute someone with it. "I didn't know the bottle was there until the officer found it."

"All that was minutes after you left Karin at the hotel."

"Quarter hour, maybe. I don't know precisely. I just know I was startled to see the cop pulling me over."

"You know, whoever made the call to the police—the one of you driving drunk—had to know your car."

McLaren's fingers encircled his glass, holding on for dear life.

"He had to know the make and the model for the cop to find you."

"You're saying it's Karin?"

"Not necessarily. I don't know how or if she's mixed up in any of this. But she had a good look at your car when you stopped to give her a lift. She could have phoned from any shop in Hathersage. Or on her mobile. Could be someone else, too. Someone who knows you."

"Like Dena?"

Jamie shrugged, reluctant to confirm McLaren's suspicion with words.

"That's daft!" He set the glass on the beer mat. "Why would she phone in a false report? How would she know I was in Hathersage?"

"You don't know, Mike. She could have been following you."

McLaren rolled his fingers into a fist and slammed it against the arm's chair. "Watch your mouth! Why the hell would she do that?"

"I don't know. I'm just saying that *someone* who knows you, who knows your car, rang up the local cop shop and reported your erratic driving. You don't have any suspicions?"

McLaren shook his head and slowly straightened his fingers. "It's absurd! This whole thing. It all started with Karin Pedersen and that damned beer bottle the cop found in my car."

"I don't suppose *he* could have planted it, could he?"

NINETEEN

McLaren's face drained of color as he stared at his friend. "*Planted* it?"

"Don't tell me you've never heard of a bad copper, Mike. There are always pay offs if you look for them, rewards for doing a favor for someone. Drugs seized during a raid, money from some bloke wanting to avoid jail time, money or gifts for your blind eye. You know what goes on."

"Sure, but I've never been a party to any of it."

"I didn't say you were. I just suggested this copper might be. You've also heard stories of evidence planted by the police to get a conviction. Maybe somebody has it in for you and paid this copper to slip the bottle into your car. Did he seem suspicious?"

"No. And I don't think he could have had it secreted on his person." McLaren reached for his glass, then saw it was empty and sank back into his chair again. "Besides, I was watching him. He didn't get that close to the passenger seat to slip it in without me seeing him. A pack of weed, sure. He could have palmed it. But a beer bottle? They're rather large and cumbersome. You ever try slipping one out of your jacket in a hurry?"

"So we're back to your wounded hiker. You're sure you don't know her?"

"I wouldn't swear to it in court but no, I don't think so. You're saying someone paid her to incriminate me?"

"Or she did it on her own. Maybe you jailed her brother or boyfriend. I don't know. Just watch out, Mike."

"I always do." But last night's attack proved that diligence didn't always work.

"Well, try harder. You're scaring me to death."

"*You're* scared? *I* was the one beaten." But he knew what Jamie meant, and he *was* scared. Scared of the unknown assailant and scared of the door that seemed to be opening before him, beckoning him to walk into the past.

"Not for long, though." Jamie opened another beer and poured it into his glass. He took a sip before adding, "Not beaten in this case."

"Why? What are you on about?"

"I spent the better part of the day nosing about in Hathersage, much to your relief."

"Relief? You must have learned something."

"Not as monumental as Copernicus' discovery—"

"I'll tell you where it ranks."

"—but you will be impressed." Jamie related what he had learned that morning, including the CCTV video surveillance. He ended, "This matches the description of the car that ran you off the road. We still have only a partial on the car registration number. The plate was partially out of camera range."

"This is outstanding, Jamie!" McLaren leaned forward, beaming. The darkness seemed to be receding. "We've got a car make and model, its color…"

"Only a partial plate number. And I'm afraid I can't follow that up and find out whose it is. It would mean my job if I was caught out."

"Sure. I wouldn't ask you to. Of course it's too dangerous." He paused as he caught Jamie's eye. They both recalled a similar event when a police officer had looked up a number on his off-duty time, only to be found out and fired. McLaren got to his feet. "You got more of the number than I did. Excellent! I can keep my eye out for the vehicle when

I talk to the main players in this case. I'll be careful. Don't worry about me, Jamie."

"I'm more than worried about you right now." He stood up. "What do you want? Can I get it? Your bruises are deepening in color. Are you sure you don't want to see a doctor? Need something attended to, stitched up?"

"I'm fine. Just a bit stiff and sore. No, I don't want anything in particular. Just couldn't sit anymore." He stretched slowly, testing his back and arm muscles. "I feel a bit better, so why do I still feel bad about this case?"

"Yeah, well, you still look unsteady on your legs. Sit down before you fall down."

McLaren snapped his fingers, and he turned toward Jamie, the moment of triumph gone from his eyes. "Fall down. That's it!"

"I told you to sit—"

"No! That's not what I mean. This whole thing is tied to my downfall. Somebody wants my undoing. Either physically," he said, massaging his bruised jaw, "or career."

"But you're not in the job any longer. That doesn't make sense."

"So it's my death, then." The words were barely above a whisper as the realization sank in.

"Maybe not your death. That's awful drastic. A lesson learned, perhaps."

"Which points to someone just released from prison."

"Unless Dena's just getting around to giving you her opinion about your broken engagement."

McLaren snorted and sat down. "Wouldn't take her a year to do that. Besides, a man attacked me. I can tell the difference, even in the dark."

"So she hired someone."

"You have no career as a comedian. This isn't funny."

"Because you still have feelings for her or because you respect women in general?"

"Just drop it, Jamie. I'm in no mood for this. My body hurts."

Jamie downed a mouthful of beer, cradled the glass in his hands, and said, "Have you given any thought to your other body, Marta Hughes?"

"In what aspect?"

"The recovery site. Why there? She didn't live in Elton. Did she know someone there?"

"That's been nagging me, too. I aim to find out before too much longer."

AFTER BREAKFAST the following day, McLaren searched for some clue to his attacker. It wasn't that he had no confidence in Jamie's exploration, but a night hunt via torch wasn't McLaren's idea of thorough. After all, most crime scenes were sealed off and reconnoitered by daylight. There was no reason he couldn't do the same. So, with the sunlight slanting through the trees, he carefully poked among the bushes, perennials, and grass. He found it some yards away from the kitchen door, as though the wind had played with it before tiring of the game and dropped it or it had slipped unnoticed from a pocket. A scrap of paper, barely larger than his index finger. Ordinarily, he would have wadded it up and dumped it into the rubbish bin, but he turned it over and glanced at it. In bold, jagged script, his house address sprawled across the paper. He set it on his kitchen table before driving back to Elton.

Elton's residents gave McLaren no new leads that Monday morning even though he asked at the pub, the bed-and-breakfast, and the vicarage. No one recognized Marta's photo when he showed it, other than from last year's splash across the newspapers. So the killer with Marta dead or alive in his car had deliberately headed here. But why? Because he knew the area and felt safe here?

Which would signify that Marta's killer had either lived in or been employed in Elton.

When asked again about family, friends, and coworkers, Alan and Chad Hughes still could not explain why Marta had been at Elton. They had no family there, nor did Marta have friends in the area. "Though," Alan suggested somewhat as an afterthought, "one of her colleagues from the Ark may live there. I really don't know. I never met them. I just knew their names."

"And they are... Would you mind giving them to me?" he said, flipping open his notebook. "I can ask them."

"It's been a while, of course. Let me think." He leaned his head against the chair back and stared at something above McLaren's head. A police siren screamed several streets away, underscoring the faint tick of the clock on the mantle. Alan nodded, evidently content with his mental list. "Right. Verity Dwyer, the coworker Marta knew best. She...she's in jail, I think. Over that trouble with the funds."

"Not in jail," McLaren corrected. "Doing community service."

"I knew it was some sort of sentence. Anyway, Verity was her closest friend at the shelter. Then there's Emlyn Gregg. He's the vet. At least, I suppose he's still there. I believe there's another assistant or two, but I don't know their names. Marta hardly worked with them. I heard only snippets about them. And of course the boss, Derek Fraser. Have I forgotten anyone, Chad?" He turned to his son, who was sitting in the chair next to him.

"That's the lot," Chad said flatly.

"I'll see if some of them live in Elton," McLaren said, standing up. "Verity lives in Youlgreave, but that's close enough for my purpose."

"Personally, I think you're on the wrong track, Mr. McLaren."

"Oh, yes? In what way?"

"I still think Tom or Rick Millington was involved in Mum's death."

"Because Tom Millington's advances were refused?"

"Yeah. Rick might've been bent on revenge for when Mum told the cops about him and Danny smoking weed."

"The Millingtons would be that angry to kill your mother?"

"Well, maybe not deliberately kill her. But stuff happens. You know…slang-matches turn into anger. And that can turn into murder."

"And you think either Tom or Rick got into an argument and perhaps went home and got a gun and shot her."

"Yeah. Something like that. They got scared and—" He swallowed, the words hard to say.

"And hid her body," McLaren finished.

Chad nodded. "It's not so daft, is it? I've heard of stuff like that happening. People panic."

"Well, motive's a bit weak, in my opinion, but deaths have happened from arguments that got out of control. I'll look into it."

"It's not that weak, Mr. McLaren."

McLaren paused in the open doorway and let Chad continue.

"Not if you know those two. They're bullies, both of them. Rick might not be too bad if it weren't for his mate Danny Mercer. Danny's two years older than Rick and I think there's a sort of older-and-wiser aura that Rick applies to Danny."

"Danny influences Rick, does he?"

"I don't know how much and I don't know in what ways, other than the marijuana. Danny got Rick involved with it."

"A shame, really," Alan said. "Rick was a nice, polite child before he took up with Danny."

"He's got money," Chad added. "Danny, I mean. He has to have or else he couldn't buy drugs, could he?"

"Does he have an after-school job, or does he get an allowance from his parents?"

"Just his mum. His dad left years ago after the divorce. He still lives at home. Well, being seventeen, he would. Last I knew he worked at the greengrocer's on Vantage Way. He'd have the money, then, if he lives at home."

"Do Danny or Rick hang out in the old barn outside of Elton?" The mental images of cigarette ends, empty beer bottles, discarded fast-food wrappers, and the half-burnt candle shone in his mind.

"I don't know," Chad said slowly. "I don't think so. Do you know, Dad?"

Alan shook his head and exhaled loudly. "Because Marta's body was there, you mean?"

McLaren nodded. When neither Alan nor Chad said anything more, McLaren said, "Well, I'll check into this. I appreciate your help."

"Uh, McLaren…" Alan followed McLaren outside and paused on the front walk. "I know Chad wants to help, but I wouldn't put much weight on what he said about Danny Mercer. We've had minor run-ins with him, but nothing major. Nothing that warrants him and my wife getting into an argument."

"I'll still talk to Danny, but thanks."

"I know for a fact that he worked during and after Marta's murder. I've seen him at the greengrocer's. So I don't know what that proves or what Chad was trying to imply."

"Perhaps I can determine that. I'm sorry to make you late for work."

"Quite all right. I'm not that important."

"Well, thanks again." He nodded to Alan and walked over to the Millingtons' house.

Danny Mercer was ringing the front door bell as McLaren came up the front walk. He turned on hearing McLaren's approach and seemed startled, slightly fearful on seeing such a tall, muscular man appear seemingly from nowhere. Danny pressed his lips together, trying to appear nonchalant, and said that the family didn't appear to be at home.

"Could be at work," McLaren suggested.

Danny snorted and rolled his eyes.

"Actually," McLaren said, standing with his feet slightly apart, "I wanted to speak to you, if you have a minute."

"Oh, yeah? Why? Who are you?" His voice had risen slightly, betraying his agitation, but his eyes darted back and forth, trying to discern McLaren's character and reason for apparently hunting him down.

"Mike McLaren, but I doubt my name means anything to you. I'm investigating Marta Hughes' death of last June. You knew Marta, I'm told."

"Yeah? Who told you?"

"Does it make any difference?"

"Yeah. You a copper?" His eyes narrowed, betraying his suspicions and his history with law enforcement.

"No, I'm not." McLaren reasoned that it wasn't a lie, though he could have added information to his statement. But Danny didn't seem the type to snuggle up to anyone in that profession, no matter how flimsy the prior association.

"You're just trying to help Chad and his dad, then."

"Yes."

"You must have some experience in this sort of thing, then."

"What do you mean?"

"Sniffing about, asking questions. You know."

"I'm not a cop."

"You said that."

"Do you want to help the family or not?"

"What do you want to know?"

"Your opinion. Chad Hughes says you're around here a lot, seeing Rick Millington."

"What of it?"

"I just wondered if you had seen anything or anyone the night of Mrs. Hughes' death."

"*Seen* anything? Like what? The bloke sneaking into her house?"

"That would be helpful," McLaren said, smiling. "I thought that since you're here so much you might have heard something. Like someone going by on the street."

"I'm just pals with Rick. I don't know what goes on around here. Ask a neighbor."

"I will. But I was hoping you might also have something to tell me."

Danny sat on the front step, declaring his position as family friend. He glared at McLaren, who still remained a few feet from him. "That sounds like you want a confession."

"You guilty of anything? Besides your drug use?" Danny started to get to his feet but McLaren pushed him back down. "I'm stating a fact, Danny, not slandering you. You've got a police record."

"So I made a mistake. That was last year. I'm clean now."

"Really? I hope so. Back then, last June just before Mrs. Hughes died, I heard you might have been angry with her over her reporting you to the police."

Danny colored but pressed his lips together.

"So angry that you might have approached her, argued with her. And that argument might have got out of hand."

"You're barmy! Over a little bit of weed? I wouldn't get mixed up in a murder. Go harass someone else." He paused, his gaze on McLaren's bruised face, then grinned as he thought of a quip. "Looks like you tried to already, but didn't succeed."

Ignoring him, McLaren said, "So what about that? Did you get into a fight with Marta Hughes, maybe get so mad at her that you went back later and shot her?"

"Leave me alone! I'll call the cops if you don't leave me alone." He pulled his mobile from his jeans pocket. "I didn't do anything to her. I got enough trouble with the coppers from the marijuana last year and from my mum. Now, get out of here."

"If you do hear anything and want to talk, let Chad know. He can get in touch with me. Thanks for your help." McLaren walked back to his car, aware that Danny was watching his every step.

THE NEXT STOP ON McLaren's itinerary was Noah's Ark. Hopefully Emlyn Gregg, the vet, would be working this morning.

Chesterfield was bustling with Monday morning traffic. He had to wait nearly a quarter of an hour for a car accident to be cleared from a road, but he breezed the rest of the way to the animal shelter. There were no other cars in the front car park, so he parked near the front door. Anything to save a bit of pain, he thought as he carefully got out of his car.

The bell at the front door announced his visit and set off a cacophony of barking from the back pen area. The young woman at the front desk looked up from the computer monitor but McLaren pointed to the man near the front window and the woman went back to her typing. The man McLaren assumed to be the boss, Derek Fraser, was arranging a display of pamphlets and a stand-up sign of a book. He affirmed that he was Derek Fraser and stopped to talk to McLaren, saying it was time the police found Marta Hughes' killer.

McLaren agreed but refrained from pointing out that if anyone found the killer it would be he, not the police, and instead asked if Derek had any idea why Marta would be in Elton on the night of her death. "Sometimes you overhear a

casual remark," he said, tacitly giving the man permission
to gossip. "If she was going to meet a friend near there…or
if she had a family member living there, that would explain
it." He smiled encouragingly and picked up a pamphlet.

"'Fraid not. I'm rarely here, and when I am…" He
shrugged, signifying he wasn't included in his employees'
social affairs.

"So you don't know why Marta would be in Elton. You
don't know if she knew anyone in the area, or if she met any
of your staff there for some reason. Girls' night out at the
pub…"

"No. Of course, I'd like to help." Derek leaned against the
edge of the counter. He was a short man, which forced him
to look up to meet McLaren's gaze. He appeared to be in his
early fifties, a graying brunet with large brown eyes that
blinked at McLaren from behind tortoise-shell spectacles.
The pamphlet he was holding sagged between his fingers as
he thought back to last year. "Of course, the whole thing was
a tragedy. Not just Marta's terrible death."

"What else happened?"

"Why, the scandal with Verity Dwyer," he said, as though
McLaren should know about it. "It was dreadful. When the
money went missing, I had no alternative but to let her go. I
hated to do it, but my hands were tied. The Board, you know."
He grimaced and looked slightly green, as though reliving the
event or hearing the board members' angry voices.

"Since the money disappeared during her shift, yes. It
must have been difficult to do, letting her go."

"And there was all the money from the back room," he
added, trying to cement his decision. "She was such an outstanding employee. Never a hint of previous trouble. But
this was rather serious. I felt rather bad about it all, about
having to terminate her position." He laid the pamphlet on
the counter. "I still keep in touch with her, you know. Still

ring her up occasionally, see how she's doing, if she wants anything."

Besides her job back. McLaren picked up the pamphlet Derek had just put down. It was a tri-panel brochure, full color, on slick paper. The shelter's logo shone predominantly on the cover. "Nice job," McLaren said, meaning it. He read a sentence aloud, admiring the wording. "'Shelter from Life's storms comes in many forms. Noah's Ark. Here for you when it floods.' Nice."

Derek beamed. "Yes, isn't it? What's nicer is that we didn't have to pay for it. Not the graphic layout or the copywriting."

"Really?" McLaren opened up the brochure and glanced at it before refolding it. "One of your staff do it, then? This looks professional quality."

"No one here could do that. We're quite lucky in that a friend of the shelter is a writer."

"A friend…like a volunteer?"

"No, he doesn't put in any hours here. But he helps out like this. He's a friend of Linnet Isherwood. Do you know Linnet? Perhaps you might, since you're working on Marta's case. Linnet and Marta were friends."

"Yes, I know Ms. Isherwood. Nice that she has a friend who can write."

"Yes, indeed. It's saved us a lot of money, which, I don't mind admitting, pleases the Board."

"I can imagine. You've saved the cost of hiring an ad agency and a copywriter. I don't know what that would run to, but I'm sure it is substantial."

"With a non-profit organization such as our animal shelter, such free services that Mr. FitzSimmons contributes are most sincerely welcomed. And don't go unrewarded," he added quickly. "We are not a greedy lot. We show our gratitude at the annual banquet that honors our volunteers and staff. And," he said, smiling broadly and picking up the brochure, "in Mr.

FitzSimmons' particular case, we're showing our appreciation in a more practical way than a plaque or certificate."

"Oh, yes? In what way?"

Derek scooted the cardboard-backed sign toward McLaren and waited for him to read it. The sign was made of the same glossy white paper as the pamphlet but a large graphic of a book cover occupied half of the paper. A date, name, and small book blurb constituted the rest of the space.

"A Dog's Calling." McLaren read the title aloud. "'Sean FitzSimmons not only captures the heart of the working dog trained to help in tragic situations but also does it with love and great understanding.' Sounds like an interesting book," he added, angling the sign squarely on the countertop. "This is the writer, I take it, who wrote your new pamphlet."

"The very one. Quite a remarkable chap. Quite talented. As you can see, we're holding a book signing this coming weekend for his new book. I believe it came out this past week."

"How nice of you."

"It's just a little thank you for the time and talent he's given us. I expect he'll sell a lot of books. Such an interesting subject, these specially trained dogs."

"Specially trained…like dogs who sniff out bombs?"

Derek laughed, shaking his head. "I don't believe Sean has had experience in that field. Of course, I'm not sure, but this book seems to be about dogs that help disabled people. Fetching things and opening doors and waking up the owner if their medical problem worsens. You know. Dogs can detect changes in breathing, I'm told."

"It does sound a fascinating subject."

"Yes. I'm looking forward to the signing. It's too bad Verity can't come."

"She fond of dogs, then?"

"Oh, yes! But she's especially interested in the subject.

She always said she'd like to have a business where she and her dog would help in disaster or emergency aid. You know, like going to earthquake zones and finding people trapped beneath the rubble, or working with dogs that could detect cadavers. I think she reads every book or watches every television program on that subject."

"So she can't come to the signing? That's a shame."

"Yes, it is." Derek lifted his glasses and rubbed the bridge of his nose. "Of course, if it were up to me, I'd have her here in a heartbeat."

"But the Board wouldn't like it," McLaren guessed.

"No." He sighed and replaced his glasses. "They are immovable as far as that topic is concerned. I've asked. They said 'no' most emphatically."

"Perhaps you can give an autographed book to Verity. Not quite the same, I know, but if she likes the subject..."

"Yes, yes. That will have to do. It's nearly like being here, I suppose. Still, it's not the same."

"She'll appreciate your thoughtfulness, I know."

"I don't know about that, but it will ease some guilt of mine. Perhaps she won't be noticed in the crush of people." He looked at McLaren, wanting his opinion, then quickly killed the idea. "It might do more harm than good if she were spotted. You never know about these parties. We've got a caterer coming in, so it should be a nice event. Of course, I've left most of the arrangements to my staff. I'm rather hopeless at this sort of thing."

"The author no doubt will be very happy with whatever arrangements you make."

"I suppose so." Derek sighed and screwed up the corner of his mouth. "They're not temperamental, are they? I mean, not like operatic singers or rock musicians?"

"Doesn't that depend on the individual person?"

"Could do, I guess. It's just that I'd never known a writer

before I met Sean. He doesn't look like I imagined a writer to look. You know," he said when McLaren frowned, "the preconceived notion that an author is all tweed suit and pipe smoker."

"Sounds rather nineteen forties."

"I suppose it does. Sean is rather unconventional anyway, so I don't know why I expected that attire when I found out he could write. He practically lives in a leather WWII bombardier's jacket and jeans."

"A bombardier's jacket?"

"At least that's what he wears in his publicity photo." He walked around behind the counter, pulled out a book, and handed it to McLaren. "Know him?"

McLaren shook his head, oddly relieved that he didn't know Sean FitzSimmons. He stared at the brown eyes looking seriously from the back of the book-jacket photo, feeling his body tense up. The pub burglar who had threatened McLaren's elderly friend and caused the altercation with Charlie Harvester had worn a leather bombardier's jacket. For one second, he thought…

"Nice photo, isn't it?" Derek went on. "I suppose he went to a professional to have it done."

"There are a lot around," McLaren said, his eyes on the jacket as he handed the book back to Derek.

"Will you be at the signing this weekend?"

"I'm not sure, but thank you for the invitation." He left with an idea taking shape in his mind.

TWENTY

McLaren didn't leave the animal shelter immediately. He sat in his car and phoned Jamie to find out about Danny's and Sean FitzSimmons' police records. As he put it to Jamie, "I know he's not the scum who attacked Nigel, but he still made the hairs on the back of my neck stand up. I can't place where I've seen him, but find out about him and ring me back."

After a quick lunch grabbed at a Chinese take-away, McLaren drove back to Elton. Killers usually dumped bodies at spots they knew, where they felt they wouldn't be seen. They knew the area, wanting a quick-in-quick-out location.

According to Neal and Alan, Marta had grown up in town, had worked during the summer in town. Had Marta's killer lived here as a child? Had he worked here, as an adult or after school?

Nothing seems different, McLaren thought as he wandered into the barn. Early-afternoon sunlight angled through the gaping windows and the hole in the roof, underscoring the forgotten, dusty farm implements and the discarded tin cans from recent trespassers' meals. He made the rounds of the barn, ground, and loft, but could find nothing new from his original search. Though what he was expecting to find, he couldn't have said. Still, he felt the pull of the place, as though something whispered beneath the straw or behind the shed door. He walked outside, inexplicably glad to be free of the darkness and the closeting walls, and made for the make-shift campfire ring.

Nothing presented itself in the fire ashes. He had picked up a castoff branch and poked through the black residue. Nothing hid beneath the large stones placed in a circle forming the pit. Other than the piece of crumpled aluminum foil left from cooking, there was nothing. He picked up the foil and flattened it out. Parts were blackened from the fire, but sunlight glanced off the clean, silvery sections. Shiny. Like the little charm he had found here.

He pulled the charm from his pocket. The charm caught the light and it threw back, brighter and mesmerizing. Was it just some lost trinket from a girl's bracelet after all? Alan Hughes had been adamant that Marta had never owned such a charm.

He shoved it back into his pocket as he walked back to his car.

SHOPPERS CROWDED the bookstore in Bakewell that afternoon, but McLaren made his purchase without much wait. A large, colorful poster on the wall above the cash register proclaimed Sean FitzSimmons' forthcoming book signing, but McLaren bought the book anyway and was soon seated in his car at the car park along the river. The sun beat down on him and he leaned against the car seat, letting his aching body soak in the warmth. The throbbing in his shoulder had lessened slightly and he closed his eyes, taking in long, deep breaths of new-mown grass, the river, and the wet shore. His left hand lay in his lap but he slowly flexed the fingers of his right hand. They were still stiff, having delivered the majority of his blows. The knuckles and back of his hand still held the small cuts and scrapes from the fight, but the swelling had resided. Soon the bruises on his face would fade and the scar on his neck would be the only lingering physical reminder of the attack.

A child ran past his car and McLaren opened his eyes. The parents hurried after her, calling her name as they reached her. McLaren sat up, rubbed his eyes, and picked up the book.

Its jacket was identical to the display graphic in Noah's Ark, showing a golden Labrador dog with a mobile phone in its mouth. Skipping the glowing endorsements on the cover, McLaren opened the book and slowly leafed through the front matter. Publisher, publication date, ISBN were duly noted without sending up flares. He turned over the page.

The dedication seemed to leap from the paper and grab his throat. He re-read the words before their implication sank in. "To my Songbird, my love and support. It's downhill from now on." Downhill. The skier charm from the area outside the barn. And songbird. There were dozens of songbirds—larks, thrushes, warblers, pipits, chats. And a dozen variety of finches. He stared at the dedication again, his palm suddenly clammy. Finches. The linnet was a finch.

He stared out of the open car window, across the River Wye, his mind superimposing the silver skier charm over Linnet Isherwood's figure. Was she the songbird and skier? Was the charm hers? If so, why was it at the site where Marta's body had been found?

Turning back to the first page of the book, McLaren read the list of Other Works by Sean FitzSimmons. Though this current book was the only nonfiction work listed, Sean had been busy producing other books. Novels, evidently. A series of thrillers, judging from the titles. Slowly closing the book, McLaren silently cursed himself. Linnet had mentioned that she had an author friend; he had even spoken to the man on his mobile when he'd met Linnet at Castleton... He hurled the book at the passenger door and sank against the seat back.

What had he got into? What did it all mean?

A group of ducks quacked noisily near the stone bridge as they fought for the bit of bread and dandelion leaves thrown down to them. Bits of bread. Pieces of the whole. Is that what he had now, pieces of the murder case?

His copper's sixth sense nagged him until he retrieved

the book from where it lodged between the door's interior and the side of the seat. Propping the book against the windscreen, he maneuvered it so the sunlight fell on it, pulled his mobile phone from his pocket, and snapped a photo of the book-jacket back. A minute later, he emailed some questions and the photo of Sean Fitzsimmons' smiling face to Jamie.

On the drive back home, Sean's charming grin seemed to dance ahead of McLaren on the road. Both the animal shelter's flyer and the bookstore's poster had touted the man's current book. McLaren slammed the heel of his palm into the steering wheel. He was an idiot—no better than a probationary copper, losing his edge—taking the phrase to mean another *nonfiction* book. He hadn't remembered the novelist, Sean FitzSimmons.

THE TEA THINGS WERE washed and drying in the dish drainer when Jamie phoned that evening. McLaren glanced at the caller ID display, not in the mood to talk to his sister, and was relieved to see Jamie's phone number. He answered with a hopeful "I'm all ears, lad" and grabbed a pen and a pad of paper before sinking back against the sofa cushions.

"You didn't mention payment in that little email you sent," Jamie said.

"Same as usual. Unless it's the knock-your-socks-off variety of information you're about to give me."

"Don't know about that, but I'm looking forward to the beer."

"You found out something, then."

"Don't I always?"

"You're a bloomin' marvel. Now, what is it?"

"In answer to your questions, in no particular order, number one: Danny Mercer has no further convictions for drug possession, distribution, or use."

"So he wasn't lying when he told me he was clean."

"Refreshing to have someone tell the truth for once. Number two: your prince-charming author, Sean FitzSimmons, has previous convictions for burglary."

"Hell."

"Ditto. He served his time in and was released from HM Prison Wealstun in West Yorkshire—"

He opened his mouth to respond but stopped short. Wealstun. Verity Dwyer's brother was currently in Wealstun. Was it important? He shoved aside the question for the moment and said, "Right. Wealstun. Category C prisoner—"

"Then to HM Prison Sudbury."

"God, what a joke Release On Temporary License is, doing community work—"

"Do you want to hear this or just make editorial comments?"

"Go on." He exhaled loudly.

"FitzSimmons was not without female company this whole time."

"Hell."

"You said that. He had visits from Linnet Isherwood—"

"Damn."

"—who brought him all sorts of lovely things a month before his release. So he'd feel right at home when he sniffed the fresh air of Freedom."

"Goodies such as…"

"A leather jacket."

"Many people wear leather jackets, Jamie. I've got one. You've got one."

"Bombardier style? Shades of World War Two?"

"I know that's what buddy Sean's wearing on that book-jacket photo that I emailed you, but—"

"It's a dead ringer for the jacket the lovely Linnet brought him in his last throes of prison life."

"How do you know?"

"I found out from one of the guards there. I rang him up when I got your questions and the photo. Of course, I can't swear it's the same jacket, but it's a hell of a coincidence, isn't it?"

"I'd hate to take odds. Did you find anything on the other question?"

"The one about Tyrone Wade Antony's restful stay compliments of Her Majesty's prison service?"

"Yeah." McLaren grimaced on hearing the name of the pub burglar and forced Charlie Harvester's grinning face from his mind. "Where is he? He still in?"

"He's still a guest, occupying a cell in Strangeways."

"Manchester. Category B convicted prisoner. Good. Close, but not the same country club, then."

"Still trying to work out where you saw Mr. FitzSimmons?"

"Maybe he was a model prisoner, learned the errors of his ways, and kept to the straight and narrow on his release. The name doesn't ring a bell with me."

"Don't let the name fool you, Mike. I knew a killer whose last name was Pope."

"I usually don't forget faces, but he has me stumped all around."

"Maybe it was a particularly nasty case and you've forgot it."

"Well," he said, stretching, "it'll probably wake me up some night."

"About your bosom pal Alan Hughes being at the theater—"

"I can tell from your voice. He was."

"At least the four tickets were used. Unless his wife went with someone else, but that still doesn't give him an alibi for her murder. That was Thursday evening and she disappeared on Friday."

"I figured it was a stupid question."

"The urge to track down every lead is still strong. I know."

He let McLaren sigh heavily before adding, "I checked on this other couple for you."

"Jamie, you're—"

"I know. Flattery is always welcome, ta."

"You're also full of—"

"Intelligence and thoughtfulness. Thanks. I know how you cherish a thorough job. Anyway, this is a tradition stretching back several years. Both couples have occupied these seats for as long as they've been going to this theater.. The Hughes and the Russells. It's a small building and the staff know them by sight."

"So there's no question they weren't there."

"Not unless they have identical twins or were swathed in actor's makeup, no."

"Which, as I said, is not really proving anything since the dates don't match. And I can't believe in a convoluted scenario such as Hughes hiring someone to kill Marta. That doesn't make sense, either. Well, thanks for the help, Jamie."

"You can thank me with a beer Friday night. Stay healthy." He rang off.

McLaren laid the phone beside him on the couch and lay back. The house was quiet, wrapped in the sounds of early evening. Gold-hued sunlight streamed in through the west-facing windows, gilding the top of the leather chair and the book spines lined up on the shelves. Leather and books. A man's room. Warming, yet solitary. Would another human presence make it more comfortable?

It had been filled with warmth and others' presence years ago. As his childhood home, growing up here, sharing everyday life with his parents and sister. Celebrating the large milestones of Christmas and birthdays, sharing the enthusiasm of smaller triumphs—a first solo bicycle ride, an outstanding school report, a first job and the first car it brought. He stared into the hallway, expecting to hear the sound of his father's whistling, his mother's laughter at a joke his sister told. He shifted his gaze to the window and the front garden. He hadn't changed it when he'd bought it. He hadn't the courage. The rope swing, grayed and smaller than he remembered, still hung from the elm in the back garden. His mother's birdbath still stood under the willow. His sister told him he was making a mistake when he bought the house, warned him the memories would be too real and painful for him to find peace there. But he purchased the house anyway, moving in last July on quitting the job and Staffordshire. Gwen was wrong. The memories were soothing. He was content to live with the ghosts and the voices that echoed down the hallway.

His eyes traveled to Dena's photo and he thought of Linnet and her comforting visits to Sean. Prison was a place to be endured, to mark time until you were free. Had Sean appreciated Linnet's friendship, supporting him even when he had made a bad choice? Perhaps the book's dedication was his repayment for her time and concern.

Dena seemed to stare at him as the dusk thickened, turning the air gray and the furniture into dark, textureless shapes. A copper's life wasn't much different than a prisoner's, in some aspects. Cops needed love and support if they were to emotionally and mentally survive their jobs. It was hard enough dealing with an abusive public who were drunk and called you four-letter names, hard working with demanding superiors and coworkers who tried to sabotage your work or who simply hated you, were jealous of you. Hard to work through cases, make arrests, clean up crime, lower statistics to please the higher-ups, get reports written up and submitted on time. To do all this without someone at home who loved you, sympathized with the pressures, understood your moods… Well, that was asking for a mental or physical breakdown. Cops needed to come home to warmth, where they could relax and be human beings and not have to fight those job-related problems. He stared back at Dena, just discerning her smile in the fading light. Was she smiling, holding out her hand? Had he made a mistake one year ago? Was it too late to bring her into his life…if she still wanted him?

He wriggled into the depths of the cushion and propped his shoeless feet on the edge of the coffee table. What had he missed that he could never regain? Was there any love left in her? In him?

He shifted position, rolling over on his hip. Something hard dug into his flesh. Leaning back into the couch, he straightened his leg and thrust his hand into his jeans pocket. He pulled out the silver charm and the scrap of paper.

The charm clattered onto the tabletop, startlingly loud in the quiet. He unfolded the paper. He didn't need to see the handwriting; he knew what it said. But the dark, spiky scrawl held his gaze as though he could still see it in the half-light. For, the obvious was clearly visible to McLaren now. His attacker had been sent deliberately to his address.

TWENTY-ONE

McLaren stared at the paper, oblivious to the mantel clock striking the hour and the fox yapping somewhere on a neighboring ridge. Who hated him so much that he would be targeted like this? Who had he hurt in his career? He wasn't even a cop anymore.

His fingers slowly relaxed, the flesh returning to its normal hue, as he thought about the criminals he had arrested. Many had uttered threats at him—that was almost expected from both sides of the law. Most he had forgotten on leaving the courtroom; many he had talked about with Jamie or colleagues; very few produced insomnia.

Still, this scrap of paper was different. It spoke of some great hatred, perhaps long standing, and the need for revenge.

Pain shot through his upper arm as he reached for the silver charm. He grabbed his shoulder and winced, settling back into the cushions. The bookstore clerk had averted her eyes when he bought the book today. Perhaps she was afraid he was a gang member and would bring the violence that obviously was a part of his life into her store. Conversely, Marta Hughes' boss at the animal shelter hadn't seemed to notice his bruises. Maybe he was more in tune with animals and their needs. McLaren gingerly touched his jaw and drew his fingers across the mottled flesh. At least the swelling had begun receding.

He took a deep breath and sat up. Grimacing, he grabbed his tea. The liquid had cooled and tasted of sugar and milk. He set the cup on the table and paced the room. The only criminal in his life right now, albeit indirectly, was Sean FitzSimmons. Were he and Tyrone Wade Antony, the pub burglar, mates? Had Sean decided to carry out some sort of punishment on behalf of his friend? McLaren shook his head. It seemed far-fetched for so short a prison sentence as burglary, no matter if Antony was a persistent offender. There had to be another connection. He paused beside the coffee table, looked again at the charm, and opened his hand. The paper scrap slowly fell onto the table, coming to rest on top of the skier. McLaren swore, turned out the light, and went to bed.

TUESDAY MORNING DAWNED with a clear blue sky and a fresh breeze from the west but McLaren didn't notice. He rang up PC Ian Shard and asked if there had been further complaints about any of the three Chesterfield teenagers and drugs. Shard replied emphatically that their little run-in with the law seemed to have dampened their taste for illicit drugs. "Obviously, I could be wrong," he added, "but I've neither heard anything further about them nor been personally involved in additional cases. And I don't believe it's because Mrs. Hughes isn't around to ring us up. There are other residents on that lane who keep an eye out for that sort of thing."

"Any more burglaries in the area?"

"You mean, like what happened at the Hughes home?"

"Yes. Was that an isolated incident, or was it part of a string—either before or since?"

"You trying to get info on the Hughes murder, then?"

"I'm simply asking about their break-in, if there were other homes broken into at the time."

"Yeah, with an eye for the big prize. Look, McLaren, I've heard about you. I know you're an ex-cop. Staffordshire's not that far away that news doesn't travel. Your Big Man Status there doesn't give you any authority around here.

So my advice is to take what I just gave you and leave well enough alone."

"Sounds like some sort of threat, Shard."

"You've got an overactive imagination, mate. I'm handing you some advice, that's all. Thought you could use it."

"The information about the Hughes case is public record."

"Really? Tell that to the Super. I've given you what you asked for. Now, trot along and repair a wall."

The click cut off McLaren's next remark.

He sat for several seconds, the noise of the disconnected phone line falling on his unhearing ears. Where was he with the case? In which direction should he proceed? He hung up the receiver, finished his coffee, and drove into Castleton.

The sun had not yet peeked above the mountain ridge when he parked opposite Linnet Isherwood's house. It would be nearly noon before sunlight slanted directly onto the road and rooftops. McLaren consulted his notebook, making certain of her address, and scanned the house nameplates. That was it—the two-story with the bright green door and trellis of morning glories. "Morning Glory," he read, thinking the house name appropriate. As he started to get out of his car, he saw Linnet rush out of her front door. He was about to call to her, but something about her determined expression made him stop. He sank back into his car seat, wanting to melt into the shadowy car interior, and watched as she jogged up to a car and unlocked its door. McLaren's hand froze on the interior door handle. The car was a gray Mercedes CLC coupé, registration plate number YV59.

McLaren sat frozen to the spot, trying to sort through the confusion and meanings of the mental images crowding his mind. Why was Linnet driving the car that had picked up Karin Pedersen in Hathersage? Was Linnet linked with his traffic stop or the beer bottle? Were she and Karin merely friends? He jammed the car key into the ignition, switched on his car's motor, and followed Linnet's flight, vowing he'd tail her until she met up with Karin.

The A6 into Buxton was heavy with Tuesday morning traffic, for which McLaren thanked his guardian angel. He could keep Linnet's car in sight without running the risk that he'd be seen. He was also thankful that she evidently was headed into the town, for tailing her to a lonely moor, for example, would have blown his whole operation. It would be hard to remain hidden behind some heather.

Having reached Buxton, Linnet drove up Terrace Road and turned right into the car park opposite the town hall. Three cars separated them as McLaren noted her slow drive through the lot. He paused to let a mother pushing a pram cross the entrance, then drove in and parked several rows from the Mercedes. He bought a pay-and-park ticket, displayed it on his car's center console, then, despite his complaining muscles, dashed off to follow Linnet.

The town-hall clock showed 11:20 as McLaren passed the building, a dark two-storey Victorian edifice showing the years of coal smoke and car exhaust fumes. He passed to the east of the hall, heading back the way he had come, jogging down the sharp incline of The Slopes, a grassy area overlooking the rest of the town below. McLaren stayed behind a crowd of tourists and office workers, glad of the near-noontime rush and the sunny day. His sunglasses and baseball cap helped with anonymity.

At a bench near St. Ann's Well, a short, dark-haired man smiled as Linnet came up to him. He tossed his newspaper into the rubbish bin before giving her an ardent kiss. More than friends, McLaren thought as he pretended to tie his shoe. And more interesting every day.

The man was Sean FitzSimmons.

McLaren didn't need the author's book-jacket photo to identify him. He'd stared at the face hard enough to burn

it into his mind. As he slowly straightened up and watched
Sean slip his arm around Linnet's waist, McLaren recalled
Jamie's information about the leather jacket. How involved
was Linnet with Sean? How long had she known him before
he'd entered prison? His past didn't seem to bother her, judging from the kiss she returned.

McLaren watched the couple walk back up the hill and
cross High Street. He followed at a slower pace. They strolled
past several shops before ducking into The Old Sun Inn.
Probably going to have lunch. He hung back from the pub's
entrance. He lingered by the doorway, giving the impression
he was studying the menu displayed in the front window and
letting several more customers find tables, before entering.

The pub smelled of hot meat pies, warm breads, and
brewed coffee. He walked partway into the front room,
scanned the area as though looking for a lunch date, then
spotted Linnet and Sean near the back corner of the adja-
cent dining area. A snug, actually, turning his back on the
smaller, intimate room. He took a table closer to the front in
the main room, putting distance and a dozen tables between
them. He also snuggled up to an ancient grandfather's clock
that leaned against the wall. Perfect. The broad front and far
side of the clock's wooden case afforded cover as good as a
boulder. He could lean forward casually and have a straight
view of them, then lean back against the wall and sink from
sight. Besides the cap, he also wore a large bandana around
his neck. He pulled it up higher, so its folded edge came up
to his jaw, and angled his chair slightly so he could rest his
right shoulder against the wall. Then he ordered lunch and
watched the show.

They had chosen an atmospheric setting for whatever they
were about to do, McLaren thought, glancing at the pub's interior. It had been a coaching inn, catering to travelers and
horses. The past still clung to the building, a whitewashed

exterior and antique-filled interior. A cheering fire would fill the stony hearth in the winter, he thought, and the leaded casement windows tattooed with frost. But now the June sun angled through the open windows, crowding the room with the warmth and scents of summer.

He leaned forward, glancing at Linnet and Sean. Even if he had been seated at the next table, McLaren doubted he could have heard their conversation, for the couple seemed to keep their conversation low, their heads bent only inches apart. He also doubted their apparent need of secrecy, for the room was noisy with the clatter of china and cutlery and the drone of other customers. Canned music plugged up any brief voids when the droning stopped. McLaren picked up his coffee mug from the low, knee-high table and held it casually in front of his face. He took slow, periodic sips, as though he were content to linger over lunch, having nothing else to do the rest of the day.

He was halfway into his ham-and-tomato sandwich when Linnet and Sean paid their bill and left the pub. They hadn't left so quickly that McLaren hadn't seen Sean's back jeans pocket. It was stuffed with a bulky envelope.

McLaren left the uneaten half of his sandwich on the plate, grabbed the bill, and thrust it and more than enough money at the cashier before sprinting from the pub. Linnet and Sean were waiting for the pelican crossing lights to change on High Street as McLaren jogged toward them. He stopped short, turned to look in a window, and wished for a horde of tourists to swamp the pavement. When the light changed they crossed the road, then turned right and walked toward the car park. McLaren slowed to a leisurely stroll, always keeping several people behind them. Sean walked Linnet to her car and waited while she opened the door before giving her a goodbye kiss.

McLaren paused at the corner of the town-hall building,

pulled his cap low on his forehead, and pretended to consult his watch. He saw Sean smile, pat the pocket that bulged from the bulky envelope, and accept something from Linnet. As she got into her car and drove off, Sean turned and crossed the car park, heading back toward the Slopes and Terrace Road. McLaren hesitated only for a split second before he dashed toward Sean and knocked against his right shoulder, throwing him off balance. As Sean stumbled and tried to keep from falling, McLaren grabbed his right arm and hand, steadying him.

"Frightfully sorry." McLaren brushed off Sean's back and shook his hand. "I do most sincerely apologize. I hope I haven't hurt you." He placed his hands on Sean's shoulders and turned him around as though inspecting for broken bones or torn clothing.

Sean shook off McLaren's hands and straightened his shirt. "I'd think you could be a bit more careful about where you're going. It's crowded, if you haven't noticed." He brushed his hands together.

"I know. I'm so sorry. I'm late back to my car. The ticket's about to expire. You're all right, then?" He said it more as a statement than as a question, but he frowned as he looked at Sean, all concern.

"Yes, yes, I'm fine. Only, be more careful. There are mothers and children about."

"I know. I apologize. Sorry."

"You said that," Sean replied, gritting his teeth. "You're either a flaming berk or you're squiffy."

"Right, guv'ner. I confess. I've had a couple. You know…" He grabbed Sean's shirtsleeve and leaned toward him, as though whispering something secret. "Boss' birthday lunch. Couldn't not go and then keep my job, could I? Had to have a couple with the boss to show him respect and good wishes of the day and all that. All the good wishes I could think of, the old bastard." He turned slightly, as though looking for the restaurant that held his employer.

"Well, you overdid it, mate. And you're tiresome, to boot. Now, hop it!"

"Certainly, sir. Right you are, sir. Immediately." He saluted Sean and nodded. "Now, where's the car?"

"How should I know? If you weren't sloshed, you'd know, you berk."

McLaren pulled himself up to his full height, blinked, and said seriously, "If I weren't drunk, I'd take offense at being called a berk, but between you and me—" He smiled and patted Sean on the shoulder. "That's okay."

"If you keep this up, I'm calling a copper. Now, lay off!"

"Yes, sir. Sorry, sir." He swayed slightly, holding onto Sean's upper arm as though it were a lifeline. "Well, if you're sure you're not hurt…"

"I'm fine." He turned quickly, shook off McLaren's clinging hands, and walked briskly down the hill.

"I'm fine, too, mate," McLaren said as he jogged to his car. He waited until he was back on the A6 before he uncurled the fingers of his right hand. In his palm lay a silver charm of a downhill skier.

TELEPHONE INFORMATION was very accommodating; it gave McLaren the home address of Sean FitzSimmons. McLaren scribbled it down on his notebook, closed his mobile phone, turned the car around, and followed the A6 southeast toward Bakewell.

He entered the town from the north, the A6 becoming Matlock Street. The Catholic church and Bath Street slipped past before he came to the small roundabout at the junction of four streets. He paused before he could ease into the traffic flow around the circle, the town busy with Tuesday business and tourists. Once clear of the intersection, he turned right onto

King Street, lined with shops, passed the huge building on the corner, and turned onto Butts Road. He parked cattycorner from the address he'd been given and looked around. It was a quiet street, several blocks from the busy town center and lined with trees. If the bulky envelope in Sean's back pocket was money from Marta's casino win—not far-fetched, since the money had never been found—Sean could afford some nice items for his home. Or a lengthy holiday somewhere exotic. Wasn't that how people usually spent their money? McLaren took off his bandana and cap, and drove to Lloyd Farmer's house.

The retired police sergeant welcomed McLaren with a grin and an offering of a cuppa, but McLaren declined, stating what he needed. "I thought you could introduce me to a friend of Sean FitzSimmons," McLaren said, twirling his car key on his index finger. "Or a neighbor."

"Someone who knows the lad." Lloyd nodded. "Nothing like a bit of info straight from the horse's mouth."

"I know you'll have kept up with everything going on in town."

"Retirement or not, eh?"

"You're a walking encyclopedia, Lloyd. And don't give me that retirement bit. Thirty-five years in the job was just the preface. You're still as interested in Bakewell goings-on as you were when you were in uniform."

"So that's why you dropped by. I should have known it wasn't for my scintillating conversation." He grabbed his latchkey and laughed. "Come on, then. I've just the chap you need to talk to if you want news about Mr. FitzSimmons."

During the short drive back to Sean FitzSimmons', McLaren told Lloyd how he had become involved in Marta's murder case. Lloyd kept quiet throughout the narrative but when McLaren had finished, he said, "So now you're shifting stones to find a murderer hiding under one of 'em."

"That's about it, yes."

"Well, I'll pray for your success. I remember that case. Nasty, it was. You need to catch who killed her."

"With your help, I hope to. This it, then?" He parked in the same spot he had a quarter of an hour ago and glanced at Lloyd.

"That's also the chap you need to talk to." He nodded to a man about sixty years old. "Shall we?" He got out of the car and walked briskly up to the older man, forcing McLaren to hurry after him.

Sam Browder was weeding his perennial border but looked up when Lloyd and McLaren approached. He shaded his eyes from the sun, his glove soiled with damp earth and bits of grass. Lloyd introduced McLaren, assured Sam it was completely unofficial and that nothing would be noted down, then walked back to the car.

McLaren nodded to Sam and wished him good day. The older man leaned against his spade, got to his feet, and asked how he could help. "I recall that incident. Last June it happened. Shocking. All I could think about for days after watching the news on TV. That poor lady gone missing. Then when they found her body later, in the wood…" His voice trailed off as he looked into the distance.

"I realize it's been a year, a long time to recollect anything, but I wonder if you remember if your neighbor Sean FitzSimmons was home all that evening, presuming he lived here then."

"That evening? When? All night? I went to bed around midnight. Yes, he was here last year. Has lived here, in fact, for years. Well, lived here except for those times when he was in prison. He'd been in twice before, I believe, before this last time. Small offences, I understand. Well, depends on how you categorize small. Things like burglary and breaking into cars. Which always surprised me, because he's a quiet neighbor. Not rowdy or prone to late-night drinking parties. Keeps his place nice. Polite, pleasant man. I understand he's written some books, too. Maybe he just got onto the wrong path for a bit but has settled down."

"Seen the light."

"Changed his way, yes. Whatever, he lets his place to a mate when he's serving time so it would still be lived in. I guess he didn't want trouble with burglars or vandalism. You know, if his place looked deserted." He snorted, shaking his head. "Sounds daft. Him in the nick and worried about others of his sort. Life's strange."

"About him being here that night," McLaren reminded the man.

"Oh, right. When that woman went missing."

"Do you know he was in, perhaps due to his car being in the shop, or if he came home when you happened to look outside? Anything like that?"

"I know exactly what happened. I remember it crystal clear."

"That would help immensely, sir."

"I remember because it stuck in my mind for days, it was so odd."

"Yes, sir." McLaren waited, nearly holding his breath. If the man's memory was good...

"I retired last year, so I was staying up a bit later than during my working days. Anyroad, Sean had been out earlier that day. I've no idea where he was, but he was probably either at his girl friend's or trying to find a job. He'd just got out of prison a while before—perhaps a month or so, I can't recall—and was applying for all sorts of jobs. I guess his writing income wasn't that regular or that much so he had to find something like office or construction work."

"His girlfriend...do you happen to know her name?"

"Certainly. She's over here often enough. Was before and

after his stretches in the nick. Linnet Isherwood. A tall blonde woman. Quite pretty."

McLaren took the information straight-faced but felt his heart jump. It made sense. If Linnet had taken Sean's favorite jacket to him prior to his release from prison, they had to have been more than acquaintances. He nodded his head. They hadn't foreseen anyone getting that jacket information when they thought up Marta's murder. The jacket definitely linked the two.

"I didn't actually see him leave or come home," the man continued. "But I knew he'd gone some place rather unusual."

"Oh, yes?"

"As I said, I first assumed he was at his girlfriend's place or out looking for work. His car had been clean that morning. I know, because I saw him washing it."

"His car looked different later in the day?"

"I saw it the next morning. I get up early to do a bit of gardening—before it gets too hot. There was the car. Muddy as hell. Like he'd driven across a newly plowed field."

Or off road in a forest, McLaren thought, recalling the spot where Marta's body had been found.

"Since I get up early, I know his car had been through something late that day, perhaps that night. I wondered where he'd been but I never asked. Wasn't my business, was it?"

McLaren replied that it wasn't but silently cursed that the man wasn't nosey.

"I learned years ago not to poke my nose into other people's lives," the man added, as though defending himself against McLaren's unspoken condemnation. "So I was kind of surprised when Sean volunteered a bit of his private life to me."

"Oh? What was that?"

"He wore a silver charm around his neck. On a necklace. I saw it on numerous occasions, so I was quite familiar with it."

"Must be unique for you to remember it."

"It seemed so to me. Most pendants or such that I've seen men wear are coins or medallions or religious symbols."

"This one wasn't."

"Not at all. I thought it was suited more for a woman. Belonged on a charm bracelet, but he wore it on that necklace."

"And it was…"

"A skier. A downhill skier. Very lovely but odd for a man to wear. Sean said he knew I'd seen him wear it so he decided that day to tell me. He was in a talkative mood, quite happy. He'd won several thousand pounds at the races, he said. I guess that was why he wanted to talk. He must have given a bit to his girlfriend, Linnet, 'cause she's been dressing a bit fancier these days. Anyroad, I was curious enough to listen, for I had been wondering about the charm. He said it was from a dear friend and he cherished it. Life's funny," he said again, picking up his spade. "Takes all sorts, doesn't it?"

"When was this? That he's had the skier charm, I mean."

"Oh, about a year ago, I guess. I think around the time his publisher accepted his first nonfiction book."

McLaren thanked the man and returned to his car. Lloyd grinned as McLaren started the motor. "That was profitable, then."

"As if you didn't know. Thanks, Lloyd."

"If you need anything else…" He left unsaid that McLaren could phone him any hour of the day or night. McLaren knew that. "Thanks for the lift." He got out at his house.

"Any time. I'll come back for that cuppa, shall I?"

Lloyd waved over his shoulder as he walked toward his house.

McLaren couldn't remember later which route he took out of town. His mind played and replayed the snippets of information and the problems they produced. If Sean had not yet found work, how did he afford to live? Is it off his savings, or the money from Marta's casino win? If the latter, what did Linnet give him at the pub? And why give him money a year after Marta's death? The questions multiplied, persistent and mocking, as he drove to Verity's home.

He stopped for a quick snack, hungry since he'd had only part of his lunch at the pub in Buxton, then got to Youlgreave and Verity's house mid afternoon. Verity was home, unloading groceries from her car. Helping her was Derek Fraser, her former boss.

McLaren remained in his car, alternately hiding behind an open newspaper and watching Derek. He and Verity weren't on bad terms as McLaren had imagined, for Verity spoke readily enough to Derek. She even laughed in response to something he said and nodded toward the house. The man picked up the last bag and followed her inside.

It was too good to pass up, as the saying goes. McLaren tossed the newspaper onto the car seat, got out of his car, and jogged up to the house. He paused slightly, judging where the kitchen might be, then walked around to the back. A small flagstone patio led off the kitchen door and held several wicker chairs, matching table, and a cluster of ornamental shrubs in large porcelain pots. He stood behind the tallest cypress and listened at the open window.

The conversation seemed to be nearly over. The thud of tins hitting the table and the squeak of cupboard doors opening and closing intruded into the speech but McLaren could make out several sentences. He leaned closer, wanting desperately to see what was happening, but reluctantly refrained from peering over the windowsill.

"Don't worry, Verity." It was Derek's voice, soothing and reassuring. A cupboard door banged shut. "I've got it figured out."

"I'd like to believe you, Derek." Verity sounded tired,

as though she'd been living on hope too long. "But I don't see how."

"Leave that up to me. What's twenty thousand pounds? The way I look at it is we owe it to you."

Another door closed, drowning Verity's reply, if there was one. A chair scraped across the floor and a cat mewed before Derek said, "Think it over. It can't miss." His voice faded and McLaren ran back to his car, just getting in and closing the door before Derek and Verity appeared at her front door. Verity waved to Derek, calling her thanks to him as he drove off.

She remained there for a moment, standing in the open doorway like a bronze statue, perhaps looking after Derek's departing Lexus. Her hand left the doorknob and crept to the doorjamb, supporting her weight as she leaned forward slightly. She plucked a spent rose from the bush nearest the door, then seemed to remember something and returned to her car. McLaren called to her as he came up the walkway.

Verity peered into the late-afternoon sun, unsure at first who was coming toward her. She had grabbed a small paper bag from inside the car and now shifted it to one arm as she shaded her eyes against the glaring light. When she recognized McLaren, she seemed to relax. She paused as McLaren grabbed the remaining paper bag and slammed her car door shut, then preceded him into her house.

"Just set it down anywhere," she said, walking into the kitchen. "Vegetables from the greengrocer's and some frozen items."

McLaren followed her and put the bag on the table. He stood there, unsure if he should offer to help put things away, if he should talk while she worked, or if he should wait until she was finished.

Verity solved the dilemma by telling him to sit down and offering him a cup of tea. "I won't be a minute, if you can wait while I get the cold things into the fridge." She opened the freezer compartment and shoved a carton of ice cream into its frozen interior. "I almost forgot about them."

No wonder, with your unexpected company. "No hurry," McLaren said, enjoying the feel of the room. It was smaller than his own kitchen but boasted the lighter color scheme of apple green, pink, and white. Appliances seemed to be new or nearly so, their exteriors free of smudges. The floor was hardwood and shone with a just-waxed brightness. He waited until she reappeared from the depths of the pantry before asking if she had heard about Marta's casino winning. "I don't mean if you heard that she won," he clarified as Verity folded one of the grocery carrier bags. "If you heard what had happened to it."

"You didn't?" she asked, picking up the second bag. "No, of course not. You weren't involved." She stuck the second bag inside the first bag and hung it on the pantry doorknob. "You think I, as an interested party, would have heard. Or at least kept tabs on the case."

"Something like that, yes." He looked at her, hoping she hadn't taken offense, then grinned as she smiled.

"It's become my main hobby. I used to knit and embroider, but not since—" She broke off, pressing her lips together.

"If it's too painful," he began when Verity shook her head and said, "You think it's too painful to talk about or think about? God! That's all I do think about! It's an obsession with me. Not like stalking, but close." She leaned against the refrigerator door and asked if he wanted a cup of tea.

"No, thank you. I just popped in to ask a question."

"Well, pop away. Anything to help, as the saying goes."

"About the money…"

"Oh, right. What happened to the money?"

"If it was ever found." He knew but wanted to hear her answer, to see if she could be trusted as truthful.

"I know it wasn't with her when the police found her body.

Well, it wouldn't be, would it, if someone found her first, or if her killer took it? But I never heard if they found it later. I kept up with the story through newspaper articles and the telly. But I never heard that anyone had found the money and turned it in. I was always hoping someone would find it. It would have meant a lot, you know."

"Kind of make up for the money missing from the animal shelter," McLaren supplied.

"Yeah. Something like that, although it still wouldn't have cleared me of the conviction of stealing that money. Still, anything found in connection with Marta would have been nice to hear." She exhaled loudly, puffing out her cheeks, and rubbed her forehead. "God, that seems a million years ago."

McLaren glanced at the Noah's Ark calendar hanging on the back of the kitchen door and took a chance. "Marta's husband wasn't implicated in her death, I know. Do you know anything about Linnet's husband?"

"Herb? I know he left her right around the time of Marta's death. I don't know when exactly. I can ring up a friend if you need to know."

"That's not necessary right now, thank you. Do you know why he walked out? I think I heard that Linnet and her children were in financial trouble because he left."

"I don't know the reason they parted. Linnet and I weren't that close for her to confide in me. But I do know she was having a rough go of it for quite a while, nearly a year, I think. Well, you would do, when your husband takes off like that, and him bringing in more than half of the household income. Linnet's back on her feet, but only just. It's been hard on her and on her kids. She's had to do without things and get a second job, working some weekends. The only saving grace is that her kids are older. Late teens and early twenties, I believe. Three of them. So even though the demand for school uniforms and such isn't there, and the oldest one lives away from home, she's still got to put food on the table and pay the utility bills. The younger one—eighteen, I believe—helps out with an after-school job, but it's not easy."

"Sounds as though she could use a bit of financial help."

"If you're hinting she stole Marta's money because they were at the casino together, you're wrong. The cops made that clear when they questioned the car-park attendant and the cashier at the casino. No one saw Marta hand over any money to Linnet in the casino or in the car park. There's nothing on the CCTV surveillance tape that even suggests they stopped in the car park so Marta could hand money to Linnet. The tape shows them getting into their separate cars and driving off. It's very clear. And I doubt they stopped somewhere on the road. That wouldn't make any sense. The police were thinking like that at the beginning because Linnet was in financial difficulty by then, but they cleared her because she and Marta left in their separate cars."

"There's no speed-camera photo of Linnet's car racing along after Marta," McLaren finished.

"That ought to prove something," Verity said. "Don't those speed cameras give a time when they're tripped like that?"

McLaren nodded, thinking it a solid alibi.

Verity continued. "I think they finally divorced."

"Do you know when?"

"No. As I said, we're not really that chummy. I think it was toward the early part of this year. End of January or first part of February. She must have got a decent settlement out of him 'cause the few times I've seen her, she's been dressed nicely. Unless she frequents the charity shops."

"Nothing wrong with that. A friend pointed me in the direction of one last Christmas. I've been thankful to him ever since."

"Nothing like a true friend to help smooth out life's bumps. Linnet was lost without Herb, but she's got a good friend in

Sean. Do you know Sean FitzSimmons? He writes, I think. Having a book signing at the shelter soon, I believe I heard."

"I think that's correct, yes."

"Linnet probably thanks her lucky stars daily that she met Sean. He takes good care of her."

"I'm sure she does. How did she meet him?" *Don't tell me it was through a prisoner welfare program,* McLaren thought. *She doesn't seem like the philanthropic sort.*

"One of those odd twists some lives take. She met Sean through a mutual friend."

"That does happen sometimes."

"Yes. Purely by chance, though. Linnet was at a pub and just happened to come upon her friend, who was drinking with Sean. The friend introduced them and—" Verity snapped her fingers.

"Instant attraction, I take it. Who's the obliging, timely friend?"

"You might know him, I don't know. He's a cop. His name's Charlie Harvester."

TWENTY-TWO

McLaren had a lot to think about on the drive home. Was Harvester somehow tied to Sean FitzSimmons, a convicted criminal, and to Linnet? It seemed bordering on the fantastic, but given Sean's criminal history and the fact that they were acquaintances, if not drinking buddies... McLaren turned onto the B6061 and stopped momentarily in a lay-by, ringing up Jamie on his mobile phone. "I need a favor, Jamie," McLaren said, his mind torn between what he'd heard about Harvester and Linnet's statement about her financial situation. What was going on? Was all this associated somehow?

"Sure," Jamie replied. "What do you need?"

"It's a bit shady," he said slowly, as though giving Jamie a chance to back out.

"Lovely. I need a bit of excitement."

"Right." He relayed the information about Harvester and Sean knowing each other but refrained from saying how he had come to know this. He added, "I need to know Harvester's work schedule."

"What?"

"When he's working. If it's tonight, that would be the best news I've had all day. Can you find out?"

"What's going on? Are you going to ambush him?"

"Is he still with Derbyshire Constabulary?" It was all he could do to talk about the man, let alone think of Harvester now working in a constabulary in McLaren's home county. He said, "H-he hasn't transferred back to his old job in Staffordshire, or somewhere else?"

"Far as I know he's still here, in B Division. Look, Mike, what's going on? Are you going to be doing something dangerous?"

"Not rushing into a burning house, if that's what you mean."

"I don't like the sound of this."

"Nothing for you to worry about."

"Now I know it's dangerous. Or at least illegal. No, on second thought, if it is illegal, don't tell me."

"You're turning into your mother, Jamie."

"I'll take that to mean personality-wise and not physically."

"Ring up the station and ask a daft question. Shouldn't be too hard to think of something."

"Thanks for the compliment. Just what am I supposed to ask?"

"Anything that sounds important, that gives the impression you need information only Harvester would have from a case he's working on."

"Oh, fine. How do I know what he's working on? He's not exactly sitting at the next desk."

"Fake it. Make it sound ambiguous. Top secret. There's enough stuff going on these days that nobody wants to stick their neck out and get involved in another officer's case."

"So what do I do when I find out when he's working?"

"Ring me back on my mobile. I should be home in about twenty minutes."

"Where are you?"

"On my way home."

"Fine. Keep your little secret. I'm going to expect some sort of payment for all this trouble I'm going to."

"Two beers, then."

"Throw in a steak dinner and it's a deal."

"You like it medium rare, if I remember right."

"I'll ring you back shortly."

McLaren rang off, feeling as though he was about to get one up on Detective-Inspector Charlie Harvester.

Jamie rang back in fifteen minutes, just as McLaren was walking into his house. McLaren tossed his keys onto the kitchen worktop and grinned as Jamie said, "I don't know what gods you pray to, Mike—"

"Whoever will get my job done."

"—but your prayers are answered. Harvester is working tonight. He's still with Derbyshire B Division, but B Division loaned him to D Division. Some sort of big case, evidently. D Division has a runner murder on. They've been at it for weeks and aren't making much headway."

Those prolonged investigations into undetected murders were always McLaren's bane, but tonight... He grinned. "So Harvester is loaned out to help the lads. Wonder if it's help as much as it is B Division wanting to get rid of him, even if it is for just a week or so."

"He's working out of Derby station. He should be there until two a.m. or so."

Lovely, McLaren thought. All the way down in Derby. A nice long drive back home to Buxton. "Did you talk to him?"

"No. He was out. But the bloke I did chat to says Harvester told his underlings he'd be working approximately that long. He'll be back in the office in Derby for about two hours. I guess he wants everyone to know how late and hard he's working."

Nothing like scoring points with the Superintendent, McLaren thought. "I hope he doesn't decide to go home early."

"The constable thought I could catch him until that time, so it seems he'll be out of your hair for a bit." He paused and swallowed, the fear suddenly building inside him. "Do you want some help, Mike? I don't know what you're about to do, but if you need help..."

"You just go home, prop your feet up and watch *New Tricks* on the telly, and leave me to do my work."

"*New Tricks* isn't on tonight."

"A figure of speech, Jamie. I'll be fine."

"Sure. You sound fine. This whole thing sounds fine. Only, it stinks like three-day-old fish."

"Thanks, mate. We'll have our dinner this weekend if it goes well tonight."

"If not, I'll order you a take-away, delivered to your jail cell."

"They'll never catch me."

McLaren hung up on Jamie's reply. He made himself a cup of tea, heated up some leftover peas and Brimstone Chicken he'd made several days previously, threw together a simple green salad, and sat at the kitchen table. Over supper, he wondered if he was about to land in jail, as Jamie had joked. He tried to remember back to when he and Harvester worked together, tried to recall the man's method of working. He sat back in his chair, holding his mug of tea, and shut his eyes. Hadn't Harvester kept case notes at his house? Besides the official documents at the station. There had always been rumors about it, how Harvester—the eager, steamrolling detective who let nothing stand in the way of his advancement goals—filled manila folders with personal notes on suspects and victims. How he spent his nights ruminating over motive and opportunity and suspect. McLaren stared out of the window, oblivious to the gray clouds rolling in from the west. With any sort of good luck, he'd find out if the rumors were true, if Harvester kept case notes—or personal notes—lovingly boxed at his home.

HARVESTER HAD NOT moved his residence since the altercation last year with McLaren. His house was at the end of a cul-de-sac in Buxton, a sleepy road thick with trees lying off Carlisle

Road. That road, in turn, was clogged with two-story brick houses and dog-legged onto the busy A515. A straight shot into Ashbourne, in the southern part of Derbyshire, which housed the police station where Harvester normally worked. But the quiet cul-de-sac was nicely removed from the rush of the A515, backing up to a golf course and a woodland of conifers and deciduous trees. The wood sheltered the cul-de-sac from Buxton's noise; it also provided a great deal of privacy, for the street was dark, despite the effort of the streetlamps.

McLaren sat in his car, staring at the house, a large two-story of red brick. It seemed a lifetime since he had last been here. And, if he were honest, it was a lifetime—someone else's life. *His* life, when he had been an enthusiastic constable with no objective in life but catching bad guys. Now he was staring at the house that belonged to a bad guy—a bad guy in McLaren's book. The images of the department Christmas party welled before him briefly, then dissolved into the blackness of the road as he shifted his gaze. Breaking and entering was always risky. It wouldn't do to be caught. Especially with the history he and Harvester had. But he had checked with some of his mates at the police station, making certain Harvester had no burglar alarm. No security cameras had been installed, either. McLaren didn't know about motion detectors on outdoor lights, but he had to chance that. So he had parked several houses down from Harvester's residence and watched the area, noting cars and lights and escape routes, feeling rather safe. Both houses neighboring Harvester's were dark, as was most of the road. He could see the occasional car pass on Manchester Road to the north and on the A53 to the south, but on the cul-de-sac nothing stirred but a prowling tomcat, the tree boughs, and the black clouds overhead.

McLaren glanced at his watch: quarter to one. Good enough. Not many people out on a work night. He pulled on his black gloves and black knit stocking cap, got out of his car, eased the door shut, and crept up to the house.

The storm seemed to blacken the night sky, for beyond the pale orange glow of the streetlamps. McLaren could make out an inky mass as a fork of lightning split the air. A gust of wind, cool and laden with dust and leaves, rushed down the road, pushing more debris before it. A metal wind chime rattled anxiously in the darkness and the cat ran for cover. Another spear of lightning streaked across the sky and a crack of thunder seemed to split open the heavens. A handful of rain pelted the road as McLaren edged toward the house.

He kept to the darker patches of the lane, where a streetlamp was burnt out or he could fade into the massive, nondescript shapes. A tree bough shivered overhead, creaking ominously as the wind hit it. McLaren slipped over the low brick wall fronting the garden and slid quietly onto the ground at the wall's base. He crouched where he had landed, listening for a dog barking, waiting for a house light to flick on. He counted slowly to three hundred before he moved.

The land between the narrow strip of front garden hugging the wall and the house was a stretch of short-clipped grass. McLaren remained bent over, running as best he could, and kept to the blacker smear of boxwood hedges that separated Harvester's property from his neighbor. He bypassed the front door for the relative obscurity of the back entrance. The hedge jabbed and scratched his forearm when he squeezed between it and the side of the house. The cracking of small twigs boomed louder than the thunder in his ears and he hugged the house, trying to avoid the hedge. As he rounded the back corner, the sky opened up. McLaren gained the shelter of the canopy as the rain drilled the ground.

He stood against the back door for several minutes, listening to the storm and to the house. He heard nothing but the wind in the trees, the rain as it drummed roof tiles and cars and terrace flagstones, and thunder. The house remained quiet and dark, as though it had curled up for the night to avoid a wetting. His hand rested against the door while he tried to steady his nerves. Planning the burglary earlier that evening seemed nearly a game; he had told himself he needed the information to help Marta Hughes. But now that he was here, at the house of his most bitter enemy, he felt his courage dissolving. Harvester had become a hazy memory these past months, a pain that had started to dull, a face that had softened as in a mist. Being at his house renewed the pain, sharpened the face into features, given voice to his threats. Do I have the resolve to go through with this? Do I want to enter my enemy's domain and feel his presence? He closed his eyes and tried to calm his labored breathing. He had come this far; Marta needed justice.

McLaren took several deep, slow breaths and opened his eyes. The door still loomed before him, heavy, black, and barred. Still there was no sound from the bowels of the house. After he had judged several minutes had passed, McLaren faced the door and flicked on his small torch. Shielding the light with his body, he opened the door with the near expertise of a professional burglar and slipped into the house. As he did, the wound seemed to split open; he felt the same terror and rage as if it were last June.

He stood in the kitchen, torn between running from the house and smashing everything he could lay his hands on. There was no time for personal agendas. Nor was he a vigilante. He would get even with Harvester some other way.

But his feet would not move. He remained as firmly stuck to the spot as if his shoes had been nailed to the floor. The linoleum was shiny with a recent waxing, throwing the light from a bedroom fixture into his face. Odors of coffee, fried eggs, and pipe tobacco lingered in the room, bringing Harvester's face out of the darkness with amazing vividness.

McLaren felt his heart leap; for one insane moment he could have sworn the man was standing next to him, his lit pipe in his hand, talking. McLaren stared into the shadowy corner near the fridge. Nothing moved, nothing spoke. Still, the room seemed to hug him, smother him with scents and memories. He lurched forward, like a sleepwalker, leaving the ghosts hovering in the dark.

Small lights had been left on in the kitchen and deep within the house. One good thing he's done, McLaren thought, snorting. He snapped off his torch and bent down as he crossed in front of the curtained windows.

The light from the front room and a bedroom streamed into the hallway, and McLaren walked slowly along the corridor, still listening for a dog or Harvester. He reached the bedroom and paused in the open doorway. If Harvester did keep personal notes of his cases, where would they be? In a wardrobe, in a filing cabinet in a spare bedroom? McLaren entered the room as the thunder broke again and walked slowly to the dresser. Linnet's photo sat to one side, angled toward him. He flicked on the torch and stared in disbelief. Above the sprawling signature Linnet had signed "This will have to do until I'm with you." He clicked off the torch, dazed. Were Linnet and Harvester lovers? Had they planned this entire thing, hiring him for some reason, perhaps as some sort of revenge for last June? McLaren resisted the urge to throw the framed photo against the wall and turned instead to the bed.

It was made, the top sheet taut and neat with its hospital-style corners. A lightweight quilt was folded at the bed's foot. McLaren gingerly lifted the pillows and quilt, then replaced them and lifted the edge of the mattress. He bent over, peering underneath. No manila envelope or file folder stared back at him. He pushed the mattress back into place and tried again a few feet farther on. Again nothing was revealed. He repeated the procedure until he checked the entire mattress, then got on his hands and knees and peered beneath the bed. The only things the torchlight revealed were a pair of slippers sitting side by side and a magazine on gardening. He snapped off his torch, stood up, and rummaged through the wardrobe and the drawer in the bedside cabinet. Nothing.

The same was true of his search of the rest of the house until he came to a room obviously used as a library and home office. He found years' worth of case notes in Harvester's filing cabinet, all neatly and accurately labeled, standing upright like cops lined up at attention on dress parade, the folder dates covering the whole of Harvester's detective career. McLaren opened one folder and scanned the pages. Harvester's notes were typed neatly and filed by date. Some points were cross-referenced but mainly it was a straightforward account. There were, however, a few handwritten notes on smaller pieces of paper, as though he had thought of things at his desk or while in his car and had jotted them down hurriedly so he wouldn't forget. Nothing seemed irregular. Harvester had evidently proceeded according to correct departmental policy.

Several pages were allocated to suspects. They were as uncooperative on the night of Marta's disappearance as some had been now. Several people had been home, with varying degrees of alibis. Tom Millington had been up and the lights on in the house. He also had been dressed, so that could be read any way you wished. Danny Mercer's mother had been asleep but opened the door quickly enough. Danny had come stumbling into the front room, his hair tousled, wearing an oversized T-shirt and boxer shorts, and blinking at the light. Harvester concluded he had been asleep. Noah Ark's co-worker Verity Dwyer had been mending hymnals at church, her presence verified by the minister and others. Same for boss Derek Fraser and the vet, Emlyn Gregg, who had all been at home when questioned. "We therefore cannot confirm that they weren't there, as there being no neighbors or witnesses to place them elsewhere," Harvester's handwritten note concluded.

McLaren closed the folder but kept his thumb inserted as a bookmark. That's why the case had boiled down to forensics. No witnesses to the slaying and her body found ten days later. He read the information about the bullet—a .38 caliber. He leafed through the pages to read Harvester's conclusions on who owned any weapons. There was nothing.

He moved a small lamp off the desk, set it on the floor, and pulled his small digital camera from his pocket. He switched on the lamp and positioned the pertinent pages so the lamplight fell onto the paper. He took two photos of each page in case his hand shook. When he finished, he shoved the camera back into his jeans pocket, returned the report to the file folder, and replaced it in the filing cabinet. He turned off the lamp and set it back on the desk.

A car door slammed somewhere in the street. Flicking off his torch he ran to the front window. Cautiously, he parted the heavy brocade curtain slightly to get a view of the street. The car's lights blinked a few times as the driver evidently clicked his remote-control lock device, then the man dashed to a house across the street, dodging and leaping over the puddles that had formed in the earthen and tarmac depressions. McLaren exhaled slowly, let the curtain fall back into place, then sprinted through the house and eased outside. He closed the door quietly and slipped back the way he had come.

THE DRIVE HOME seemed inordinately long to McLaren, the road stretching to a distant point that appeared unobtainable. Lightning streaked across the blackness overhead as the tree branches scrambled to catch it. The windscreen wipers continued their mesmerizing sweeps in front of his eyes, pushing aside the rain that slid down the glass. His car headlights caught a fox running along the side of the road, his tail sodden and mud-splattered. He turned into his lane and felt the soggy earth beneath the car tires, heard the splash of water as he slogged through the puddles. When he finally sat down in his front room with a cup of tea and the photographed pages printed out from his computer, he stretched his legs out on the sofa and reread Harvester's notes.

Nothing glared at him, new and important, on this more thorough read. But Harvester's personal life had sneaked into the pile of Police Officialdom. Scrawled on the edge of a page was a note: "Linnet, 7:00, dinner, The Barking Dog."

McLaren sat up, nearly spilling his tea. He set the cup on the saucer and stared at the page. The date at the top indicated they had known each other at the beginning of the case; known each other so well that Harvester was calling Linnet for a dinner date. McLaren threw the papers at the far wall, his animosity building. Harvester had violated one of the primary rules of police investigation: do not become involved with a witness or suspect, thereby jeopardizing your case. Just how far had Harvester become involved with Linnet? Had it destroyed his case? Had he overlooked certain things she had done?

McLaren got up, picked up the spilled papers, and returned to the couch. He leafed through the pages, noticing that there were other similar notes jotted in page margins. All were suppers and all were a discreet distance from the police station in Ashbourne. After all, McLaren thought, still fuming, it wouldn't do to be caught in public with a witness or suspect.

He laid the sheets of paper on the coffee table, walked into his bedroom, and undressed. As he got into bed, he listened to the thunder rolling across the sky. It seemed to echo his own grumblings. Harvester had left the Staffordshire Constabulary at the same time McLaren had. But, unlike McLaren, who left the job, Harvester transferred to the Derbyshire Constabulary. And on that fateful day when Marta's body

had been found, officers from B Division had been thin on
the ground. Harvester, in A Division, had been called in to
help. The rest, as they say, was history. McLaren closed his
eyes, cursing the past year, cursing Fate. He fell asleep to the
sound of the rain against the windows, still cursing, but now
it was at Harvester.

A MENTAL NUDGE so quiet, yet persistent, muscled into his
dream. He'd been wrestling Harvester, had him around the
neck, and was about to plunge with him into a river when
the obstinate whisper woke him. He blinked, staring into the
night, trying to determine where he was. As the room grew
recognizable, he sat up, the sheet falling from his chest. He
rubbed his eyes and glanced at the alarm clock on his bedside cabinet: 4:17. He groaned and sank back onto the mattress. His hands grabbed the sheet but he made no other move.
Frowning, he looked at the ceiling. What was the problem?
What bothered him so much that he'd woken?

He closed his eyes, trying to remember his dream. Was
that it? Was it something about Harvester or Linnet? He
propped himself up on his left elbow and stared out of his
window at the night sky. He'd been fighting Harvester. They
were about to plunge into a river… He rubbed the back of his
neck, trying to loosen his tight muscles. But there had been
something else. A voice calling to him. There had been no
other people in his dream—just him and Harvester locked in
a death-like grip. Where had the voice come from? A spec-
tator on the shore?

He sat up, his body tensing as the voice sounded in his ear.
It was feminine and sounded vaguely familiar. Dena? No. He
concentrated, trying to recall the dream. The woman was
short and thin and seemed to know him. Her voice was soft,
barely audible, yet persisted, calling his name.

He stared at the clouds as they skidded across the sky. It

was like that, he thought. She was obliterated by a mist on the shoreline. He strained to see her but the darkness thickened.

As he sank back onto the bed, the moon broke from an imprisoning cloud. The mist in his dream evaporated in a sudden gust of wind and the voice grew louder. McLaren sat up. The woman was Verity Dwyer.

Exhaling slowly, he wiped his forehead with the edge of the sheet. Why was she calling to him? Because maybe she was mixed up in Marta's death after all, he reasoned. Because maybe she had stolen the casino winnings to finance her disaster-dog business. He lay down and hadn't realized that he'd fallen asleep until the early-morning rain rattled against the gutters, prodding him awake.

Two HOURS LATER he was in Castleton. He had showered, shaved, and dressed hurriedly, as though he had to meet a deadline, but he had taken a few minutes to fill his travel mug with hot coffee. Breakfast was a cold slice of pizza, left over from dinner several nights ago. He ate it while he drove.

He was not in such a hurry, however, that he was careless. He drove slowly the length of the wet road on which Linnet lived, looking for her vehicle. It wasn't there. She wasn't home. He parked several cars down from her house, in case she returned before he left, grabbed the photo of Harvester, and walked up to one of Linnet's neighbors.

"'Morning," he said, smiling hopefully at the man.

The man, in his early thirties and dressed in a suit, had just locked his front door and was shifting his briefcase to his other hand. He paused, looked at McLaren, and asked what he wanted.

"Just a bit of help. It'll take only a minute."

"If you're lost—" the man began.

"No. I wonder if you'd take a look at this photo and tell

me if you've seen this man around here." He held out Harvester's photo and the man stepped closer.

"Why? What's he done? You a copper?"

McLaren explained who he was and that the man in the photo might be involved in an old murder case.

"That right? Let me have a look." The man took the photograph, looked at it for perhaps several seconds, then nodded. "Yeah. I've seen him. Used to be around here quite regular. Haven't seen him for a while. He the dead bloke?"

"When did you see him? Do you remember?"

"What…like a specific date?"

"An approximation will do. Last winter, this spring…"

"No. It was longer ago. Last spring. Yeah. That's it. Last spring. Last year. He was here for a couple months. He was seeing Linnet, my next-door neighbor. They were dating for a while, probably until the end of May or so, then they must've had a hell of a row 'cause I've not seen him since."

"When you say you saw him a lot, what does that mean? Did he pick up Miss Isherwood for dates? Mow her lawn? Fix things around her house?"

"He was around her house, all right, but I think it was more like a sort of live-in boyfriend. I'd see him come in the evenings and he'd still be here the next morning when I left for work. You figure out what that means." He glanced at his watch and started toward his car.

"Sorry. One more question, please."

"Sure. I thought you had finished. What else?"

"Was he here regularly, like every night, or every other weekend?"

"It was every weekend, or just about. This went on for the entire time I saw his car here. Then, he leaves the end of May. Must've been real sudden."

"Why do you think that?"

"Well, Linnet must have been crazy in love with that man.

I've never seen her smile so much or even sing when she was pottering about in her garden. Her husband had left her, I guess you know, and I thought she'd never get over that. Then along comes this chap—the one in your photo—and it was like instant love. She was over the moon. Then I don't see his car or him anymore and she's back in her depression again, just like when her husband left. She cried for weeks. Literally. Sobbing. I didn't think she'd ever get over him."

"It does take some people a long time to recover from a broken heart."

"Probably a bit more than just a boyfriend-girlfriend breakup, if you ask me, 'cause she took to wearing a ring around her neck."

"Sounds like an engagement ring."

"Could be. I don't know. But he must've made it up to her."

"Oh, yes? Are they back together, then?"

"No. At least, I haven't seen him around. Maybe she goes to *his* place. I don't know. But someone sent her that fancy car of hers. Last August, I think."

"Why do you say that? She couldn't have bought it?"

"With her husband gone and her working those piddling jobs? I don't think so. This came from someone with a lot of cash to spare. That Mercedes must've cost something. Sorry, mate, I've got to hop it. Hope that helps." He was down his walk and out his front gate before McLaren could thank him.

McLaren sat in his car, turning over the new information in his mind. End of May last year was around the time he and Harvester left the Staffordshire Constabulary. After the pub-burglary incident when he threw Harvester into the rose bushes. Was this the reason for the beer bottles that kept cropping up in his life? Were they a subtle reminder about the pub burglary and Harvester's absence from Linnet's life? Had she been in love with Harvester and he left her due to the pub incident?

He rubbed his forehead, trying to understand the whispers that echoed in his mind. Linnet wore a ring on a chain. He'd seen it the first time he had met her. Was it Harvester's ring or her engagement ring? And now she had evidently taken up with Sean FitzSimmons. What did that mean? Was it nothing more than looking for a meal ticket, or was it something more?

He stared at her house, picturing her again as she got into her car. Her husband had left her; Harvester had left her. She had been financially strapped. So how does a woman desperate for money get expensive clothing? And a Mercedes a mere two months after Marta Hughes is killed? He turned the key in the ignition and headed for Danny Mercer's home.

TWENTY-THREE

THE QUESTIONS KEPT whispering to McLaren as he drove to Danny Mercer's house. He needed a few more bits of information before he could hand the case over to the police. He was surprised to feel the prickles of excitement coursing through his blood, the adrenalin start to surge and shove him into a state of being he thought long lost. The same sensation grabbed him now as it had when he had heard police sirens as a kid, or when he was deeply involved in a case featuring a child or elderly person. He always expected and accepted the euphoric rush; he was astonished it still could claim him a year after leaving the job.

As he approached the Mercers' home, McLaren thought again about Linnet. When her husband had left her, she'd been nearly desperate for money. Whether intentionally latching on to Harvester or not, she reasoned she would soon be financially safe. The diamond ring—most probably an engagement ring— she wore spoke mutely of that brief episode. But when Harvester left Staffordshire, Linnet tried to get money from Marta when she won at the casino. McLaren felt sure of that. He also needed to find out if Linnet had access to a gun.

He parked the car in front of the house but made no move to get out. Something wasn't right. It didn't make sense. If Linnet was mixed up in Marta's murder, why did she hire him to find Marta's killer? Then the photograph in Harvester's bedroom stood out with alarming clarity. If she still had feelings for Harvester, as the ring implied, and Harvester had broken the engagement—perhaps due to his Staffordshire disgrace and his uncertain future—then maybe all this had been set up for McLaren's failure. He nodded, sitting back in the car seat. Linnet had known he wasn't in the job anymore, that he had never worked as a private detective. Yet she had come to him when she could have hired an experienced investigator. She probably was assuming he would fail and then she and Harvester would get a huge laugh over it, with Harvester spreading the news around the office. McLaren sat up, looking at the Mercer house. Sure. The beer bottles were just a little touch to remind me of my tangle with Harvester during the pub burglary, to rub it in and hint that I wasn't clear of him yet.

McLaren swore softly and grabbed the ignition key. Was Harvester involved in this? McLaren couldn't see how he would be, if he were busy with the runner murder in D Division. No. Harvester was just a personal sideline with Linnet. She had used someone else to help her. Probably someone used to being a thug and in constant need of money. Who better to fit both criteria than her ex-con friend Sean Fitz-Simmons? McLaren got out of the car, slammed the door, and strode up to the Mercers' house.

Danny's mother answered the door. She was dressed in a tailored suit, a mug of coffee in one hand. She kept her free hand on the edge of the door, as though barring McLaren's entry into her home or guarding some secret. Her reaction on hearing McLaren's introduction and the reason for his visit was to take a sip of coffee and look incredulous. She also protested.

"You're on the wrong track," she said, her voice faint, keeping the conversation between the two of them. Her eyes held a mixture of fear and denial, as though the topic exhausted her and she didn't want to deal with another authority figure. "Danny's a good boy. He's not doing drugs any more. That was last year. He's left that all behind. He's learnt his lesson."

"Good to hear it. I hope he has. Is he home now? May I speak to him?"

"He left about a half hour ago. He's looking for work. He'll be back in time for tea, if you want to come back then…" She eyed him, not knowing what a talk between her son and this man involved.

"If I have time, I shall, thank you."

"Trouble is," she said, leaning against the doorjamb, "once you're labeled as a druggie, you got it for life. People always look at you queer, especially the police. They think you're up to no good, whatever you do. Even just walking along the street or on his way to his friend's house. But Danny's quit all that. He's a good boy. He always has money, so he's not a drain on society or on me."

"Contributing to the household, is he? What is he… seventeen? That's commendable."

"Yes, it is. I suppose he feels like the man of the house since his father died last year. There's nothing he can't do for me, helping with the housework, mowing the lawn… He gave me a lovely gift for my birthday this last May. A lovely garden sculpture. He even installed it in the back garden all by himself. Now," she said, squaring her shoulders, "doesn't that show you he has money and is thinking of me? Lots of boys his age wouldn't give much thought to their parents, but Danny does. He's always bringing me some little something."

"You're fortunate to have such a caring son. Some parents can't say that."

She set her coffee cup on the hall table and picked up her briefcase and car key. "Yes, I am. I realize that and compliment Danny on many things. Even when he lost his job just after Christmas last year, I commiserated with him. I made certain he felt all right about it, that it didn't affect his self-

esteem. So many times it does, you know. You work hard
and then you get fired for no fault of your own, really. Just
because the economy is down or the after-Christmas rush is
over. It's hard on anyone's ego to be let go like that, without
warning, so I made it a point to praise his job-finding efforts
each day. It's hard to find work when you're so young and
haven't much experience. He needs the praise right now."

McLaren nodded reassuringly but thought it odd. If
Danny wasn't working since last December, how did he get
the money for the garden sculpture this May? Sculptures
weren't cheap.

He thanked Mrs. Mercer for talking to him and walked
back to his car. He sat there, pretending he was talking on
his mobile phone, but he kept an eye on the house. When
Mrs. Mercer drove off several minutes later, McLaren remained in his car in case she returned for a forgotten item
or Danny came home. It wouldn't be the first time a teenager
had drawn the wool over someone's eyes. Even with a mother
so adamant about his good behavior, Danny could still be up
to something when his mother was working. Or late at night
when she was sleeping.

He leaned his head against the headrest, the conversations
with Alan and Chad Hughes echoing through his mind. It was
certain Danny had been involved in drugs—Marta had seen
it and reported him to the police. But was Danny's mother
telling the truth when she said that was past behavior? Did
breeding tell or did environment mold you? Danny's grandfather held a distinguished World War II record; Danny had
been reared around the relics of that record. Had the stories
he heard steered his life's path or had his hooligan mates ne-
gated all that?

When a quarter of an hour passed without any further
house activity, McLaren walked into the back garden. The
sculpture rested in a small grassy clearing surrounded by

clumps of Siberian iris, hosta, and rhododendron. It seemed a perfect place for it, shady and quiet, reminiscent of fairy haunts he had imagined as a child. The sculpture, in fact, was a three-dimensional metal fairy. Her open wings could have lifted her in flight at any moment, but she balanced on top of an elaborate metal pedestal, one leg bent and the toes of the other leg firmly soldered to the pedestal.

Stifling a groan, he laid the ornament on its side. The ground beneath the pedestal's base was bare. No yellowed, dying grass had been smothered by the pedestal. Meaning, the ground had been disturbed for some reason. Odd for something that had required no concrete platform or inner support rod.

McLaren scanned the yard. A three-pronged cultivator sat on a garden chair near the back door. He grabbed it and quickly clawed at the soil. The digging was easy, unlike the hard-packed soil that greeted him whenever he planted something in his garden. It took him only seconds to scrape away the earth and reach the object buried inches below. He leaned closer to the hole and laid the cultivator beside him, wanting to use his fingers for the final few seconds' work. Carefully he maneuvered his fingers beneath the object, feeling the cardboard give slightly against his grasp. As he pushed the box up, he brushed the remaining soil from its top, finally lifting it and holding it in his hand.

He grinned as he set it beside the garden tool and gingerly removed the lid of the shoebox. Inside were a carton of .38-caliber bullets, a Webley Mk IV .38-caliber revolver, and a woman's silvery shoe that was missing its heel.

TWENTY-FOUR

THE WEBLEY MK IV WAS a relic of World War II, McLaren thought, staring at the revolver and the box of ammunition. Were these items part of the glory-day relics of Danny's grandfather? Was it the service revolver he had used in the war and retained on returning home? Many soldiers kept their sidearms when the war ended, either their British pistols or German Lugers, souvenirs of their years overseas. McLaren stared at the weapon. This had to be the grandfather's revolver. And it was a .38 caliber, the same size as the bullet that had killed Marta Hughes.

It might not be evidence, but the shoe fit that definition. Especially if Danny's fingerprints were on it.

McLaren pushed the soil back into the hole, tapped it down with his foot, then righted the sculpture and returned the garden tool. He replaced the lid on the shoebox and picked it up. Danny had hidden the revolver after using it to kill Marta, McLaren realized as he got into his car. Or Linnet had used it. Either way, the shoe and revolver linked Danny to Marta's murder just as Linnet's car and expensive clothes linked her to the stolen casino money. He set the box on his back seat and rang up Jamie, telling him about the gun and the missing shoe. "I know that heel I found at the stone barn will fit this shoe," he said, the volume of his voice underlining his belief. "You'll see when you get it to the lab. Right now I need you to accompany me if you've got the time when you get off."

"Accompany you where? To the Mercers' house?"

"No. I need Official Police Presence when we confront Linnet Isherwood."

"When *we* confront her? This is your case, Mike. You're doing very well without the lads in blue."

"I'll need you to make the arrest. I'm a civilian, remember?"

"Just barely," Jamie said, laughing. "Maybe I should loan you my warrant card."

"I'll take that as a joke and not as a serious suggestion. Bring your handcuffs and anything else you want. You can follow me in your squad car."

"Uhh, Mike…"

"Yes?" His breath caught in his throat, fearful that Jamie was going to suggest he contact the Chief Constable.

"You're not going to be doing anything illegal, are you? I mean, I'm not going to get a reprimand or something for helping you."

McLaren let out his breath. Jamie hadn't suggested that McLaren go it alone. "We'll review the case before we drive over to Linnet's. If you feel I'm totally round the twist, I'll bend to your opinion and call it off."

"Fair enough. Thanks."

"I'll be on the street when you get out. Find me." He rang off and waited for Jamie, feeling he owed himself a celebratory meal and a hand washing.

EARLY TWILIGHT WAS descending on the village of Castleton and the last vestiges of color clung to the western sky. The eastern side of Peveril Castle loomed dark and forbidding against the curtain of pale pink and yellow, gray shadows slowly consuming the land. Down in the dale where the village nestled, the sunlight had already vanished, yet still anointed the rooftops and treetops with an ochre-hued mantle. McLaren and Jamie parked halfway down the road from

Linnet's house—a precaution in case she remembered the make, color, and model of McLaren's car or happened to see the police car. They also checked the back garden, making certain no one was there who might be a potential problem. When they were satisfied they weren't walking stupidly into a trap, McLaren rang the front doorbell.

Through the open window he heard the bell ringing deep with the house. Music sounded and a wooden-legged chair was shoved back. The soft padding of shoes thudded on a hard floor, then the click of metal as the dead bolt moved in the doorframe. There was a squeak of protesting hinges and moments later Linnet Isherwood opened the front door.

"Mr. McLaren!" Linnet's exclamation nearly caught in her throat on seeing him. She forced a smile but it quickly faded as her hand went to her throat. "I—I didn't expect to see you so soon. You've something to discuss about Marta's case?" Her eyes had drifted from McLaren's face to Jamie's, then to his uniform. She glanced back at McLaren. "You brought a police officer? You've solved the case, then? Are you going to make an arrest?" She smiled again but remained in the open doorway, unsure if their presence warranted a private talk or if a brief sentence or two on the doorstep was sufficient.

McLaren answered her questioning look by asking if they could come in.

"Why…certainly. Of course!" She stepped aside, opened the door wider, but remained there as they walked into the front room. "You'll have to excuse my attire. I—I wasn't expecting anyone. I was exercising." By way of confirmation, the music in the back room erupted into a loud tattoo of drums, brass, and strings. She gave a half-hearted smile, unsure if she should turn off the music or not.

"Would you care to join us?" McLaren asked, motioning to the sofa. "This is Constable James Kydd. Derbyshire Constabulary," he added as if it were an afterthought.

Linnet nodded, closed the door slowly, and leaned against it. She was dressed in designer-label black leotards, a halter-top, and soft-soled ballet-style shoes. A red-and-purple-print scarf was tied around her waist; a matching hand towel lay across the back of her neck. She eyed the two men as they waited for her to sit down, then hesitantly moved to a chair near the front window. She sat but the men remained standing.

She looked up at McLaren. "A police officer? Then you *are* making an arrest in the case." Her voice cracked but she pulled a limp smile from a recess of her soul. "Th-that's wonderful news. Who is it? Can you tell me?" Her gaze switched to Jamie, as though mutely inquiring if it would be proper police procedure. When Jamie didn't speak, she focused on McLaren. She turned toward Jamie, though, when he cautioned her. She listened, unbelieving her senses, his words making no sense. When he finished, she got to her feet. Her mouth had gaped open in surprise but she closed it as she alternately stared at each man. In the stillness McLaren could hear the last bars of her recorded exercise music, a selection of Handel, he thought. Or Haydn. Then abrupt silence filled the house as the CD ended.

Linnet's hand went to her throat again, as though she needed a physical touch to convince her she was not experiencing a nightmare. Her voice shook from fright but it was abnormally loud as she said, "*Me!* This is absurd. You've made a mistake. I went straight home after our casino outing. Anyway, why should I kill Marta? We were best friends."

"Exactly," McLaren said. "Being best friends, you expected Marta would bail you out of your financial difficulty with her big roulette winning."

"That's ridiculous. I was nowhere near Elton."

"Maybe not that night, but you were later."

"Oh, really? When was that supposed to be?" Her voice

had regained its strength and her anger underscored her words. "Why would I even go there?"

"You planted a silver charm. The type used for bracelets and necklaces."

"Amazing. The police never said anything about a charm, and they searched the area when Marta's body was discovered."

"No, they didn't find it because you hid it there after I took the case."

She glared at him but fright shone plainly. "Absurd."

"I found it, though. Just as you hoped. Look familiar?" He took the silver skier charm from his jeans pocket and held it so that Linnet could see it.

"No, it doesn't."

"It should. You've seen two of them. The first one you gave Sean FitzSimmons on the publication of his novel. There's the author photo on the dust jacket. He's wearing it on a chain around his neck. The dedication of his book even mentions it. And links you to it," he said, pointing to the silver skier. "It was probably some token between you two. I don't know and right now I don't care. You got it away from him and planted it at the crime scene to implicate him in the murder."

Linnet started to protest but McLaren cut her off.

"The second charm you gave him in Buxton. I saw you hand it to him just before you parted after lunch. *This* is that charm." His fingers closed over the charm and he returned it to his pocket.

"What a furtive imagination you have. This doesn't prove a thing. You could have bought that charm at any jewelry store."

"I could have done, but I didn't. I got it from Sean. But if you're so sure I'm lying, ask him." He pulled out his mobile phone and held it out for her. "What's the matter? Don't you want to know if I'm lying or not?"

Linnet made no move for the offered phone, instead chewing her bottom lip. Her face had drained of color but she did not reclaim her chair. A car backfired in the street before she said, "I—I believe he's out of town."

"The phone reaches around the world."

"No." She shook her head but her eyes held the desperation of a caged animal. "I—I don't want to disturb him."

"That had bothered me for a while." McLaren shoved the phone into his pocket. "I thought for a while that Sean killed Marta. He was a good choice, wasn't he?"

"What do you mean? Sean and I are—"

"Friends? Lovers? No. Not really. Maybe that's what he believes, but he's nothing to you. Not in that sense. He's a tool, isn't he? You tricked him into believing you cared for him but you used him. He's a great decoy, Miss Isherwood. I congratulate you on finding him."

Linnet shifted her weight onto her other foot and tried to look nonchalant, but the fear still shone in her eyes. "Decoy?"

"Certainly! You thought I'd zero in on him, didn't you? Sean FitzSimmons, ex-con and perfect murder suspect. The police would find out about him and look no further. He had many skills you needed. One was his record as a burglar and car thief. You asked him to break into my car—subtly so I would begin to doubt my reason—and steal anything he could find. I applaud his skill. He accomplished it in broad daylight without leaving a trace on my car. But he was probably surprised to end up with that bag of beer bottles. Did he show them to you?"

Linnet remained silent, her arms crossed on her chest.

"To ice the cake, in case the coppers were a bit slow in suspecting him, you planted the charm near the spot where they found the body. Was it supposed to have been lost when Marta fought Sean for her life?" His last words exploded in his anger and he stepped toward Linnet.

"You're insane. You have no proof for any of this. Now, if you're quite finished, I wish you'd leave. I have other things to do than listen to fiction. I would sue you for slander if it weren't so laughable."

"Fiction is another element of it, isn't it? Sean is a fiction writer, an author of thrillers. He's good at thinking up plots. Did you get him to plan where, when, and how to kill Marta? Or had you thought of it by the time you'd met him? I'm sure you didn't talk this over with your friend Charlie Harvester."

Her eyes widened and she opened her mouth, but McLaren went on. "I know about you two. I heard it from a very reliable source, how matey you once were. Might still be, for all I know. After all, you've still got his ring."

She'd had enough time to think and pounced on McLaren's statement. "What ring? Am I wearing any ring?" She held out her hands so the men could see her fingers. They were bare. "You're obsessed, McLaren. Was your mother frightened by a jeweler?"

"*This* ring." He strode toward her. His hand shot out and he grabbed the necklace she wore. He yanked on the chain, pulling the bottom length of it out from beneath her halter-top. A diamond ring slid down the length of the twisted silver. He threw the chain at her and her hand clamped over the ring. "You must still love him, though I don't know why, after he broke off your engagement."

Jamie's hand wrapped around McLaren's upper arm, pulling him away slightly from Linnet.

"You may have killed Marta for her money—after all, she won more that night at the casino than you had ever seen, and you were desperate for money after your husband left."

"Ridic—"

"But you hired me for revenge."

"Revenge? For who? When?"

"Revenge for Harvester. You still love him. You found

out—probably from him—about the pub incident. You thought I needed to pay for Harvester's ultimate disgrace and reprimand. So you hired me, probably thinking I'd fall on my face with this case and make a fool of myself. The beer bottles were a nice touch. Did Sean give me my lesson?" His hand went to a bruise on his cheek. "It took me a while to realize where I'd seen him. I thought it was from my days in the job, but it was the night of my beating. I just had a glimpse of him by the lamplight from my kitchen table, but I couldn't place his face for a while."

A smile gradually claimed Linnet's face as she stared at McLaren. She leaned against the fireplace mantel, her fingers toying with the ring that hung from the necklace. "At least he did *something* right. I'd written your home address down for him so he'd know where to find you. I dashed it off, in a hurry, never thinking I should have typed it out. He told me how he ambushed you." She gave a short laugh and shook her head. "We thought you'd mess it up," she said, her voice bitter. "We thought all the fight had gone out of you and that the case had grown too cold for you to discover anything. We—" She took a deep breath before correcting herself. "I thought you'd latch on to Sean as the killer and I'd get my revenge when Charlie proved Sean's innocence in court. I didn't really want you to solve Marta's murder. You were smarter than we thought."

"Too bad you weren't a tad bit smarter."

She frowned, fearful she had overlooked something. "What?"

"You wrote down my address for him."

"So?"

"I have no doubt a handwriting expert can match that to the check you wrote me to retain my services. Rather distinct handwriting you have, Linnet—bold, jagged script."

She stepped toward him, her hand raised, but Jamie

caught her wrist and forced her arm down. Shrugging, she relaxed. "You think you know it all, don't you, McLaren? But you don't. You haven't any idea what happened to Karin Pedersen…or about those beer bottles."

"Your doing, I suppose."

"Of course. I knew where you were going after you left me in Castleton when we talked. I had an idea the route you'd take and let Karin know. She's a friend."

"Mobile phones are a wonder, aren't they?" He snorted.

"We weren't one-hundred-percent certain you'd drive that way, mind you, but it was no big deal if you didn't. Karin faked her wound and sat by the roadside. I gave her your car description. It was simple—all she had to do was wait and wave away other offers of help…if there'd been any. As I said, if you didn't show up…well, no harm done. It was just a bit of fun designed to annoy you."

"And the beer bottles?"

"That was Sean. We wanted to remind you of that little pub episode with Tyrone Wade Antony and your dismissal from the Force. And Charlie Harvester. Did it work?" She smiled, lowering her eyes like a 1920s vamp.

"Harvester didn't have anything to do with the murder, did he?" McLaren said as Linnet shook off Jamie's hand. "Or with framing Sean."

"No." She said it almost as a shout of victory. "We just talked about 'wouldn't it be wonderful if one day Michael McLaren fell flat on his face?' but Charlie had nothing to do with any of this. I was the only one involved."

"Hardly you alone, Linnet. You had to have help. As you pointed out to me, you were home. Danny Mercer wasn't." The faintest smile played at the corners of his lips as he watched the shock register on her face.

A faint noise, like a door latch catching in place, came from the back of the house. Linnet pushed herself away from the mantel and said rather loudly, "Danny Mercer? Whatever made you think Danny is mixed up in Marta's death, Mr. McLaren? Is that why you brought this police constable with you?"

Another sound, louder and sharper, cracked the brief silence. The bang of a door slamming and the rattle of Venetian blinds hitting a window jabbed McLaren into action. As Jamie handcuffed Linnet, McLaren ran into the kitchen.

TWENTY-FIVE

THE BLINDS WERE SWINGING as McLaren yanked open the door. He paused momentarily on the threshold, looking for Danny, wary of an attack or weapon. The sound of running feet came from the direction of the road, and McLaren dashed down the alley and to the front of the house.

Danny ran down the center of the road, dodging oncoming cars and glancing back, his figure bright in the car headlights. He paused at a new Skia and tried to insert his key but he couldn't control his shaking hand. As McLaren charged up to him, Danny abandoned his car and sprinted down a side road.

The daylight was rapidly failing, the parked vehicles, rubbish bins, and clipped shrubs dark shapes against a murky backdrop. McLaren paused at the mouth of the side road, trying to distinguish forms in the gloom. A movement to his left centered his attention for an instant, but it was a dog sniffing at the refuse bins. McLaren jogged slowly down the street, landing lightly on the balls of his feet, making no noise other than his ragged breathing. He kept a zigzag course, crossing and recrossing the road to peer behind bushes and cars, any place Danny might be hiding.

He turned sharply toward the sound of scraping metal, his body tensing, his heart rate increasing. A man was dumping rubbish into his refuse bin.

At the house next door to him, an older woman opened her front door and the light from her front room spilled onto the front pavement. McLaren dashed over to the cypress stand-

ing like a sentinel at her front gate and glanced behind it.
No Danny.

Neither the man nor woman had seen Danny, either. Or
at least they didn't admit to it when McLaren asked them.

He had jogged to the end of the road and was about to re-
trace his steps when a shape emerged from the front garden
ahead of him. He stopped abruptly, startled by the sudden
movement and the realization that the massive form was two
people walking close together, holding hands. As the couple
moved into the faint light from the house, the girl smiled
tentatively at McLaren. The boy, however, mumbled something in her ear and nuzzled her neck with his forehead. His
left hand, McLaren noticed, was around the girl's shoulders.
His right hand was in his jeans pocket. The girl shifted her
eyes from the boy to McLaren, then repeated the gesture as
her lips silently formed the word "help." McLaren nodded
and walked past them.

The older woman eyed the couple as she finished setting
out her rubbish, then called her dog and went inside. The
front door closed with a dull thud and the road sank back
into darkness.

McLaren turned and charged after the couple, covering the
scant distance in seconds and shouting for the girl to run into
the road. As McLaren grabbed Danny's left arm, he angled it
behind Danny, using it as leverage to simultaneously release
the girl and force Danny to the ground. The girl scooted behind a parked car and crouched down, her fingers gripping
the back bumper, her head peeking above the boot as she
watched the fight.

It was brief. Danny swung at McLaren with his right fist
but missed. His foot lashed out at McLaren's legs and he suc-
ceeded in landing one blow with his heel before McLaren
brought him to the ground. He kept his hand on Danny's arm

and placed his foot on Danny's back, pressing him against the pavement as he regained his breath.

"Are you all right, miss?" he asked from his bent-over position.

As the girl got to her feet, she slid her hands to the car's boot in an effort to support herself. "Yes, thanks." Her voice quivered slightly as she looked at Danny, then at McLaren. "He grabbed me. I was walking up to my car and he jumped out of the shadows and grabbed me. He made me walk with him, pretend I knew him. Who is he? Do you know him?"

Ignoring her question, he said, "Get up." He grabbed Danny's shoulder and helped him to his feet. Eyeing the girl again, McLaren said, "You're sure you're all right? He didn't hurt you?"

"No, I'm fine. Just a bit scared." She dusted her hands on her jeans. "I expect I'll laugh about this tomorrow. Or at least be the envy of my friends. You know," she said when McLaren smiled, "helping catch a burglar. Or whatever he's done." She tilted her head, trying to make out Danny's features in the darkness. "He do something like that? Are you the police?"

"I'm taking him to the police." McLaren tightened his grip on Danny's arm. "And yes, he did something like that."

"Oh."

"I'm afraid, miss, I'll have to send a police officer to your house to ask you a few questions about this, since it is a police matter." His voice trailed off as he studied her face, assessing if she were emotionally stable for the interview.

"Yes, certainly. You'll need some kind of witness statement, I expect." She pointed to the last house in the row. "I live just there. Will it be tonight?"

"An officer will contact you to let you know. He'll tell you he's calling on behalf of Michael McLaren. That's me, by the way. Michael McLaren."

"I'd like to help, if I can." She glanced again at Danny, perhaps memorizing his features and clothing. "Whenever the officer comes is fine. Thank you for helping me."

"Enjoy your fifteen minutes of fame tomorrow." He left her on the pavement. It wasn't until he had turned the corner that he could no longer make out her figure in the darkness.

THE REST OF THE STORY came out as McLaren walked Danny back to Linnet's house. Though sullen and angry at first, Danny finally admitted he and Linnet had split the casino winnings when he killed Marta. He used some of the money to buy his car, some he still had, and some he used to buy drugs. Marta had got into his car that fateful night because he said he wanted her advice about a problem he had. "She was like that—trying to help me get back on my feet, so she never suspected a trap." Marta had broken the heel off her shoe as she tried to run from Danny at the barn. "I never could find that heel," he confessed after explaining that he'd kept the shoe as evidence in case he needed to blackmail Linnet at some future date. The broken poker chip at the body dump site had been Marta's, kept as a souvenir of her big win, and must have been broken as she fell after being shot. McLaren felt his stomach tighten as he imagined the small, thin woman trying to run through the wood, but he said nothing. He was neither judge nor jury. Nor God, he thought, wondering briefly what would become of Danny. The boy had begun his narrative by answering McLaren's questions in short, thunderous snaps, but by the end the replies had subsided into muffled whimpers.

Jamie cautioned Danny and handcuffed him as a second police car drove up. He nodded to the officer, opened the back door, and settled Danny in the back seat. Linnet, in Jamie's car, sat sullen and silent, and stared straight ahead. The village had grown quiet. A ribbon of ash-gray clouds seemed pinned just above the horizon in the west. There was no moon or stars in the blackness that stretched above their heads. No fox barked, no owl called, no breath of wind stirred the tree branches. It was as if they were the only souls awake in the bleak landscape.

McLaren tilted back his head, taking a deep breath of cool air, looking into the vastness of the somber sky. He felt small, as he always did when standing in the throat of the Winnats. Or when walking through Dove Dale. The enormity of nature welled up around him, threatened to engulf him in its wildness and beauty. The thud of the car door slamming pulled him from his reverie and Jamie walked up to him. "The Governor will want you to write up a few things," Jamie said as he closed his fist around his car key. "Can you fit it in between your stonewall work?"

"I'll have to, won't I?" McLaren's lips curled into a half smile. "Never ends, does it? I thought I left report writing behind when I left the job."

"You're either optimistic or a fool. And I don't think it's the latter." He slapped McLaren on the back. "Nice work, Mike. The Super will be in touch soon."

"Sounds like a threat. Thanks for the hand, Jamie." He waved as he walked back to his car.

On the drive home, McLaren thought about the case. He would get nothing more than the retainer Linnet had already given him, but he was strangely unaffected by the loss of the rest of his fee. Perhaps he did live to see injustices righted after all. Was it a remnant of his police training, the siren song of the job and what it stood for, or was it a quality deep within him?

He wondered briefly how Danny had known when to kidnap Marta, when she would arrive home. Linnet had no way of knowing Marta would win at the casino that night. Perhaps it was as simple as Linnet ringing Danny, using her mobile phone from her car in the casino car park, to tell him this was The Night. McLaren squinted at an approaching car's headlights as he imagined the short one-sentence message. Perhaps Linnet said something months before. "I'll let you know when we go to the casino, so you be ready any time. She's bound to win big one of these nights." Danny would drive to Marta's house when he got the word and wait for her in the shadows.

McLaren exhaled loudly. His fingers curled around the steering wheel in anger. Of course, he didn't have to prove that. The police could search mobile-phone records in preparation for the trial. It was enough right now that he had given Jamie the probable murder weapon and the missing shoe. Danny's fingerprints would be on both. He smiled, for the first time in months feeling happy about the future.

He turned the car around in the lonely stretch of The Winnats, the wind-swept mountain pass of the Pennines. Without thinking he headed back the way he had come, driving through Castleton and heading south toward Kirkfield. He had several miles of dark highway to cover and he settled back in the car seat, the B6061 rolling beneath the car wheels and his mind rolling through the week's events. His fingers loosened their grip on the steering wheel and he turned on the car's stereo. The cassette-tape recording started up, the strains of the guitars and viola as familiar to him as Dena's face, which hovered before his eyes. As his folk group's rendition of "Near Woodstock Town" began in earnest he realized it was Wednesday. Unless things had drastically changed in the past year, Dena would be at her sister's house in Hathersage tonight. He turned the car again and headed for Hathersage as he cranked up the tape's volume and sang along.

Several songs and several miles later he entered Hathersage. The village was a splash of light in the surrounding dark countryside, its restaurants and pubs open for the night crowd. McLaren passed The Hanoverian Hotel before turning onto the road housing the local police station.

It was long past regular office work hours and the road was deserted. A few streetlamps shed orange-tinted light on the landscape but outside these pools the street was dark. The familiar blue police lantern shone above the police station door and McLaren parked his car opposite it and got out. He took his time assessing the area, wanting no wayward pub-crawler or village resident to spot him. So he sauntered up to the police station, pretending to window shop in the closed establishments nearby. He stopped short of the entrance to the station and picked up a beer bottle lying at the curb. The brown glass caught the light from the police lamp and seemed to wink at McLaren. The irony was not lost on him, and his pent-up rage and hurt broke from him in an unstoppable rush. He felt the weight of the bottle, its curve sitting snuggly in his hand rather like a rock for mending stone-walls. Taking a deep breath, he threw the bottle at the lamp. A satisfying shattering of glass rewarded his effort and he ran back to his car.

He slumped against the car seat, imaginary newspaper headlines flashing through his mind. "Ex-Cop Caps Cold Case." "Ex-Cop Comes Thru When Chips Are Down." "Killer's Second Mistake: Hiring Ex-Cop." He smiled at the reaction the story would undoubtedly cause, both in the media and throughout the Force. He'd again be the topic of conversation around police-station water coolers and break rooms, but this time he wouldn't mind. The talk would be about good police work, not the titillating gossip of a ruined career.

Opening his mobile phone, McLaren punched in Dena's number. The police lamp's blue glass was broken on two sides where the beer bottle caught it; the light bulb was shattered.

The street lay dark and unpopulated. Police…beer bottles. His thought broke off as Dena's voice came to him over the phone. Grinning, he said, "Dena, sweets. I'd like for us to try again. I'm learning to release my emotions."

* * * * *

REQUEST YOUR FREE BOOKS!

2 FREE NOVELS
PLUS 2 FREE GIFTS!

W(◗)RLDWIDE LIBRARY®

Your Partner in Crime

YES! Please send me 2 FREE novels from the Worldwide Library® series and my 2 FREE gifts (gifts are worth about $10). After receiving them, if I don't wish to receive any more books, I can return the shipping statement marked "cancel." If I don't cancel, I will receive 4 brand-new novels every month and be billed just $5.24 per book in the U.S. or $6.24 per book in Canada. That's a saving of at least 34% off the cover price. It's quite a bargain! Shipping and handling is just 50¢ per book in the U.S. and 75¢ per book in Canada.* I understand that accepting the 2 free books and gifts places me under no obligation to buy anything. I can always return a shipment and cancel at any time. Even if I never buy another book, the two free books and gifts are mine to keep forever.

414/424 WDN FEJ3

Name	(PLEASE PRINT)	

Address		Apt. #

City	State/Prov.	Zip/Postal Code

Signature (if under 18, a parent or guardian must sign)

Mail to the **Reader Service:**
IN U.S.A.: P.O. Box 1867, Buffalo, NY 14240-1867
IN CANADA: P.O. Box 609, Fort Erie, Ontario L2A 5X3

Not valid for current subscribers to the Worldwide Library series.

Want to try two free books from another line?
Call 1-800-873-8635 or visit www.ReaderService.com.

* Terms and prices subject to change without notice. Prices do not include applicable taxes. Sales tax applicable in N.Y. Canadian residents will be charged applicable taxes. Offer not valid in Quebec. This offer is limited to one order per household. All orders subject to credit approval. Credit or debit balances in a customer's account(s) may be offset by any other outstanding balance owed by or to the customer. Please allow 4 to 6 weeks for delivery. Offer available while quantities last.

Your Privacy—The Reader Service is committed to protecting your privacy. Our Privacy Policy is available online at www.ReaderService.com or upon request from the Reader Service.

We make a portion of our mailing list available to reputable third parties that offer products we believe may interest you. If you prefer that we not exchange your name with third parties, or if you wish to clarify or modify your communication preferences, please visit us at www.ReaderService.com/consumerschoice or write to us at Reader Service Preference Service, P.O. Box 9062, Buffalo, NY 14269. Include your complete name and address.